# THE CHANNELER
# TRILOGY

*A Tale of Liamec*

J. Steven Lamperti

## The Tales of Liamec

*The Wolf's Tooth*

*By the Sea*

*Twilight's Fall*

*The Channeler Trilogy*

*Sunshine over Hero*

*The Pirates of Meara*

*Endymion and the Fae*

## The Channeler Trilogy

*Moon & Shadow*

*Sun & Dream*

*Death & Dragon*

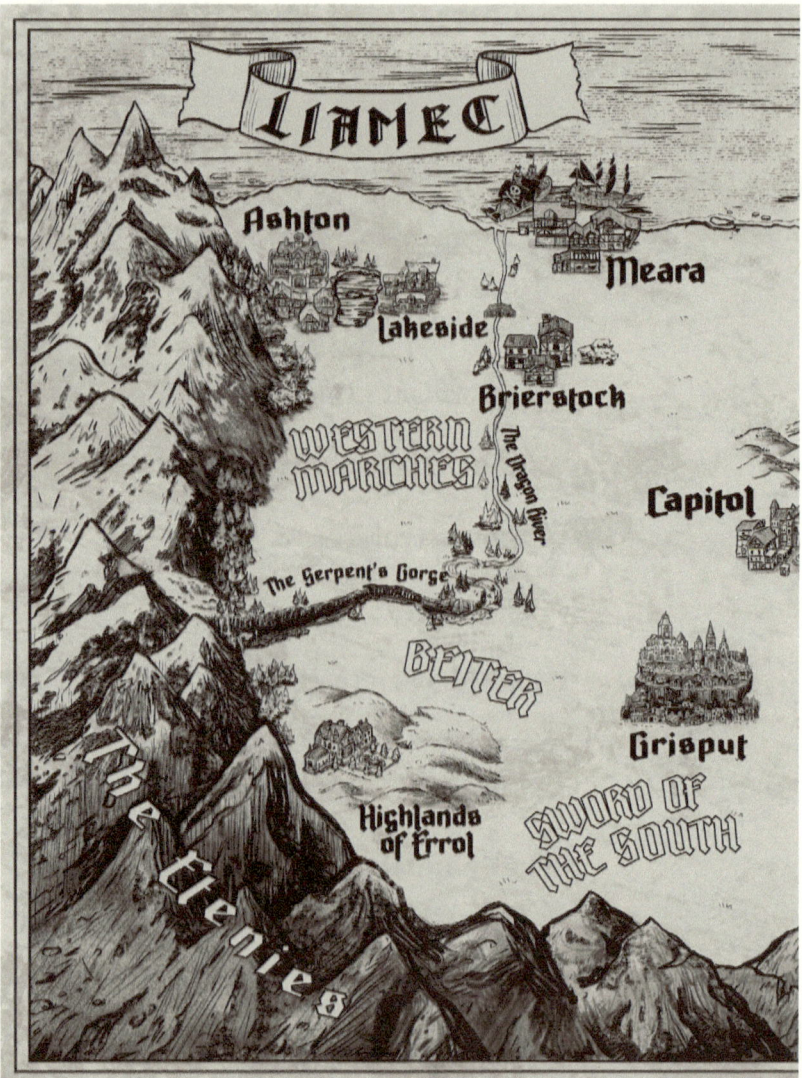

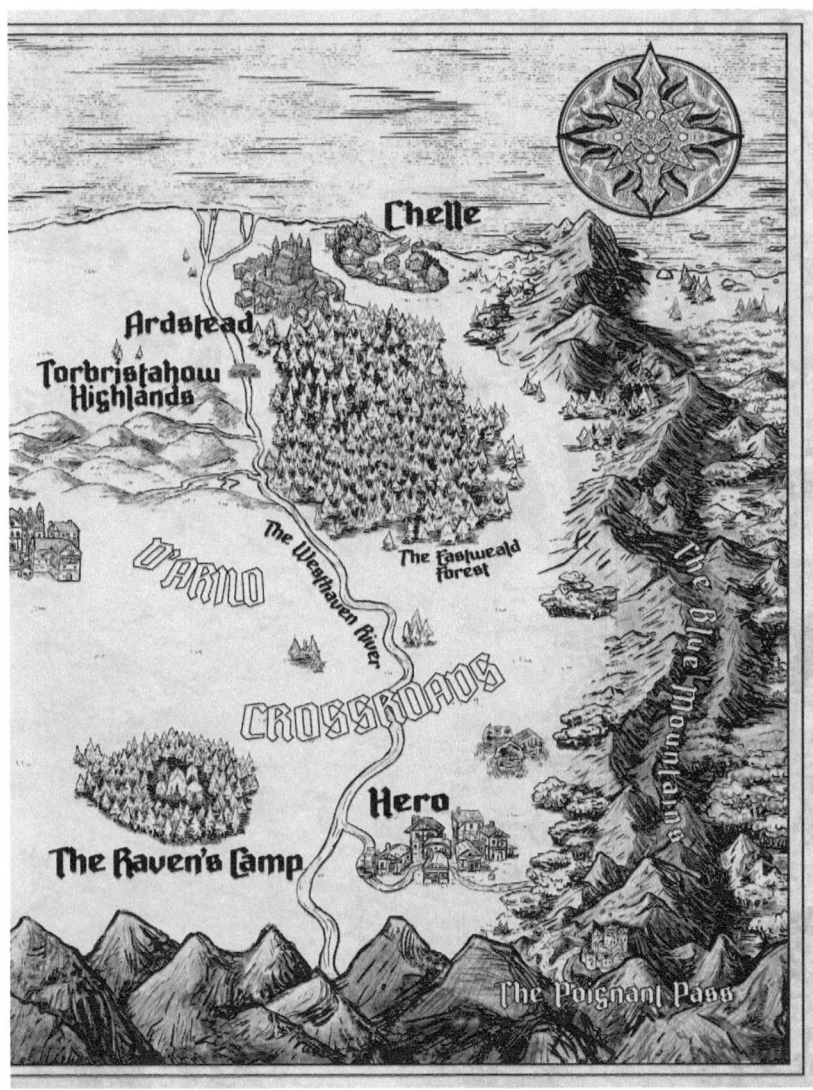

# AUTHOR'S NOTE

I wrote these three books as parts of a single story. Some questions are answered quickly, others take longer to surface, and a few only make sense once you've reached the end.

Moon & Shadow, Sun & Dream, and Death & Dragon follow different moments of the same unfolding tale. The story begins simply, with a farmer named Sebastian and a girl named Anise, and grows outward over time—into dreams, gods, and the quiet forces that shape the world of Liamec.

Whether you are new to Liamec or arriving from other tales set in this world, I hope this story deepens your understanding of the kingdom and the people who inhabit it.

Thank you for reading.

—J. Steven Lamperti

# MOON & SHADOW

J Steven Lamperti

*For Andrea,*

*Who heard every word before anyone else did.*

# 1

There was a young man in the village, Sebastian, who went out late one evening when the moon was full, took the moon down from the sky, and hung it over the mantelpiece in his home. He didn't try to do this in secret; he didn't hide what he was doing from the other villagers. He simply did it, like he was bringing the cows home for the evening, as he had earlier.

Now in those days, people were more likely to believe things. They were more likely to believe things they saw, they were more likely to believe things they felt, and they were more likely to believe things they heard. So when a couple of villagers who saw Sebastian do this described what they had seen in the village pub, they weren't greeted with disdain and denial. Instead, they were greeted with wonder and fascination, followed by disdain and denial.

"I saw it," said one older gentleman while dunking his cheese bread into his tankard of ale. "Our Sebastian is tall, but he couldn't quite reach, so I watched him climb up onto Swenson's fence out in his cow pasture and try to grab it. Still, he couldn't reach, so he climbed up completely onto the fence and jumped. He caught the edge and swung out on it until it detached. Then Sebastian and the moon fell into Swenson's pasture. I was thinking then that he had barely missed a cow patty. And a good thing too 'cause when he came away carrying the moon, I thought it was just about the prettiest thing I had ever seen, and I wouldn't have wanted to see it all covered. If you know what I mean."

"No," said a younger man, his voice filled with disdain and denial. The expression on his face clearly showed that if the older man hadn't been dunking his cheese bread in his ale, he would have been more believable. Who does that, after all?

"No," continued the younger man, Gerard, as he

swept a well-maintained cowlick off his forehead. "No one can take the moon down from the sky, and if someone could, it wouldn't be Sebastian."

There was a chorus of approval at this comment. While most everyone (except possibly Gerard) liked Sebastian, the consensus was he wasn't anyone very extraordinary. If anyone could take the moon down from the sky, it probably would be someone special. Gerard was confident in his opinion it would have been he, himself, who would have been able to do this before a nobody like Sebastian.

Sebastian was born in the village and spent his not very special youth there. The only thing anyone at the pub could think of that was even a little unusual about him was being so young and living alone in his father's house. Of course, in some ways, his father was special. He had moved to town a long time ago, with his young pregnant wife in tow and with some kind of mystery about him, something about having been a soldier. He had settled down to farming until his wife died, giving birth to Sebastian. After that, it was farming and raising his son. And until the fever took him a few years back, he hadn't given the villagers much to talk about, which was how they liked it for the most part.

The mayor, who felt he had to take charge of this conversation to assert his stamp of authority on the crowd, said, "Like father, like son. The father was some kind of big-wig soldier, and now the son thinks he can take the moon down from the sky."

The older gentleman, dismayed at how he was losing the crowd's attention and still smarting at the way Gerard had shown him such disdain and denial, spoke up.

"If you don't believe me, go outside. I bet the moon was up when most of you came into the pub. You know it should be rising, not setting. Go outside and look for it."

There was a bit of a rush outside. It was a sparklingly

clear night. Seeing as the moon was no longer in the sky, the stars were taking advantage to show themselves at their best and brightest. The night sky was beautiful, the stars were shining like diamonds, but being from a small village, they all knew where the moon should be, and it was gone.

After filing back inside and muttering to themselves a bit about the disrespect the youth of today showed for the natural order, they looked at the mayor for some answers. The mayor, realizing there were upsides and downsides to being in charge, announced,

"All right. I need to talk to our young man and see what he thinks he's up to."

# 2

Sebastian's house was on the outskirts of the village, just barely inside the town wall. (The town wall was mainly just a fence. Some parts were a little higher, and some sections were more substantial, but much of it was just a fence like you would have around a field on a farm. The mayor liked to refer to it as the town wall, as that made him feel like the mayor of a town with a wall, not just a village with a fence.) Sebastian's father had maintained a little distance from the other villagers. Not that they minded this, as quite a few of the villagers liked to keep to themselves.

As the mayor approached Sebastian's house, he felt a little nervous. He thought about why that might be for a moment. He had known Sebastian since he was born, and Sebastian had always been a quiet and careful youth, not inclined to cause trouble or really to stand out in much of any way at all. Still, a little nervousness was perhaps called for, as the pulling down of the moon from the sky was a bit of a surprising thing. When one surprising thing was happening, others might as well.

Sebastian's house was nothing unusual for the village. There were some one-room cottages, but most homes in the town had more than one room. As one might expect from a bachelor living alone, he hadn't done much with the exterior decoration. The house was white, whitewashed rather than painted. Like most houses in the village, Sebastian's home was built of wattle and daub over a wooden frame. A few of the wealthier villagers had clay brick houses. The mayor prided himself on his.

* * *

The mayor knocked on the door, noticing an unusually bright glow coming from a window as he did so.

"Sebastian?" he called out.

"Come in," came a voice from behind the door.

The mayor opened the door and stepped inside. The door opened into the house's central room, with other doors opening back to the bedrooms and the kitchen. There was a hearth in the center of one wall. There, hanging just above the mantel, was the moon. It was a radiant moon. The sort you would look at and marvel at how full and beautiful and shiny it was. For those who could see him, the man in the moon's face was staring down, his mouth opened in shock. Perhaps at the fact that he was now in a house living room instead of in the night sky. The mayor thought it was the sort of moon where you would look at it and marvel at the feeling it was almost close enough to touch.

It took the mayor a moment to notice it, as the moon's presence was a little distracting, but hanging on the wall just beneath the moon was a well-polished old sword. The sort of sword a veteran of battle might keep to remind himself of his past.

Sebastian stood in the center of the room between the mayor and the moon. The light was outlining him a bit, and it surprised the mayor to notice how tall he had gotten. The mayor still had the tendency to think of him as just one of the kids running around town. Though, now that his father had died and he was a property owner, the mayor might have to start thinking of him differently.

"So, look at that," said the mayor.

"Yes," said Sebastian, looking at the moon. "It's pretty, isn't it?"

\* \* \*

The mayor questioned Sebastian for an hour, but all he could get out of him was, "I thought it was pretty, and I wanted to hang it over the mantel." Sebastian didn't seem to have a deeper reason for what he'd done and no idea how. So with no answers which would help him with the pub crowd, the mayor decided he had to look for more expert help.

## 3

Lilith lived in her own small house on a hill just outside the village fence to the north of town. No one called her a witch, though that's what everyone knew she was. When the mayor knocked on her door and stepped inside, she cackled and said, "I know why you're here."

This startled the mayor for a moment, then he remembered that was also how Lilith had greeted him the last time he came in to talk to her.

When we said everyone knew Lilith was a witch, that was not entirely correct. Everyone was aware that Lilith could do and knew things they couldn't do and didn't know. If two women from the village were sitting at the bar in the pub, and one said to the other, "Eh, my John, he just isn't doing the things in the bedroom that he used." The other might reply, "Oh, only give our Lilith a shout. She's a cunning one. She'd come up with a potion or summat that'd help."

If two men from the village were leaning against the back fence looking over the cows, and one was to venture, "Bossy is not for the best today. I think she might have a touch of the bloat." The other might well reply, "Talk to the cunning woman Lilith. She helped when our grandson Ralph ate the entire pot of beans we meant to keep for the week. Don't know what she did, but she fixed him right up. Taught him a lesson as well; she did. He's been a right good lad since that day."

Lilith wasn't a witch, per se. She was the village's cunning woman. She had learned her cunning from the previous cunning woman, who recognized something in Lilith as a girl and had passed on her secrets. They were genuine, those secrets. Lilith could cure bloat. She could help with many ailments and injuries. Lilith couldn't make a potion that would make a young person fall in love with another young person. But she could produce one which would make them reconsider whether a specific person was a prospect for romance. Which, if you think about it, is in some ways more real and more difficult. She could do some other more impressive things, though she tried not to do too much when the villagers were around. The idea that all magic was wrong was not common; the idea that some magic was wrong was.

The most important thing (at least at the moment) that the previous cunning woman had passed down to Lilith was the knowledge that what she knew and what she taught was just the beginning. There was magic as far beyond what she had learned as she was beyond the magical knowledge and power of a child. Speaking of children, another thing Lilith had learned was to recognize the potential for cunning in others. There was very little in this village.

* * *

In Lilith, the mayor recognized the need he often felt himself to make sure of his position with a certain amount of facade. So, he ignored Lilith's comment about knowing why he was there. Lilith's facade extended a little beyond this comment, as the mayor well understood. Listening carefully to Lilith's cackle, you might recognize the pleasant laugh of a relatively young woman concealed beneath a little attempted senile cackle sound overlay. Lilith had also been known to try to dress the part, with hoods and a little attempted shadow lurking as well. Let's say her cunning exceeded her acting skills.

The mayor filled Lilith in on how Sebastian had pulled the moon down from the sky with no further delay. She made no attempt to disguise her excitement at the report. After she confirmed that the moon was actually missing through a convenient window, Lillith eagerly followed his request to go and try to find out more. It wasn't far from Lilith's house to Sebastian's, and anticipating the most exciting thing which had ever happened in this village, Lilith fairly flew across the distance.

* * *

Sebastian wasn't much more forthcoming to Lilith than he had been to the mayor. The mayor had a different priority than Lilith did on the two main questions they wanted answered. The questions were *Why* and *How*. The mayor was very concerned about *Why*. He had difficulty putting himself into the shoes of a young man who would go out one evening and pull the moon down from the sky. That's the kind of thing that people would talk about forever. It would be challenging to become mayor of a town when people could find something like that in your past. He didn't care so much about *How*. He knew *How* was somehow important, but he felt it was above his intellectual pay grade.

Lilith didn't give a flaming cow patty about *Why*. She understood that *Why* might be interesting to someone like the mayor. She couldn't bring herself to care about the motivations of a guileless boy like Sebastian. *How*, however, was a burning, blazing torch for her. If she could get any glimpse into *How* from Sebastian, she might be able to master some of it for herself. There were also hints from the person she had learned her cunning skills from that there were places to contact and things to do if indications of real power showed themselves in the village.

* * *

Lilith could feel the power in the room (it came off the moon in waves). Unfortunately, Sebastian was still pretty much the same innocent villager she had thought him to be. He didn't have anything helpful to say about how he had pulled the moon down from the sky.

* * *

There was nothing left but to report the lack of news to the mayor and go to bed.

# 4

The village of Westhavenfieldbrook was seldom referred to by name. Everyone who lived there simply called it the village, except, of course, the mayor, who refused to say anything but "town." Nestled between the Blue Mountains to the east and the Westhaven River to the village's west, it was a quiet, peaceful village. Too quiet and peaceful for some.

The village boasted a mill, a brewery, a smithy, a one-room schoolhouse, any number of small farms, and not much else. The mayor bragged about his civic improvements- the cobblestones in the market square and the town wall and gatehouse. Really there wasn't too much to brag about. It was a quiet village.

Quiet, yes, but prosperous. No one went hungry in Westhavenfieldbrook. Many of the residents had houses or cottages with more than one room.

There was a brook that flowed through the village. After beginning its journey in a trickle high in the Blue Mountains, it ran through the millwheel on the east side, through the village's center, and finally into the river.

From the miller's perspective, it was an excellent thing that the mill was on the east side of town. As in many villages and towns, sanitation was an issue in Westhavenfieldbrook. By the time the brook's waters made it to the west side, you wouldn't have wanted them flowing over your millwheel.

The most prominent street, which led out of town, didn't connect directly to the main road. You could head north out of the town gate, and after half a mile or so, you would intersect with the main road, which ran from east to west. It ran east toward the blue mountains and west toward an old stone bridge over the Westhaven River. Most people traveling along the road wouldn't bother heading south to the village.

The village was very scenic. Looking west from beyond the last row of houses, you would overlook green fields with old stone walls rolling gently down to the shores of the Westhaven River.

Looking east from many places in the village, including the market square, the majestic Blue Mountains showed themselves on the horizon.

# 5

The following day was market day. The previous night's events had shaken people, and many were still trying to wrap their heads around what had happened. But, market day was market day, and things had to get done.

Sebastian had been planning to sell a cow on this market day. This was long in the planning. He needed some roof repairs, more than he could do himself, and selling the cow was intended to finance the job. Surprisingly, though, he found himself walking toward Main Street on his way to the square on this bright market morning without a cow in tow. Also, surprisingly, he found he wasn't going to turn around to go back and get the cow. Suddenly, the selling of the cow was not compelling for him. He found he was going to market for different reasons. He didn't know what those reasons were, but he was confident he would know them when he saw them.

Sebastian felt good as he stepped down Main Street toward the market square. The sights and sounds of people getting ready for the market surrounded him. He skipped a little as he strode down the street, kicking up a small cloud of road dust. The village's streets, even Main Street, were still dirt, in a way like the town wall was still a fence. The market square was cobbled, one of the points of pride of the mayor's tenure, but cobbling was expensive, took time, and hadn't yet been a priority on the streets.

Main Street was broader than the lanes and alleys leading off it, but it was still a narrow village lane. With carts transporting goods to the market square and early risers walking to the market, the street was crowded.

Sebastian waved to Mr. Arkwright, the blacksmith, as he loaded up a cart with worked metal objects he would bring to his booth.

Mr. Smith, the fishmonger, always had a friendly smile. It was often best, however, to maintain a little distance. The more exotic of his wares were imported, and the nearest ocean fishing ports were not very close. It was best to buy local fish from the river. His cart had a special double-wall, which was supposed to be filled with ice, but he had been finding ice hard to come by, and the best he could come up with was cold water from the mill brook.

Mr. Shepherd, the miller, was up ahead with two carts. One loaded with various-sized bags of flour and the other with different varieties of bread. It was a mark of pride in the village that they had their own mill. Unfortunately, Mr. Shepherd and his family weren't the best bakers, and their baked goods left a little to be desired. Many people in the village bought or bartered for flour and baked their own bread.

# 6

**M**rs. Fisher, the village carpenter, led a cart pulling from a side street into Main Street. She had loaded it with beautifully worked chairs, chests, and small cabinets. Mrs. Fisher was a skillful carpenter, and the market day was her day to shine. Also shining, as far as Sebastian was concerned, was her daughter Isabel, who was supporting the load from the side.

As the cart pulled into the street, Sebastian found himself face to face with Isabel. His skipping missed a step, as perhaps did his heart.

Sebastian hadn't spoken to Isabel in years. Not since his father had died and not much before then. The closest he had come to doing more than talking to her was looking at her ponytail.

* * *

The village had a small one-room schoolhouse. Mrs. Shoemaker ran the school with a temperament of iron and a ruler that felt like steel. She had been the village school teacher since before the mayor was born. When the children were in school, they sat at wooden desks in tight rows. Moving was not tolerated, not in class. When recess was called, a flock of children would flee barefoot into the dusty school courtyard. Or perhaps you could say a horde if a group of eight to ten children could be called a horde.

While seated, Mrs. Shoemaker could monitor whether or not you moved. She could tell you off if she saw your eyes wandering, but she couldn't tell you off if you sat quietly and stared straight ahead. For years Sebastian had the desk directly behind Isabel. He stared faithfully straight forward, his eyes taking in every detail of her dark brown ponytail and the hairs on the sides of her neck that escaped that ponytail. The thought had occurred to him, more than once, that if he was one of those hairs, he wouldn't have tried to escape.

Somehow, Mrs. Shoemaker had gotten hold of some very satisfactory wooden desks with seats, a top which opened, and a built-in inkwell just above the hinge on the desktop. They were a bit worn but very serviceable. When practicing penmanship, the inkwells came in quite handy. There was another use for the inkwells, which Sebastian was familiar with. A couple of times, one of his male classmates had helped the female student seated in front of them to a new hair color by dunking her hair into the inkwell. The perfect hairstyle for the execution of this maneuver was, of course, the ponytail.

There were several reactions to this, only slightly different each time. Mrs. Shoemaker, of course, would implement the harshest punishment she could. This was some combination of smacks with the steel ruler, sitting in the corner with the dunce cap on, and an extended period of social disgrace. The other children, especially the other boys, seemed to accord the lawbreaker a new measure of respect. But the most significant reaction, and the one which weighed most heavily on Sebastian's awareness, was the reaction of the girl in question to the perpetrator of the act. Was it an act of ultimate disrespect, or was it an act of ultimate love?

Sebastian had spent several years pondering this question. If there was any way of knowing that ponytail dunking would have been taken as something positive, nothing would have stopped him from doing it.

# 7

Sebastian almost cried when he looked at Isabel on this bright market day morning. She had cut her hair. The new hairstyle was fetching, but the ponytail was gone. She was moving so quickly that he nearly ran into her.

\* \* \*

Sebastian and Isabel both came to a stop, facing each other.

Here is where the little dance we all do when running into someone starts. Both stop; One moves left as the other moves right. Embarrassed smile, one moves right, as the other steps left. Eventually, it gets disentangled. That's not what happened here.

Isabel looked up at Sebastian. For a moment, she wondered who this tall, confident-looking young man was, then she recognized him. *Of course, it's just Sebastian*, Isabel thought. She started to smile and step past him, but he didn't move meekly out of the way as she expected.

"I'm sorry, Isabel. I wouldn't ask this of you if it wasn't important," he said.

Isabel nodded uncertainly, not sure what he was asking.

Then Sebastian did something rather unexpected; he knelt in the dusty road at Isabel's feet. She thought he was proposing for a moment and didn't know what to think of that. But instead, he reached out and took a firm grip on her right ankle. The grip wasn't hard enough to make her fall, but the unexpected nature of the contact made her lose her balance. She slipped backward, and with a small flurry of yellow dress and white petticoats, she landed on her rear. Sebastian still had a grip on her right ankle. For a second, she thought about how strong his hands felt, then indignation filled her, and she let out a grunt of protest.

She felt an unfamiliar pulling sensation at her ankles as he seemed to do something to them. Then Sebastian stood again, offering her his right hand to help her up. There was something dark in his left hand. Perhaps a pair of dark things. They were moving around in his grip. With a scowl, she took his hand, and he pulled her back to her feet.

"This is my market-day dress," she complained.

"Sorry," Sebastian repeated, "I'll have them back to you as soon as I can." He kept hold of her hand for a moment and pressed it to his lips before releasing it.

"Them?" she said.

Sebastian turned and headed down the road in the direction of the market.

* * *

Isabel indignantly started to stride off after him to demand an explanation but found her feet weren't working right. They didn't hurt, and they looked fine, but when she tried to move them, they seemed lighter, and she felt wobbly.

Mrs. Fisher came over to her.

"Isabel, are you all right?" she said.

"Mama, my feet feel funny," Isabel said.

Mrs. Fisher gave a gasp and pointed at Isabel's shadow. As mentioned, it was a sunny morning, and Isabel's shadow was painted clearly on the road dust. That is, most of her shadow. Her shadow from head to ankle, including the shadow of her pretty, slightly-dusty, market day dress, was clearly visible. There was nothing there from the ankles down. There was a six-inch gap in her shadow from the bottoms of her feet to the tops of her ankles.

# 8

Sebastian continued on toward the market. It felt like a great day. He felt like he had some idea of what market day was about today. He stuffed the dark shadowy things he held in his left hand into a pocket. He started skipping again. The sunlight shone through the dust kicked up around his feet.

Gerard walked down the street toward the market square, ahead of Sebastian. If Sebastian felt good, Gerard felt great. He loved market day. There wasn't anything to sell, but that wasn't what a market day was about for him. He had a new shirt, a fine-looking thing with many glorious colors mixed in a beautiful pattern. He had a bright sunny day, and with it, the expectation of many of the fine young ladies of the town fawning over him as they often did on a market day. Gerard was even hopeful someone from a neighboring village, or perhaps even further afield, was here for the market. It didn't happen often, but sometimes someone interesting would arrive. Gerard was eager to make sure any newcomers to the village met the right people. That, of course, meant Gerard.

A peddler had come through town a few days ago. Not an altogether unusual occurrence, they were frequent travelers on the roads. Peddlers sometimes had some cunning knowledge. Sometimes they could repair things. But, primarily, especially for Gerard, they had goods to trade. The peddler had had the shirt which Gerard was wearing. The first thought that crossed Gerard's mind when he saw it was that he needed it for market day.

The peddler had some silly patter about the shirt. "Glorious weaving," "fine eastern fabric," "colors of a peacock's feather," and other similar stuff. All Gerard thought when he saw it was how good he would look in it. If he left the top two or three buttons open, a bit of his chest hair would peek through. *The colors* are *reminiscent of a peacock's feather,* he thought, *blue and green with a touch of yellow and purple.* Shirts of more than one color were unusual in the village, and Gerard was excited to see people's reactions.

* * *

Sebastian, due to his skipping, was catching up to Gerard. Gerard turned and looked to see who was coming up behind him. His smile changed to a bit of a scowl when he saw it was Sebastian. He had never been terribly fond of Sebastian. Of course, as children, they had often been part of the same games. The village was small enough that all the children had known each other as they grew. As they got a little older, Sebastian had put a bit of a damper on Gerard's effect on the ladies. For some reason, some of them went for the quiet, respectable, modest type of presence that Sebastian offered. Of course, he had no idea how to leverage this, but the simple fact of the contrast turned some of them off of Gerard.

Also, Gerard was annoyed at Sebastian about the pulling down the moon thing. If anyone was supposed to do something that got the entire village's attention, it was supposed to be Gerard, not Sebastian. Someone who knew how to dress, not someone dressed like a beggar, or worse yet, a farmer.

*Pulling the moon down from the sky, what was that?* Gerard thought, *An attention-getting move if I ever heard of one.* Gerard wished he had thought of it first.

Sebastian stepped up beside Gerard, clapped him on the shoulder, and directly met his gaze. Gerard was a little taken aback at this. As part of the whole modesty act, Sebastian usually let Gerard control the eye contact when they interacted.

"Gerard, if it's not too much trouble, I would like to borrow your shirt," Sebastian said.

More than a little taken aback, Gerard was

astonished to find himself starting to take off his shirt. *Why am I doing this?* He thought. *Sebastian can't tell me what to do.*

Perhaps to justify the shirt removal to himself, Gerard thought, *It is a bit warm. The shirtless look always works for me, anyway. Didn't I see Isabel back there a little way? It wouldn't hurt for her to see my chest.*

His hands got stuck a little in the sleeves, and he felt Sebastian reach out to help him. He felt an unfamiliar pulling sensation in his chest like something was being tugged out of him, along with his shirt being pulled off. Then he stood next to Sebastian, who held his beautiful new shirt in his hands.

"Thank you, Gerard," said Sebastian. "I'll give it back as soon as I can." He turned away to start walking down the road.

Gerard felt empty. As if he had lost something.

"Wait, Sebastian," he said. He was surprised to feel tears starting to form in his eyes. "What do I do now?"

"You'll be all right, Gerard," Sebastian said. "Just try to think about what you *want* to do."

Sebastian headed on down toward the market and started whistling as he kicked up a little more sunshine and dust with a skip.

\* \* \*

Gerard stood for a moment in the middle of the street. He wasn't sure he felt like going to the market anymore. He watched Sebastian skip off with his shirt and thought that the shirt was awfully bright. It seemed to glow in Sebastian's hands. It was a little much, with all those colors. He thought he might go home and find another shirt, a more modest one. And maybe, he'd take a nap.

## 9

S ebastian reached the market square. The market wasn't in full swing, but people were milling about, and many booths and carts were open. He felt the cobbles beneath his feet. The mayor was right to be proud of the cobbling. It helped keep the dust down and made the square feel elegant and respectable. It made the village feel more like a town.

Sebastian didn't notice, but he was drawing stares from the villagers. Most of those who weren't directly involved in the action last night had been told something about what happened by somebody. They weren't sure what to do with him, but they were very interested to see what he would do. Sebastian still had Gerard's shirt in his hands. It was too big to fit into a pocket, so he tied the sleeves around his waist. If he'd known he would be collecting stuff, he might have brought a backpack.

\* \* \*

The town hall bordered one side of the square. It was more of a village town hall than a town town hall, but there it was. On both sides of the stairs leading to the main door were grassy areas, with a bench on each side. On the one to the left of the stairs, a small man was resting.

Leonard was the town fool. On this day, he was resting in the shade, enjoying the market's noises and sights and smells. No obligations were placed on him, and the village took care of him as best it could as a community. If he was hungry, he could ask anyone for food, and they would provide him with some of what they had. If he needed a place to sleep, someone would have a spare bed or at least a pile of hay in the corner of a barn. This wasn't an official thing, just something that had happened and continued to happen.

Mrs. Shoemaker, the schoolteacher, was at least partly responsible for Leonard's status. She was the one who despaired while trying to teach Leonard when he and Sebastian were fellow students. Leonard, Gerard, Isabel, and Sebastian were all of a similar age. Leonard and Sebastian had been friends during school times. Sebastian still thought of Leonard as his friend, though they had grown apart as they took on their adult roles in the village.

Leonard smiled as he saw Sebastian approach.

"Moon and shadow, Sebastian," he said, "Moon and shadow."

Sebastian smiled back.

"Moon and shadow, Leonard," he said. Someone must have told Leonard something about the events of last night. What he'd been told and what he understood were probably quite different. Still, Sebastian was confident his own understanding of what was going on probably wasn't much better.

Sebastian didn't feel Leonard was missing anything in terms of his intelligence, just that the way he thought and perceived the world differed from other people. It made it hard for Leonard to fit in in the village. When he was having trouble with Mrs. Shoemaker, Sebastian had tried to help. But Leonard couldn't say or do things how Mrs. Shoemaker needed him to, so it had never worked out.

"Are you enjoying the market and the morning, Leonard?" Sebastian said.

"The sun is shining through people today, Sebastian," Leonard replied.

Leonard wore homespun brown clothing, plain and functional. Today, as on most days, he wore a brown linen cap. Sebastian reached out, grasped his old friend on both sides of his head, and pulled their heads together so that they were face to face, only inches apart.

"Hey Leonard," he said, "I need to take something

from you. Is that all right?"

Leonard looked startled, a little frightened, then he nodded.

Sebastian gently gripped the cap on Leonard's head. He tugged upward, and it seemed like there was effort involved in pulling the hat up. Still inches from Sebastian's, Leonard's face took on an expression that looked awestruck, like what he was seeing was something marvelous he'd never seen before. As the cap raised, something dark, gray, and cloudy was suspended between the inside of the hat and the top of Leonard's head. The gray cloud pulled out of Leonard's head and into the cap. Sebastian took a step back, hat in hand, and waited for Leonard's reaction.

Leonard rose to his feet and looked around.

"Thank you, Sebastian," he said. "I'll be seeing you."

Sebastian folded the cap in two and tucked it into his belt.

"Good luck, Leonard," he said.

Leonard started walking briskly away, heading down a side street. He was leaving the market square as quickly as he could. He took one look behind himself and sped up a bit as if fleeing from something.

# 10

Sebastian looked around himself and realized he and Leonard had had a bit of an audience. The village children usually took advantage of market day to travel around the square as a group, looking for fun and minor trouble. It hadn't been so long since Sebastian, Isabel, Leonard, Gerard, and their peers had done the same. Some children were hiding behind a tree on the other side of the town hall stairs. There were several watching from the edge of the cobbles of the square. A few more were scattered around in other places.

Sebastian smiled to himself, clapped his hands, and called out, "Scat!"

They scattered, embarrassed to have been spotted. One boy, hiding behind the tree, tripped as he tried to run. Sebastian noticed some blood on his pant leg. Striding over to where the boy was scrambling to his feet, he called out, "Hey, you, wait!"

Sebastian continued, "What's your name?"

"Marcus," said the boy with a tremor in his voice.

Sebastian remembered now, Marcus Arkwright, the blacksmith's son.

"Hey, Marcus," he said, "what happened to your leg?"

"Old Widow Clark's dog. He's a mean old thing. We were trying to sneak by, and he bit me."

Sebastian remembered this as well. It really hadn't been so long ago since he was in Marcus's shoes. Old Widow Clark, who Sebastian thought of as Mrs. Clark, had been told by the mayor to keep her dog tied up any number of times. When the dog was loose, he terrorized the street. He had been young when Sebastian and his peers had to deal with him, but it didn't seem like age had mellowed the dog any.

"Let me see if there is anything I can do about that,"

Sebastian said. After offering Marcus a hand up, he headed off toward Blackbird Lane.

Blackbird Lane was where the Widow Clark had her brewery. It was a mark of pride in the village that they had a brewery. The Widow Clark's brew actually had a reputation that extended a bit beyond the town borders. Not too far, but a couple of neighboring villages bought from her in addition to the local trade. Sebastian noticed the gang of kids following him, led by Marcus. They kept a discreet distance behind him but seemed very keen to keep him in sight.

Sebastian reached Blackbird Lane. He could see the dog a little way down the street. Loose again. When Sebastian and his peers had dealt with him, they speculated that Widow Clark kept him for additional security. The further speculation was that she was rich from her product's sales, and there was wealth to guard. Sebastian tried to remember the dog's name. It was something he had always found ironic, like Pico or Tiny. Something that really didn't fit with the snarling, barking monster who had just spotted him and was charging down the lane toward him.

Sebastian's recollection was that Pico wasn't really a killer. He mostly liked to scare and enjoyed watching people run away from him. Sebastian also noticed Pico was definitely getting older. In addition to the gray flecking his muzzle, he was a step slower than Sebastian remembered. He was already panting from the effort of charging down the lane.

Sebastian sidestepped the rush, and Pico wheeled around for another pass. He was panting again but determined to show who was in charge.

As Pico rushed again, Sebastian stepped forward and reached out both hands toward the dog. One hand landed on top of Pico's head, and the other went down his throat. Pico seemed to stop in midair for a second as the hand that had gone down his throat emerged with something clenched in it. The dog dropped to one side, rolled on the ground, and started gagging. The thing in Sebastian's hand looked like a piece of leathery fabric. It was white or off-white and looked light and airy.

Pico climbed to his feet, still gagging, and started barking in indignation at Sebastian. The dog tried to bark, at least. As he opened his mouth and made all the actions that should have turned into a bark, no sound emerged. Confused by this failure, Pico tried whining, with a similar result.

Sebastian inspected the white thing in his hand for a second, with a puzzled look on his face. Then he folded it as best he could and tucked it through his belt next to Leonard's cap. Turning back to Pico, he attempted to approach, his hand outstretched, lowered a bit, to allow Pico to sniff it.

Pico stood his ground for a second, looked at the approaching hand, attempted again to bark with a similar failure to produce any sound, then turned and charged back down the lane toward home.

# 11

There was a small informal gathering of concerned citizens in the pub that afternoon. Convinced this was a meeting he had called, all indications otherwise aside, the mayor addressed the group. He banged his empty ale mug on the bar to get some attention.

"I know everyone is very concerned about what's going on with Sebastian," he said, "but don't worry. I've got it all under control."

The chatter he had momentarily interrupted resumed.

"Did you hear what he did to old Widow Clark's dog?" One voice said.

"Leonard's left town," someone else said.

"Leonard's left town?" came a third, "Where will he go? How can he travel?"

"Isabel's mother is worried. She says Isabel's feet still don't have any shadows."

\* \* \*

The mayor wished for a second Gerard was with them in the pub. He sometimes appreciated how Gerard could make people listen to him. It wasn't that Gerard always said the most intelligent things. Still, they were stated with such confidence. The mayor had asked Gerard if he wanted to come to the discussion, but Gerard said he wasn't feeling up to it.

The barroom of the pub was all dark wood and beams. The ceiling was low, and the doorways even lower. When Sebastian came to the pub, which wasn't very often, he had to duck his head to enter.

Lilith chimed in. Everyone stopped talking and turned to look at her. For a second, the mayor was jealous. Then he imagined he had asked everyone to pay attention to Lilith, so that was all right.

"I still don't think Sebastian has any power of his own. What's happening is being done to, or with, or at him, not by him. On the other hand, it doesn't seem like he's being controlled by anything, so he still has his own free will. There's power flowing through and around him," Lilith said.

There was a moment of puzzled silence as the listeners tried to process and respond to this information, then the chatter resumed again.

"What do you think will happen next?"

"Should someone try to catch up to Leonard to see if he's all right?"

# 12

I n the late afternoon, Sebastian returned to his house. There were still things to do. He had to make up for spending most of the day at the market. He stepped over to the mantel, admiring how the moonlight reflected off his father's sword. He had to change before heading out to the fields. He hadn't dressed up fancy for the market, but he hadn't worn his work clothes either. Also, he had to unload all this stuff he had collected.

He gazed at the various things stuffed into pockets or hung on his belt and, for a moment, had no idea what to do with them. Then he took the shadowy black things that he had taken from Isabel's feet out of a pocket. By the full moon's bright light, they were even darker and more substantial than they had looked under the light of day. He held them for a second, then smoothed them out with a stroking motion. They looked like just what they were, the shadows of a woman's feet. Sebastian took them and placed them on the floor a bit to the left of the mantelpiece. As they hit the floor, they took on an even more substantial look, and by the bright light of the moon, a pair of dark shadowy boots stood there.

Sebastian pulled the thing he had taken from Pico out from his belt, unfolded it, and looked at it by the moonlight. It was light and felt like a piece of fabric. White with an airy texture. It seemed like a piece of cloth woven out of wind and air. Placing the material carefully on top of the boots near the mantel, Sebastian watched as it shaped itself into a pair of trousers standing on top of the shadowy footwear.

Untying Gerard's shirt from his waist, Sebastian put it on the trousers. Hardly surprised now when it stood upright on top of the pants, he pulled Leonard's hat from his belt for the finishing touch. He put the brown cap on top of the neck opening of the shirt. Something was holding all these things up. If you looked out of the corner of your eye, it looked like a person standing guard by the mantelpiece. Sebastian didn't spend much time speculating about what held it all together. It seemed like a small thing compared to what he'd been living through recently.

After finishing his evening chores, making sure the animals were safe for the night, and securing the farm, Sebastian stepped back into his living room. The moonlight lit up the figure standing next to the mantel. Sebastian proudly thought it was like a suit of armor guarding a castle, though more colorful. The black boots, white trousers, peacock-styled shirt, and brown cap presented a look that made Sebastian smile. After taking in the sights of his living room for a moment, Sebastian sighed with satisfaction and headed to bed. He had the feeling it had been a good day.

* * *

Lilith had gone to bed early. The stress of trying to explain things to the villagers was very tiring. When strange things happened, though nothing this peculiar had ever happened before, the villagers thought of the cunning woman as the one who could help. She'd repeatedly explained that she had no more idea what was happening than they did. She'd finally gone home exhausted and dropped into a deep sleep. Her sleep had ended, with a start, just now. She sat up in bed and wiped a bead of cold sweat off her forehead. Something was coming to the village. Something bad.

# 13

I n addition to not having a stone wall, the village didn't really have a night watch. The mayor had set up a schedule, but it wasn't updated as often as it should be, and people had a tendency to skip out on guard duty every now and then. Because the fence which circled the town wasn't complete or maintained terribly well, the urgency of guarding the main gate didn't seem too high. There was a gate, however. Like the cobbled marketplace, it was relatively recent. It was part of the mayor's attempt to upgrade the village to a town. It was mainly wood instead of stone and iron, but it was closed and locked at night.

Tonight, in a significant victory for village security, the gate was closed, locked, and two guards were present. William and Reynard had decided to play cards. As William was on guard duty and it was a pleasant evening, they had pulled a wooden table and a pair of chairs out into the road behind the gate and were enjoying a game. When Reynard spotted some people approaching the gate, he brought them to William's attention. William grabbed the two tankards of ale sitting on the table and tried to hide them behind his chair.

It was very unusual to get unexpected visitors, especially at night. The excitement of meeting strangers was almost enough to offset the disappointment of interrupting the game. William stepped up to the gate. Putting on his most official voice, he called out, "Who goes there?"

There were five of them, though one seemed to be a child. A woman approached the gate with the child beside her. She said, "We're from the ruin of the village of Anesbury. We seek refuge. We've been traveling a long and weary way. Can you open the gate and let us in?"

William turned to Reynard and said, "Reynard, go

get the mayor and Lilith."

* * *

The woman looked dusty from the road, but none of the five seemed threatening. They all had backpacks or improvised bags as if they had fled their village with just what they could carry on their backs. The child holding the woman's hand was a little girl. She couldn't be more than ten years old. Her swollen, red eyes made it clear she had been crying, and not long ago.

* * *

William made an executive decision and opened the gate. He ushered them in. The other three, two more women and an older man, moved carefully inside. They seemed to assume the woman who had spoken first would be their spokesperson.

"If you'll have a seat," said William, "I've sent for the mayor."

"My name is Rose," said the woman who had spoken first. "Have you heard what happened to Anesbury?"

"They say in other parts of the kingdom, news travels as fast as a swift horse, but around here, it travels as fast as a lame, cranky mule," said William with a smile. Then he flushed for a second as he realized how inappropriate joking might seem to these people who had just apparently undergone something horrible.

Rose didn't seem to notice. She settled with a sigh into one of the chairs which William and Reynard had been sitting in. William felt embarrassed again. He realized he couldn't offer them much hospitality without leaving to go get someone to help. William had the feeling he shouldn't leave them here by themselves.

"Let me get some more chairs," he said, rushing off toward the gatehouse.

* * *

To William's great relief, it wasn't long before the mayor and Lilith showed up, with Reynard trailing behind them. Rose hadn't told him much, just that the girl's name was Anise, as she didn't want to have to repeat herself too many times. The other three had continued their silence as if they were in shock.

The mayor suggested they retire to the meeting room in the town hall, arrange some food and drink, and figure out where their visitors could sleep. He sent William and Reynard off to rouse people to help prepare.

After they settled at the main table in the town hall meeting room, and each of their guests had something to eat and drink in front of them, Rose told them her story.

# 14

Rose began, "I've lived in Anesbury my whole life. My whole family lives... lived there." For a moment, she seemed like she might break down in tears. All five of them looked exhausted. Anise was resting her head on her arm on the table. Her hair was draped over her face, so it was a little hard to tell, but from the gentle moving of her shoulders, it seemed she was sobbing quietly into the crook of her arm. The other three adults still looked shell-shocked and were content to let Rose do the talking.

"Anise is my sister's daughter. My sister and her husband were the first to see the thing coming."

Anise lifted her head at this.

"I saw it first," she said. "I was out in the field, and I saw it standing behind the fence. It was huge and looked really scary. When I saw it walk through the fence, without stopping or even slowing down, I ran to get mama and papa." At this mention of her mother and father, who obviously weren't with them, she lowered her head again, and the quiet sobbing resumed. When Anise looked up and started speaking, Lilith focused on her with a curious look on her face.

Rose continued. "It was, as Anise said, big and scary. On our journey here, when we were sharing our stories of what we saw, we took to calling it 'the beast,' so I guess I'll call it that. My sister, her husband, and Anise ran to the central square. The sun was starting to set. We had a bell tower, which was a landmark in the town. We rang it on the hour to mark the hour. Still, everyone in the village knew that it meant something was wrong if it rang twice. It hadn't rung twice in my lifetime, but if you grew up in our town, it was trained into you from an early age. There were still people in the square, so someone was there to help ring the bell.

"People came running. As I said, the bell had never rung twice before, but we all knew what it meant. Our cunning woman, Robin, arrived early and grilled my sister and brother-in-law about what they saw. We didn't have a mayor, and Robin was, for all practical purposes, the leader of the village."

The mayor felt an involuntary shiver run down his spine when he heard this.

Rose resumed her story, "Someone climbed the bell tower to see what was happening. Other people arrived who had seen the beast as well. It didn't seem to bother with roads or paths. It just walked through anything that got in its way. It headed straight toward the square. The people who were ringing the bell kept ringing it. There didn't seem to be any reason to stop.

"At this point, those of us in the square, which was most of the village by then, could hear the sounds it made as it came toward us. Crashing and crunching sounds. Louder, as it got closer than anything I've ever heard before.

"It arrived at the edge of the square and then just stopped. It stopped and stared at us expectantly like it was waiting for something. As I said, at this point, pretty much the whole village was there, and both the villagers and the beast just stood there waiting for someone to make the first move. I wish I could describe what it looked like, but I literally can't. We've talked about that, and it seems that it looked different for everyone."

"I've told you, Aunt Rose," said Anise, without lifting her head. "It was a nightmare."

"I know, Anise," said Rose, "it was. For me, at least, it must have been ten feet tall and an indeterminate gray color. It didn't have a face but somehow still had a mouth. As Anise said, a nightmare.

"That's when I saw the bravest thing I have ever seen or will ever see. As I said, it was just standing there, expecting something, and we were all frozen too, waiting to see what it would do. So Robin stepped forward, moving towards it, and tried to talk to it. I could see her gesturing and tell that she was speaking, but I couldn't hear what she was saying.

"It waited for a second, perhaps trying to see what she was doing, then advanced forward itself and just ate her. It basically just engulfed her. It somehow opened up, moved on top of her, and she was gone.

"That broke the paralysis. There were screams, and everyone started running in all different directions. It was total chaos. I lost track of my sister and brother-in-law but somehow kept hold of Anise's hand.

"I looked back over my shoulder as we were running and saw it ripping pieces out of the bell tower. The whole thing started shaking, and a little later, I saw it fall. After that, it just started attacking people and tearing down buildings. I've never seen anything like it.

"We got out of the village and just followed the first road we came across. We've been walking for days. As far as I know, we're the only survivors, though I hope others escaped in different directions.

"Nobody in our village even had a weapon, except hunting gear. There was nothing we could do."

# 15

T he following morning, as promised, the mayor took their visitors on a tour of the village. They seemed to be feeling a bit better. The mayor thought *A good night's sleep and a good meal can work wonders. Also, the return of the feeling of everyday village life might be helping as well.*

There wasn't too much to show in the village, though the mayor didn't let that stop him. Or even, truth be told, slow him down too much.

He showed them the gate and the gatehouse in the town wall, though they had seen that last night when they came through it. It had been dark then, so they hadn't seen much. He didn't mention that the gatehouse had the town's entire armory, comprising two spears, which the night watch didn't even really know how to use. Of course, he did mention that the gatehouse and the wall were built under his tenure.

He led them on a walking tour of the entire village, including showing where the prominent citizens lived. This didn't, of course, include Sebastian's farm. However, they saw him coming into the market square from another street as they walked into the market.

Anise cried out and grabbed her aunt's arm. "That's him, Aunt Rose, that's my hero, my knight, the one I told you about!"

A little annoyed that they weren't appropriately impressed by his cobblestones, the mayor said, "That's no hero. That's just Sebastian. Something strange has been going on with him, but he's not a knight. We don't have any knights in this village, little girl."

"He *is* a knight!" said Anise. "I wished for him, then I dreamed him, then I asked him in my dream, and he said he would help me. I knew he was here. That was why we had to come to *this* village."

"Anise," said Rose, "The mayor's been kind enough to show us around town. The least we can do is be polite and listen to him." She turned to the mayor and, addressing him directly, said, "She's been having strange dreams lately. Not too surprising considering what she's been through. Please continue."

Relieved he would get the chance to talk about his cobblestones, the mayor did so.

\* \* \*

The townsfolk settled the refugees into extra rooms and provided them with food. Rose and Anise, because there were the two of them, were offered the opportunity to move into an unoccupied cottage. The villagers were happy to help them get back up on their feet. Though the implication was if they were staying on, they would need to find a way to contribute to the local economy.

\* \* \*

Rose had been a baker in Anesbury, and though the cottage she and Anise were in didn't have the best kitchen she had ever seen, she made do. She had to borrow the ingredients for her first baking attempt, but it was well-received, and she was able to barter loaves of bread for ingredients for her next batch. Within a few days, she had the beginnings of a business, or at least the beginning of a way to keep herself and Anise clothed and fed.

\* \* \*

Anise, in the meantime, spent a few days getting the lay of the land. She got orientated and learned how to get from their cottage to critical places in the village. She met a few local children, but she didn't have time for them, as she was on a mission. With a bit of detective work and a little sneaking, she managed to figure out where Sebastian lived. She knew he was the hero of her dream.

She was hiding behind a bush across from Sebastian's house. When she saw him come home after bringing the cows in from the fields, she waited just a moment longer. The light from the setting sun shone across the house front as Anise got up the courage to cross over and knock on his door.

.

# 16

Sebastian opened his door. "Hello there," he said, looking down at Anise. He hadn't been very involved with the refugees or their stories. Aside from some strange looks received while walking around the village, his life had returned to routine the last few days. He didn't mind that so much, although the feeling of adventure he had had when unusual things were happening had been exciting.

Anise was nervous, but she knew what to do. She stepped forward, just over the door's threshold, and dropped to one knee. She didn't know what to do with her hands, so she folded them together in front of her.

"Hail, Sir knight," she said.

Sebastian looked startled and paused for a second before he started laughing. He held out his hand to help her up and said, "My name is Sebastian. Where did you get the idea I was a knight?" He continued, "Also, I don't think people need to kneel to knights, anyway."

"But you are a knight," Anise insisted. "You told me so yourself. You're the Knight of Moon and Shadow."

"I told you?" Sebastian said.

"In my dream. I wished for you, and then I dreamed you. You told me you were the Knight of Moon and Shadow and that you would help me."

"I can assure you," said Sebastian, with the echo of the laugh still in his voice, "that I am not a knight of any kind. By the way, even if I am not the Knight of Moon and Shadow, I still need to know your name?"

"I'm Anise," she said. She realized what was wrong. "You're not the Knight of Moon and Shadow yet," she announced.

"I'm not?" said Sebastian. "I thought I was?"

"Not yet," said Anise. "You need to have a squire, and

you need to be knighted."

Anise looked into the room and saw the moon and the sword hanging over the mantel. Beside them was the stack of outlandish things Sebastian had collected. She smiled a self-satisfied smile.

"I'll be your squire," she said in a tone which brooked no discussion, "part of my job will be to help you put on your armor," and she gestured toward the stack of things.

"Armor," said Sebastian, "that's not armor, it's just some weird things I borrowed....," his voice trailed off as he realized that the way the things were piled up did make it look like an odd-looking suit of armor.

"I can help some more," said Anise. "I think I know what to do to make you the knight." She headed over towards the mantelpiece and tried to reach up toward the sword. She was quite a bit too small to reach it, but even so, as soon as he saw what she was trying to do, Sebastian interrupted.

"Careful with that. It's sharp."

*　*　*

Sebastian's father had taught Sebastian many things. One of the most emphasized was that a weapon should be respected and well maintained. The sword was sharp because Sebastian took it down once a week, every week, and repeated his father's ritual of cleaning, polishing, and sharpening it. He had done this ever since his father died.

Sebastian stepped over to the mantel and pulled the sword off the wall. He grabbed the sheath also and sheathed it before handing the scabbarded weapon to Anise.

"You'll have to leave it in the scabbard," he said, "it's too sharp to play with otherwise."

"I guess that'll work," said Anise uncertainly. She turned to Sebastian. "Now kneel," she commanded.

Sebastian took a knee, and Anise tried to raise the sword above his head. Even kneeling, he was too tall, or she was too short, or some combination of the two. Anise motioned for him to wait and pulled a chair over from the table. Pushing the chair in front of Sebastian, she climbed up onto it.

Anise lifted the sheathed sword as far over her head as she could. "I dub thee...," she started to say. Her speech was interrupted as her attempt to flourish the blade around in a flamboyant swing failed. She lost her balance and almost fell off the chair. After a moment of stabilization, she lifted the sword and tried again.

"I dub thee, the Knight of," and here she touched the sheathed sword to his right shoulder, "Moon and," and she carefully lifted the sword over his head and touched his left shoulder, "Shadow."

* * *

With her goal achieved, Anise was almost glowing like Sebastian's moon as she walked home. The knight from her dreams was here to protect her.

## 17

The following morning was bright and cheery. Lilith walked through the marketplace, enjoying the sunshine and the sounds of the village. Since they had arrived, she had wanted to talk to the refugees, the new villagers, but hadn't had time until now. She passed through the market and headed down the lane that led to Anise and Rose's new cottage.

Rose and Anise fascinated Lilith. Especially Anise, though Rose seemed interesting herself, in her own way. But Anise was setting off Lilith's cunning sense. There was something special about the girl. The way Lilith perceived a person's cunning ability differed for each person. Anise was showing something which Lilith had never seen before.

She reached the front door of the cottage and knocked. It seemed like Rose had already been doing some gardening in the few days she had been here. Newly planted rose bushes lined the path on both sides of the doorway.

"Who is it," came a voice from inside.

"It's Lilith," Lilith said with a cackle. She and Rose had met when Rose arrived and had interacted a bit since, so Lilith was sure Rose would remember her. The cackle was just insurance, playing the part of the old village cunning woman.

Rose invited her in and made some tea. The cottage kitchen, where they were sitting, smelled pleasantly of the bread Rose was baking. Rose and Anise had begun to settle in, and the kitchen looked happily lived in. Rose's baking had been going well, though it meant early mornings. People wanted fresh bread to break their fast, so bakers were busy before everyone else got up.

Handing Lilith her tea, Rose noticed her looking around and said, "Anise isn't here. She's been going out early and wandering around the village. I'm glad to see her occupied. I know she won't forget, but I want her not to be thinking about the recent past."

Lilith nodded. "I need to ask you about her."

"What do you need to know?" said Rose.

Lilith hesitated a second, weighing her words carefully.

"My mistress Evelyn, she who taught me the ways of the cunning folk, showed me how to see that which is cunning in others. I think I see something in Anise. I need to train her."

Rose hesitated as well. She dropped her voice a little, though no one other than Lilith was listening.

"She's just lost her parents," her voice broke slightly as she said this. "I need her to have some time to be normal for a while before starting anything new."

"Have you noticed anything unusual about Anise," said Lilith. "Anything about her you thought was strange as you saw her grow up?"

"Anise has always been a happy child. She seems normal to me. Imaginative and bright, but not unusual."

"Of course," said Lilith, "we'll talk about this again some other time."

Rose looked a little relieved that Lilith was not going to press the issue.

"There is one thing," she said. "She has always had strange dreams. She'd dream about some problem or worry and then dream someone was helping her solve it. That's why I didn't worry about what she was saying about your Sebastian. It was just another one of her dreams."

Lilith thanked Rose for the tea and reassured her with a comforting press of the hand as she left. She promised to be in touch in the future about the training.

* * *

That evening, just as the sun was starting to set, the beast arrived.

# 18

I t started just as it had in Rose's story of Anesbury. The beast appeared on the edge of the village and slowly made its way directly toward the center. Instead of traveling down roads or lanes, it walked in a straight line, crashing through everything which stood in its path.

\* \* \*

It happened that the direction the beast took went directly toward the main gate. Reynard was on guard duty this evening. He heard the crashing noises and stood up to see if he could tell what was making them. Everyone in the village had heard some version of Rose's story by now, but Reynard was there when she arrived, and he heard her tell it directly.

In the days since the refugees arrived, Reynard had heard lots of talk about the story. Many people didn't believe it. Some people accepted parts of the story, but the idea of the "Nightmare" or the "Beast" left them skeptical.

Reynard believed. He had seen Rose's face when she was telling the story. Reynard believed, and in some ways, had been waiting for this. He thought he knew what the crashing sounds were even before seeing anything.

Reynard got one of the spears out of the gatehouse with a resigned sigh. They were kept sharp and well maintained, as what use is a poorly maintained spear. Reynard took his spear and went to stand behind the gate.

The sun was setting. The gate was closed and shut at the first trace of sunset, so it was already locked. Reynard peered through the bars of the gate. The crashing sounds were awfully close, so he was surprised he couldn't see anything yet. Then he did.

With bricks and thatch scattering everywhere, the beast burst through the wall of a house-the house just on the other side of the street from the gate.

How to describe the indescribable. As mentioned, it looked different to each person who saw it. Perhaps it was, as Anise had said, a nightmare. Maybe it was taking something from the fears of the observer and building something fearsome for them personally.

Reynard thought for a moment about running, but he was on guard duty. He braced the spear on the dirt road behind him and kept the point aimed at the beast.

The beast hesitated for just a second, then stepped up to the closed gate and made a backhand sweeping gesture with its left arm, tentacle, or whatever it was. The motion swept the part of the fence it touched, the gate, Reynard, the spear, and the gatehouse aside like so much debris. The beast stepped forward, over the remains of the gate, and continued toward the town center. It ignored the pile of rubble to its left.

* * *

The village didn't have a bell tower as Anesbury had. But many people were gathering in the market square, anyway. The crashing sounds of the beast's arrival had alerted many to events, and others had been told. The market square was the central meeting place for the village. It was where the town hall was, and the villagers seemed to gravitate to it.

The lamps had been lit, and the sun was still not fully down, so there was enough light to see the signs of the beast's progress. It was heading right toward the market. It's not clear if the market square was actually in the center of town or if the creature somehow knew where it was, but regardless, that's where it headed.

Aside from the crashing sounds, another unavoidable racket was all the dogs in the village barking insanely. The dogs knew from the noise and the barking of the other dogs that this was their moment. Years of alertness, waking up in the middle of the night to alert their people about strange events, led to this. This crowning moment, this was their time.

Rose stood in the square, surrounded by the other villagers. Fear was flooding her mind, making her limbs feel heavy. *Not again*, she thought. She felt an absence to her right. Hadn't Anise been holding her hand? She looked around, even more panicked.

"Anise!" Rose wailed.

# 19

A nise pounded on Sebastian's door. Somehow he hadn't heard all the noise. The beast's progress toward the square was in the direction opposite to his house. He opened the door, and Anise dashed in.

She filled him in on what was happening. After he had some idea, Sebastian started to rush out the door. Anise stopped him.

"Sir knight," she said, "aren't you forgetting something?"

"Anise, this isn't the time for games," Sebastian said.

Anise just pointed at his father's sword over the mantel.

Sebastian hesitated a moment and then realized she was right. Even if there was no chance to do anything, there was no reason to leave a perfectly good weapon sitting on the mantelpiece of his home.

He walked over to the mantel and pulled the sword down. Sebastian accidentally bumped the moon as he reached for the sheath. His heart stopped beating. He had a feeling of great responsibility for the moon. He was just a caretaker.

The moon fell off the wall with a clatter and dropped to the floor. It looked fine, with no cracks or scratches. Sebastian knelt carefully to pick it up. As he did so, he noticed straps on the back, which was otherwise flat and black as a moonless night sky. The straps made it clear it was intended to be worn like a shield.

While Sebastian crouched, looking at the shield straps, he felt something cover his eyes. Anise had taken Gerard's shirt from the pile of things by the mantel and was trying to pull it over his head. It was easier to finish pulling it on than to fight it. He felt a surge of confidence and strength as he stood, his father's sword in one hand, the moon in the other, and Gerard's shirt on.

Sebastian laughed. He felt good. Why was he always so careful? There was nothing he couldn't do if he set his mind to it.

He took a look at the shirt he was wearing. He saw why Gerard had liked it. The colors were stunning. And why shouldn't a man try to look good if he was a good-looking man? Somehow, though it looked the same, the shirt felt thicker and more substantial than it had.

Anise handed Leonard's cap to him, and Sebastian folded it over his belt. He knew the cap was not to be worn until the right moment.

"I'll help you put on the boots, but you're going to have to put on the pants yourself," she said.

\* \* \*

Sebastian stepped out the door of his house, followed closely by Anise.

"You said it was headed to the market square?" he said, puffing out his chest a bit, so the moonlight from his shield reflected a little better on the peacock colors of his shirt.

Anise just nodded, and the two of them set off together. Sebastian had to keep consciously slowing down to keep pace with Anise for some reason. It felt like they were moving at a snail's crawl.

\* \* \*

Sebastian and Anise arrived at the market square from one side, just as the beast arrived from the other.

# 20

The beast stepped up to the edge of the square, stopping right at the beginning of the cobbles. It stood there as if it was waiting for something. The villagers were facing it, so no one saw Sebastian and Anise enter the square from the opposite side.

It momentarily crossed the mayor's mind that he should do something as the village leader. The thought crossed his mind quickly and then continued on its way. Even if he hadn't heard Rose's story, his idea of what being mayor of this village meant was cobblestones and walls, not nightmare monsters.

Isabel and her mother were standing in the crowd as well. Isabel had her hand on her mother's shoulder, partly to reassure her and partly for balance, as she was still a little shaky on her feet.

Rose was the only one who wasn't looking at the beast in the crowd. She was still frantically looking around for Anise. When she spotted her arriving at the far side of the square, her shout was loud enough to get everyone's attention.

"Anise!"

As the crowd turned at the shout, Sebastian stepped into the square. He stepped forward, his chest thrust out, the moon shield on his left arm, his father's sword strapped to his belt.

He presented a curious sight. The black boots on his feet seemed to blend into the flickering shadows. At certain moments, they looked like leather boots colored black. At other moments, it looked as if Sebastian didn't have feet at all, as if his lower legs just faded into the night shadows.

His pants, glowing as the white color reflected the light from the lamps around the square, looked sturdy yet still flexible. Something about the material made it look like you could blow it away with a breath, but it seemed substantial, anyway.

Sebastian still had Leonard's hat folded over his belt. The color combination of the hint of brown at the belt, the bright blue and purple shirt, the white pants, and the black boots might not have been a hit at a fashion show. But in the flickering light of the setting sun and the lamps, there was something very striking about it. The glow of the full moon strapped to his left forearm brought the whole appearance to an otherworldly look.

The crowd of villagers parted as he stepped forward. The beast was still standing, waiting at the other side of the square. Sebastian headed directly toward the creature through the parting crowd. Anise made as if to follow him, but Rose sprang forward and grabbed her arm.

Some of the villagers gasped as they recognized Sebastian. Some just stared with their mouths open. Sebastian sped across the square, moving more quickly than seemed possible. When he got within a certain distance of the beast, he stopped, and the two stood for a moment, facing each other.

The beast still seemed to be waiting. It stood, if stood is the right word, immobile as a rock. Rose remembered how it had behaved in Anesbury. *It's waiting for a challenger,* she thought. *It's a nightmare, and it needs a dreamer.*

\* \* \*

As mentioned, the beast seemed to look different to each viewer. Here, it stood in front of a crowd. Each person was seeing something they feared the most. Perhaps because he stood close to it, or maybe because he was challenging it, Sebastian now saw what all the people perceived at the same time.

Sebastian's heart skipped a beat, even with the brashness he was drawing from Gerard's shirt. It was the hardest thing he ever did to pull himself together and take a step forward toward the beast.

# 21

The beast seemed to accept the challenge. It took a step forward as well, reared back its head, and let go a roar that shook the buildings around the market square. If they hadn't been paralyzed with fear by the spectacle before them, half the crowd would have fled at that moment. Something about that roar shook you down to your deepest fears.

Sebastian also thought about fleeing. Brashness is brashness, but it's not quite the same thing as bravery or recklessness. Though his hand was shaking, he reached down to his belt and pulled Leonard's cap out.

Hesitating for a moment, Sebastian held the cap in his hand, worried about what putting it on might do and whether he would be able to take it off. Realizing there would never be a better time, Sebastian slapped the hat onto his head.

Sebastian's confidence jumped through the stratosphere. *There was nothing to worry about here; this would be a piece of cake. The beast was history.* Sebastian straightened his back and lifted his eyes to meet the creature's gaze. He momentarily remembered the saying, "Give me an army of the foolhardy or the brave, I don't care which."

The beast pulled back its left arm/tentacle/limb and prepared to give a blow to Sebastian as it had to the gate. The crowd saw what was coming and moved collectively back to avoid the impact. When it hit, cobbles were flying everywhere, but Sebastian, or his body, was nowhere to be seen. The mayor, somewhere toward the back of the crowd, gave a despairing groan.

Abruptly, from the beast's left, Sebastian emerged from the shadows. He crouched down and lifted the moon on his left arm toward the creature. The bright light from the full moon shone into its face, and it staggered back momentarily.

Afterward, those who were there said it felt like Sebastian could disappear into one shadow and emerge from a different one.

The beast roared again, and the crowd recoiled. Sebastian seemed utterly unfazed.

He darted back between the beast and the crowd. With his movement to avoid the blow, he had left an open path from the creature to the villagers. He seemed to be trying to prevent this. The villagers gasped again when they saw how fast he was moving.

One of the villagers turned to his neighbor. "How is he moving like that? It has to be faster than old man McGinty's fastest horse. You know the one. The one who won the race at the last midsummer fair?"

"But," the neighbor replied, "did you smell that smell? Every time he moves, there's a smell like a dog's bad breath."

* * *

Sebastian stood facing the beast again. It couldn't get to the villagers without going through him. In fact, though, it didn't seem to be eager to avoid that. Going through him seemed to be precisely what it wanted to do.

Sebastian lifted his shield, seeing the glow of moonlight spilling over the beast. He reached across to his sheath and drew his father's sword.

# 22

The sword felt comfortable in his hand. It was the first time he had drawn it, with intent, in a real fight, but not the first time he had drawn it, not by a long shot. In addition to teaching him the importance of cleaning and maintaining a sword, his father had spent a respectable amount of time teaching him how to use one.

"Parry in four, for that attack," his father said. "Remember to use the forte, the strong section of your blade, against the weak part of his. You don't need to whack his sword out of sight. Just displace it enough so that it doesn't hit you."

In addition to fencing, the civilized sport of sword fighting, where he learned the rules, his father taught him when his opponent would break the rules and when he should as well.

"In a real fight, it's not about whose fencing is the best or who's being the most honorable. It's about who lives and who dies."

Sebastian had hated the drilling. He always told his father he would be a farmer, and he was the son of a farmer. There didn't seem to be a point. They'd trained with sticks most of the time, and he'd often told his father he felt like a fool, waving those sticks around.

"Who knows," his father had said, "maybe someday this foolish stick waving will turn out to have been a good idea."

They'd spent countless hours drilling and practicing. Much more than Sebastian was happy with. They'd mainly trained in the yard behind the house. Sebastian's father had trellises growing wine grapes there. He made a couple of barrels of wine a year from them. They would dodge back and forth between the rows of vines. The clatter and clanking of the sticks hitting against each other echoed off the trellises. Sebastian often wondered what the neighbors thought the sounds were.

Sebastian's father never talked about his past. Whenever he was asked, he'd said something about leaving the past in the past. Pressing hadn't worked and seemed to make him mad, so Sebastian learned to let it be.

Sebastian also never learned much about his mother. Like his past, talking about his wife made his father uncomfortable.

In the end, though, Sebastian's father had to admit Sebastian was getting good. If there were any fencing competitions to enter, who knew if he would have been winning them but, by the same token, who knew if he wouldn't have been.

Sebastian was almost certainly the only person in the village who knew how to use a sword or any weapon, really. The night watch's training with the spears primarily taught them which end was the pointy end.

\* \* \*

Anyway, this is only to say when Sebastian drew his sword, it felt comfortable in his hand.

# 23

The beast swung one of its arms or tentacles at Sebastian. Instead of dodging the blow or fading into the shadows, Sebastian took the impact on his shield. The jolt drove him backward, but the moon bore the shock without denting or scaring.

Sebastian launched a counter-attack with his sword. He swung at the tentacle. It looked like he hit the beast, but it hardly seemed to notice. It would take a lot more than that to do any real damage.

Anise, listening to some villagers in the crowd wondering about Sebastian's unique armor, said with pride, "That's the Armor of Gifts. I dreamed it up for him. He'll have to give it back." She looked a little sad at this.

Then there came a brief period of feeling each other out. Sebastian and the beast launched attacks and counter-attacks, each trying to see how strong their opponent was, trying to learn what would be the best strategy. Here was where the creature showed itself to be more than just an animal, as it seemed to be willing to take its time and not just launch mindless attacks.

Sebastian stumbled on the edge of the broken cobblestones while taking a step backward, recovering from a lunge. His foot slipped among the cobbles. The sound was loud in the night's absolute stillness and the hushed crowd. The chorus of dogs had quieted. Either they had said all they needed to say, or something about the beast's closeness silenced them.

The creature sensed an opportunity. It charged forward and slashed at Sebastian with the edge of a tentacle that looked at that moment, razor-sharp.

Off-balance from stumbling, Sebastian partially managed to get his sword up to block the swung tentacle. He mostly blocked the blow, but the razor edge bent around the sword blade and cut into his abdomen. There was the sound of ripping fabric and the smell of blood in the air.

Sebastian gasped and retreated more quickly. He looked down at his side. There was a rip in Gerard's shirt's purple and blue fabric. There was blood on the edges of the tear, but it didn't look or feel too bad. What did feel strange to Sebastian was the change in his mind. The confidence he was drawing from the shirt, or whatever of Gerard's he took with the shirt, wasn't gone. It just felt different.

The beast was still advancing on him, and Sebastian felt the need to slow it down or make it back up to keep it away from the crowd. His side ached a little, but he didn't feel like it would be enough to hinder him.

Sebastian launched a series of attacks, and the beast backed off a little in its attempts to avoid his sword. It was the first time he got it on the defensive, and it reassured him, as it meant the beast felt like he could hurt it.

The creature came at him again and thrust with one limb. He parried and riposted. He felt his sword sink into the beast's flesh. There was a smell like rotting meat, like something dying. Sebastian tried to pull his sword back, and it caught in the creature for a moment. He felt a flash of panic, and a bead of sweat distracted him as it dripped from the back of his neck down his spine. Then the sword came free, and he was able to step back. A trickle of dark blue fluid ran down the beast's side from the wound.

The beast roared again and charged toward Sebastian, enraged by the wound. This was the moment Sebastian was waiting for. Taking advantage of the beast's momentary mindlessness, Sebastian sped into the nearest shadow and disappeared. He emerged right beside the creature. He lifted his shield, shining the moonlight full onto the creature's face, and thrust his sword deep into its side.

The beast gave another roar, with a different tone this time. The cry sounded puzzled. It was as if the creature hadn't imagined that it could lose this fight. It fell to the ground, with a crash that shook the entire village and a splash of cobblestone fragments.

Sebastian stopped for a second, breathing heavily, then the sound of the crowd of villagers' cries of delight reached him.

## 24

The beast's body lay on the shattered cobbles for a moment, then it started to fade. What had seemed so substantial a second ago, so solid, faded away to nothing. After a moment, Sebastian had trouble recalling what it looked like. If he'd ever known in the first place.

The villagers remembered, or at least if they didn't recall what it looked like, they didn't care. They knew that it had been there and that they were sure it would kill them all. They crowded around Sebastian, clapping him on the back, congratulating him, and praising him.

Anise tried to get through the press to talk to her knight, but too many people were around him, and she couldn't. Anise saw Isabel standing on the edge of the crowd. She was looking at Sebastian with a puzzled look on her face like she'd never seen him before.

Somebody retrieved some strips of cloth from somewhere and carefully bandaged Sebastian's injured side. At first, they tried to rip Gerard's shirt to get to the wound, but Sebastian would have none of that. He pulled the shirt up as far as possible to give them access.

Someone else talked the Widow Clark into donating a keg of beer, and the occasion seemed well on the way to turning into a party. Then, some of the villagers remembered it might not feel like a party for everyone and went off to check what had happened at the main gate.

The gate was a ruin, and both the gatehouse and gate had been swept into a pile of rubble, but imagine everyone's delight when they found Reynard after digging through the debris. There were a few broken bones, and at first, he didn't know where he was, but he was alive, and recovery was just a matter of time.

The mayor was with the people who went to check

on Reynard. He was excited to see Reynard alive but not so happy to see the main gate's ruin and what was left of the gatehouse. A little later in the evening, he was seen slumped over a beer, bemoaning the state of his civic improvements. Someone tried to cheer him up by suggesting that the place where the beast had fallen would make a perfect spot for a historical marker or statue. He went over and looked. The cobbles that weren't damaged were stained with the creature's blue blood. The body was completely gone by now. He perked up a bit and was overheard muttering something about tourism.

Someone started playing some music. There were no traveling musicians in town, so it wasn't particularly good music. The villagers who could perform weren't as skilled as they might have been. Still, it was music nonetheless, adding to the party atmosphere.

At one point, Anise noticed Sebastian had managed to slip away. She wasn't sure how long he had been gone, but he wasn't in the square anymore. Avoiding Aunt Rose, who had been looking for her for a while now (Anise was sure it was to tell her it was time to get to bed), she ran off to find him.

## 25

S ebastian was looking through the contents of a box he pulled from under his father's bed. He had left his father's room untouched since his death, except for a bit of dusting. This box contained everything his father had kept that had been his mother's. There wasn't much in there. He opened the box because his mother had been the keeper of the family sewing kit.

When Sebastian arrived home from the market square, he first placed all the gifts, as he had started thinking of them, onto their places. Then he got dressed in more simple clothes and headed directly for this box. For some reason, the rip in Gerard's shirt was bothering him, and he felt like there was nothing more urgent.

Sebastian took the box and went to find a seat in the front room. He took the sewing kit and put it aside for the moment. There were two pieces of jewelry in the box as well. One was a locket he had seen before, which contained a tiny painted portrait of his mother. He had seen his father looking at it and crying a few times. The other was a jade pendant in the shape of a heart. He didn't know the exact story behind this piece, but his best guess was his father had given it to his mother.

Sebastian put both jewelry pieces around his neck, then got up and got Gerard's shirt from its place. He settled down and retrieved some purple thread from the sewing kit. Sitting there and mending the fabric with his mother's sewing kit made him feel close to his parents.

Sebastian's father had taught him how to sew. He wasn't particularly brilliant at it, but mending your clothes was a lot more thrifty than getting new ones.

There came a knock at the door.

"Come in," said Sebastian.

The door opened, and a breathless Anise rushed in.

"Sir Knight...," she said.

"Anise, I've said, please call me Sebastian." Sebastian had the tone of a patient person whose patience was being tested.

"Sebastian," Anise said, sounding a little uncomfortable with the name. "Why did you leave the celebration?"

He just held out the shirt with the threaded needle attached.

He resumed sewing, and Anise sat quietly and watched him for a moment. The appearance and disappearance of the needle in the fabric and the steady motion of Sebastian's hands were hypnotic. Anise felt like something was being done that was more significant than just the mending of a shirt.

"I'm almost done," he said. "With the shirt, I mean," he continued. "I know I'm not done yet with being a knight."

"I know too," said Anise.

## 26

The following morning Sebastian got up early. He dressed in his gifts and packed as best he could for an extended journey. Sebastian had never been on such a long trip before, and he felt very unsure about it. It helped when he got dressed, especially when he put on Gerard's shirt, but some uncertainty remained.

He wrote a note, offering the farm's produce to a fellow villager who would maintain it for him while he was gone. He had no one specific to ask, but one of his fellow villagers should welcome the offer. He planned to give the note to the town watch as he left town. Assuming that anyone was watching what was left of the gate.

Sebastian packed a backpack with the food he could find in his pantry that would travel well. He didn't know how long he would be on the road, so he packed carefully. The townsfolk usually bartered for things they needed, so Sebastian didn't have much money in coins. He put what he had into a small pouch and put it at the bottom of his pack.

It was early enough that he hoped he wouldn't run into anyone on his way to the gate. As he stepped over the threshold and closed the door, he felt a momentary pang of sorrow. This would be the longest time he would spend away from this house in his life.

Sebastian didn't run into anyone on his way to the gate, but as he approached the gatehouse ruins, he saw a group of people standing there. His first thought was he should have snuck out a different way. The fence around the town was not very secure, and there were many ways to get through. In fact, the backyard of Sebastian's house had a gate that led outside the village fence. If he hadn't been planning to give his note to whoever was on watch at the town gate, he would have gone that way.

Sebastian thought about heading back and leaving

the village by another route. But they had already seen him and were heading toward him. In fact, it seemed like they were waiting for him specifically. Anise was there, and Rose. The Mayor, Isabel, and her mother. Mr. Thatcher, the farrier, was there holding the lead of a mule. There were several other people there as well.

The mayor stepped forward and announced, "Sebastian, my boy, I need to thank you again for your service to this community. When Anise told us of your quest last night, your community spirit struck me dumb. You already did so much for us by defeating that creature. To think you're still at it astonishes me. What did she call it, 'The Quest of the Dreamer'?" The mayor grabbed Sebastian's hand and pumped it up and down with an almost painful vigor.

After leaving Sebastian, Anise had gone around the night before and told everyone in the village he was planning to leave town to track down where the beast came from. "There's nothing to stop more nightmares from coming unless he tracks it down," she told them.

Several of the people waiting had prepared supplies for Sebastian to take with him on his journey. Rose had been up since before dawn baking goods intended to travel well. Besides other kinds of baked goods, she had a specialty that was a flat raisin cake with a slightly sweet breaded crust. She had prepared a bundle of these for Sebastian to take with him on the trip. Sebastian didn't have the heart to tell her he hated raisins.

After being presented with the supplies people were so generously offering him, Sebastian thought about his simple backpack. There was no way he could take a fraction of this with him. Mr. Thatcher stepped forward and handed him the lead to the mule's halter he held.

"Her name is Betsy. She's a bit moody, but she's a hard worker," he said. Betsy peered at Sebastian as he took her lead. She put both her ears back, which he hoped meant she was considering whether Sebastian's taking the lead was acceptable to her and not that she was about to head-butt him.

Sebastian was overcome. "This is all too much," he said. He felt a little moisture seeping into the corner of his eyes, which he resisted, as it felt like an inappropriate moment.

"Nonsense, my boy," said the mayor. He slipped a small pouch containing some coins into Sebastian's hand. "In case you run into any unforeseen expenses," he said with a wink.

With a bit of help, Sebastian distributed the supplies onto Betsy's back. Once she was loaded, Sebastian took her lead and started to head out of the village.

Anise turned to Rose. "Aunt Rose, are you sure I can't go? A squire needs to be with her knight."

"Not a chance, Anise," said Rose.

"Good luck, my lad," called out the mayor.

Isabel ran forward, and putting her hand on Sebastian's chest, she stood on tiptoes to reach up and kiss him on the cheek. The morning sun shone right through her feet.

## 27

Sebastian floated on air as he left the outskirts of the village. It was a beautiful day; the sun was shining; there was an open, blue, almost cloudless sky; she had kissed him. Sebastian led Betsy. She gave him a look and cocked one ear forward while putting the other one back.

"She did," he said defensively. "I think she really wanted to, too. It wasn't just because she felt sorry for me."

Betsy looked skeptical.

It *was* a beautiful day. Not too hot, with just enough of a crisp edge in the early breeze to make the morning sunshine feel pleasantly warm instead of hot.

Anise and Sebastian had agreed that the first step he needed to take would be to travel back to whatever was left of Anesbury. From there, he might be able to track the beast further back toward its origin. It didn't strike Sebastian as odd that he was taking advice from a ten-year-old. There were even more unusual things going on.

Sebastian looked to his right as he walked along the road. He admired the sweep of the blue mountains on the horizon. To his left were the fields between the lane and the Westhaven river. He wouldn't have to walk far down the path before reaching the main road. Anesbury was to the north and east of his village. He'd been given some directions as he left town, but he also knew that each of the road's intersections would be marked. A series of old stone markers were put up a long time ago. They were old but serviceable.

It was hard to imagine that just yesterday, he'd been in a battle with a nightmare. Sebastian allowed himself a moment of pride. "I really did save the village," he said quietly to himself.

"Heee Awwwwwwww!" said Betsy. It was clear to

Sebastian she was thoroughly dismissing his heroism. He got a little defensive.

"I did," he said. "Imagine what could have happened if I hadn't been there?"

Betsy snorted, and Sebastian gave up. There was no use arguing. He knew mules and knew how stubborn they could be. He was just happy she was following the lead without complaint.

He reached the intersection with the main road. The signs were there-old stone markers, carved many years ago. The one pointing back down the lane he had just walked read 'Westhavenfieldbrook.' That stone was longer than those indicating the other directions. The last few letters of the name were carved more lightly than the earlier letters as if the stone-workers had gotten tired of carving.

The name 'Anesbury' was not yet on the markers, but his directions were clear. Usually, the stones were carved with two engravings, the next village's name and one of the larger towns in that direction.

Sebastian turned to the right, to the east, toward the mountains.

# 28

Sebastian walked all that day. (Betsy did, too, of course). The weather continued to be mild, though the balmy sunshine that was enjoyable in the morning hours became a little less pleasant later in the day.

During the hottest time of the day, Sebastian pulled off the road when he saw a shady spot near a stream, and he and Betsy took a little rest. It was cool and refreshing in the shade, and Betsy certainly appreciated a few minutes to graze on some fresh green grass by the bank of the stream. It surprised Sebastian to discover he wasn't half as tired as he thought he should be. They'd been walking for quite a while, but his legs still felt fresh and energetic. They continued as soon as he could drag Betsy away from her grassy stream bank.

\* \* \*

Later, Sebastian looked for a spot to camp for the night when the sun started to set. He couldn't find anything as welcoming as the spot by the stream where they had stopped earlier. Still, he found a place where he could tie Betsy up, pitch the tent that he found in one of Betsy's saddlebags, and lay a fire. Sebastian unloaded the mule and tied her up near the fire. For one thing, he wanted to be able to keep an eye on her, but he also thought it would be nice to have her close.

Sebastian knew how to build a fire, and he was used to being by himself. (In fact, with Betsy's company, he was less alone than he had been since his father died). He was unaccustomed to being outside with a campfire, preparing and eating dinner under the stars.

It was a moonless night, of course, but Sebastian was the only one in the world who had a solution for that. He took the moon off of the pile of Betsy's saddlebags and leaned it up against a rock near the edge of his fire pit. Sebastian dined under the stars with an excellent lady companion, who only occasionally grunted and snorted, by the light of a beautiful, full summer moon.

Sebastian told Betsy in great detail about his feelings for Isabel. He told her what life was like, growing up in the village with Gerard, Leonard, Isabel, and their peers, for company. Sebastian told her about his doubts about this quest. He told her he had no idea what had happened the last few days and how that worried him.

Betsy grunted at the appropriate moments. She encouraged him to continue with a thoughtful ear flick when it was correct to do so. At one point, when he mentioned something particularly interesting, she gave her mule whinny, a cross between the he-haw of a donkey and the whinny of a horse. A "Heee Awwwwwwww!" sound.

Just before Sebastian retired to his tent, he told Betsy, "You're a good conversationalist. You really know how to listen."

## 29

I sabel was watching her mother putting the finishing touches on a cabinet. She was planing the top smooth. Isabel's mother was a perfectionist. Anyone else would have been finished already, but she saw some barely detectable flaw on the cabinet's top surface. The final step would be sanding and staining it, but that couldn't be done until everything else was exactly perfect.

Mrs. Fisher and Isabel made most of the wooden furniture for the village. Their workshop was attached to the house. It was well equipped.

Isabel was supposed to be helping. She was 'officially' apprenticed to her mother as a carpenter. Usually, Isabel was a hard worker, but this evening she seemed distracted.

"Mama," she said. "What do you think of Sebastian?"

Mrs. Fisher grunted. Perhaps not the most ladylike response, but appropriate for the occasion to her mind.

"You mean the fact that he stole the shadows from your feet or that he just saved us all from a horrible death?" she replied.

"No, I mean Sebastian," said Isabel. "What do you think of him? Do you think he's good-looking? Do you think he's nice? That's what I mean."

Mrs. Fisher was a widow. Isabel's father had died several years ago. It was unusual for a widow not to remarry and run her own business. But, Westhavenfieldbrook was a progressive town in its own way.

"You mean, if he were to make a pass at me, would I respond?" said Mrs. Fisher with a smile.

Before Isabel could reply, she continued, "Well, he is a good-looking young man. I always thought of him as a very nice boy when you two played together as kids. I'd be tempted, but I have to say, I think he's a bit young for me."

"No, Mama, I mean for me," Isabel said.

"Oh," said Mrs. Fisher, with an expression of mock surprise. "I didn't realize he was for you."

# 30

Sebastian and Betsy traveled the following day without incident. There were few other travelers on the roads, and those few didn't seem interested in talking. The weather was still clear and bright and not too hot. They passed through several intersections, but each time Sebastian's directions were enough to allow him to determine which way to go. Finally, the last set of stone markers they passed included "Anesbury" on one of the arrows.

Sebastian knew they wouldn't make it to Anesbury before dark. So as the sun began to set, he looked for a place to make camp.

\* \* \*

The sun was getting low in the sky, and he still hadn't found a place. Sebastian had been hoping to set up camp while it was still light.

The welcome sight of a campfire off the side of the road ahead caught Sebastian's attention. Hopefully, the rules of traveler's hospitality would apply. He pulled Betsy's lead forward and headed toward the firelight.

As Sebastian entered the circle of light, he saw a large man sitting by the fire. Not large in the meaning of tall, nor excessively broad, but more in his presence. The man looked up, smiled when he saw Sebastian standing there, and waved a greeting.

Sebastian walked over, still holding Betsy's lead, smiled, and returned the greeting. He noticed the man had an enormous handlebar mustache. Some traveler's stew simmered in a pot hanging over the fire. Sebastian's stomach growled. He and Betsy had been trying to make some distance today and hadn't eaten much.

"Come join me, lad," said the man. "It seems I've made too much stew for one man to eat."

"Gladly," said Sebastian. "Let me make Betsy comfortable first."

The man nodded appreciatively and pointed towards the other side of the fire.

"My two horses are over there. Maybe somewhere near them?"

Sebastian saw a pair of horses tied to trees just outside the firelight circle on the other side. He headed off in that direction. As he got closer, he saw a wagon beyond the horses. An ornate roofed wagon painted in bright colors; a showman's wagon. The light was too dim to read the writing on the side, so he moved a little closer. "Lorenzo's Cunning Goods and Services," it read.

Sebastian found a place to tie up Betsy. Close to the two horses, but hopefully not close enough that they would bother each other. He got her some food and water, then gratefully returned to the fire and took a seat.

"You must be Lorenzo," he said.

Lorenzo laughed and replied, "Indeed. And you must be hungry." He scooped some stew from the pot into a bowl and handed it and a spoon to Sebastian.

Sebastian took a closer look at his new companion. Or, he tried to. It was challenging to look at Lorenzo without being distracted by his handlebar mustache.

It was glorious. For one thing, it was lush and thick. It also stretched out well beyond what one would have thought possible on both sides of Lorenzo's face. But these things, noteworthy as one might think them, were not the most remarkable thing. The mustache hair had been trained, or perhaps educated, into an intricate spiral on each side. *Some kind of wax?* Thought Sebastian. Even though it seemed to spin around when you gazed at it, it wasn't just the spiral; it was also the texture. The spiraling curls of hair seemed to glisten and gleam in the firelight.

Sebastian tore his gaze away. Staring was rude.

"Lorenzo, this stew is delicious."

"My friends call me Enzo."

## 31

Lorenzo gazed at Sebastian inquiringly. "So what brings a young man like you out to the middle of nowhere like this?" he said. The spirals on the ends of his mustache moved up and down as Enzo spoke. When he ended the question, they rose with the pitch of his voice.

"I'm on a quest," said Sebastian. He wasn't sure if he was ashamed to say it like that or proud, but it felt like it would be letting Anise down if he didn't do things the right way.

"A quest!" said Lorenzo. "I haven't met a young person on a quest in a month of Sundays. That's very exciting!"

"My name's Sebastian, by the way," said Sebastian. "What are Cunning goods and services?"

"Well," said Enzo, "that's a question with a potentially involved answer. How much time do you have?"

Sebastian looked a little puzzled. "I guess I've got all night," he said.

Enzo laughed. "That was a rhetorical question," he said. "Cunning goods and services are the goods and services a traveling cunning man or woman might sell or provide."

"So, you sell stuff," said Sebastian.

"Exactly," replied Enzo with another laugh. "You have a very precise way of cutting through the garbage, don't you?"

"Do you sell snake oil?"

It was Lorenzo's turn to look puzzled.

"I suppose I do. I have a couple of different things I sell that you might call snake oil. I have an oil-based potion I brew that is supposed to be useful for repelling snakes. I think I have a formula somewhere for a potion intended to turn someone into a snake on the more expensive side of things. I haven't actually tried brewing that one before, and I'm not sure I have all the ingredients, but I could give it a try if you need it."

"Oh, I don't need it," said Sebastian. "It's just my father used to talk about snake oil salesmen, and I was wondering if you were one."

Enzo looked surprised for a second, then he started laughing again. "Oh, you are a gem, aren't you?" he said.

Sebastian wasn't sure if this was a compliment or an insult, so he decided to ignore it.

"So," he said, "tell me more about cunning goods and services."

"Well," said Enzo, "I have some expertise with alchemy, so a lot of what I sell on the goods front is potions, but I was always best at elements, so that's a lot of the services. I was never much of a channeler or illusionist, so I mostly leave those for other people. I provide a bit of stonework, plumbing work, and chimney sweeping. It's amazing how useful elemental magic is for household maintenance. I can do a moderately good controlled burn if you need a field or some brush cleared."

Sebastian had a sudden thought. He wasn't sure how relevant it was, but he didn't want to forget it.

"Do you like raisins?" he said.

It occurred to Lorenzo that if laughter really was the best medicine, then Sebastian would be an excellent tonic for his health. He laughed again.

"Love them," he said.

Sebastian got up and walked over to his saddlebags. He walked by the back of Lorenzo's wagon as he reached the bags. There were rows of little bottles on shelves inside the open back wagon door. *It makes sense*, Sebastian thought. *He needs to use every square inch of the inside of the wagon.* He read the label on one of the bottles before grabbing the package containing Rose's raisin pastries from one of his saddlebags.

He sat back down at the fire and tossed the package of raisin pastries to Enzo.

"Everyone says these are great, but I don't like raisins," he said.

"My good fortune," said Enzo. He pulled one of the pastries out of the package and took a bite. "They *are* good," he said with a smile.

Sebastian thought of the rack he'd seen on the back of Lorenzo's cart.

"I saw the bottles on your wagon. One I saw was labeled 'Grains of paradise.' Are those potion ingredients?"

"No, that's only my spice cabinet. I was using it for the stew. I'll give you a tour of the wagon tomorrow when there's some light if you want," said Enzo.

Sebastian made the mistake of looking at Enzo's face again. His eyes were drawn irresistibly to the swirling glistening spirals of Enzo's mustache.

Enzo saw where Sebastian was looking.

"You know, when I pull into a village, driving this wagon, the villagers all expect a show. I try to oblige. I use the back of the cart as a stage and describe my goods and services. They want a show, so I do some magic. You know, sparks and small bursts of flame, little clouds of smoke, levitating pebbles, stuff like that. As I said, I'm not much of an illusionist, but after I'm done with the elemental tricks, I do a few small illusions.

"The stache helps. I've enchanted it with a couple of little spells of my own invention. I bet you've noticed it seems to glisten a bit. That's water magic. The spiral effect is a combination of illusion and air. If people spend enough time looking at my mustache, they don't notice any flaws in my performance. Also, it makes 'um more interested in coming to talk to me about my goods and services.

"Anyway," said Enzo. "That's enough of me talking. It's your turn. Tell me about your quest!"

## 32

Before Sebastian could respond, Enzo continued, "And this story better include a complete description of why you're dressed like that. Gotta be the most interesting outfit I've seen since I saw my first girlfriend in her birthday suit."

Sebastian was wearing Gerard's shirt, his white leather trousers, and the shadow boots. He also had his father's sword at his waist. It felt like it was right to wear it, though he wasn't expecting to need to use it on the road. The road in these parts was usually safe. Leonard's cap was in the same saddlebag as the moon.

Sebastian told Enzo his story. He couldn't think of a reason he shouldn't. It took a while. Lorenzo had to get up to put a new log on the fire at one point. Sebastian noticed he had quite a pile of firewood. He wondered momentarily if Lorenzo had collected it at this site or if he kept it in his wagon.

Lorenzo looked thoughtful for a bit after Sebastian finished.

"That's quite a story, son," he said finally. "I would call you a liar except for a couple of things. For one thing, everyone's been talking about the missing moon for days. And for another, after our conversation of this evening, I don't think you're even capable of lying."

Lorenzo mumbled a few words under his breath and made a quick hand gesture. He reached out and put his hand lightly on the white fabric of Sebastian's trousers. "Also," he said, "I'm surprised I didn't feel all that power. I must be getting old."

"I am *so* capable of lying!" said Sebastian indignantly.

"Not sure that's the most important take-home message from what I said," said Enzo.

Enzo leaned back a bit and gazed at Sebastian thoughtfully. "Son, it sounds like you got yourself caught up in the middle of a powerful channeler battle."

"Channeler. I heard you use that word before. What's a channeler?"

Enzo grunted in disbelief.

"My word, what are they teaching these kids in school nowadays?"

"The teacher at our school didn't think much of magic," said Sebastian. "She wouldn't talk about it and didn't like it when we did."

"Primitive," said Enzo. "Well, if you're interested, I could fix one mistake she made in your education."

Sebastian looked around at their surroundings and replied, "There's not much else going on. Go ahead."

Enzo looked pleased and settled himself a little before starting. It occurred to Sebastian that salespeople and teachers had one thing in common. Both of them liked to hear themselves speak.

"I'm sure you know the difference between us cunning folk and those who call themselves mages. But to summarize, the biggest difference is that we cunning folk teach each other out here in the real world. Mages all learn at the magic academy." Here Enzo waved off in a vaguely northwestern direction.

"They're arrogant. They don't believe anyone who hasn't studied at their precious academy can do real magic." Enzo looked genuinely angry about this, though Sebastian felt he saw some hurt in his expression.

"Anyway, at their academy, in addition to training students to become mages, they do research, write papers, things like that. One thing they've done is to categorize magic into specific disciplines, and they train people in those areas. The four main specialties they define are; elemental magic, alchemy, illusion, and channeling.

"There are those of us who think they missed a

couple. There are debates within the academy as well. For example, people specializing in healing would like the academy to have a healing discipline. They use some alchemy, channeling, and elements in their magic. Still, the sum of the whole could be thought of as a new discipline. There are others like that.

"Elemental magic controls and uses the four elements: earth, air, wind, and fire. Alchemy is the mixing and enchanting of potions. Illusion magic is the discipline that allows the creation of illusions. Things that fool the senses but don't really exist. Finally, channeling, the one we're really interested in, is the conjuration and control of powerful magic spirits."

Sebastian reconsidered and reached over to the open package of raisin pastries and picked one up. He took a bite.

"Actually," he said, "these aren't too bad."

Enzo grabbed the package and pulled it closer to himself.

"No," he said with a wink, "Mine.

"But to continue, as I was so rudely interrupted. Channeling is interesting because it's indirect. Each of the other disciplines I listed allows direct control over the spell you're casting or the thing you're creating. In the case of channeling, the mechanism involves non-conscious thought.

"In its most uncomplicated form, a channeler dreams about something they want to happen. The wish is sent to the dreaming world, and a spirit may respond by coming to our realm and attempting to make the dream a reality. Sometimes the spirit comes here directly. Other times it controls animals, people, or things in this world.

"The complexities of channeling are many. For one thing, unless trained, people don't have control over their dreams. It also isn't immediate. The dreamer makes the request to the spirit world, and then the response may or may not happen sometime later.

"As I said, I have never been much of a channeler myself. The closest I ever came was one time when I dreamt some squirrels were storing their nuts in my spice cabinet, and when I woke up, I found them trying to get in through a window.

"That brings us to your situation. I think your nightmare is an attack by one powerful channeler and what's happening to you is a defense by another. I'm afraid I don't know any more about it than that, and that's just a guess, but I would call it an educated guess."

# 33

L ilith caught up to Anise just as she was leaving the clearing where the gatehouse had been. Not that there was much of the gatehouse, or the main gate, remaining. They had just started rebuilding. Lilith found out from Rose that Anise asked every day to see if the watch had heard from Sebastian.

"Anise," Lilith called out. Anise turned and waited for her.

"I wanted to ask you," Lilith said, "about the Knight of Moon and Shadow."

Lilith had decided this would be a better way to get Anise talking than to ask her anything about herself.

It seemed as if it might work. Anise perked up as soon as she heard the name.

"What do you want to know about the Knight?" said Anise. Her tone conveyed that she thought Lilith had come to the right source for the information.

"Tell me about his armor," Lilith said.

Anise was very excited to talk about the knight's armor. She had named each piece. There were the Shadow Boots, the Pants of the Wind, the Fool's Cap, and finally, the Tunic of the Peacock. The moon was just called the moon, and Sebastian's sword didn't really have a name. She told Lilith about each piece in great detail.

"He hasn't come back yet," she said sadly. "I think it'll still be a while."

"Did you say you dreamt about the Knight?" said Lilith.

"I dreamt him, and I wished for him. No, I mean I wished for him, and then I dreamt him," said Anise.

Anise started fidgeting, and it was clear to Lilith she was eager to leave.

"One more thing, Anise," she said. "Do you have

other dreams which are real?"

"All my dreams are real," said Anise. Her expression made it clear this should be obvious.

Anise ran off, calling out in an attempt to be polite, "Sorry, I have to go."

# 34

In the morning, Lorenzo remembered his promise to show Sebastian the inside of his wagon. Sebastian found the tour fascinating. The potion ingredients were quite interesting, but Lorenzo's collection of magical artifacts was even more absorbing. Lorenzo had a small selection of items that had somehow gained permanent magical properties. He kept them near his desk/workbench, where he worked on developing potions and spells.

"Permanent enchantments on items are rare," Enzo told Sebastian. "Most spell effects are temporary, and the process of making them permanent isn't well known.

"That's one of the debates at the magic academy, by the way. There used to be a discipline called crafting, which studied creating permanent magical items. Most of that knowledge has been lost."

Enzo had a small silver ring, which made Sebastian feel warm all over when he put it on. Enzo told him it would keep him warm even if it was freezing outside and he was naked. There was a small clockwork bird that sang and flew around the room when wound up. Enzo said he supposed it might be possible to make such a thing without magic. The windup mechanism controlled the spell and was mainly used as a timer to determine how long the bird would fly and sing. It sang beautifully and seemed to be able to avoid bumping into things as it flew around the inside of Enzo's wagon.

At this point, Enzo asked if he could see the other things Sebastian had told him about over the fire last night. He was intrigued by the moon and wanted to see Leonard's cap.

"You know," he said, while admiring the moon, "there are two different ways enchanted items can come into existence.

"Crafting, as I was saying, is the art of making spells and magical effects permanent. It's mostly lost, though there are hints and indications people used to know more about it than they do now. But the other main way items can become enchanted is through channeling. After the spirit summoned by a channeler leaves the world, the things they do here can persist. If you were to give away, keep, or sell these items you have, they would most likely keep their magical properties."

"They were gifts! I have to return them," Sebastian said, shocked at the suggestion.

"Oh, I'm not suggesting you should," said Enzo, smiling. "I'm just telling you what would happen if you did. You are, at the moment, a walking treasure trove of magic. It would be best if you were a little careful. Not everyone out here is as goodhearted as I."

After the tour was over, Sebastian thanked Lorenzo for his hospitality of the previous night. Sebastian was heading into Anesbury, and Lorenzo was going the other way.

Lorenzo had been through Anesbury the day before and told Sebastian a little about what he saw there.

"I didn't spend much time looking around, as there wasn't much to see," he said, "the town looks like it's been flattened. I didn't even see anyone trying to rebuild. Nothing dangerous to warn you about, but on the other hand, like I said, nothing positive to look for either."

Lorenzo wished Sebastian good luck on his quest and headed off. Sebastian and Betsy traveled on to Anesbury.

# 35

Anesbury was both worse and better than Sebastian expected. It really had been flattened. There was hardly a beam or piece of a wall standing above the ground. It was as if the beast had gone through each building and knocked over every structure and standing timber.

On the other hand, there weren't any bodies. After Rose's story and the beast's actions in Westhavenfieldbrook, Sebastian expected to see dead villagers. It relieved him that he didn't.

Anesbury had been about the same size as Sebastian's village. Maybe a little bigger.

Sebastian and Betsy didn't run into anyone as they walked into the ruined village, so Sebastian headed toward the central square where Rose had said the bell tower stood.

In addition to not seeing any people, there didn't seem to be any signs of reconstruction. Perhaps any survivors had given up because of how much damage the beast had done. Or maybe they hadn't yet returned to the village.

The feeling of the ruined village was ominous. Sebastian felt the hairs on the back of his neck stand up. It was morning and a bit overcast. The feeling Sebastian had didn't have anything to do with the weather. Betsy had both of her ears plastered back on her head. In the last couple of days, Sebastian had figured out that this meant she was seriously considering refusing to do something. She was still following the lead for the moment.

Sebastian and Betsy stepped into what had been the main square. The bell tower's ruins were on the other side of the space from where they were standing. Between them and the tower ruins were six recent graves. A simple wooden unnamed grave marker was positioned at the head of each pile of earth. An enormous pitch-black raven was perched on the first of the wooden signs.

Betsy balked and nickered fearfully. Standing just on the other side of the graves was a man dressed in black. He was a little shorter than Sebastian. He had his arms folded, and he was leaning on a shovel stuck into the dirt mound of one of the graves. His face was hidden behind the black-dyed cap he had pulled down almost over his eyes.

Sebastian was momentarily relieved to see someone but changed his mind as he looked at the man. Betsy absolutely refused to move any closer. Sebastian tied her lead to a broken and burned section of timber. After the beast had destroyed the village, fires had started.

He headed over toward the man. It was hard to tell with the cap pulled over his eyes, but it seemed he watched Sebastian's every move. As Sebastian started into the square, the raven on the first grave marker spread its wings and cawed as it flew away.

"Good day to you," said Sebastian.

The man grunted. As he got closer, the man looked even more unusual to Sebastian. His black clothing was one piece; there didn't seem to be a division between the pants and the shirt. He kept his head tilted down, so Sebastian couldn't see his face.

"Do you know what happened here?" said Sebastian. "Are there other survivors?"

"I'm a caretaker," said the man. His voice rasped, a little like a chain dragged over a washboard. "There were three of us; the others have moved on. I stayed behind in case other things needed to be done. He tasked us with cleaning up."

"There was a creature, a beast," said Sebastian. "Do you know which direction it came from?"

The man waved to the northeast.

\* \* \*

Try as he might, Sebastian couldn't get anything else

out of him. He untied Betsy and led her around the square. She refused to go through it. They made their way to the northeast corner of the village. They found the remains of a farm, which Sebastian speculated was Anise's parents', where the beast first entered the town.

There was a trail leaving the village in more or less the right direction. Sebastian had no better plan than to track the beast back to where it came from, so he and Betsy followed the trail out of town.

# 36

M r. Shepherd, the miller, was waxing eloquent on the subject. He was grinding the words like his mill ground wheat. "She just moved to town, and suddenly she thinks she's in charge of making bread for everyone?"

Sitting a little way down the bar, the mayor perked up at hearing the word "town."

"My family has been making bread for the folk of this village for ten years," the miller continued. "We don't need two bakers in a village this small."

The mayor sagged back down and sadly took a sip from his ale mug.

There was a muttering from the group. It seemed they agreed with part of what the miller was saying. Specifically, there didn't need to be two bakers in the village.

"As I said, we've been making bread for the village for years. We make great bread!"

The muttering seemed to be veering toward the skeptical.

Mr. Smith, the fishmonger, rose to his feet. In the evening, at the pub, the respectful distance people kept from him during the day was waived. After an ale or two, the fishy aroma which seemed to cling to him was less bothersome.

"Byram, you know we all love you," he said as he clapped the miller on the shoulder. "But your family bakes bread that tastes like boiled leather."

There was a chorus of positive responses when this was said. It seemed to have struck a chord with the group.

"Earwax," said one voice from the crowd.

"Toe cheese?" said another.

"I'd rather eat the boiled leather," said a third.

Mr. Smith interrupted before the chorus could get completely out of hand.

"Byram, maybe it's all right that someone else is doing the baking. You and yours still mill all the flour."

Byram didn't look particularly happy at this. Still, he sensed the crowd's mood was against him and decided to fight this battle another day. He sat back down on his barstool and pulled his ale mug closer.

# 37

Sebastian and Betsy were some ways northeast of Anesbury. They'd been following the road, as it was heading in mostly the right direction. The evening came on, so Sebastian found a place to camp. He was worried about their aimlessness.

Anesbury had been a clear destination, but now it felt like they were lost. Despite his concerns, there was nothing he could do about it until morning. Sebastian tied Betsy up and provided for her. He set up the tent so thoughtfully given to him as he left the village, and he started trying to cook something over the fire.

The sun was setting over the mountains in the east. Sebastian had never been this close to the mountains. His whole life, they'd stood off in the distance; majestic, unapproachable. Now it felt like they were very close. In fact, people probably considered the hills rising to the east of the road he and Betsy were traveling to be part of the foothills of the Blue Mountains.

"Ho, the traveler!" came a voice from over toward the road.

Sebastian looked and saw a worn-looking wanderer heading toward him.

"Ho," he called out.

"Need any company?" said the man as he approached.

"Feel free to join me," said Sebastian. He looked over the man as he unloaded the most massive pack Sebastian had ever seen. It seemed to Sebastian the wanderer was a traveling peddler. Sebastian was surprised he didn't have a horse or other pack animal with him, but from the ease with which he unloaded his massive pack, perhaps he didn't need one.

The peddler settled down across the fire from

Sebastian. He offered to help with the cooking. Sebastian gratefully accepted the help. He hadn't yet figured out the details of cooking over an open fire.

As they got their food ready, Sebastian couldn't help but notice the peddler kept looking curiously at his shirt. Seeing as the peddler was already inspecting him, Sebastian did the same. The man was probably somewhere in his mid-thirties, and it seemed the road had worn him down a bit. The enormous pack had a pair of saddlebags attached to it, so the peddler had a donkey, mule, or horse at some point. Maybe the fortunes of a traveling peddler were subject to ups and downs.

His clothes were worn, and he hadn't shaved in a while. Perhaps he hadn't bathed in a time either. Though maybe the smell Sebastian was smelling was the smell of the spices being added to the meal. However, his gear looked well taken care of, and though worn, his clothes were carefully and well mended.

"I know that shirt," the peddler said. "I sold that shirt to someone not long ago."

Sebastian told the peddler about borrowing the shirt from Gerard, which led to talk of Westhavenfieldbrook and his and Betsy's journeys. The peddler let Sebastian know he'd like to hear the rest of the story over their meal.

After Sebastian had gleaned a few tips about preparing meals over an open fire and the meal was prepared, they settled back to enjoy their supper and the conversation.

The peddler told Sebastian a little about life on the open road. It fascinated Sebastian. He'd seen just enough of this life in the last few days to know he wouldn't want to live it, so he was quite interested in hearing stories from someone who did.

After telling some of his stories, the peddler turned to Sebastian.

"So, I've been sharing my stories. Why don't you

share yours?"

Sebastian hesitated a moment, remembering what Enzo had cautioned him about. But the warmth of the fire and the enjoyable conversation had left him feeling very agreeable, and he decided there was nothing to worry about. It might have helped with this decision that he and the peddler had been passing a bottle of old Widow Clark's best back and forth.

Sebastian told the peddler what had happened to him since he had pulled the moon down from the sky. The peddler seemed interested and encouraged the tale with interjections and appreciative sounds from time to time.

The peddler looked thoughtful when Sebastian finished and said, "That's quite a tale, son."

After another pause, he continued, "I have a couple of things to share with you in return that you may find interesting."

"First off, I hear a lot of things in my travels. There's a story they tell in these parts which might be relevant. The local folk talk about a cave in the hills that houses a wizard hermit fellow. The hermit mostly keeps to himself, though he has to contact people occasionally for food and other supplies. The stories they tell about his cave, though, are intriguing. They call it the cave of nightmares, and no one dares go near it. They talk about horrible sounds, and there are stories of locals who entered the cave but didn't return.

"The other thing," continued the peddler, "is a story I've heard. If you're interested, I'd be glad to tell it."

"Of course," said Sebastian.

# 38

The peddler seemed experienced at telling stories. Perhaps it was part of what he did as he traveled around selling his wares. He sat up straight in the firelight and made a dramatic gesture as he began to recite in a sing-song voice.

"The boy who hid behind the moon." After the briefest pause to clarify that this was the story's title, the peddler continued.

"There was a village in a southwest corner of the kingdom. It was not the largest village. There was nothing particularly noteworthy about it, except that the citizens had recently come into some good fortune. Their income mainly came from mining. The village had grown up around a small gold mine. The mine was not particularly successful; it produced just enough gold to keep the citizens in their jobs.

"The stroke of good fortune they recently had was hitting a rich vein in the mine. This had changed things in the village. Suddenly there was an influx of wealth. Unfortunately, this wealth was not being evenly distributed. The chief and the wealthy profited off the gold, and the rest of the villagers did not.

"It's not clear if the bandits were disgruntled villagers unhappy with the status quo or real bandits who heard of the new village riches. Regardless, they stormed the village and took over. They seemed to know who was wealthy and who was not, and they targeted the wealthy. After the attack was over, rumors were that the gold taken from the rich was distributed to the more needy citizens.

"The village chief somehow got wind of the attack. Or perhaps he just reacted faster than the other wealthy villagers. He was nowhere to be found when the bandits took over. They searched his home and couldn't find any hidden stash of valuables.

"Now, the chief's son, who was not particularly popular in the village, was one of the people who were being held by the bandits. When they realized they couldn't find either his father or his father's money, it occurred to them he might know something about where one or both of those things could be found.

"Somehow, the young man escaped from the bandits. He knew the area around the village well and took off into the countryside."

Sebastian stood for a second, gesturing for the peddler to continue, and went to throw another branch on the fire. As he threw the new wood on the fire, there was a burst of flame from the existing embers and a brief shower of sparks.

"If he had been anyone other than the chief's son, the bandits would probably have just let him go, but the chief had been the main profiteer from the mine, and they needed to find his gold. The bandits got hold of some dogs and gave them the young man's scent from his room in his father's house.

"The chief's son was holed up somewhere in the woods when he heard the baying of the hounds. His plan to hide from the bandits wasn't going to work with dogs tracking him, so he took off running through the forest.

"The sun was setting as he tried wading upstream in a narrow creek. It slowed the dogs down, but he could hear them as they figured it out and resumed the chase.

"Night fell, and by the light of a full moon, the young man entered a clearing in the forest. He had no more options and was about to collapse on the grass when he heard a voice.

"'Climb up, and you can hide behind me,' it said. The chief's son had no idea who was speaking initially until suddenly, he realized it was the moon. He climbed a tree near the moon, jumped over, and found a convenient hiding space behind the glowing orb.

"The young man was getting used to his hiding place when the dogs, followed closely by the bandits, entered the clearing. The dogs sniffed, especially around the base of the tree he had climbed, but the bandits couldn't see anyone in the tree by the full moon's light.

"The young man saw and heard everything from his vantage point. Imagine his glee when he overheard the bandits discussing how the dogs had lost the trail. They were ready to abandon the chase when he failed to contain it and let out a laugh.

"The bandits heard the laugh and knew he was there even though they couldn't see him. They set up camp for the night and kept a watch.

"The chief's son was able to stay awake and alert for a while, but the stillness and his exhaustion from the evening's events eventually got to him, and he fell asleep. Sleeping, he tumbled out of his hiding place and fell to the ground.

"The bandits collected him and returned to the village. They found his father and the gold with the information they got from him."

The peddler lowered his voice and then his gaze to show he was done.

"That's the end?" said Sebastian. Maybe it was old Widow Clark's best speaking, but he was indignant. "What's the moral? What's the point? Where's the happy ending?"

The peddler smiled. "Who says every story has to have a happy ending? Or a moral?

"Maybe it's just something which really happened," he said.

## 39

L ilith had a customer. She usually liked to put on a bit of a show. She pulled the hood of her cloak down over her eyes. It made her look more mysterious. She had something simmering in the large cauldron she kept over her fireplace. (It was only some water she had added a bit of coloring and some exotic smelling spices to, but it definitely added to the ambiance.)

"Well, my dear," she cackled. "What can I help you with today?"

The customer was young and female. Lilith estimated her age at about fourteen. Lilith recognized her by sight but not by name. The town was small enough so that it was hard not to know everyone, but she didn't spend too much time with the village children.

The girl seemed nervous. It must have been a struggle for her to muster the courage to ask for help. Lilith felt a touch of admiration for the effort.

The girl was still dressed in her school clothes. Mrs. Shoemaker had tried to enforce a school uniform, but it hadn't worked. She had, however, implemented a dress code.

The young customer looked around at the interior of Lilith's cottage. In addition to the cauldron, Lilith had some of her spices hanging from hooks on the ceiling. She had arranged rows of jars containing interesting-looking things on both sides of the fireplace. Most of the items were spices or just decorations, but some legitimate potion ingredients were among them.

Lilith's black cat Brinley stuck his head out from behind one of the jars. He hissed at the girl. She jumped and took a step backward. Lilith appreciated the gesture from Brinley, but she wished he had saved it for a more significant time. Impressing this girl was a little too easy.

Lilith decided this was enough. She stepped forward, reached out, and took the girl's hand. "Don't be scared, my dear," she said. "How can I help you?" Brinley saw the way things were going, jumped down off the shelf, walked over, and started rubbing against the girl's legs.

The girl hesitated a moment, then noticeably relaxed a little. She reached down and petted Brinley.

"I'm Constance," she said. "I … I heard you can make a love potion?"

This was not too different from what Lilith expected. More often than not, when a young person asked for help, it was something along these lines. Lilith had a standard disclaimer she gave.

"It's not really a love potion," she explained. "It's a potion which makes a person reconsider their attitude toward you. It gives you a new chance at a first impression. So is this boy you're interested in someone at school?"

"She's not a boy. Who said anything about a boy? She's beautiful, and she ignores me," said Constance.

Lilith was intrigued. At least a little different from the usual.

"The price is one copper coin and the memory of a summer day."

Lilith had no idea how to capture the memory of a summer day and even less of an idea what to do with it if she did. Adding something magical to the price gave her a certain mystique. It also made the customer think twice about whether or not they really needed their purchase.

Constance didn't hesitate. She produced the coin in a flash and waited for whatever magical extraction Lilith would need to do.

Lilith pocketed the coin and put on a little show of extracting the memory. She gave Constance the potion and a description of how to use it.

Constance thanked her and started to walk out the door.

"Constance," said Lilith, smiling, "come back and tell me how it went."

# 40

Sebastian dreamt he opened his eyes. He dreamt he sat up and looked around the campfire. The peddler wasn't there, but a glowing form sat across the fire from where Sebastian lay. Sebastian didn't recognize the figure, but he knew the glow. It was the same glow that came from his shield. It was the soft, gentle glow of a moonlit night.

*The man in the moon*, Sebastian thought. Though it was evident that she was a woman. *Of course she is*, he thought, though he couldn't remember why it had seemed so obvious when recalling the dream the next day.

She had her mouth open in the expressive "o" of shock he always saw when he gazed at the moon. Though it looked less like shock and more like mild outrage at this moment. Her expression changed to a friendly smile when she saw Sebastian looking at her.

"Sebastian," she said, "at last, we meet."

Sebastian didn't know how to respond. Several things struck him dumb about this. First off, this didn't feel like a dream to him. It felt more real than many waking moments he had had. Second, the moon was beautiful. She wore a flowing gown that glowed with the same soft moonlight which shone from her face, and that face was just stunning. He felt like he was in the presence of royalty, and although he didn't really know what that felt like, it was clear this was it.

"No reason to be alarmed about this," she said. "But I'm here to let you know you're being robbed."

Sebastian started and looked around himself. There was nothing to see except himself, the circle of firelight, and the moon.

"Don't worry," said the moon. "No time will pass in the waking world while we talk. We have a moment.

"I just wanted to say," the moon continued, "I am enjoying this calling. They're not all pleasant, and it's nice to have one that feels worthwhile."

Sebastian made a conscious effort to make the expression on his face look a little less befuddled. He had no clue what was going on, but he didn't have to make that obvious.

"Be easy on him," she concluded. "He has his reasons."

# 41

Sebastian was using the saddlebag with the moon and Leonard's cap in it as his pillow. He woke up with the feeling that his pillow had moved. Sebastian sat bolt upright, with his hand flying immediately to the hilt of his sword. He wasn't sure where that reaction came from, but it served him well at this moment, as the peddler was only inches away from him with his hand on the laces of the saddlebag.

"Stop right now," Sebastian said.

The peddler stepped back, waving his hands, and tried to make some excuse.

"Don't even try," said Sebastian. "I know what you were doing." He looked over at his other saddlebags and saw they were all open. It seemed the peddler had looked through the easier ones before getting to the one under Sebastian's head.

Sebastian pulled the sword from its sheath. He meant to keep it ready, though he really didn't want to have a reason to use it.

"Did you take anything out of those bags?" he asked.

"No," said the peddler, looking sincerely ashamed. "I was looking for the moon. You don't have any idea what you have there."

"I know it's not mine to give away, sell or keep," said Sebastian. "And it's certainly not yours."

It was still the earliest stages of the dawn twilight.

"That thing," said the peddler, "would be worth a fortune to some people. I would have enough to buy a castle for my family.

"Times have been tough," he continued. "I had to sell my donkey to replenish my stock."

"You have a family?" said Sebastian.

"I haven't seen my family in almost a year. And I

haven't had enough money to bring them anything for even longer."

"Pack up your stuff," Sebastian said. "I shouldn't do this, but I'll see if I can do something for you."

While the peddler got his belongings together, Sebastian plucked some grass blades and wove them into a grass ring. He kept an eye on the peddler as he did this to make sure he didn't get anywhere near the saddlebags.

Sebastian opened the saddlebag with the moon in it and took the little grass ring he had woven. He reached into the bag and touched the grass to the moon. There was a brief flash of light, then the woven grass started glowing with a shine that resembled the moon's glow. The weaving seemed to tighten and solidify.

Sebastian walked over to the peddler and handed him the ring. "Here," he said. "Take this. You can call it a moon ring. See if you can sell it. Now get going. I don't want to see you again."

The peddler looked curiously at the ring and took it eagerly.

"What does it do?" he said.

"How would I know?" said Sebastian.

"Can you make me another one?"

"Don't push it," said Sebastian. "Now, go!"

# 42

The mayor was in a private meeting. Mr. Arkwright, the smith, was one of the town aldermen. The town council comprised the mayor and the five prominent citizens who were the aldermen. Mr. Arkwright and the mayor were discussing critical town business. The mayor liked to think of all town business as critical.

"I've got four sketches of different proposed designs for the monument," said the mayor.

"The cobbles near where the beast fell seem to be permanently stained blue," said Mr. Arkwright.

"That's great," said the mayor. He rubbed his hands together as he spoke. "We'll put the monument right where it died."

"Where's the list of possible new names?" said Mr. Arkwright.

There was a knock on the door. The mayor sighed as he called out. "Come in." If this were a real town, no one would interrupt the middle of an important meeting.

The town hall didn't have a regular assistant, so different villagers volunteered to help. Anne, the miller's eldest daughter, was helping today.

"Mrs. Fletcher is here to see you, sir," she said. "She's very insistent."

The woman in question pushed past her through the doorway as she spoke. Mrs. Fletcher was the cobbler's wife. Also, Gerard's mother. Of course, being the cobbler's son was why Gerard always had the most elegant shoes in the village.

"Of course," said the mayor. "There is never a wrong moment to check in on the status of the merchants of our great metropolis."

"That's not what I'm here about," said Mrs. Fletcher, never one to bandy about an issue.

"Well then, my dear lady," said the mayor, "may I ask what you're here about?"

"It's Sebastian," she said. "When he comes back, you need to arrest him."

The mayor hesitated a moment before saying, "May I ask why?"

"He did something to my Gerard," she said. "He's always been such a strong boy. So sure of himself, so confident. Now, he won't hardly leave his room. He won't do anything. He says he's just waiting for Sebastian to come back."

"And you think Sebastian had something to do with this," said the mayor.

"When he took his shirt," said Mrs. Fletcher. "He took something else from him."

"Well, thank you, Mrs. Fletcher, for bringing this to my attention," said the mayor. "I assure you I will look into it." He realized as he spoke that there hadn't been any accounts of issues with Gerard in a while. In the past, he'd had to deal with a relatively steady stream of reports of someone feeling harassed, bar fights, or other altercations, and that had died down.

As Mrs. Fletcher thanked him and turned to leave, the mayor stepped back to his desk to look for the list of new town names for Mr. Arkwright.

# 43

S ebastian and Betsy were feeling aimless again. Sebastian was excited when he heard the peddler talk about a cave called the cave of nightmares in the foothills. That really seemed like something he should check out. So after scaring the peddler off in the morning, they tried to look for it. Unfortunately, there were no road signs which read, "Cave of Nightmares," and they didn't run into anyone to ask.

So far, they had been staying on the paths and trails. Sebastian worried that maybe the cave of nightmares was somewhere off the beaten path. If that were the case, they would never find it without some help.

They wandered around aimlessly for several hours. It was about noon, and the noonday sun blazed overhead. Sebastian dripped sweat and was not in a great mood.

He turned to Betsy and said, "Why do I have to be in charge. Why can't you take care of things for a while?"

He loosened his hold on the lead and gave her a look. She stared right back at him and, sensing the slackness on the strap, took off down a grassy bank on one side of the road. Sebastian hadn't expected this effort to succeed and was a little startled. She was moving quickly, and he struggled to keep up with her.

"Betsy," he called out. "Wait for me!" Sebastian hoped whatever spirit was guiding him, and this expedition had taken hold of Betsy. Maybe she would lead them to the cave.

She seemed to know where she was going. Sebastian followed her for what felt like a long time but probably wasn't more than a few minutes. Sebastian heard a splashing sound as they pushed through some thicker underbrush. He put his hand on the hilt of his sword. Maybe they were getting close to the cave.

As they cleared the brush, he saw a babbling stream ahead. There was a green meadow between him, Betsy, and the creek. Betsy was making a beeline for the water. Sebastian gave up. The green field and the flowing water looked fresh and inviting. He let Betsy drink a bit, removed her saddlebags, and settled her down to graze. He lay down for a nap in the shade of a weeping willow whose branches trailed into the stream's water. He plunked his head down on a saddlebag and was sound asleep in no time.

## 44

Sebastian dreamt again that he opened his eyes. He dreamt again that he sat up. The glow of the full moon was shining around him. He looked around and wasn't surprised to see the woman in the moon sitting cross-legged on the grass a little ways away from him. It did surprise him to see Betsy standing between where he was and the stream. Betsy nickered with gratitude. She was pleased to be part of the dream this time.

Even sitting cross-legged on the ground, the moon lady was more elegant and graceful than anything Sebastian had ever seen. He really had no idea how to speak to her. She reached somewhere in her glowing robe and pulled out a carrot that she held out in Betsy's direction. Surprising Sebastian, as he'd never seen Betsy hesitate to do anything, except listen to him, Betsy inched hesitantly over to the lady. The mule reached out, pulling her lips back from her teeth, and gently pulled the carrot out of the moon lady's hand.

Raising her voice a little to be heard over the crunching carrot sounds, the woman said, "Sebastian, you seemed a little lost today."

Sebastian felt this needed a response, so he mustered his courage and asked, "Have you been watching me?"

"It's a little hard to see much from inside your saddlebags, but I have my ways," she replied.

"Yes, we are lost," Sebastian said. "I'm not even sure I know how to get back to the road from here. Miss... What should I call you?"

"Call me, Luna," said the woman with a smile.

"Miss Luna," said Sebastian.

"Just Luna," she said.

"That feels a little informal," Sebastian said

sheepishly.

Luna laughed. The sound was like the babble of a moonlit stream running over mossy rocks at midnight on a beautiful clear summer night. Betsy stopped crunching her carrot for a moment and looked over at her. Then she snapped up the last bite and started sniffing at Luna's robes for more.

Luna produced another carrot from somewhere and spoke again. "I think I can help."

"We will appreciate whatever you can do," said Sebastian. "We're really lost."

"It should be evening twilight when you wake," Luna said. "Look for help in the twilight. I'll send someone to help you."

## 45

William knocked. The door muffled the sound, but he thought he heard someone call out. He opened the door and stepped inside. It felt a little stuffy. William thought maybe he should try to get some air flowing.

"Reynard?" he said.

"Back here," came the reply from a back room. "They're not letting me get up, or I'd answer the door."

There were various foodstuffs and other supplies on the table in the front room. William added the bread and the other food he was carrying to the rest.

He headed back into Reynard's bedroom.

"You hungry?" he said.

"Hi, William," said Reynard. "I was wondering when you'd get around to visiting."

William flushed, then he saw that Reynard had a big smile on his face.

"Oh, well," he said, "I figured you had enough visitors with the whole town looking in on you."

William inspected Reynard and was genuinely embarrassed. Reynard looked terrible. One side of his face was still bruised and scraped up. One leg and one of his arms were in splints. He should have checked in sooner.

"None of them will play cards with me," said Reynard.

"Well, it's a good thing I'm here then," said William, and he pulled a deck of cards out of a pocket.

## 46

When Sebastian woke, he noticed a small puddle of drool on the side of the saddlebag he was using as a pillow. He flushed and hoped Luna hadn't somehow seen him drooling. Betsy leaned her head over him and started pushing up against him. He realized Betsy must have seen him drooling, but that didn't bother him as much. He also thought the way Betsy was pushing her head against him was very reminiscent of how she had sniffed at Luna's robes in his dream.

"I don't have any carrots," he said.

The sun was setting. Sebastian looked around to see any sign of the help Luna had promised. There was no one there but him and Betsy. He got up and reloaded the mule. The night shadows were getting thicker, but he hoped his dream would help him find his way, and he didn't want to miss the promised help.

Betsy and Sebastian started off toward the mountains. They didn't really know which way to go, but Sebastian concluded that caves would be more likely in the foothills.

They walked for quite a while without seeing anyone. Sebastian even called out at one point, though he felt foolish as he didn't know who he was calling out to. The oncoming darkness made it hard to keep going. Sebastian had an idea. The idea had occurred to him earlier, but he hadn't wanted to try it on the main road.

He held Betsy's lead to stop her so he could open the saddlebag containing the moon. His idea was to wear the moon on his arm and travel by its light. The full moon's light was usually enough to allow one to see pretty well at night. Even though nights were dark since Sebastian liberated the moon from the sky, the night didn't have to be dark for him.

As soon as he opened the saddlebag, a brilliant light beam shot out into the darkening twilight sky. The glow seemed to twirl around in a descending spiral. Something about how the little ray of light shot out of the saddlebag, through the night sky, and back toward Sebastian and Betsy made it look joyful. As if it was glad to be free of the saddlebag.

The beam of moonlight formed into a ball and danced in the air in front of Sebastian's face. It bopped up and down as if nodding. Sebastian had let go of the open flap of the saddlebag when the light shot out. The flap closed, but the glow didn't go out.

"Hi," came a voice. It was gleeful, high-pitched, and sounded distant like it was a voice and the echo of the same voice simultaneously.

"Hi," said Sebastian carefully.

"I thought you'd never find me," said the voice. "Luna sent me to help. I'm Moonbeam."

# 47

Moonbeam chirped, "This'll be so much fun. I haven't spent a whole night down here in a really long time." The light ray bopped up and down excitedly, though it slowed toward the last word.

"I'll have to leave in the morning," it finished sadly.

Sebastian watched, trying to see how the voice came out of the bouncing ball of light. The light pulsed and bounced up and down with the rhythm of the words. That was about all he could make out. There was a shower of motes of brightness whenever the voice finished speaking and the feeling of an echo.

"We're not too tired," Sebastian said. "I had a good nap under the willow tree, but I'm not sure we can walk all night."

"Follow me!" said Moonbeam, and he, she, or maybe it, zoomed gleefully up the hill. Moonbeam was zipping back and forth over the hillside and glowing almost as brightly as a full moon.

"Hey, Moonbeam," Sebastian called out hesitantly. "Maybe you could slow down a little? Also, maybe we should turn down the light show a bit?"

Insomuch as a floating ball of light can look embarrassed, Moonbeam did. "Sorry," it said. "I got excited."

The glow seemed to dim a bit.

Moonbeam floated over to Betsy. It drifted around her head. Betsy cocked one ear forward and the other back as she snapped her teeth at the floating ball of light.

Moonbeam zipped hurriedly out of the way of Betsy's teeth. Its light dimmed and then brightened again as it spun in a spiral around the mule's head. Betsy swung her head around to follow the glow, then gave up. Moonbeam continued up the hill more slowly.

"Why do you have to leave in the morning?" asked Sebastian as he pulled Betsy's lead up the hill.

Moonbeam flitted over to hover in front of Sebastian's face. Somehow he got the impression he had said something ridiculous. "Moon spirits aren't much good during the day," said Moonbeam. "No one can see or hear us."

They reached the top of the ridge, and Moonbeam led them on confidently. It seemed to be leading them further into the hills. The pleasant moon glow it cast over the way was enough to see where they were going.

"How do you know which way to go?" said Sebastian. "Is there a trail leading to the cave, or do we have to cut cross-country?"

"You wouldn't believe the view from up there," somehow Moonbeam indicated the sky as it said this. "You want a trail? Isn't that dumb? Why don't you just fly, like me?"

There was a moment of silence as Moonbeam considered what it had just said.

"Sorry," it said. "I forgot."

The direction Moonbeam was leading them seemed to change a little, and Sebastian hoped this showed it was trying to find a trail for them to follow.

Sebastian noticed Betsy's ears plaster back on her head a half-second before hearing what she heard. It was a howling sound, the call of a wolf. It was too close for comfort. Sebastian's hand went instinctively to the hilt of his sword.

Moonbeam noticed them stopping and started bopping up and down like a firefly.

"I'll go see," it said.

The beam of moonlight shot straight up into the air and raced off toward the sound. Moonbeam's absence left Sebastian and Betsy in almost complete darkness. Sebastian thought about opening his saddlebag to let a little light out, but he decided to wait. Betsy was quivering on the lead. He felt around in the darkness until he found her side and stroked her to calm her.

Moonbeam returned just as quickly as it had left. It dropped to the level it was at before and bopped up and down again.

"It's all right. The wolves are going the other way," Moonbeam said.

Moonbeam led them on through the night. After a little while, they pushed through some brush onto a narrow meandering trail.

As they walked along the trail, the lunar spirit commented, "plod, plod, plod."

It seemed to enjoy the sound it had made and started singing a little song.

"Plod, plod, over the sod. Trudge, trudge, through the sludge.

"Clump, clump, around the stump. Tramp, tramp, to the camp."

Moonbeam sang the same song for what felt like hours. It started becoming less enjoyable for Sebastian. Eventually, even Moonbeam seemed to tire of it, and it stopped. They trudged on in silence for a while.

As the first glimmer of dawn showed in the morning sky, Sebastian realized how tired he was. They had walked through the night. Betsy showed signs of exhaustion as well. Her head was down, and her nostrils were flaring. Sebastian expected laid-back ears and a refusal to continue at some point.

Moonbeam stopped and indicated the trail ahead. "You're almost there. I did good, didn't I? The cave is just a little further on."

"Are you sure you have to leave us?" said Sebastian. He'd only just met Moonbeam, but he was sad about this. It'd been nice to have someone take charge, and Moonbeam was so cheerful.

"Gotta go," said Moonbeam. "But just remember, once we're back up in the sky, you'll see me every night!"

Moonbeam drifted over to Betsy. The flap to her saddlebag flew open, seemingly by itself. With a flash of light, or perhaps *as* a flash of light, Moonbeam disappeared into the bag. The flap dropped closed, and then the only light was the morning twilight and the twinkling stars.

Sebastian found a spot he didn't think was visible from the trail and set up his tent. He took off Betsy's saddlebags and tied her in a place where she could graze. Then he crawled into his tent and fell sound asleep.

## 48

T he mayor banged his gavel hard enough to make at least one tired alderman start. "This meeting of the Westhavenfieldbrook city council will come to order." As much as the word town always gave the mayor a little pleasure, the word city sent an electric shock of joy through his body.

The mayor and the five aldermen sat in the town hall meeting room. Rows of chairs were facing them, but only one villager was present. It was Mrs. Fletcher. The mayor was reasonably sure she was here to raise the idea of arresting Sebastian. He hoped to put off talking to her as long as possible.

The mayor banged his gavel again. This time everyone started. He wasn't sure what the protocol was on when he was and wasn't supposed to use it, but it seemed to get everyone's attention, and he enjoyed doing it.

"If I could have your attention, please," he said. "This portion of the meeting is a closed session. If I could have the bailiff clear the room, please."

There was no bailiff. Today, Anne, the miller's eldest daughter, was the town hall volunteer. She looked a little surprised, but she stepped forward. She walked over to Mrs. Fletcher and held out her hand to help her stand.

After Mrs. Fletcher had left the room, the mayor continued, "If we could have the secretary read the minutes from the last meeting," he said.

Anne stood again, lifted a paper, and read a detailed description of what happened in the last meeting. They had discussed funding a monument to commemorate the recent battle between Sebastian and the beast. They had also discussed ways to make the village of Westhavenfieldbrook attractive to tourists.

"New business," said Mr. Arkwright. "As you all

know, we've been talking about a new name for the village. Westhavenfieldbrook is descriptive, but it's at the very least a mouthful."

There were some muttered responses from the other aldermen. It seemed this idea had some fans and some opponents.

"Our esteemed mayor," continued Mr. Arkwright. The mayor preened a little when he heard himself mentioned. "Has come up with a proposed name which has some potential advantages. Let's give him our attention."

"We'd have to redo the road signs," one alderman muttered.

"It's been the name of the village since before I was born," another one said.

The mayor began, "the issue we have had in times past with the discussion of a possible new town name has been that we couldn't agree on a name. You all know about my plans to see if we can get a bit of a tourist industry going in our town. In light of that effort, I propose we rename Westhavenfieldbrook to Hero. Welcome to the town of Hero!"

# 49

I t was twilight again when Sebastian awoke. At first, he wasn't sure if morning or evening twilight was lighting the canvas walls of his tent, but he felt rested, so he quickly realized he had slept the day away.

He stepped out of the tent into the last rays of a fading sunset. Betsy was contentedly cropping grass not far away. It was a very peaceful moment, and Sebastian hated to leave it, but he had things to do. He opened the saddlebag containing the moon and brought out both the moon and Leonard's cap. When Sebastian lifted the moon out of the bag, it seemed like a piece of light shining from the moon isolated itself and spiraled gracefully around his hand.

As he adjusted his armor, including checking his mending of the rip in Gerard's shirt, he felt a momentary flash of pride. "The Knight of Moon and Shadow" was not such a bad thing to be called. He could also be called "The Bearer of the Gifts." Though he thought the first one had more of a ring to it.

Sebastian hung Leonard's cap through his belt. In case he needed some foolishness or some foolhardiness. He put his forearm through the straps behind the moon and checked to make sure his sword was loose and free in its sheath.

Moonbeam had said the cave was nearby, so Sebastian left the tent set up. Betsy was contentedly grazing and looked very comfortable, so Sebastian thought she would be fine. He loosened the lead. Not enough so she could leave immediately, but just enough so if he didn't come back, she should be able to free herself with a bit of effort.

He scratched her between the ears, in the spot where he thought she liked it. She nickered and licked his face. She put one ear back and the other forward in the way he read as inquisitive.

"I'll be back soon," he said. "Unless I'm not."

Sebastian stepped over onto the path. He followed it a little further. As Moonbeam had said, it wasn't far to the cave. Around the next bend, the trail led into a clearing.

On the far side of the clearing was a rock face with an ancient opening. A jagged crack in the rock opened broadly enough at the bottom that two people could walk in side by side. The cave was clearly lived in, as the trail led right into the crevice.

The clearing was lit by starlight, the last trace of fading light from the setting sun, and the moonlight from Sebastian's shield.

Sebastian immediately knew he was in the right place. Standing in the middle of the clearing was another nightmare, twin to the one that had attacked the village.

# 50

S ebastian took a second to assess the situation. Either the beast hadn't detected him yet, or perhaps it just wasn't feeling challenged. It seemed to be ignoring him for the moment. On the other hand, there was probably not going to be any way around it. The path led, both figuratively and literally, right through the nightmare.

It looked the same as the other beast he had fought, in one way. In another, it seemed entirely different. When he faced the monster back in the village, there had been a crowd of people there. The creature took on something of the fears and dreams of the people watching. Now, it was just the beast and Sebastian.

Sebastian stepped into the clearing. Immediately the creature turned in his direction. A rushing sound like rocks scraping together as they rolled down a hill filled the air as the beast charged toward him. Sebastian lifted his shield and drew his sword.

He thought about pulling Leonard's cap from his belt, but he felt sufficiently in control of this situation. It wasn't time to look for Leonard's help yet. Sebastian held the shield between himself and the beast to deflect whatever blow it would throw. Then he sidestepped the attack using the speed he felt flowing into his legs from Pico's pants.

The beast roared as it rushed past Sebastian and its tentacle clanged off the moon. It was close enough that the wind of its passing surrounded him. His sense of smell felt heightened. Perhaps something to do with Pico's gift. He smelled the beast. It smelled of moss and mold. It smelled of the mushrooms you might find growing in a crevice at the base of an old oak tree in the middle of a shadowy forest.

Sebastian felt like laughing. He felt full of daring. He knew how to fight this beast. It was old news. He wouldn't need Leonard's cap, but he knew where his confidence came from. He had the gifts. He had support. He had Isabel, Luna, Moonbeam, Pico, Leonard, his father, and even Gerard helping him.

From there, the battle was mainly rote. Sebastian felt for the creature. He was faster than it with the pants of the wind. He could fade into the shadows if he needed to. Gerard's shirt was giving him confidence. He could deflect the creature's blows with the moon. It was almost unfair.

There were a series of feints and parries like the battle in the village, but the conclusion seemed preordained. Sebastian tried to think of some way he could spare the beast from the coup de grâce. But as far as he could tell, the creature was mainly mindless and wouldn't stop until he killed it.

As he delivered the final blow, Sebastian felt sorry for the creature. It disappeared, like the one in the village had, leaving the stones and earth of the clearing stained with the same blue that covered some of the village square cobblestones.

Sebastian walked over to the cave entrance and entered the cave of nightmares.

## 51

T he cavern led back into the mountain. Soon after passing the rough rock of the cave mouth, the walls looked smoother. Someone had worked the walls of this cavern into a smooth tunnel at some point. The moon glow from Sebastian's shield, and the light from a series of glowing stones about eye height on the cave walls, broke the tunnel's darkness. The glow from the rocks was a sickly blue color, but the warm moonlight from Sebastian's arm overpowered it.

The air in the tunnel was damp and smelled a little moldy. Sebastian heard nothing. He tried to keep quiet to not announce his presence, though the battle outside with the nightmare might have already spoiled that effort.

The walls of the tunnel opened outward as it widened into a chamber. Sebastian thought the space was empty for a second, then he shivered as he saw what was filling the cavern. It was packed from top to bottom with webs. Not spider webs; these webs were the weaving of tent caterpillars. Sebastian heard a rustling sound like thousands of tiny legs scurrying over webbing.

Sebastian's memory flashed back to one summer when, as a child, he had been climbing a tree on a quiet summer evening while his father tended to the cows. He was high in the tree, disregarding his father's warnings. As he reached the top of the tree and raised his head to see the view, he lost his footing.

Sebastian didn't remember the details of the fall, except for the sensation of falling, which he never forgot. But he remembered the landing. He didn't make it to the ground. There was a stunning impact, which knocked the wind out of him, and he lost consciousness for a moment.

He had landed flat on a broad branch, with his arms and legs straddling both sides of the limb, somehow balanced, so he didn't fall further. The part that stuck in his memory and nightmares was how he landed with his face right inside a tent caterpillar's nest.

Sebastian had recovered awareness with the caterpillars climbing over his face and with one in his mouth. He couldn't see anything except the insects and the white of the silk tent. He tried to call out for help, but the insect in his mouth and the silk around his head muffled his cries.

Since that day, Sebastian's idea of hell was slightly different from most people's. What he saw in this cave was that hell.

He stood in the tunnel mouth. The scuttling noise he had heard earlier was growing more intense. Sebastian was convinced he could see shapes moving in the silken tent webbing. Whatever was scuttling about there was long and thin and bigger than any insect had a right to be.

Sebastian thought about drawing his sword and trying to cut through the webs, but he couldn't even start to move his hand. He took a step backward. He shook his head. This really wasn't going to work.

It occurred to him that a change of perspective might help. He pulled Leonard's cap out of his belt. Sebastian hesitated. His worry about putting Leonard's gift on his head was whether he would ever be in the frame of mind to remove it again.

Sebastian slapped the cap on his head. Immediately things did feel different. It wasn't that he wasn't afraid anymore. Or that he disregarded the fear. It was more like his priorities had changed.

The quest was unimportant. The fear was insignificant. What interested Sebastian now was the notion of a caterpillar more than a foot long.

Sebastian stepped forward. Reaching out toward the nearest web, he looked for one where there seemed to be something moving behind it. He tried to grab the webbing to pull it aside like a curtain. His hand went through the web as if it wasn't there.

He stuck his head through the web. He felt nothing. He could still hear the scuttling sound and see the webbing. He could even smell something like his memory of the tent and the caterpillars from his fall. But when he tried to touch it, there was nothing there.

Sebastian was confused; perhaps the word baffled might apply. He stood there partway through the tent wall, having trouble figuring out what was going on. He reached up to his head and pulled Leonard's cap back off.

Sebastian blinked. Things seemed clearer. He remembered Lorenzo's description of the discipline of illusion. He tucked the cap back into his belt. Lorenzo had described an illusion as a spell that fooled your senses, specifically vision, hearing, and smell, but wasn't physically there. Sebastian waved his hand through the web again. He felt nothing.

He knew what he had to do. He had to walk through the chamber, ignoring the visions, sounds, and smells, until he got to the other side.

Sebastian drew his sword and tapped it like the cane of a blind man to find his way across the cavern. The sights and sounds still brought back bad memories but knowing they were not solid helped.

He made it across the chamber and found a tunnel continuing further into the earth on the other side.

# 52

I sabel was delivering some chairs for her mother. She led a cart loaded with five chairs down Main Street toward the market square. The chairs were being taken to the town hall. One was the original, which her mother had needed to create perfect copies, and the other four were those copies. Her mother had spent more than an hour on just the color of the stain. She made sure the shade was precisely right, so you couldn't tell the copies from the original.

The mayor had ordered the chairs for the meeting hall. He expected town hall meetings to have more attendees in the future, and the chairs were one small step to prepare for that. He assured Mrs. Fisher there would be more orders coming.

Anise was helping with the delivery. At the moment, her help was slightly less than helpful. She had an apple and walked next to George, the draft horse, who was supposed to be busy pulling the cart.

Isabel sometimes thought of George as "George, the dragon slayer." Not because he had slain any dragons, but because he had a mighty kick. He had broken down his stall door at least once, forcing Mrs. Fisher to make a new, stronger one. Isabel imagined if a dragon were ever to stand behind George, the dragon slayer part of his name might come true.

Anise's apple kept causing George to pull to the side, so Isabel had to keep pulling the opposite way on the reins to keep the cart straight.

"Just give him the apple, Anise," said Isabel.

Anise did so, and soon the sound of contented crunching filled the air.

"Are you and Sebastian going to get married?" said Anise.

"What?" Isabel flushed.

"Are you going to get married?"

"Why would you ask that?" Isabel's flush got a bit deeper.

"Well," said Anise. "You kissed him when he left on his quest."

"Anise," said Isabel. "I kissed him on the cheek. It was to thank him for saving the village. Anyway, one kiss doesn't mean you have to get married."

"It doesn't?" said Anise.

"No. It doesn't."

"Oh," said Anise. She paused thoughtfully for a moment before continuing. "Well, I wouldn't mind if you got married. I might even like it."

Isabel smiled. "Well, thank you for your blessing, Anise," she said.

# 53

Sebastian stepped into a larger open chamber. It was still carved from the rock, but this chamber was set up as a living area. Tapestries warmed the rock walls, and carpets covered the stone floor.

A man stood in the center of the room. He wore a worn robe, the sort you might see at an educational institution or on a monk. It was threadbare, nearly in tatters, but it might once have been made of exquisite material. In some ways, the man looked as worn as his robe. He was old, by Sebastian's standards, ancient. He looked alert, however, and perhaps dangerous.

Sebastian's mouth dropped open in shock. He hadn't recognized him, at first, as he was dressed differently and looked older. But his face was the same, and it was impossible to fail to acknowledge his mustache. It was Lorenzo.

"Enzo?" Sebastian said. "What are you doing here?"

"Trying to get rid of you," said Lorenzo, with a trace of the same smile he had worn as they sat by the campfire. As he spoke, he made a curious gesture with his hands. He held them together, all ten fingers spread out, and made a pushing motion toward Sebastian with his arms.

A small darting flame shot out from the tip of each finger. The ten little darting bolts of fire all homed in on Sebastian. He stepped back and raised the moon between himself and the fiery darts. They splattered against the moon, one by one, with Sebastian being knocked back another half step as each one broke on the shield.

Sebastian lowered his shield and stepped forward. Lorenzo's face drew his attention. It was the same face he had grown to like as they had shared a meal a few days ago, but today the expression was harsher. There was cruelty showing there that Sebastian hadn't seen before. As he studied Lorenzo's face, Sebastian was careful to avoid looking at the whorls of his mustache. Probably that was more dangerous than Lorenzo had told him as well.

"I don't understand. How did I meet you on the road if you've been here?" Sebastian asked.

"I had to see what I was facing," said Lorenzo, and Sebastian recognized the signs of him starting to cast a spell. This time Lorenzo held both hands together and swept them from left to right across the open space in front of himself. A mighty wind started, blowing from Sebastian's right. It was fiercer than any wind Sebastian had felt before, and it would have swept him aside if it hadn't been for his trousers. Where the wind touched the white material of his pants, it seemed to blow through the fabric without any pressure. With the wind not affecting his legs, Sebastian could resist the tempest and continue to move forward.

Lorenzo took a step backward when that attempt to slow Sebastian failed. He seemed like he was considering what to try next.

Sebastian stopped moving for a second. He had a moment of grief, like someone he knew had died.

"Lorenzo," he couldn't bring himself to use the nickname Enzo, as it felt like that was the name of a person who was gone. "So, everything you said to me was a lie?"

"Not really," said Lorenzo, "a lot of that is who I used to be." He made another gesture, with one hand this time, a cupping gesture, and a globe of water rose from a tub on the other side of the room. Lorenzo swept the cupped hand in Sebastian's direction, releasing the fingers as he did so. The ball of water swept toward Sebastian, moving at an incredible speed. But Sebastian was already gone when the liquid broke over where he had been. He used the Boots of Shadow to step into the darkness and reappear in another place in the room.

Lorenzo sighed wearily. He rubbed his hand over his

eyes.

"Well, this isn't getting us anywhere," he said. "Perhaps we should sit down and talk. Would you like a cup of tea?"

## 54

S ebastian warily made his way over to the table and chairs that Lorenzo pointed out to him. He sat and waited a moment while Lorenzo bustled about making some tea. The contrast with what had just been happening was disturbing for him. He tried to calm his breath and let his adrenaline settle.

"What did you mean when you said that was what you used to be?" he called out to Lorenzo.

Lorenzo walked over to the table with a loaded tea tray.

"The man you met on the road is pretty much who I used to be, years ago, before I went to that damn academy I told you about. I learned many things there, some of which I'd be happier not knowing."

He put the tray on the table and put cups in front of Sebastian and himself.

"I used to travel around in that cart, giving shows and selling services, exactly like I told you. I haven't used it in years. It was nostalgic to dig it out and go on the road with it, if only for a while."

Sebastian remembered something he should have noticed at the time. The corners of the cart and some of the supplies were dusty and cobwebbed. He should have known something was up. He'd just thought of it as poor housekeeping.

Sebastian rested the moon beside him as he sat, leaning her against his leg. He wanted to have her near to hand, just in case.

Lorenzo continued. "Then, I got the idea that I wanted to learn. I wasn't actually as hostile to the academy as I made it sound. Anyway, I enrolled. One thing I told you, which was a lie, was about me and channeling. Channeling was actually my strength." Lorenzo looked proud for a moment. "In fact, they didn't know what to do with me, as I was a stronger channeler than most of my teachers."

Lorenzo paused for a moment and took a sip of his tea. He gestured towards Sebastian's cup with his chin, encouraging him to try it.

"Try the tea," he said. "I make it myself from local herbs."

Sebastian reached for his teacup. A mote of light from the moon shone out and flitted over by his hand. The slender light beam spiraled around his forearm as it moved toward the tea. The glowing mote blocked him from touching the cup. He pulled the hand back and dropped it to his side. The light faded back into the shield.

Lorenzo watched the ray of light block Sebastian from drinking the tea. He looked interested and disappointed at the same time. "You have a lot of friends helping you." He smiled. Again, Sebastian saw a hint of the smile he remembered from before.

"So what was it you said about learning things you would be happier not knowing?" said Sebastian. "And what does all this have to do with why you're attacking villages?"

"Those are both essentially the same question," said Lorenzo.

Sebastian had his right hand on his sword hilt. He wore both the locket with his mother's picture and her heart-shaped jade medallion around his neck. While Lorenzo was talking, he played with them with his left hand.

"That's nice," said Lorenzo, referring to the jade heart.

"It was my mother's," said Sebastian.

## 55

Old Widow Clark was talking to Mr. Thatcher, the farrier, in a stable attached to the side of his house. It was his place of business. The town didn't have a veterinarian. If you had a problem with an animal, you would either ask Mr. Thatcher if there was anything he could do, or you would talk to Lilith.

"My Pico," said old Widow Clark. "He won't bark anymore. He's so quiet and sad. I swear I don't know what to do."

Mr. Thatcher wondered why he was thinking of Mrs. Clark as old Widow Clark when she wasn't actually any older than he was. It just seemed that was what people were calling her nowadays.

"I'm sorry, Mrs. Clark," he said, "I don't know much about dogs. Wasn't it something Sebastian did to him? That's what I've heard people saying."

"I don't know anything about that," said Mrs. Clark firmly. "Maybe you need to express his anal gland?"

"I'm sure I don't need to do any such thing," said Mr. Thatcher, even more firmly.

## 56

Lorenzo continued, "I studied at the academy. Graduated. In fact, a few years after graduating, I went back and became a teacher. I taught channeling. I was good at it. Teaching, I mean. I think I helped the students.

"The infighting among the staff got to me. I told you a little about that the last time we talked. I didn't tell you how bad it was. The teachers and administrators all had their domains. They would fight over the stupidest things.

"As I told you, one thing they fought over was which were true disciplines. But often, their reasons for arguing one way or another were about power or position at the academy, not whether it would help the students. Anyway, I had a student, a young woman, who was a good student but wasn't a channeler, an illusionist, an alchemist, or an elemental mage. Instead, she was a clairvoyant. I tried to argue that to help her, we should adopt the study of clairvoyance as a discipline, but no one would have anything to do with that. It would weaken their authority too much.

"She was haunted by what she saw of the future, by what she knew. No one would help her. No one could. I tried; I left the academy; I took her with me. I did my best to help her deal with her demons. I failed. I failed her. To this day, the fact that I couldn't help her torments me."

Sebastian interrupted. "I'm still not seeing how this connects to the nightmares."

"I'm getting there," said Lorenzo, "kids nowadays. No patience.

"I was recording her prophecies. Her predictions," Lorenzo continued. "There is no record of what she knew, what she saw, except what I wrote down.

"I retired here to study what she had known. A lot

of it came true. Some important things, some more minor. Even the things that didn't come true left you feeling you knew why they hadn't.

"I guess I lost touch with the world a little. I've been camped out in this cave for years. I've been trying to help in my own way.

"Her most significant prediction was that a channeler would be born. More potent than any there had ever been before.

"I've seen the signs. This channeler has been born. The prophecies predicted this powerful channeler would fracture the world. Would disrupt things beyond belief; would cause reality to shatter into pieces. I have to eliminate the source before that can happen. Based on my reading of the signs, this channeler should still be a child, so I am trying to get rid of them before they can develop their powers.

"Channeling is the most powerful of the disciplines. It's also the hardest to control. An out of control or evil channeler can do enormous damage."

"Like you've done with your nightmares," said Sebastian.

"It's hard to target channeling," said Lorenzo, "I'm sorry about the collateral damage, but the ends justify the means."

"Collateral damage!" said Sebastian. "These are people's lives we're talking about!"

"I was trying for a surgical strike," said Lorenzo. "The nightmares were just supposed to kill the channeler."

"Surgical strike!" said Sebastian, "Anesbury was leveled. My village would have been as well!"

"That's why I sent the caretakers in," said Lorenzo. "I hoped they would help fix things up."

"All they did was bury the dead," said Sebastian.

# 57

Lorenzo got angry. It was the first time Sebastian saw him show any emotion other than amusement. "You stupid boy," he shouted, "why didn't you do what the peddler suggested. Just take your things, move somewhere, sell them, and settle down to a rich life."

"I couldn't," said Sebastian.

"I know," said Lorenzo sadly.

Lorenzo made another quick gesture. This time he clenched each hand into a fist and made a pulling motion like pulling two things toward himself.

Sebastian heard Luna's voice in his head.

"Sebastian," she said. "Behind you, quickly."

Sebastian grabbed the moon from beside his leg. It leapt into his hand. He whirled around and held up the shield. There were two loud thuds as two rock spikes crashed into the moon. Sebastian was forced back a step, but the protection held.

"Sebastian," said Lorenzo, "I had to do it. You don't know what this channeler will be capable of. Can you blame me?"

"Yes," said Sebastian. He spun quickly to face Lorenzo, raced over to him, and reached out to grab his hands. He thought that keeping Lorenzo's hands still might prevent him from casting a spell.

Lorenzo had looked vigorous when they sat at the campfire, but he must have been using illusions to hide his age. Sebastian found himself able to contain the older man.

Sebastian felt he had a dilemma. In some sense, the correct thing to do might be to kill Lorenzo. It could be the only way to stop him, and perhaps it was deserved for the damage he had done and the people he had killed.

But Sebastian couldn't bring himself to do it. For one thing, the idea of the cold-blooded killing of a helpless person wasn't something he could conceive. For another, he still had some sympathy for Lorenzo and his story.

He had an inspiration. Holding Lorenzo's wrists in his right hand, he pulled the jade heart off his neck with his other hand. As the stone pulled away from Sebastian's chest, a small gray shadow moved with it. Sebastian lifted the necklace up and brought it toward Lorenzo. Lorenzo's eyes opened wide as he saw what was coming, and he struggled to get free of Sebastian's grip. But the younger man was stronger, and he dropped the necklace over Lorenzo's head.

As the jade pendant settled onto his chest, Lorenzo dropped to his knees and began to cry. Sebastian let go of the grip he had on Lorenzo's wrists.

Sebastian stepped over to Lorenzo. Lorenzo didn't seem to see him, as he was too involved in his grief. Sebastian reached out his index finger, placed it on the jade heart on Lorenzo's chest, and gently pushed. Nothing happened at first, then Sebastian felt another presence. Luna was with him, and he could feel the pressure of her invisible finger on top of his. His finger pressed into the jade heart and then through it. The force of his and Luna's fingers pushed the shadow out of the jade heart and into Lorenzo's chest.

## 58

Anise and Rose were having breakfast. Shining past the flowered curtains on the windows, sunshine spread across the kitchen table. With a bit of help from Anise, Rose had been baking all morning. The baked goods covered the counter. The delicious aroma of warm bread filled the kitchen.

"Isn't it a beautiful day, Aunt Rose?" said Anise.

"It is, Anise," said Rose, "You're in a good mood

today."

"I'm happy," said Anise. "Sebastian is coming home soon. And Isabel's going to marry him."

"Is she, now," said Rose with a smile. She put some fresh pastries from the day's baking onto a plate in front of Anise.

"Now, Anise," said Rose, "Don't get too excited about Sebastian coming home soon. As far as I know, we haven't heard anything from him since he left. There's no way for him to let us know what he's up to."

Anise took a bite from the pastry in front of her. "He is coming home. I dreamed it last night."

"Anise," said Rose, "you know we talked about this. Dreams aren't real."

"I know yours aren't, Aunt Rose, but mine are. In my dream, Sebastian had a fight with the bad man."

Anise continued. "He beat him, Aunt Rose. He beat him, and he gave him a piece of his heart. The bad man's not a bad man anymore."

## 59

Sebastian and Betsy were camping just outside Anesbury again. Sebastian had set up the tent, and Betsy contentedly grazed near where Sebastian was starting a fire. They'd traveled for two days since leaving Lorenzo's cave. It relieved Sebastian to think they were halfway home.

Lorenzo hadn't taken well to his change of heart. He wept for ten minutes, then got furiously angry for another ten. When he switched from being sad to being angry, Sebastian kept a careful eye on him to see if he did anything dangerous. Especially for the start of a spell.

It was hard to get a coherent word out of Lorenzo while he was so angry. Still, it seemed like he was raging about how the academy hadn't listened to him when he tried to get them to accept the prophecies.

After his raging, Lorenzo became confused. Almost befuddled. Sebastian thought maybe he was trying to reconcile his thoughts with his new heart.

In the end, Lorenzo calmed down. When Sebastian could finally talk to him, he found a calm, quieter man struggling with regret for some of what he had done, but not all of it. Lorenzo still felt the prophecies' predictions were vital, but he regretted the violence of his methods.

Lorenzo found something in the prophecies that made him believe the new channeler would eventually make their way to the academy. He decided his best course forward was to help the academy prepare for this arrival.

Sebastian helped Lorenzo pack up his cart and prepare for a journey. Lorenzo would travel back to the academy and make them see the error of their ways. He would convince them to prepare for the coming of this predicted channeler. He would persuade them they needed to take clairvoyance seriously as a discipline.

"When this new channeler gets to the academy," he said, "we need to be ready to train not just the student's skills, but also their ethics and morals."

Sebastian and Betsy saw Lorenzo off on his journey. He was eager to head to the academy to see if he could change their culture. He said the time spent in the cart on the trip would remind him of his younger days.

\* \* \*

A few days later, Sebastian and Betsy reached the lane that turned off the main road toward Westhavenfieldbrook. Sebastian was very excited to be almost home. It was noon, so the sun was high overhead. Sebastian had hoped to get back a little earlier, but they had been a bit slow getting started this morning.

He saw the stone marker that showed the town name directions. Someone had changed the stone pointing toward Westhavenfieldbrook. Someone had replaced it with a much shorter stone that just read "Hero." Sebastian wasn't exactly sure what to make of this. He looked around to see if they were in the right place. Everything else looked the same, except for that stone.

He pulled on Betsy's lead and headed down the lane toward his village.

## 60

Rose and Anise stood on both sides of the lane leading out of the village outside the rebuilt town gate. They had been waiting there for hours. Rose was trying to convince Anise that it was time for them to go home.

"Anise," Rose said, "I don't think he's coming today."

"Aunt Rose," said Anise with a quaver in her voice, "I told you. He is."

A banner lay on the dirt of the lane between them. Anise held the cord attached to the top of one side, and Rose had the one attached to the other. The writing couldn't be read at the moment as the written side was face down.

"Anise," said Rose with parental patience in her voice, which somehow had crept in there in the last few weeks, "everyone thinks it's great how much you care about Sebastian's quest, but...."

"There he is!" called out Anise. She jerked on her end of the cord to lift the banner so quickly that the other end was almost pulled out of Rose's hand.

When Rose lifted her end of the cord, the sign rose off the ground. She looked down the lane.

Anise was right. Sebastian and Betsy were headed toward them. She saw the conquering hero, who seemed like a tired and dusty young man to her. She looked over at her niece. Anise's eyes shone through the swollen cheeks and dried tear tracks. Rose wondered what she saw.

Anise held her cord as high as she could. She had her arm up-stretched over her head. The top of her side of the banner was just about at Betsy's nose. The banner read, "Welcome home to Hero, Hero!" The mayor had had several banners and other signs made up. He was planning a welcome home parade.

Betsy walked up to the banner. She sniffed it to see if

it was something to eat.

"Anise, Rose," said Sebastian. "It's good to see you."

Anise dropped the cord, ran over to Sebastian, and wrapped her arms around him.

"I'm sorry, Sebastian," she said, crying again. "I'm sorry, it's just us. They wouldn't believe me when I said you were coming today."

Betsy gave up trying to eat the banner and started sniffing at Anise, who had a carrot stashed in her smock.

"Thank you, Anise," said Sebastian, giving Anise a big hug. "I couldn't imagine a nicer welcome home."

# 61

T he following morning Sebastian awoke to a pounding on his door. Somehow the night before, he had managed to avoid getting too much attention. This morning wouldn't be as easy.

When Sebastian made his way to the door to open it, he found the mayor waiting for him.

"You don't look ready, my boy," said the mayor.

"Ready for what?"

"The parade! Your welcome home parade. You need to get dressed, my boy. Don't forget your shield and sword."

While Sebastian was getting ready, the mayor gave him a pep talk to get him excited for the parade. It quickly became apparent this event wasn't about Sebastian for the mayor but about finishing the adventure and the story for the tourism industry, which would put the town of Hero on the map.

When Sebastian and the mayor stepped out the door, a cart was in front of the house. It was a hay cart, with the sides removed. There were banners attached to both sides of the base of the cart. The phrase "The hero of Hero" was written on both.

"I'm not getting on that thing!" said Sebastian.

With talk of his civic responsibilities, how it was for the town, and not for himself, the mayor convinced Sebastian to stand on the back of the cart. The mayor had gotten Mr. Thatcher to lead the horse pulling the wagon. He had recruited Mr. Arkwright, who fancied himself a musician, to play the bagpipes to lead the parade with music. Mr. Arkwright was a masterful piper if you judged the quality of the music purely by the volume. His son Marcus came up with a drum and tried to find the rhythm in the tunes his father belted out.

The mayor had two young daughters and a son. He

had dressed them in their market day best and given each of the girls a basket of flower pedals. The parade started out with the two girls in the front, scattering the petals. The son followed the girls, looking uncomfortable in his Sunday best.

Mr. Arkwright started into his first tune. Marcus bravely attempted to locate the appropriate places to bang on his drum. The parade turned onto Main Street and headed toward the market square.

Sebastian was having difficulty finding a place to hide on the back of the hay cart. It was early enough that some village roosters hadn't started crowing yet. It mortified Sebastian that his reintroduction to his fellow villagers would be waking them up with this unholy racket early in the morning.

As the cart drove slowly down Main Street, the villagers came out of their houses. To Sebastian's surprise, the reaction seemed to be mainly positive. Instead of yelling about the noise, most people coming out of their homes seemed in good spirits. They started following the cart down Main Street.

By the time the cart approached the market square, the parade felt different. The flower petals the girls scattered were shining colorfully in the morning sunshine. Most of the village's population walked down the street behind the cart, murmuring and talking among themselves.

Even Mr. Arkwright seemed to have taken inspiration from his first voluntary and perhaps most appreciative audience ever. For the first time, you could describe his play by other adjectives than just "loud." Marcus seemed to have figured out how to find the beat in his father's tunes.

The parade pulled into the market square. On the opposite side of the cobbles was a large object covered in canvas with a temporary-looking wooden platform standing next to it. Mr. Thatcher pulled the cart up next to the wooden platform, and Sebastian stepped off the wagon onto the platform. The mayor climbed up the slightly rickety wooden stairs on the platform's side to stand next to Sebastian.

The villagers spread out into the market square. Sebastian scanned through the crowd, picking out Isabel and her mother and then Rose and Anise.

The mayor looked out over the crowd and, in his best "addressing a crowd" voice, called out, "May I present, Sebastian! The hero of Hero!"

# 62

There was a roar of applause from the crowd. This was almost entirely the same group of people who had been standing here when Sebastian fought the beast. He flushed and felt overcome with gratitude himself. The sense that the people of his village appreciated and valued him made him feel warm all over.

"Speech!" came a cry from the crowd. Soon, it was echoing all over the square.

The mayor stepped forward and started to speak.

"Not you!" came a loud voice from somewhere in the crowd.

The mayor looked skeptical, trying to spot who had called out, but he stepped back.

After a few more cries of "Speech!", and the mayor pushing him forward, Sebastian stepped to the platform's railing.

His first reaction was he couldn't speak to so many people, even though he knew them all. But he grabbed the bottom edge of Gerard's shirt with both hands, tugged it down, so the front of the shirt tightened across his chest, and pulled himself together.

"Thank you," he said. Sebastian tried to raise his voice to a crowd addressing volume as the mayor had. The height of the platform helped a bit.

"As some of you know, I left the village to find out where the creature that attacked us came from and see if there would be more attacks."

Some crowd members started murmuring, and several leaned forward in anticipation.

"You'll be glad to hear I found out where it came from, and I was able to stop it. We should not be attacked again."

There was a roar from the crowd, and someone

started chanting Sebastian's name. He stepped back from the railing, flushing red with embarrassment.

The mayor stepped forward. This time when he started to speak, there were no interruptions.

"You've heard him," he said. "Our hero of Hero has saved us again!"

The mayor paused for a moment as the crowd applauded and then continued. "Our newly renamed town of Hero will forever remember the brave actions of our heroic son," and here he clapped Sebastian on the shoulder to more applause.

"And, to ensure we never forget," the mayor paused dramatically. He gestured to Mr. Arkwright, who had put down his bagpipe and stood near the sizable canvas tarp-covered object, a cord in his hands.

Mr. Arkwright gave the cord a sharp tug. Nothing happened. The mayor made a panicked gesture with his hand as Mr. Arkwright looked over at him to see what he should do. Mr. Arkwright reached over and grabbed the heavy canvas covering the large object with his hands and tried to move it.

The canvas was hardly moving. Some crowd members joined in, and with several hands helping, the tarp finally dropped off the object. Many of the cobblestones formerly hidden by the canvas were stained blue.

It was a large stone obelisk with a metal plaque embedded in it. Sebastian couldn't read it from where he stood, but the mayor resumed talking, and Sebastian was sure the gist of what was written on the plaque would be in what he was saying. Sebastian was enormously relieved what was revealed wasn't a statue. A historical marker he could deal with. A statue of himself would have been a new nightmare.

"On this spot," the mayor intoned. "Sebastian, the Knight of Moon and Shadow, defeated a nightmare creature which threatened to destroy the town of Hero. This creature had already destroyed the village of Anesbury, and Sebastian defeated it in single combat.

"Paraphrased a bit," said the mayor, "but there it is.

"Let's show our hero what we think of him.

"Hip, Hip, Hooray!"

The crowd joined in.

"Hip, Hip, Hooray!"

# 63

T he following morning Sebastian got up early. He finished his morning chores as quickly as possible, as he still had some unfinished business. As he stepped out his front door to get started, Anise, waiting for him, pounced.

"Anise," said Sebastian, "I've got things to do this morning." He held a folded piece of white-colored fabric in his hands.

"I want to help," said Anise.

Sebastian thought about it for a moment. He'd been used to being alone most of his life. Especially since his father died. He'd been planning to finish this quest by himself today. He realized he didn't mind having Anise tagging along. In fact, he thought he liked it.

"I'm not sure I know how to do this myself," said Sebastian.

"Then, we'll learn it together."

Sebastian set off down the lane, with Anise trailing after.

Anise skipped and bounced as they walked through the village, practically bubbling over with delight.

"Which one is first, Sebastian?" she said.

Sebastian held out the folded white fabric he held in his hands.

Sebastian and Anise turned off Main Street onto Blackbird lane.

"When are you going to ask Isabel to marry you?" said Anise.

"What?" said Sebastian, eloquently.

"Are you going to ask her today, or are you going to ask her after you give her shadows back to her?"

"Who told you I was going to ask her at all?" said Sebastian.

"No one told me. I figured it out by myself. Isabel said it was all right, though."

"Isabel said it was all right?" said Sebastian.

They were approaching the Widow Clark's house. Pico's dog house was in the side yard. There was a fence around the yard, but it was always in a state of disrepair. The same people who speculated that the Widow Clark wanted Pico free for additional security thought she kept the fence poorly repaired on purpose so Pico could get out.

The opening in the fence was big enough that Sebastian and Anise could climb through. They hadn't seen any signs of Pico. Anise told Sebastian nobody saw Pico much. He'd been very withdrawn since he'd been silenced.

Sebastian stepped up to the doghouse and leaned over to look inside. It was dark in there, but he thought he saw Pico curled up in the back of the house. He pulled the white fabric, the Pants of the Wind, from his belt.

Anise reached over and grabbed the pants out of Sebastian's hands. "Let me," she said.

"Be careful," said Sebastian. "We're not sure how he'll react."

Anise walked over to the doghouse door and looked in. She could see Pico at the back. He looked at her and tried to whine. Anise partly unfolded the pants and waved them in front of the door opening of the doghouse.

Pico came charging out and started bouncing up and down in front of Sebastian and Anise. He looked for all the world like he had just been offered the biggest treat a dog could imagine. It was strange to see the large dog making excited barking motions but not a sound. Sebastian thought that if Pico had embraced his change, he could have been the terror of all the cats in the neighborhood, sneaking up on them entirely silently.

Anise held the white fabric out to Pico while putting her hand on his head, trying to calm him. Pico opened his mouth, and the material seemed to flow down his throat. It wasn't that Pico ate the fabric. Instead, it seemed to turn to wind and blew down his gullet.

The fabric disappeared instantly, and Pico barked excitedly. His tail wagged like a metronome, and he started licking Anise's face, almost knocking her down in his excitement.

Pico headed back into his doghouse. As Sebastian and Anise turned to leave, they heard joyful grunting noises coming through the door opening.

"Well," said Sebastian, "that seems to have been successful."

# 64

Sebastian's next visit was to the mayor. He had had difficulty deciding what to do with Leonard's cap. He couldn't return it to Leonard, as Leonard had left town. Sebastian had heard that he was all right, but there wasn't any word of when, or if, he was planning to come back. Also, Sebastian thought that the giving of Leonard's cap had been a blessing for Leonard, as well as being a gift for Sebastian.

Sebastian had given it a great deal of thought, and he concluded that in some ways, the mayor was the kind of a fool who is a fool because he's not enough of a fool. If he were to put the cap on, he would become more foolish, which would allow him to take his foolishness less foolishly.

Sebastian left Blackbird lane and headed back down Main Street toward Market Square. Anise was still close on his tail.

"Anise," said Sebastian, "you don't have to stay with me all day. I've got a lot to do today."

"I know I don't have to," said Anise. "I want to."

Sebastian and Anise entered Market Square and started toward the town hall.

"You said something about Isabel saying it was all right for me to ask her to marry me?" said Sebastian.

"Yes," said Anise. "She also said that you couldn't get married because she kissed you when you left town. Or something like that. But I think you should ask her anyway."

Sebastian felt like he was getting whiplash. They approached the main door of the town hall. Sebastian opened the door, and they entered.

Mary, the miller's second daughter, was working as the town hall assistant today. Mr. Shepherd, the miller, was trying to curry favor with the mayor, so he'd been asking his daughters to volunteer. He was trying to get the mayor to appoint him and his family the official village bakers. Unfortunately for Mr. Shepherd, the mayor had secretly grown very fond of Rose's lemon custard tarts.

Mary greeted Sebastian and Anise with a friendly smile. She nodded to Anise, who she had seen around town.

"Good morning. How can I help you today?" Mary said very officially. She'd been practicing her official greeting. She'd just said the same thing to the empty room several times before they walked in.

"I was hoping to see the mayor," said Sebastian.

"Just a moment," said Mary. "I'll check to see if he's in." Mary knew quite well that the mayor was in. He had the habit of bouncing a ball off his office wall when he was bored. She could hear the regular thumping of the ball hitting the wall. It wasn't loud enough to be distracting unless you knew what it was.

Mary got up and knocked on the door of the mayor's office. She stuck her head in, and Sebastian and Anise heard a quiet conversation. Mary stepped back to her desk and gestured them toward the door.

The door opened as they approached it, and the mayor came out. He clasped Sebastian's hand in both his hands and shook it vigorously up and down.

"Sebastian, my boy," he said, "I've always got time for the hero of Hero. What can I do for you today?"

"I'm hoping it's more what I can do for you, Mr. Mayor," said Sebastian.

The mayor looked at Sebastian inquiringly.

Sebastian pulled Leonard's cap from his belt. "Mr. Mayor," he said, "as you know, this is part of the armor of the Knight of Moon and Shadow. I want to present it to you for the official use of the office of mayor of this village."

The mayor looked slightly irked. "Town," he muttered under his breath.

"As you may not know," Sebastian continued, "when I put this cap on during the battle with the nightmare which attacked this town, it gave me courage."

"Of course, I'm honored," said the mayor, "but in most of the situations I have to deal with daily, courage isn't an attribute I need."

"And," said Sebastian, "it's not exactly what you would get from wearing this cap."

The mayor waited expectantly for Sebastian to continue.

"What I believe wearing this cap will give you is a change in perspective. I would recommend putting this cap on when you have to make critical decisions. It should help you form wise opinions about difficult questions.

"A couple of additional pieces of advice about how to use this powerful item," Sebastian continued. "You should not wear it unless you're imminently about to make a decision, and you should remove it immediately when you're done."

The mayor reached out carefully and took the cap from Sebastian's hand. "I'll take that under advisement. Thank you, Sebastian," said the mayor.

## 65

Sebastian knocked on the door of the Fletcher family's house. Anise stood behind him. Above his head, hanging over the door frame, was a large wooden pair of shoes. The shoes were there to mark this as the home and place of business of a cobbler.

The door opened, and Mrs. Fletcher stuck her head out. She took one look at Sebastian and said, "What do *you* want?"

"Good afternoon, Mrs. Fletcher," said Sebastian. "Is Gerard at home?"

"He is," said Mrs. Fletcher, "he always is, recently. But I'm not sure I want you to see him."

"Mrs. Fletcher," said Sebastian, trying to put on his most winning tone. "I need to talk to Gerard for a moment. I borrowed something of his which I need to return."

"He'll feel better," said Anise from behind Sebastian.

Mrs. Fletcher reluctantly opened the door and led them up a narrow flight of stairs. The Fletcher family lived on the second floor above Mr. Fletcher's workshop.

She knocked on a door and opened it without waiting for an answer. She stuck her head in, and Sebastian and Anise heard a mumbled conversation. Mrs. Fletcher opened the door wider and stepped to one side so they could walk in.

Gerard was lying on his bed on one side of the room. On the opposite side was a large open wardrobe. There were several nice-looking pairs of shoes littering the dresser's floor. Some glamorous clothes were hanging inside. However, they weren't arranged as nicely as they might have been, and a few expensive shirts lay casually on the floor.

Gerard was wearing a simple cotton nightshirt and looked tired and sad.

Sebastian went over to where Gerard was lying. Gerard rose to his feet. Sebastian said, "Gerard, I am grateful to you for your gift."

"Thank you, Sebastian," said Gerard.

"I've come to give you your shirt back."

Gerard took a step back and raised one hand, palm outward. "No, thank you," he said. "I may be a little sad now, but I don't like who I was when I wore that."

"It's all right, Gerald," said Sebastian. "It won't be the same, I promise."

Sebastian held the shirt out toward Gerard. It still seemed to glow bright with color. The place where it had ripped in the battle with the beast and Sebastian had sewn it up was clearly visible.

"Are you sure, Sebastian?" said Gerard. "I like plain simple things now. I don't want to stick out."

"Look at it, Gerard," said Sebastian, gesturing toward the shirt and almost incidentally toward the mended tear. "It's not the same as it was."

Gerard took the shirt carefully. He put it on over his nightshirt. As it settled down over his shoulders, he seemed to stand a little straighter and taller than he had.

Sebastian reached out and clapped Gerard on the back. "How does it feel?" he asked.

Gerard stood up even a little straighter and shook Sebastian's hand. "It feels good," he said. "I feel good." The handshake with Sebastian grew firmer as he spoke.

"Thank you, Sebastian," he said. "And I don't just mean for the shirt. Thank you for what you have done for the village as well."

# 66

Sebastian and Anise had just one more stop. As they headed down the street toward the Fisher house, Sebastian felt nervous for the first time that day. Until now, everything they were doing was quest business. The Knight of Moon and Shadow had taken care of it. This next errand felt more personal.

The small-scaled wooden cabinet hanging over the door frame to the Fisher's carpentry shop swung a bit as the door opened, and Mrs. Fisher and Isabel stepped out. They started walking down the street away from Sebastian and Anise.

"Mrs. Fisher, Isabel!" called out Sebastian, speeding up his pace toward them. Anise struggled to keep up.

The sun was setting behind them as Mrs. Fisher and Isabel turned to see who was hailing them. The setting sun's rays shone straight through Isabel's feet as they stubbornly refused to cast shadows.

"Sebastian," said Isabel, a little breathlessly.

"Isabel," said Sebastian, "I have something of yours." He pulled the shapeless dark shadows folded over his belt out and held them in his hand.

Isabel and Mrs. Fisher waited a second for Sebastian and Anise to approach. As soon as they were close enough, Sebastian dropped to one knee in front of Isabel.

"Not this again," said Mrs. Fisher, with a smile.

Sebastian reached out with one of the dark shapes in his hand and gently held Isabel's ankle. There was a small amount of pressure as he massaged the substance into her calf and foot. Sebastian took the second shape and, holding it in one hand, pinched a small amount of the dark material off of it. Then he massaged the second shadow into Isabel's other calf and foot.

Isabel's shadow now showed her feet and ankles as

it stretched across the ground. Sebastian took the slight pinch of material he held in his hand and worked it with his fingers for a moment.

Still on one knee in front of Isabel, Sebastian turned his face up to her. He held a small dark object out toward her and said, "Isabel Fisher, will you marry me?"

Anise clapped. Isabel looked at the object in Sebastian's hand. It was a small dark ring, woven of material that looked at the same time substantial and also wispy like it could blow away at any moment.

\* \* \*

Now, suppose you're worried Sebastian made the ring out of part of the shadow of Isabel's feet, leaving her still incomplete. In that case, you'll be happy to know that he used the shadow cast by the shoes Isabel was wearing that day. Those shoes were still lying sadly shadow-less in Isabel's closet.

## 67

A few days later, on a night when the moon would have been full had it been in its usual place, Sebastian went out to Swenson's cow pasture. The moon obviously was not in the sky, as Sebastian had it with him. He held it in front of himself, lighting the way as he walked through the field toward the back fence.

Sebastian had to weave a bit as he walked to avoid the cow patties. The Swensons kept more cattle in this relatively small field than Sebastian liked. He preferred to give the cows as much room to roam as possible. The bright light from the moon in his hands made navigation easy.

Sebastian reached the back fence and climbed up. The climbing was awkward with the moon in his hands, but he got up on the crossbar just below the top. He gave the moon a kiss for good luck, held it up as high as possible, and jumped.

There was a clank as the edge of the moon thudded against something in the sky, but nothing held, and Sebastian and the moon wound up lying on the grass of the Swenson's field. Sebastian landed with a cow patty just a few inches in front of his face. He thanked his lucky stars and perhaps the little kiss he had given the moon that it hadn't been closer.

He got up and climbed back up onto the fence. This time, he made an effort to climb to the very top. The balancing act of standing on the very top of the top crossbar while holding the moon was challenging. It helped that he didn't have to stay long once he got there but could immediately take a leap upward.

Sebastian jumped and felt the moon collide with something invisible above him. There was a satisfying click, and the moon latched into place. Sebastian hung for a second, holding onto the moon's lower edge. For a moment, he was reluctant to let go. It had felt magical and unique being the Knight of Moon and Shadow. He wasn't sure he was ready to return to being just Sebastian, the farmer again. Then he remembered Isabel's answer to his question from a couple of days before, and he smiled.

Sebastian let go of the moon and dropped to the grass, narrowly missing another of the Swenson's cow pies. Just as it was time to let go of the moon, it was time to let go of the Knight of Moon and Shadow.

The full moon's bright light lit Sebastian's path as he made his way from Swenson's pasture back home.

# EPILOGUE

That summer, Isabel Fisher and Sebastian were married. Anise was the ring bearer. She was very proud to bear the ring, which she immediately named "The Ring of Shadow." The whole village came to the wedding. The mayor made sure it was a spectacle that added to the tourist reputation of the town.

The mayor appointed Rose the official town baker, with the condition that the town hall would be well supplied with lemon custard tarts. Mr. Shepherd, the miller, was initially indignant at this. But, he had recently discovered Rose's rhubarb pie, so he complained less than he might have.

Anise spent almost as much time at Aunt Isabel and Uncle Sebastian's house as she did at the bakery. Rose wasn't always happy about this, but it seemed Isabel and Sebastian didn't mind, so she let it go.

It wasn't long before Isabel and Sebastian were expecting. They named their first son Twilight and called him Twi for short.

Lilith kept a careful eye on Anise. She knew she had to bring the girl's potential to the academy's attention, but she thought there was no hurry.

* * *

But those are tales for another time.

# SUN & DREAM

## The Channeler Trilogy Book Two

J. Steven Lamperti

*Dedicated to the one I love,*
*and hopefully,*
*loved by the one I dedicate it to.*

# PROLOGUE

Nestled in the foothills of the Etenies mountains, in the northwest corner of the kingdom of Liamec, was a lake. A pretty little body of water, the lake was a beautiful crystal blue. Cold, it was fed by streams flowing from the mountains to the west. It was high enough in elevation that many of the trees on the lake's western shores were evergreens. The outlet from the lake was a stream that wound east down toward the lower lands. Eventually, this stream gathered force until it joined the Dragon river from the south. Together, they roared into the ocean far to the north and east.

Deer, bears, and wolves came from higher hills and drank the crystal waters. There were smaller creatures living in the woods also. All manner of birds flew through the skies and sang among the trees. Hares and badgers scurried through the underbrush. There were rumors and stories of larger, darker creatures coming down from the mountains.

On the lake's eastern shore was a small, undistinguished town called Lakeside. Lakeside was so small and undistinguished that it's hardly worth mentioning, so we'll leave it in peace for now.

On the western side of the lake, among the evergreens, was the town of Ashton. Ashton was supposedly so named because it had been burned to ash by a dragon's flames and then rebuilt in the distant past. No one in living memory had seen a dragon, and there were other theories as to why the town was named that. One of the industries in Ashton was the production of soap.

Ashton had other distinguishing features. In

addition to contributing to the cleanliness of Liamec by producing soap, Ashton made magic, and people trained in magic. In and around Ashton were buildings, places, and people that, put together, constituted an academy of learning. A place where people from all over Liamec, and sometimes further abroad, came to learn how to control and direct forces that allowed the manipulation of reality.

The Academy, as it was referred to throughout Liamec, was housed in a walled enclave adjacent to Ashton. There was also an island in the lake. This island, a short distance through lake waters from the Academy, was known as the Isle of the Wise. The Isle was only accessible to students and faculty of the Academy. Stories and rumors about what was on the Isle were rife among the non-magical citizens of Ashton.

But that's not where our story begins. Our story begins in the village of Hero, in the opposite corner of the kingdom of Liamec.

# HERO

# 1

Anise did not particularly enjoy feeding Uncle Sebastian and Aunt Isabel's chickens. Aunt Isabel had a certain specific way she wanted the feeding done. It wasn't enough to scatter some feed on the ground and let the chickens fend for themselves. The worry was that some greedy ones would take all the food, and others would starve. Isabel said it had happened before. So, she was supposed to put the food in the feeders located around the chicken coop run. Also, she was supposed to feed them in waves. First, put down some food for some, wait a while, and afterward, put down food for the rest.

Anise felt it was a lot of work for some dumb chickens. She knew they were dumb because she'd been playing a game to keep herself amused while feeding them. The game was fun, but it didn't work as well as it should have because the chickens were so stupid.

The game worked as follows: first, she would think of something that she wanted a specific chicken to do. Then, after imagining what she wanted the chicken to do, she would daydream about the chicken doing it and see what happened. For example, she had this one hen that she had been trying to get to fly up on top of the coop. It was a bit hard because while she was daydreaming about getting the chicken to do what she wanted, it was hard to keep feeding them. The first time she tried to do her daydreaming, she started to really fall asleep and only woke up when she felt herself falling down.

After she stirred herself from her daydream, she was excited to see that chicken start to flap its wings and actually take off and fly in the direction of the coop's roof. Unfortunately, at that point, it just flopped around a bit, looked confused, and then landed. That was when she decided that they were too stupid to exist.

The rooster, who she had named Sure, followed her

around. He had become excited when she had imagined something about one of the hens. It seemed he had gotten the wrong idea. He followed Anise around, flapping his wings sometimes and scratching at the ground.

Anise slipped into her daydream again and visualized Sure, sitting quietly in the corner of the chicken run. When she woke herself up, he did wander off and seemed to be leaving her alone. Maybe he wasn't quite as stupid as the rest of the chickens.

Betsy stuck her head over the chicken run fence and gave a loud "Heee Awwwwwwww," her mule bray, that was a combination of a donkey's bray and a horse's whinny. The chickens all scattered. Anise was startled as well.

"You dumb mule," said Anise. "You scared me."

Immediately Anise felt awful. For one thing, she loved Betsy, and for another, that was no way to talk to the noble steed of the Knight of Moon and Shadow.

Betsy had been slowing down a little in the last few years, and she'd never really been that noble anyway. Still, she deserved respect for how she had helped Sebastian. When Anise's uncle had transformed into the Knight of Moon & Shadow and saved the town, Betsy had traveled with him throughout the entire quest.

Anise walked over to the chicken run door and out into the yard. Aunt Isabel had asked her to stop by the house when she was finished feeding the chickens. She had something else she wanted to talk to Anise about.

# 2

Hero was a small settlement in the southeast corner of the kingdom of Liamec. Some called the quiet little town of Hero a village, though the village's mayor would be sure to correct anyone who said that within his hearing. "It's a town!" he would retort, though he wished he could be saying that it was a city in his heart of hearts.

The main street that led past Hero was marked, as were most of the roads in Liamec, by stone way-markers engraved with the names of nearby towns. Travelers on that road would usually keep going past the side lane that led to the town's gates.

Those on their way to the rest of Liamec to the west, the other towns of the Crossroads to the north and east, or sometimes, rarely, to the southeast and the Poignant Pass, would ignore the stone marker reading, Hero. They had more critical destinations in mind. Perhaps the mighty city of Capitol, with the glorious King's Seat where the kings of Liamec had resided for hundreds of years. Maybe the exotic land of France on the other end of the Poignant Pass or other even more exotic lands beyond it.

Those who walked past the turnoff toward Hero did miss something, however. They missed a scenic little town nestled between the Westhaven River on the west and the distant Blue Mountains on the east. It had a mill house, cobbled streets (mostly), a market square, and a solid wooden town gate.

Hero's claim to fame, and the source of its name, was an event that had happened several years ago. Towns and villages that were part of the loose confederation of communities called the Crossroads were suddenly attacked by creatures out of nightmares. Anise and her Aunt Rose had come to Hero, then called Westhavenfieldbrook, as refugees, fleeing an attack on their town by one of those nightmare monsters.

An unremarkable villager named Sebastian had suddenly acquired extraordinary powers and magical artifacts, which enabled him to defend the village against the attacks. After Sebastian's defense of the town, and his subsequent defeat of the channeler behind the attack, Lorenzo, things returned to normal.

The mayor, sensing an opportunity to grow his village into a city, had renamed the sleepy little town of Westhavenfieldbrook: Hero and built a monument to Sebastian's victory in the town square.

The story of Sebastian's adventures became well known, and songs were written that entertained many people in other parts of Liamec. Unfortunately, this hadn't translated into income or growth for Hero. Life in the peaceful village went on much as before.

# 3

**A**nise opened the door of the house that had been her second home for the last few years. Uncle Sebastian and Aunt Isabel weren't really her real aunt and uncle. She didn't have any real family, except for Aunt Rose. But, since Anise and Aunt Rose had moved to Hero, Anise had adopted Sebastian and Isabel as her aunt and uncle. She spent almost as much time at their house as at the bakery with Aunt Rose. Of course, Anise slept at the bakery. Sometimes she still missed her parents. Sometimes she cried quietly in bed at night. But not as often as she used to.

Sebastian's house's white-washed wattle and daub exterior still looked the same. But, since Isabel had been living there, the interior had been redecorated with a woman's touch. Linen curtains waved in the gentle breeze coming in through the open shutters, and there were throw cushions on the wooden bench against one wall. The seat had been lovingly crafted by Isabel's mother, the town carpenter.

In a throwback to Sebastian's bachelor past, his father's sword still hung in its place of honor over the mantle. Above the blade, in the spot where Anise felt it should be, was an image of the moon. To honor the Knight of Moon & Shadow, who he called the "Hero of Hero," The Mayor had had a portrait painted of the moon for Sebastian. The full moon shone down on a fence running through a cow pasture in the picture. There was a face on the moon in the painting. The face was partially the artist's idea of the Man in the Moon. And, partially, it was his interpretation of Sebastian's description of his encounters with the lunar spirit.

Anise once told Sebastian that she didn't think it was an accurate likeness of Luna. He had just given her an odd look as if he was surprised she was familiar with Luna's appearance.

Even though it didn't really look like Luna, Anise sometimes felt the portrait was trying to talk to her.

Anise looked around the room. She didn't see Isabel, but in the corner was Twi's crib. She started. Twi stood in the corner of his crib, staring fiercely at her. He looked intense, not making a sound, just focused on what she would do next. Twi's crib was a little unusual in that Sebastian had installed slats across the top to match those on the sides. He had been capable of climbing out of his crib for months.

Anise laughed. She shook her finger at him.

"You don't even know that you're a baby, do you," she said indulgently.

Twi was Sebastian and Isabel's son. Anise thought of him as her brother. She had, she felt, helped raise him. He was only a bit over one and a half, but he sometimes acted like an old man. "An old soul," Lilith said. His full name was Twilight, but they all called him Twi for short.

Anise was often given the job of watching Twi. She complained to Sebastian, Isabel, and anyone else who would listen that he was a trial to watch as he tried to escape any chance he got.

"I have no idea where he thinks he's going to go," she grumbled.

Anise had a theory. She had heard how the wee folk sometimes snuck into people's houses and swapped babies. A changeling, they called the baby that they left. She told Sebastian this once.

He just smiled at her. "He has my hair and his mother's eyes," he said. "I don't think we can blame anyone other than ourselves for him."

After Sebastian said that, Anise inspected Twi's and Isabel's eyes. Blue-green: a perfect match. The color made her think of how she imagined the sea looked. There were rumors that Isabel's father, Isiah Fisher, had come to Hero from somewhere near the sea.

Anise had asked Lilith about changelings as well. Lilith was the village's cunning woman. She knew about things that other people didn't. Her answer had been less reassuring than Sebastian's. She had said, "Oh, probably not. The wee folk don't do that so much anymore."

Anise stepped a little further into the room. "Aunt Isabel?"

# 4

A unt Isabel had given Anise the job of watching Twilight. She and Uncle Sebastian had somewhere that they needed to be that evening. Aunt Rose had told her something similar. The coincidence made Anise suspicious, but she didn't mind, as she had nothing else to do. Her friend Mary had to cover for her sister, Anne, who had skipped out on her turn to work at the mayor's office. So, Anise would have been at home anyway.

Mary and Anne were the miller's daughters. Mary was Anise's best friend. They shared an interest in things like reading that most of the rest of the villagers didn't have time for. Anne, Mary's older sister, had become boy obsessed and was always sneaking off to meet someone.

Twilight was quiet in his crib for the moment, so Anise used the time to try to solve a wooden puzzle that Isabel's mother had made for her. It was a little wooden bird in a cage. It was cleverly carved and put together so you could work the bird between the bars if you knew the trick or sometimes if you just fiddled with it enough. She had managed to get the bird out of the cage and was trying to put it back.

Anise looked up from the puzzle. The quiet in the room made her suspicious. Twilight was sometimes calm, but not usually for very long or without some reason. She looked over at the crib.

The baby was crouched in the corner of the crib, with his back turned toward her. His body was moving rhythmically back and forth. A low rasping sound that she hadn't noticed came to her attention.

Anise stood as quietly as she could and walked over to the crib to see what he was doing.
She gasped. Twilight had gotten hold of one of the table knives, and he was using it to cut at one of the slats on the crib.

"You monster," she cried and reached through the slats to grab the knife from him. There was a little pile of sawdust on the floor beneath the slat.

She put the knife on the table, unfastened the latch on the top of the crib, and swung it open. Reaching into the crib, she grabbed Twi, lifted him out, and pressed him to her body. She squeezed him against herself hard, trying to determine the exact amount of pressure necessary to compress all the rebellion out of him.

Twilight grunted. He met her eyes with his own, reached out, and grabbed her nose, his thumb inside her nostril and the other fingers gripping firmly.

Anise loosened her grip, her eyes tearing, and reached one hand up to the little baby's hand on her nose, trying to free herself. She put him on the floor, blinked tears from her eyes, and said, "All right, you want some attention?"

The baby stood, balancing precariously on his little feet. He smiled at her as he swayed back and forth.

There was a game that Sebastian played with his son. They both loved it, and it was one of the few tricks that calmed Twilight down when he got overwrought. Sebastian had crafted two little swords out of wood, so small as to be more like knives than swords, and he and his son would have little duels. Anise used this sometimes to calm the baby.

She got the sticks and gave the baby his. She laughed when he took it and turned his body to the side to present a smaller target to his opponent. He almost tumbled backward and barely kept his footing.

Sebastian had asked his mother-in-law if she could craft improved swords for the game, but she turned the job down. As the town carpenter, Mrs. Fisher was very skilled with wood, but she responded as a grandmother.

"You can't teach a baby to sword fight," she said, "it doesn't make any sense. And, anyway, you shouldn't be doing that. That's how you lose an eye!"

Sebastian had insisted that his father had taught him at that age. "'Sooner learned, never burned,' my father always used to say."

"He always did have the strangest sayings," said Mrs. Fisher. She shook her head. "No one around here says anything like that."

After an hour of vigorous battle, Anise finally got Twi to bed.

# 5

They were all sitting on the bench in a row. Uncle Sebastian, Aunt Isabel, Aunt Rose, and Lilith. The other side of the table was free. They were all looking at her, obviously expecting her to sit down opposite them.

*What have I done wrong now?* Anise thought.

It was the dining room table at one end of the main room of Isabel and Sebastian's house. Twilight was on his feet in his crib at the far end of the room. He was holding onto the slats with both hands. His face showed that he was astonished that he wasn't sitting at the table with his parents.

Anise trudged haltingly toward the table. She gazed down at the tabletop to avoid meeting the adult's eyes.

*It must have been something terrible*, she thought. *They all look so stern.*

The surface of the table wasn't a bad distraction. Isabel's mother, grandma Fisher, had made the table as a wedding present for Sebastian and Isabel. She had spent months working on it in secret. The tabletop was a miracle of inlaid wood. The patterns and shapes in the inlay were seemingly random but made you feel like they weren't. Anise had spent quite a bit of time admiring it.

"Have a seat, Anise," said Sebastian. He didn't sound angry, more worried.

Anise sat down. After studying the tabletop for another moment, she glanced up. Isabel was smiling at her, Rose was looking down, Lilith looked grim, and Sebastian met her gaze with an earnest expression.

Rose glanced up. Her eyes were a bit red as if she had been crying. Anise was sure that couldn't be it. She had never seen Rose cry.

"Anise, dear," she started.

"What's this about?" said Anise, "What did I do

wrong?"

Lilith leaned forward. She put her arms in front of her on the table and met Anise's gaze. Being among friends, Lilith wasn't wearing her hood or trying to put on her village cunning woman act. She wasn't trying to put on a show like she sometimes did, but she had gained a certain gravitas in the last few years. The touch of gray in her hair at the temples didn't hurt either.

"Anise," she said, "when a young woman gets to be a certain age, changes start to happen in her body..."

"This isn't going to be about the birds and the bees, is it?" said Anise. "I know all about that from school. Mrs. Shoemaker won't let us talk about it during school hours, but the kids talk at recess."

Lilith leaned back, defeated.

"Anise," said Sebastian, "in the foothills of the Etenies mountains is a lake, and on that lake's shores is an academy—"

"I know all about the Academy. Lilith told me," said Anise. "Why are you all here? What did I do wrong?"

Sebastian turned and exchanged a glance with Isabel.

Isabel ventured. "Anise, dear," she said, "if you'd let anyone finish, we're trying to talk to you about something."

Rose started crying.

Anise stared; Rose never cried. Something was really wrong.

# 6

Sebastian tried again. "Anise," he said, "we're trying to tell you, without much luck so far, that we've talked about it, and we think that it's time for an important and necessary change in your life."

Rose started crying harder.

Sebastian looked grim. "It doesn't have to be a bad thing. That Academy I mentioned? Lilith says you need to be trained there."

It became clear to Anise why Rose was crying. Lilith had hinted at this to Anise before, but she hadn't taken it seriously. She scanned the faces across the table. Rose wouldn't meet her eyes. Isabel was smiling with what was clearly supposed to be an encouraging smile. It was clear that Lilith wanted to say something.

"Do I have to go?" Anise said. A little knot of nerves started to form in her stomach. Her voice broke, and she felt she should have waited to speak.

"There was some resistance," said Sebastian, glancing sympathetically at Rose, "but I'll let Lilith address that question."

Lilith was eager to speak. She met Anise's gaze directly and firmly. "That's why I mentioned your age, Anise. The beginning of adulthood corresponds with the onset of the full powers of magic. We've talked before about your potential, and I've given you what training I can, but you have a great deal of power in you, and I'm not equipped to help you bring it out fully."

Anise shook her head. "I don't need to know magic," she said, "I'll stay here, and those stupid people at that academy can do their magic without me."

Lilith shook her head as well. "I'm sorry, Anise, it doesn't work like that." She looked thoughtful and smoothed a lock of brown hair with a streak of gray out of her face. She continued, "If you had less potential for power, or were showing signs of being good at alchemy, maybe, but you're going to be a channeler. Channeling is the wild card of magic. It's hard to control, hard to understand, and hard to use constructively. If you don't learn how to control and understand your abilities, they will be a danger to you, us, and the whole village." She frowned. "The country, possibly. Your uncle, Sebastian, has offered to travel with you." Lilith turned to look at Sebastian.

"It could be fun, Anise," said Sebastian. "It'd be just you and me on an adventure."

"I can't leave," said Anise. "Who would watch Twilight?" She turned and looked over at the baby. He was still watching the meeting intently. It seemed he thought he had something to contribute.

Sebastian smiled at the comment. "I think we can keep an eye on him," he said, "He's just a baby, after all."

"I don't want to go," said Anise. She felt like she was facing an oncoming storm.

"I'm sorry, Anise," said Lilith. "There isn't any choice. Channeling the spirit of a squirrel or even a dryad from a local tree is one thing. But, two years ago, the moon itself took an interest in us and our village."

Anise looked down at the ground. She felt defeated. "Could we take Betsy?" she said.

Sebastian hesitated. "Betsy's getting a little older," he said. "I guess we could ask Mr. Thatcher the farrier if he thinks she'd be up for the trip."

# 7

T he crowd gathered at the main gate to see Anise, Sebastian, and Betsy off, reminded Anise of the Knight of Moon & Shadow's quest. The mayor was there, Isabel, Isabel's mother, and Lilith. Mr. Thatcher, the town farrier, was there. Whenever anyone in the village had a question about animals, especially horses, mules, or donkeys, they would turn to him. He had given Betsy an extensive medical exam, mainly just opening her mouth to look at her teeth. She hadn't liked it and had tried to bite him. He had pronounced her ornery but healthy.

The morning was stressful. It was a long journey, and Anise wasn't going to be able to travel back and forth very often. It wasn't clear how or when she would next be back in the town of Hero. Rose wasn't taking this well. People had been trying to get her to stop crying all morning.

Sebastian would be traveling with Anise, and once he helped her settle, he would be coming back. Still, the Academy was all the way on the other side of Liamec, and he would be gone for a long time. Isabel was not terribly happy about this.

Isabel held Twi on her hip. He was looking around at all the action with enormous interest. Apparently, he was contemplating how he'd manage a departure gathering differently if he were in charge.

The mayor was relieved to see that Mr. Arkwright, the smith, wasn't there. They had had a falling out about a year ago or so. It wasn't about the cobbling of the town streets of Hero. The cobbles that proudly covered the main square now ran all the way down Main Street to this very gate that they were standing beneath. No, Mr. Arkwright had dared to run in the last Mayoral election.

It hadn't been a real challenge. The mayor had won handily. Still, the notion that one of his own aldermen, someone he had taken under his wing and mentored, would stab him in the back like that had left a bitter taste in his mouth.

"Citizens of Hero," cried the mayor, using his best 'talking to a crowd' voice. "Good morning to you all!" Most of the town was still asleep, but the mayor thought it was best to keep up appearances. "Our Sebastian, Our Hero of Hero, is leaving us on another quest."

Isabel and her mother shared a 'who does he think he's talking to' look.

The mayor turned off the voice, walked over to Sebastian, and clapped him on the shoulder. "Take good care of our little Alice, my boy," he said.

Perhaps it's a good thing that Anise was just starting her journey to magic, as otherwise, the look she gave the mayor might have made him burst into flame.

Rose approached with a bundle of pastries wrapped in wax paper in her hand. She had stopped crying for the moment, but her eyes were lined in red. She handed the bundle to Anise. They had already loaded the mule with supplies. *These must be something extra*, thought Anise.

"They're for Sebastian. Raisin cakes. He loves them," Rose whispered.

Rose started crying quietly again. She reached out, gathered Anise to herself, and hugged her tightly. "You be careful out there," she said. "Listen to your uncle. Don't talk to strangers. Be strong and proud."

Isabel ran forward. Awkwardly, because holding Twilight offset her balance, she put one hand on Sebastian's chest and stood on tip-toes to kiss him. The morning sunlight cast her shadow across the ground behind her. The black ring on one of her fingers seemed like it absorbed rather than reflected the light. Sebastian grabbed her around the waist, pulled both her and the baby into himself, and returned the kiss.

# 8

Once they were out of sight of Hero and Rose's tears, Anise felt a little better. The sun was shining, she was walking beside her uncle and her favorite mule, and they were on an adventure. Betsy was getting excited too. She announced it to the morning and the world with a big, "Heee awwwwwwwww!"

They turned left at the intersection on the edge of town. The leftward way led west, away from the Blue Mountains and toward the heart of the kingdom of Liamec. They crossed the old stone bridge over the Westhaven River. The wide road led on as far as they could see to the west. It was cleared for ten feet on each side for visibility and safety. Now that they had left Hero's fields behind, there were untended forests on the roadsides.

Anise ran ahead down the dusty lane, turned toward her uncle and Betsy, raised her arms up like a bird, and charged back towards them as if she were flying. Betsy flicked her ears disdainfully.

"Isn't it a beautiful day, Uncle?" she said breathlessly.

"It is, Anise," said Sebastian. "Though that morning sunshine you are enjoying will feel less friendly in a few hours when it gets hot."

It was late summer, about the hottest time of year. They were hoping to reach the Academy in time for the start of the fall session.

Anise fell into step beside her uncle. She looked up at the blue sky, the few clouds, and the bright morning sun. She looked thoughtful. "Does the sun have a spirit, like Luna and the moon?"

"Of course," said Sebastian. "Helios is the god of the sun. He's up there right now, looking down on us. They say he sees everything. If you look at the sun directly and squint the right way, you can see his face, just like you can see the face of Luna in the full moon."

Anise turned obediently and started to look at the bright morning sun.

Sebastian put his hand between her eyes and the blazing orb with a laugh. "I was kidding, Anise," he said. "You shouldn't look directly at the sun. It's bad for your eyes."

# 9

Anise ran through a dark wood. The branches of the trees grabbed at her clothing. Moonlight filtered through the trees, barely, just enough for her to see the narrow trail by the faint glimmer. Her heartbeat was a drum roll through her chest.

*Where's Aunt Rose?* she thought. *I just need to make it to a clearing, and I'll find her.*

The next howl was closer.

*They're catching up with me*, Anise thought.

In her mind's eye, she could see the face of one of the wolves chasing her. The wolf was panting, her tongue hanging out of her mouth. Her eyes looked fierce, but they also looked fearful.

*They're not just angry—they're scared*, thought Anise. *They're scared because they're angry, which makes them more scared.*

*Where's Aunt Rose?* she thought again. *If I can only find Aunt Rose, I'll be all right.*

There were rustling sounds and the sound of bodies rushing throughout the underbrush around her. Somehow she was running fast enough to keep ahead of the wolves.

*They're scared because I am*, she thought.

"Anise," said Sebastian urgently in an anxious whisper. "You need to wake up now." He shook her shoulder as she lay tightly curled up in her bedroll.

Anise opened her eyes. Her uncle stood over her. He was fully dressed in the outfit that Isabel had prepared for him for the journey. Anise had helped her. The white dyed thick linen britches were intended for protection, but they had spent more thought on the jerkin. It was double-layered durable cloth, with stitching quilting the fabric into compartments. Anise had had the inspiration to stuff the quilted pockets with thistledown. It had taken her a long time to gather enough from the fields around Hero.

Isabel dyed the padded jerkin purple and Sebastian's leather boots black. The intent was to give him the look of the Knight of Moon and Shadow. Sebastian was a little unsure when he saw it, but he wore it for Isabel.

Anise looked around. The campfire was still burning, though it had burned a little low, and the firewood was in short supply. The fire illuminated the circle of large boulders that stood around the spot they had picked to camp. Betsy stood over on the other side of the campsite, nickering fearfully. Her lead was lashed to a tree. Otherwise, she might have bolted.

"There's something out there. I think it's wolves," said Sebastian. He was holding his sword in his hand. "I need you awake in case we have to run."

A howl cut through the night air.

# 10

Anise stood. She looked groggy to Sebastian. He saw her make an effort to pull herself together. "It's all right, Uncle," she said. "They don't want to be here any more than we want them here. They're just here because of my dream."

"Anise," said Sebastian, "this is serious. The fire is keeping them at bay for the moment, but we're running out of firewood."

"Just a minute," said Anise. "I'll get rid of them." She raised one hand, palm outward, toward Sebastian. She shut her eyes, her breathing slowed, and she swayed back and forth.

Sebastian gazed at her. *Had she fallen back asleep, standing up?* He resisted the impulse to shake her again and looked around the campsite. It had seemed a safe spot to camp for the evening. What felt like an eternity ago. The circle of large boulders sheltered them from the wind. There was already a circle of smaller stones forming a firepit where numerous previous travelers had made fires. There was a place to tie up Betsy close, but not so close that she would be putting her nose into their dinners.

He re-evaluated the site from a more defensive perspective. There were several spots where there were gaps in the boulders. If the wolves launched a coordinated attack, they would be hard to stop. *They wouldn't do that, would they?*

He held his sword in front of himself as he walked toward one of the gaps.

Anise shuddered and opened her eyes.

"There," she said. "I've told them as best I could. Some of them didn't listen, though."

She looked thoughtful. "They really don't like the fire."

The firelight lit up the circle of standing boulders.

With a loud howl, a wolf burst into the light. The flames and light from the fire's glowing embers reflected off its eyes. It was a gray wolf, not too big, but plenty big enough to be terrifying.

Betsy reared up onto her hind legs. Her forehooves lashed through the air. For a moment, where a tired mule had stood, there was a mighty war stallion. The steed of the Knight of Moon & Shadow. Then Betsy flopped back down, and her forelock fell over her eyes.

With his sword in one hand, trying to hold the beast at bay, Sebastian grabbed a brand from the fire with the other. He moved to stay in between the creature and Anise. The wolf crouched by the edge of the clearing, between two boulders, growling. Sebastian didn't see or hear any others coming.

Sword in one hand, burning brand in the other, Sebastian took a step toward the creature. He had the feeling that Anise was right. The wolf didn't want to be here, especially with the rest of the pack not making an appearance. It snarled, baring its teeth.

Sebastian swung the blazing brand and managed to nick the creature on the top of its back. It yelped, and he saw embers off the flaming wood scatter like sparks around it.

The wolf decided it had had enough. It turned and ran back through the gap between the boulders.

# 11

The sun was shining brightly in another beautiful sky the following morning. Betsy was ambling along behind Sebastian and Anise. Even though Sebastian walked in front, holding Betsy's lead, she still set the pace. Nobody could hurry Betsy up if she didn't want them to. It didn't seem like the mule was in any rush to get to their destination.

Sebastian turned to Anise and said, "Anise, what did you mean about the wolves being there because of you?"

"It's channeling. Lilith told me about it. Apparently, I have the potential to be a very good channeler," Anise said proudly. She smiled in a way that lit up her face. "Channeling is when you make people, animals, or spirits do things in your dreams. The wolves were coming to get us because that's what was happening in my dream."

Sebastian looked at her sternly. "Anise," he said. "We almost... We almost... We could have died. If I hadn't woken you or the wolves hadn't left, we could have died."

Anise looked a little shamefaced, "That's what Lilith said. I need to go to the Academy for—" She hesitated. "—control. She said they could teach me control. She said that the cunning folk don't do much channeling. They do illusions, elemental magic, and potions, but they don't do channeling."

Sebastian said thoughtfully, "Well, I guess we'll have to keep you happy so that you don't have any more bad dreams until then."

Sebastian stood by the stone way-markers at an intersection. He had pulled the map that Anise and Mary made for the trip out of Betsy's saddlebags. He was glaring at the parchment, the furrow between his brows deep enough to get lost in.

"Anise," he called out, "can you help me with this

map?"

Anise came closer and looked over his shoulder. "What's wrong?"

"The town names on these way stones don't match any of the town names on the map." Sebastian waved the parchment in Anise's face.

Anise and her friend Mary had visited the town library in preparation for the trip. They had managed to get a piece of parchment from Brone Tailor, the town scribe.

Anise had always been very impressed with the town library. It was just a modest room in the town hall, but the bookshelf against one side of the room must have had twenty books in it. Anise hadn't thought that there were that many books in the world.

When Brone pulled the map out of a drawer and spread it out on a table, Anise had no idea what they should do. The parchment was covered with pretty little pictures, lines, and dots. There was no way they could make a copy of it.

Brone helped them. They didn't copy the pictures, just the town names of the bigger towns and lines to show roads. They had a spider web of lines connecting dots with labels written on them when they were done.

Anise and Sebastian compared the labels on the map with the names on the stones. At each intersection on the major roads of Liamec, there were stone way-markers. The stone way-markers pointed down roads, listing the name of the closest village and then usually the name of another larger town further off in the same direction. Eventually, they found a label on the map that matched one of the names carved on a stone and continued on their way.

# GRISPUT

# 1

Sebastian and Anise were gathering wood and kindling for the evening fire. Sebastian told Anise that they should collect more than the previous night. "I don't think it'll happen again, but better to be safe than sorry," he said.

He was dumping a load of firewood near the fire pit when he saw someone approaching from the road. Betsy looked up and flicked her ears toward the approaching person.

As Anise drew near from the other direction, Sebastian studied the figure.

It was a young man. He was dressed in rags, dirty, faded britches, and a torn linen tunic. He had a beat-up backpack on his back, a small knife in a sheath belted at his waist, but didn't seem to be carrying anything else. Sebastian assumed the young man was looking for a hand-out from the disheveled clothes and the grime.

Anise reached the fire-pit and dropped the wood and kindling she had found. Sebastian called out, "We don't have much money, but I suppose we could spare a copper." He reached for one of Betsy's saddlebags, looking for his coin purse.

The young man stepped closer. He looked indignant. He stood up straight, met Sebastian's eye, and said, "I am no beggar. I am Briac, the magnificent, world-famous minstrel!"

He opened his backpack and pulled out a battered lute. Holding it in one hand, he executed a smooth minstrel bow, one leg stiff, the other bent, as he leaned forward.

"Uncle!" said Anise. Sebastian wasn't sure what she was reacting to. He didn't feel like his assumption had been unwarranted.

Briac played a few notes on his lute. He again bowed toward Anise, "At your service, my lady," he said.

Anise giggled and glanced down at the ground. He nodded toward Sebastian. "And you, sir."

Sebastian noticed that the lute was missing a string. Briac still managed to make a pleasant sound with it. He was young, just a few years older than Anise. Through the dirt, he looked healthy and fit. Sebastian started to regret his unwelcoming behavior.

"Briac," he said, "as a fellow traveler, would you care to join us at our campsite this evening?"

Briac smiled. "I would be honored," he said. He reached once again into his backpack and pulled out a withered turnip. "I will, of course, contribute," he said, flourishing the vegetable. "For the soup."

## 2

Sebastian hadn't planned on making a traveler's stew that evening, but he changed the menu to include Briac's turnip. Rose, Isabel, and Mrs. Fisher had packed them food and supplies that should last a long time. Still, they didn't know how long the journey would take, so he was careful to first use the more perishable things.

Sebastian made a point of adding the turnip to the stew at a moment when Briac was looking, so he knew his offering was accepted. As they gathered around the campfire, Sebastian studied the young man. At one point, as he walked past, Sebastian detected an unpleasant smell. Given the state of his clothing, that wasn't surprising.

Sebastian noticed that what he thought was dirt on the young man's face was a trace of hair on his upper lip. Either he was trying to grow a mustache, or shaving was also not part of his hygiene regime. His hair might be a light shade of brown after a bath.

His tunic was ripped down the front. A few chest hairs showed through the rip. Sebastian thought it seemed like the first shoots of new growth from a garden. He caught Anise looking at Briac admiringly.

"Isn't he pretty?" she whispered to Sebastian when Briac was on the other side of the campfire.

*Pretty smelly*, thought Sebastian, but he didn't say anything.

After they got bowls of stew and sat, Briac announced, "I just played for the gentry and mayor of the town of Hero. They loved my new song."

Sebastian sat up. "We just came from Hero," he said.

"Oh, did I say Hero?" said Briac. "I meant Hercule. A different town."

"You write songs?" said Anise. "Can you play us one?"

"Of course," said Briac. "What minstrel doesn't play

for his supper?" He stood and took another bow in her direction. "As soon as we are done with our stew, I will play you my new song, the *Lay of the Knight of Moon & Shadow*."

The young man looked at Anise and Sebastian inquiringly. "You know the story, of course? The tale of how the small-town farmer was summoned by Luna, the lunar spirit, to save his village?" Then he smiled. "Of course you do. You said you just came from Hero."

Anise shot a glance at Sebastian.

Briac continued, "The *Ballad of the Hero* felt too long to me. *The Man Who Pulled the Moon From the Sky* has a boring melody. I think I've improved on them both."

# 3

T he flickering firelight cast a warm glow over the evening as the three sat around the campsite. The meal was over, and Briac pulled his lute out of his battered backpack. He played a little introductory riff and then began to sing.

A hero born of night and dream,
From farmer's field, across hill and stream.
The wind, the moon, the dark, his might,
He saves the world through moonlit night.

A night, oh Knight, a night so dark,
Stop evil dreams to take their mark,
Lo, moon & shadow will not fall,
A knight, oh knight, please heed our call.

The hero rises when nightmares come,
The moon his strength. Her will be done.
His father's sword, his good right arm,
his heart so true, shields all from harm.

A night, oh Knight, a night so dark,
Stop evil dreams to take their mark,
Lo, moon & shadow will not fall,
A knight, oh knight, please heed our call.

And when at last, the nightmares' gone,
struck down by virtue, shadow, and brawn.
Our hero, humbly, fades into night
until he's needed to resume the fight.

A night, oh Knight, a night so dark,
Stop evil dreams to take their mark,
Lo, moon & shadow will not fall,

A knight, oh knight, please heed our call.

There was a moment of silence around the campfire when Briac finished. He strummed the last chord, then paused; Anise released her breath. She sat up straight and clapped her hands. "That was beautiful," she said. She smiled at Briac. He returned the smile.

"Well sung," said Sebastian, "I really admire how you play around that missing string."

Briac laughed and said, "It'll be hard to get used to having it back once I get a new one."

Sebastian threw Briac a water flask. "Here, son, I think singing must be thirsty work." He smiled gently at Briac. "After you've taken a drink, you might want to wash your face. I think you've got a bit of dirt on your lip there."

Anise gave Sebastian a disgusted look. Briac looked hurt.

"It is a lovely song," Sebastian continued thoughtfully. "Did you think about adding more of the story's facts into your lyrics? It's a pretty song, but it doesn't really tell the story, does it?"

Briac scoffed. "Does no one understand abstraction anymore? Everyone knows the story."

Sebastian replied, "If you're writing a song about an event, aren't you usually trying to communicate with the people that don't know the story?"

Anise interjected, "I think you should keep your eyes open when you sing. It will help you connect with your audience."

# 4

Anise was sitting by the campfire. The moon was shining down on the campsite. She wasn't sure it had been full when she went to sleep, but it was full now. Anise recognized that she was in a dream. She thought she saw Luna, the lunar spirit, wink at her from her position in the sky. Sebastian, Betsy, and Briac were nowhere in sight. Once she knew she was in a dream, she felt in control.

There was a circle of firelight shining on the stones around the campfire. Around and across the fire from her were nine elegant ladies. Anise was more impressed by how elegantly dressed they were than by who they were. They didn't look like they were sitting around a campfire at the side of the road. They could have been dressed for a ball. A little out of fashion, perhaps, but elegant nonetheless.

"So," said Anise in a business-like manner, "you're the muses, right? Who's who?"

One of the ladies swept forward confidently and pronounced, "I am Calliope, the elder sister."

Behind her, there was a chorus of name declarations. Anise could only make out a few.

"Poly."

"Clio."

"Thalia."

Anise sighed wearily. "Who's in charge of music?" she said.

"That's me. I'm Euterpe," one of them said. She wore a laurel wreath on her head, a light red gown, and she met Anise's gaze with a warm smile.

"If I might have a word," said Anise.

Sebastian awoke with a start. He felt a surge of adrenaline. He reached to his belt for the hilt of his sword and rose to a sitting position. *Where are Betsy's saddlebags?*

*Someone's trying to steal the moon.*

Sebastian looked around the campsite. Anise and Briac were still asleep. The first hint of light was just showing in the eastern sky. He wasn't even wearing his sword. There was no one there but them.

Before Anise opened her eyes, the strains of distant music reached her ears. It was pretty, exotic sounding. She recognized the sounds of Briac's lute, but the tune was unfamiliar.

She smelled something as well. She opened her eyes and saw Sebastian bustling around the embers of the fire. He was melting some cheese onto slices of rye bread on a flat rock near the warm coals.

Sebastian saw her open her eyes. "I know we're not supposed to break our fast until midday," he said, "but I thought a bit of bread would give us strength for walking today."

Anise looked around for Briac. She didn't see him, and the sounds of his lute were a bit distant.

Sebastian noticed her look and said, "He didn't want to wake you. He said something about musical inspiration. I think he's not far. It sounds pretty, doesn't it?"

## 5

After eating, Sebastian started getting Betsy ready for the day's travels. She grumbled, as she always did when he put on her saddlebags. At one point, she tried to nip his hand. "What kind of gratitude is that for finding us this lovely campsite?" said Sebastian.

When they made their way over to the roadway, Briac seemed in no hurry to leave. Sebastian turned to him and said, "Which way are you going, son?"

Briac pointed down the road in the same direction they were heading.

Sebastian, somewhat reluctantly, said, "Well, I guess we'll be traveling together, at least for a little." Anise smiled.

Briac put his hand on the hilt of his dagger and said, "There's safety in numbers."

Sebastian walked a bit ahead. Anise held Betsy's lead, and Briac walked beside her.

"This is Betsy," said Anise. "Betsy, meet Briac." Briac started to reach out to touch Betsy's nose. "Careful," continued Anise. "If she's not in a good mood, she might try to bite you."

Betsy assessed Briac's hand skeptically. She flicked one ear forward and the other back. She might have spun one of them around in a circle if she could. It took her a while to get used to new people.

"Betsy," said Briac thoughtfully. "You named her after the mule in *The Man Who Pulled the Moon From the Sky*." He looked again at the gray hair around her muzzle and continued, "Or, renamed her." Anise laughed.

"I had a dream last night," said Briac to Anise.

"Uh-huh," said Anise, looking at him.

"There was a woman in my dream. She encouraged me with my music. That tune I was playing this morning felt like it came from that dream." He looked bemused.

Sebastian went to the way-stones at the next intersection and pulled out his map to check the names. Briac came over and looked over his shoulder. "What kind of map is that?" he complained. "There aren't any pictures or colors. Shouldn't it have the emblems for the towns or the flag colors of the houses on it?"

"That would be nice," said Sebastian. "But this is all we have. You've traveled quite a bit. Maybe you can help me."

Briac scoffed. "Not with that map." He walked back to where Anise and Betsy were standing. It occurred to Sebastian that it was likely that Briac couldn't read. Hero was an unusual town in that it had a schoolhouse, and all the town's children got a school education.

Sebastian thought that maybe Briac would split off and go a different direction at the intersection. He seemed content to continue traveling the same way they were.

# 6

An arrow came arching through the air. It hit the hard-packed earth of the road right in front of Sebastian and skittered off to one side. He stopped walking forward immediately. "Hestia's hips!" came a voice from the woods off to one side of the roadway.

"Stand and deliver!" a deeper voice called out.

"We're standing, we're standing," said Sebastian quickly. He stepped back to be just a little in front of his traveling companions.

Five men stepped out from the tree line, though there might have been more hiding in the underbrush. Two of them stayed back in the trees, bows trained on the travelers. The other three walked forward to the edge of the roadway.

As they walked forward, Sebastian took stock of Briac and Anise. Anise seemed calm. She was still young enough to assume that her uncle would take care of her. Briac had his hand on the hilt of his dagger. He was watching the oncoming men very intently. Sebastian met the young man's eyes, moved his own hand toward his belt, and shook his head. Briac moved his hand away from the hilt. *He's not a coward*, Sebastian thought.

The men reached the travelers. They were roughly dressed: worn leather clothes, well-traveled but patched and maintained. The one in the middle, probably the one who had called out, was one of the largest men Sebastian had ever seen. He looked more like a bear than a man between his size and the thick brown hair that mostly covered his face.

The man to his right said apologetically, "The arrow was supposed to hit the ground and stick there, quivering. It would have been more dramatic."

Briac stepped forward next to Sebastian and said, "I am Briac, the splendid, and these are my traveling companions. They are under my protection."

The bear-man ignored Briac and casually said to Sebastian, "Are you rich, or do you work for the prince regent?"

"I can honestly say no to both," said Sebastian.

The big man looked disappointed. The third man, who hadn't spoken yet, said, "Well, can't we take their money anyway?"

The second man, who had mentioned the arrow, went to retrieve it. The big man turned to the third one. "You remember what the Raven said. The rich and powerful, not the common folk."

Sebastian held back a start when the bear-like man mentioned the Raven. He'd heard of the Raven. The outlaw band called the Raven's men was getting a bit of a reputation in these parts.

The big man turned back toward Sebastian, a momentary hopeful gleam reappearing in his eyes.

"You aren't by any chance a tax collector, are you?"

"Sorry," said Sebastian.

The big man looked disappointed again but resigned. He waved to his companions, and they started back towards the woods. He turned again to Sebastian and said, "You folk be about your way. Be careful out there. The roads can be dangerous." He and his companions all disappeared into the shadows under the trees with that final word.

# 7

A nise dropped behind Sebastian, Briac, and Betsy. Sebastian and Briac were discussing sharpening blades as they walked down the road. Sebastian was very insistent that it was essential to sharpen your blade frequently. Briac argued that excessive sharpening of an edge that wasn't used was unnecessary and could wear it out. Anise found the topic excruciatingly dull.

She heard a rustling in the underbrush just behind her. She turned, a little wary after their encounter with the outlaws.

A family of quail burst from underneath a bush and started across the trail. It was a mother quail followed by her brood. The mother looked from side to side as she led the babies onward. The baby birds were tiny. Each was just a feathered dot on little legs following behind the mother in a line.

Anise held her breath as they scurried across the way. She didn't want to scare them, and she also didn't want to alert Sebastian and Briac to the bird's presence. She wasn't sure if they would, but she didn't want them thinking of the mother bird as a way to supplement the traveler's diet.

She tried to reach out with her mind and connect with the birds as she had with the chickens at Uncle Sebastian's farm.

She could feel each little spirit and the larger one of the mother bird. Each baby felt like a tiny dot of life, heartbeat, and fear. They were nervous at the open road's exposure, and there was no room for anything else in their tiny minds.

Anise felt a mental 'pop' of disconnection as each little bird scurried into the underbrush on the far side of the road.

"Anise," called Sebastian from down the way. "Don't

fall too far behind."

At each intersection, Sebastian wondered if this would be the point where Briac remembered which way he was heading and left them. He selected the same direction they were going every time by some happenstance.

## 8

Anise, Briac, and Sebastian were standing on a low hill. Betsy stood a little way behind them. She wasn't as interested in the view as the rest of them. They had left the road and climbed the hill to get oriented, to see exactly where they were.

The view, Betsy's opinion aside, was impressive. There was a busy four-way crossing in the road below them. The road they were following joined the intersection and continued to the gates of a dark high-walled city. Purple flags with a black silhouette of a serpent flew from the battlements. The dark high stone walls curved away to the left of the city gates. To the right, they merged with an imposing rock cliff face. The cliffs towered above the gates and the lower part of the city. They could see that the walls resumed on the top of the cliffs high above them.

Although it was still early afternoon, parts of the lower city were already shaded from the sun by the towering cliffs.

"Grisput," said Briac.

"We're not going in," said Sebastian. "We'll take a route around the city walls."

Briac shivered. "No argument from me."

"But I wanted to see a big city," said Anise.

"Not this big city," said Sebastian firmly.

Approaching the city, the foot and cart traffic on the road increased steadily. As soon as they turned off the main way, it lessened again. The carts with goods, people walking, and troops of guards were more interested in traveling into Grisput than they were in going around it.

The road wound through a wood, drifting further from the city walls as they went. When it began to get dark, Sebastian suggested that they should find a less well-traveled place to camp. They found a smaller track leading off the main road and followed it for a while.

As they passed some trees on the track, a small village of perhaps fifteen houses came into view. Sebastian heard some sounds and gestured his companions to silence. They crept forward and found a place where they could see what was happening without being seen.

The little town was bristling with armed men wearing tabards with the same purple color and silhouetted serpent that had been on the flags flying over the city walls. Anise started to ask what was happening, but Sebastian held his finger over his lips.

"Grisput guards," whispered Briac.

Sebastian glared at him and repeated his gesture.

The guards were searching the houses. They were everywhere. Sebastian estimated that there were at least two dozen or more. A cart rumbled into the center of the small town. A second one followed it. One of the guards opened the door of the largest building and made a beckoning gesture through the opening.

The guards led a line of manacled people out of the door and toward the cart.

## 9

T he whole population of the town was being loaded into the carts. There were twenty or more people in the chain lines. Anise turned to Sebastian and started to say something. Sebastian repeated his shushing gesture again.

The town looked small and destitute. Sadly, Sebastian thought that there wouldn't be anyone coming to rescue these people. He pulled on the shoulders of his companions, and they backed away from their vantage point.

As soon as they were far enough away that they could talk, Anise said pointedly, "What was going on back there? What were they doing to those people?"

"I don't know, Anise," said Sebastian sadly, "but I can come up with a guess."

Anise waited impatiently for him to continue.

"We avoided going through Grisput because Grisput is one of the few cities in Liamec that supports a system of indentured servitude."

Anise gazed at him blankly. "What's that?"

"It's almost like slavery. If you owe a debt, they make you work to pay it off, and you have to keep working until your debt's paid."

"What debt do those people owe?" Anise asked.

"I don't know," said Sebastian. "Sometimes, they make something up to get free labor."

"That woman on the end of the line, with the red hair, was carrying a baby. How can a baby owe anyone a debt?"

"We don't know the whole story," said Sebastian, "but you're right. Something wasn't right back there."

Briac was watching the exchange. He looked as sad and troubled as Sebastian.

"We have to go back. We have to help those people!"

Anise was almost shouting. Sebastian cast a worried glance back toward the town to be positive they were far enough away that she wouldn't be heard.

"Anise," said Sebastian soothingly, "there were two dozen heavily armed and armored men back there." The calm in his voice just made her angrier. "If we'd approached them to talk, they might well have just added us to the end of the chain. If we attacked them, how long do you think the thistledown in this fine padded jacket you and Isabel made for me would last once they start whacking at me with their swords? I told your aunt and the rest of the town that I would take you safely to the academy. I'm going to do that."

Anise started crying, and Sebastian put his hand on her shoulder.

"Anise," he said gently, "sometimes you have the power to effect change, and sometimes you don't. We're not strong enough to fix this. Life's not fair. The best we can do is use what power we have to make that bit of the world we inhabit a little fairer."

Anise wished she had the power to bring down lightning from the skies. She thought, *One day, I will be strong enough to help people who need it.*

# THE CARNIVAL OF WONDERS

# 1

T he light from the fire flickered and reflected off the boulders around their camp. As one traveled around the roads and byways of Liamec, one would often come across circles of boulders with a site for laying a campfire in the middle. It wasn't clear if these had been put together by some age-old traveler's organization or were perhaps magicked into position by wandering mages from the Academy.

Regardless, they were convenient places to camp and often were situated in perfect spots to break one's travel for an evening.

Anise had asked about their progress and how far they still had to go. She'd fallen just a little short of saying, "Are we there yet?" but the meaning had been clear.

They had eaten, and Sebastian was ready to address the question.

He held the map in his hand.

"Well," he began, "we started in Hero. Or, at least some of us did." He nodded to Briac. "We traveled some way due west, leaving the east side of the kingdom and the Blue Mountains behind us."

He looked at the map, met Briac's eyes, and said, "You know, Briac. You're right about this map. It's not very visually pleasing." The spider web of lines representing roads and the dots for towns were helpful for navigation but not very pretty. He pulled a stick from near the fire and sketched in the dirt with it.

He drew a vertical set of inverted v's representing the Blue Mountain range that was the eastern border of Liamec. He followed that with more mountain symbols on two other sides of the map.

"The Etenies mountains border the kingdom to the south and the west. We've been paralleling the southern arm of the Etenies as we've traveled west."

Sebastian stabbed his stick angrily into the dirt, leaving a divot. "That's Grisput." The divot was northwest of the mark he had made for Hero. "We've been traveling west and north. Ashton and the Academy are here." Sebastian made another mark in the soil. It was near the northernmost end of the mountains in the west.

"Of course," said Sebastian, "the sea is Liamec's northern border." He drew a straight line across the top of his sketch.

Briac leaned over for a closer look at Sebastian's map. "If I was a skilled tracker and saw that set of marks in the earth," he said, with a wink at Anise, "I'd be pretty sure that I'd seen the spot where a pair of rabid badgers made love."

Undeterred, Sebastian continued. "As you can see by the distances on my most excellent map, we're more than halfway. If we skirt around that little pebble, go over or under that twig, we're there!"

Sebastian looked thoughtful. "If we deviate from our path just a bit, about here," he pointed with his stick to a spot near the Western arm of the Etenies, south of the mark that represented Ashton. "We could visit The Serpent's Gorge. It's supposed to be impressive."

"Oh, yes, let's," said Anise.

"I know you're going to Ashton, but are you planning to attend the Academy?" said Briac.

"I think I have to," said Anise.

It wasn't cold, but Briac shivered a bit. "I don't hear good things," he said. "They say people that go to school there come back different."

## 2

There was a man in the blue tabard of the king's guard coming toward them. Of course, they had encountered the king's guard troops going about their business on the road. They were very distinctive in their chain-mail and tabard. The blue background and the black silhouetted lion's head marked them for all to see and for some to avoid.

Sebastian tried to keep Betsy and his companions on their side of the roadway. They didn't need any trouble with the law.

The man staggered a bit as he walked toward them. Sebastian saw that the guard wasn't much older than him as he got closer. He was also clearly drunk. It was unusual to see a guardsman alone.

As he drew closer to them, he stepped into their path or, more correctly, lurched.

"Are you going to pay the prince regent's toll?" he slurred.

Briac moved forward. "I am Briac, the fabulous," he said. "These are my companions."

The guardsman gave Briac a once-over and said, "Are *you* going to pay the toll?"

Sebastian looked at the man. All musings on being drunk in the middle of the day aside, they didn't want any problems. He sighed and got his coin purse out of Betsy's saddlebag. "I can give you a copper," he said.

The guardsman turned his gaze to Sebastian. "Just throw me the purse."

Sebastian frowned. "No."

The guardsman put his hand on the hilt of his sword. "Throw me the purse," he said. His speech sounded a little clearer with each word.

It occurred to Sebastian that he might have been pretending to be drunk. "No. We need this money for our trip."

The guardsman's sword caught the sunlight as he drew it from his sheath. "Now," he said.

Sebastian drew his own sword and turned his body to angle his right side and his sword arm toward the guardsman. "No."

The guardsman looked shocked at first. He clearly hadn't been expecting resistance. Then, his face broke into a wide smile. The smile made Sebastian feel like he liked the man for a moment. Then, he felt an edge of cruelty underneath it, and whatever illusion of friendliness he thought he had seen vanished.

"We don't have to fight about this," Sebastian said. "Just sheath your sword, and we'll be on our way."

"It's too late for that." The guardsman lunged low and to the right.

Sebastian parried in the seventh position, the years of training with his father serving him in good stead. He hesitated on the riposte, however. He was reluctant to try to injure one of the king's guards.

"Where'd you get such a good sword, boy?" said the man. "That's too good for the likes of you. That looks like a guardsman's sword, or better." He took a mighty swing at Sebastian's head.

Sebastian avoided the blow. It helped, however; it helped in a couple of ways. Despite the guardsman's seeing that Sebastian had a good sword, he hadn't recognized that Sebastian was a worthy opponent. That swing was what you would do if you were fighting someone who had never held a sword before. It also had been powerful enough that it would have taken his head off if Sebastian hadn't avoided it. His opponent was underestimating him and trying to kill him. The underestimating gave Sebastian an edge, and the man's trying to kill him permitted him to fight back.

They met blades a few more times, moving back and forth on the roadway. Anise and Briac watched anxiously.

Briac with his hand on the hilt of his dagger. Sebastian knew he had to act fast. His underestimation advantage wouldn't last if they kept this up for long.

Sebastian didn't hold back on the riposte on the next attack where his opponent over-extended himself. He did, however, try as best he could to hit the man with the sword's side rather than the edge. The flat of his blade smacked into his opponent's head. The guardsman slumped to the ground and lost consciousness.

Sebastian stepped over to the man and checked on him. He hadn't been wholly successful with the flat of the blade. The edge of the sword had given him a cut on his face. It ran from the left side of his cheek, through his lip, and across to below his nose. Sebastian knelt to see if he could stop the bleeding. The cut was probably going to leave a scar.

Sebastian looked around to see if anyone had seen the fight other than Briac or Anise. There was no one on the road except for them. He worried that they would get in trouble with the man's unit. Hopefully, the guardsman wouldn't want his extracurricular thievery to be known. Also, he might not want to admit that a farmer had beaten him.

Sebastian grabbed Betsy's lead and waved Briac and Anise into motion. The best thing they could do was be far gone when the guardsman woke up.

## 3

A few days later, they reached an intersection where one of the stones had the words 'The Serpent's Gorge' carved into it. The main road led off just a little east of due north. The path marked with 'The Serpent's Gorge' led to the northwest.

That way was more narrow, less traveled, and led up in the direction of the mountains. It looked steeper.

"The Etenies," said Sebastian with some satisfaction. "The snowmelt of the Dragon River comes down from the Etenies mountains, makes its way through the hills, then north, and eventually to the sea. Along the way, as it cuts through the foothills, it carves the gorge. I haven't seen it, but it's supposed to be spectacular. Are we still going that way?"

Anise nodded eagerly. Briac looked stoic. He had told them that he'd already seen the gorge. Sebastian wasn't sure if he believed that. Briac didn't like to admit that he didn't know something or hadn't done something.

They headed off up the trail toward the gorge. Immediately the nature of the trip changed. The major roads in Liamec were well maintained; broad, flat roadways. In some places, preternaturally so. As with the circles of stones that travelers used for campsites, there were rumors that the roads might have been formed or influenced by ancient magics.

The trail they were traveling was more narrow, rougher, and steeper. Betsy was not happy about it. She took to complaining. She didn't voice her annoyance with her mule bray but rather with a constant steady, low grumbling sound. Once Anise knew where it was coming from, it became part of the background noise.

At first, there was no sign of the Dragon River, then there was. The river showed itself and then kept them company for a while. When they first saw it, they took a break for a bite to eat and a wash. The water was cold. Sebastian pointed to the mountains in the distance. "It's snowmelt. That's why it's still so cold even this far from the Etenies."

They filled their water flasks. Betsy took a long welcome drink.

As they continued up the trail, it followed the river at first. Then it took a turn to the left, toward the mountains, away from the roaring waters. They climbed. Betsy's grumbling got louder. The trail switch-backed up a steep slope. As they climbed, Anise caught sight of the river below several times. Each time it seemed more distant.

The trail crested unto a relatively flat plateau. The Etenies towered over the travelers to the west. It felt like the plain extended to the base of the mountain range, but it was a little hard to see through the low windswept trees, rocks, and brush. The pathway turned to the north, crossing part of the plateau.

The travelers walked across the plain. After a while, it started feeling much the same: the same small scrub trees, low bushes, rocks, and dirt. Anise picked a few wild blueberries.

The trail took a slight dip, and their destination came into sight. Anise stopped short. The world dropped away in front of them. At the bottom of the short slope, down into the dip, was the edge of a cliff. Someone had constructed a wooden railing right at the brink. The gorge opened up beyond it.

To Anise, it looked like the other edge was miles away. From where they stood at the top of the rise, the bottom was invisible. The trail they were on led forward toward the railing. Anise thought the path dropped off into the chasm below for a moment. Then she saw a bridge across the gulf, a narrow stone bridge.

The stone bridge must have been formed by magic. It was a single unbroken rock structure. It seemed narrow when they first saw it, but it became clear it was as broad as the roads they'd traveled to get here as they got closer.

There were low barriers on the sides. They were formed of the same stone that made up the rest of the bridge. Anise inched slowly to the corner where the wooden railing on the cliff's edge met the bridge's stone barrier. She didn't think of herself as afraid of heights. Still, this didn't feel like a height; this felt like *the* height.

She peered carefully over the edge. The gorge walls dropped almost straight down. The cliffs were rough brown and gray stone, gradually easing into brown and tan soil and greenery far below. She could barely make out the Dragon River at the bottom. However, It took her a moment to do so because something else distracted her from trying. As she looked below, she tried to understand what she was seeing.

There were spots of brilliant purple of various sizes between her and the greenery around the river far below. Anise blinked, trying to clear her vision. Patches of uniform purple floated between where she was located at the top of the cliff and the bottom. She stared, trying to make sense of it.

Hundreds of feet high, multiple stone columns rose from the gorge's floor. The columns rose to various heights between the river and the canyon's top edge. They were made of a denser stone than the surrounding land. And the purple? The flat tops of the columns had accumulated soil and were supporting fields of flowering purple blossomed thistles.

# 4

**B**riac was leading Betsy. She had given Anise a look when Anise handed the lead to him. Skeptical, the expression clearly meant, "He's only been traveling with us for a week. You already trust him with my safety?" When he put a little pressure on the line, she lashed both ears first forward, then back, but she started moving.

Anise walked a little ahead and caught up to Sebastian. She hadn't told Briac about her dreams and why she was going to the Academy. She wanted to share something with her uncle.

"I had a dream last night, Uncle," she said.

"Should I be scared?" said Sebastian.

"It wasn't bad," said Anise thoughtfully.

"So?" said Sebastian.

"I met Helios, the sun god," said Anise. "You told me about him, and I met him in my dream."

"How did you know it was him?"

"In the dreams, you just know," said Anise. "Sometimes. Sometimes you don't. That might be part of what I learn at the Academy."

"So, what was he like? What did you talk about?"

"You were right," she said. "I couldn't look at Helios' face directly. It hurt. I tried at first, but it hurt. Then he took his crown off when he saw me squinting, and it got better."

"So, it was the crown that was bright and not him?" said Sebastian.

"It was both, but the crown was brighter."

Anise paused, then continued, "He was nice but a little strict. He said he might be able to help me later if I needed it."

"That's nice," said Sebastian. He wasn't sure how to take Anise's dreams. They felt like they were something that was beyond him.

"He said his sister said to say, 'Hi,' to you."

"His sister?"

"Selene. The spirit of the moon. We've been calling her Luna."

# 5

They were passing another circle of boulders when a voice called out. "Ho, the travelers!" A man was leaning against one of the stones. After getting their attention, he sauntered casually over toward them.

He looked young, perhaps between Anise and Briac in age, probably closer to Briac. He was dressed in linen britches and a brown tunic. The thing that struck Anise as he walked over toward them was his hat. The hat was a green felt cap. It had a crimson feather attached to the brim. The red of the feather almost burned in the afternoon sunlight.

"Ya seem a likely group o' travelers," the young man said, smiling. He swept his cap off his head and made a deep bow. "My name is Alan, an' I'm mighty pleased ta meet you." Anise watched, heart in her throat, as the feather in the cap swept within an inch of the dusty road. She didn't want to see that brilliant red color smudged.

Briac bowed back. "Briac, the brilliant. The honor is all ours. These are my traveling companions: Sebastian and Anise." He gestured toward them.

Betsy cut loose with a complaining, "Heee Awwwwwwww!" It was clear to Anise that she was complaining about not being introduced. Briac didn't seem to get the message.

"I'm out here ta greet an' welcome travelers," said Alan. "Welcome ta the Carnival o' Wonders!" He made a flamboyant open-armed gesture of invitation.

Sebastian, Briac, and Anise looked a little confused. There was nothing behind Alan except the circle of boulders. Alan turned and looked. "Sorry," he said. "Let's walk an down the road a bit. I guess I was waiting in the wrong place."

He fell in line with them, and they walked further down the road in the direction the travelers had been going.

"I'm supposed ta encourage people ta come ta the evening's show," Alan explained. "I'd offer ya discount coupons, except there ain't any. The show's nat very expensive, anyway."

They turned a bend in the road, around the circle of stones. There was a large tent in the process of being set up off the side. People were bustling around driving stakes, pulling on ropes, unrolling canvas sections, and setting up poles. Beyond the workers and the rising tent were rows of wagons: showman's wagons, some of them, and some animal cages.

Alan bowed again and said, "Welcome ta the Carnival o' Wonders!"

# 6

Alan swept an arm across the air like he was opening a curtain. "The Carnival o' Wonders. Thespians, acrobats, jugglers, dancers, tumblers. We have exotic animals; we have clowns. Our ringmaster is a wordsmith beyond compare. We even have a mime, if ya would believe it, though we keep him hidden inna invisible box between shows."

"Magic?" said Anise, a little breathlessly.

"What's a mime?" said Sebastian.

"And a thespian?" said Briac.

Alan frowned, the lines of the frown momentarily breaking the features of his boyishly handsome face. "Magic! Na magic. Magic is cheating. We use sweat, training, an' talent ta accomplish our magic."

Alan got excited. More so than he already had been. "A thespian is a practitioner o' the dramatic arts. I count myself a member o' this profession." He took another bow: deeper this time.

"We have two wagons in the caravan. We perform a short play during the big show, but we also have a stage set up in front o' our wagons." He gestured over toward the rows of wagons beyond where the tent was being constructed.

Alan shuddered. "A mime is a practitioner of a certain form o' performance called pantomime. He comes from the exotic far-off land o' France. Parlez-vous francais?"

The three just stared at him blankly. Alan shook his head sadly and mumbled quietly, "Liamec. So provincial."

More loudly, he said, "As I said, we mostly keep him in his box."

Alan winked at Anise. "Now, at this point, I'd usually encourage ya an your way and tell ya ta come back later for the show, but ya seem a likely lot. How would ya like the backstage tour?"

# 7

Alan wanted to show them the animals first. As they walked by the crew setting up the tent, he commented to a man working there, "Good job, Bernhard, but I think ya missed a spot there." He pointed at the spike that the man was pounding into the ground.

If Bernhard wasn't the tallest man Sebastian had ever seen, he was the most muscular. He wasn't wearing a shirt, and the biceps and chest glistening with sweat from the hammer blows were impressive. Bernhard straightened, lifted his massive hammer lightly to his brow, and saluted Alan.

"Bernhard's fresh from Almany," said Alan, "he doesn't speak much English yet. Right now, he's mostly working crew, but he's in training ta be our strong man."

"How'd you get out of working on the tent?" said Sebastian with a smile.

"We need a greeter," said Alan. "Besides, look at me an' look at him."

It was true. While Bernhard was seemingly built of pure muscle, Alan was slight, almost to delicacy. He carried himself well, but it made sense that he might be doing the job he was.

"How old are you, anyway?" said Sebastian.

"Nat that it's any business o' yours," said Alan, a smile undercutting the bite in his words, "but I'm twenty-two." Sebastian was skeptical. Images of kids running away to join the circus occurred to him. He wasn't sure Alan's voice had entirely dropped yet.

They passed the tents and reached the wagons.

"The Menagerie o' Wonders!" called out Alan in a showman's voice.

They were standing in front of two of the wagons in the group. These wagons were divided up into cages with wooden walls separating them. The outer walls were iron bars. Wooden slats could be added over the iron bars for inclement weather.

The nearest cage held a chicken with a hood on its head. There were a couple further on with animals the size of horses. Beyond that, Anise couldn't see what was in the other cages. Alan waved them closer toward the chicken.

"Don't be scared," he said cheerfully. "I'll protect ya."

# 8

They moved closer to the hooded chicken. An ominous hissing sound was coming from the cage. It sounded to Anise more like a snake than a chicken. "Behold," said Alan, "the mighty Cockatrice!" The chicken turned its head toward the sound of the words.

Anise inspected it more closely. Its belly had scales instead of feathers.

"As ya know, a Cockatrice is born of a serpent hatching a chicken egg. There's supposed ta be death in their gaze." Alan reached between the cage bars and stroked the chicken under its beak. "I call her 'Baby,'" he said. "We think she might be only half Cockatrice. Maybe half Cockatrice an' half chicken? Which would make her three-quarters chicken? Anyway, it's complicated. She doesn't kill ya if she looks at ya; she just gives ya a headache. Rufus is our apprentice in the thespian troupe. He got the job o' Cockatrice victim. Rufus plays dead when she looks at him. He says he wakes up the next day feeling like he's hungover. I told him he's young enough that he shouldn't know what being hungover feels like."

Anise studied the chicken again. Did it have a small leathery-looking tail poking out from under its feathers? She felt grateful for the hood it wore.

The next cage contained a horse. Its backside was turned toward Anise, and it looked to her like an old gray nag. Betsy poked her head over Anise's shoulder to get a closer look.

"Our unicorn, Lucky," said Alan. He came up with a carrot from somewhere and tried to get Lucky to turn around. The wagon stall was just wide enough for Lucky to turn. Eventually, he smelled the carrot and shifted to face them.

Anise was disappointed. Lucky looked just like an old gray mare. The image she had in her head of the spiraling shining unicorn horn from stories was nowhere to be seen. Lucky had a wide squat gray horn on the top of his head. It came to a point and was clearly a horn, but it was nothing like she imagined.

"Lucky's a sweetheart," said Alan. Alan let him crunch on the carrot. Betsy pulled against the lead Anise held, craning her neck to see if Alan had another one.

"We don't think he's a real unicorn," said Alan, "but the horn's real."

The stall next to Lucky's held another animal of about the same size. Anise braced herself for another disappointment.

She was disappointed in her expectation of disappointment. The next stall held an animal, the likes of which she had never seen. It was about the same size as a horse, but black and white stripes covered its body.

"Our hippotigris, Barbara." Alan produced another carrot. Betsy was now clearly expressing her displeasure on her face.

"Barbara is one a' our biggest draws," said Alan. "She comes to us from the far-off land o' Africa."

As they approached the next stall, Anise made eye contact with the creature inside. It was smaller than the horses, about as big as a dog. It was easily the biggest lizard Anise had ever seen. Anise felt intelligence and anger from those eyes that gave her a chill. She thought about reaching out with her mind and trying to touch the creature's presence, but the idea scared her.

"Flambé," said Alan, "our dragon. Keep a little way away from the bars. Sometimes she likes to snap at people."

Like the unicorn, the dragon didn't meet Anise's expectations. She looked like a big lizard, a little potbellied, with short legs and a long thin neck.

"Where are her wings?" asked Anise.

"Maybe she's young. Maybe she's nat really a dragon. Maybe dragons don't fly. I don't know. She's *our* dragon, aren't you, girl?" Alan threw a little piece of meat he got from somewhere through the bars. Flambé's snake-like neck whipped through the air as she gobbled the morsel.

"Besides being an actor," said Alan proudly, "I'm also the carnival's dragon wrangler."

Sebastian had fallen a little behind as he studied the hippotigris. He came up to stand next to Anise and Briac. As he approached the bars, Flambé hissed. The reptile's mouth opened, and along with the sound, which reminded Anise a little of a kettle boiling, a bit of steam came out.

"Huh," said Alan, as he motioned them back from the bars, "she really doesn't like ya." He looked curiously at Sebastian. "I've never seen her react that way ta anyone before."

## 9

Alan pulled them on past the menagerie to the thespian area. Two carnival wagons were positioned side by side. The front sides of both wagons were pulled down on massive hinges and connected to form the boards. The backstage area of the stage was the interiors of the wagons.

There were people on the stage. They were rehearsing a performance.

"The thespian troupe is the heart an' soul o' our carnival," said Alan with a certain self-satisfaction. He frowned. "Though, I guess some might argue that that back there is the heart." He gestured back toward the people setting up the big tent. "Well," he said philosophically, "at least we have the soul. Tragically, I don't have a part in this part o' the play."

There were rows of chairs already set up in readiness for the evening's performance. They sat to watch.

The scene being played was a duel. It was for the heart of a young maiden. The battle was exciting, though Sebastian couldn't help but notice the difference between the stage fighting and genuine fencing. The goal was often to hit the opponent's sword instead of the opponent.

Anise found her attention drawn to the hero and heroine of the piece.

The heroine was riveted by the duel, unsure if her hero would win or die. She was a picture of innocence; blonde, beautiful, youthful, and petite.

The hero was dueling for his life with his opponent, the villain. He was the most handsome man Anise had ever seen. Tall, with a presence that filled the stage, he had a thin mustache that set off his piercing eyes and noble nose.

Anise found herself as riveted to the performance as the heroine was to the duel.

Alan leaned over to her and whispered, "He wears

lifts."

When the scene ended, the actors left the stage. The petite actress that played the heroine walked down the rows of seats toward them.

"Alan," she called out happily, warmly hugging him.

"Rufus," said Alan with a smile.

"Rufus?" said Anise.

The blonde woman reached up and removed her beautiful curls, revealing a short-cropped head of red hair.

"At your service," said the young man with a bow.

"I think I mentioned Rufus," said Alan. "Our cockatrice victim."

The young man with the short red hair in the stunningly beautiful dress clutched his chest. With a low moan, he fell to the ground and died.

Alan seemed not to notice. "If ya have a moment, we could stop by the pub before I have ta start getting ready for the show tonight," he said.

"Sure," said Rufus from the ground.

# 10

T he pub was another of the wagons. The hinge on the front wall of this wagon was at the top. The wall lifted out to form a roof over the seats and small tables set up in front of the wagon. "Grab a seat," said Alan. He walked over toward a counter.

Anise, Briac, and Rufus settled into chairs around one of the tables. Sebastian found a place to tie up Betsy's lead, where she'd be out of the way, and joined them.

"So, what's special about you lot?" said Rufus.

People were sitting at the other tables. Anise found herself staring. The performers had already started getting ready for the show. They were all manner of people and were dressed in all kinds of outfits. Anise found herself lost in spangles, colors, faces, and figures. Acrobats dressed in skin-tight sequined costumes, clowns, she thought she saw someone who must be the ringmaster, it started to feel like too much, and she looked down at the ground under the table.

"What do you mean?" said Briac.

"Alan's spending a lot of time with you. He must have seen something he liked in you. What was it? I must know." Rufus winked at Briac.

Anise looked up. "Why were all the people in the play, men?"

Rufus frowned. "Some misguided people don't think much of actors or acting, especially when women do it. In England, it's against the law for women to be thespians."

Alan walked back to the table as Rufus spoke. He was carrying a tray loaded down with ale mugs. He set one down in front of each of them.

"I watered yours down a little, young lady," he said to Anise, smiling.

He sat down. "As Rufus said, there are lots o' people who don't think women should be actors."

Alan took a sip of his ale. "If ya all don't mind, I'll just slip into something more comfortable." He reached behind himself, quite agilely, and loosened something in the small of his back, then reached up, pulled off his cap, and shook his head.

Alan's chest seemed to expand, and at the same time, long silky hair cascaded down from under the cap.

Briac found himself staring with fascination at this process. Like a farmer watching the first shoots growing on a newly sown field, the expansion of Alan's chest was, to him, the bursting forth of new life from a formerly barren waste.

And the hair. Briac gazed at it in wonder: Chestnut, caramel, umber, walnut, russet, he couldn't figure out which color it was. It draped over Alan's shoulders like a silken mane.

"Pleased to meet you," said Alan, holding out a hand. "My name's Elaine."

Sebastian took the hand and held it gingerly, with a bemused look.

"I've had to play a man - playing a woman, a couple of times. It gets a little awkward," said Elaine.

"What happened to your accent?" asked Sebastian.

"Alan has an accent. He grew up in the highlands of Errol, in the southwest corner of Liamec. They talk funny over there. I grew up just outside Capitol." Elaine shook her head again, and her hair settled further into place.

Briac tapped Sebastian on the shoulder and whispered, "What color is her hair?"

"Brown," said Sebastian.

# 11

T he carnival was everything Anise hoped it would be. There was a fair each summer in Hero. At least that's what the mayor called it. People showed off their animals, there was a pie-eating contest and a beauty pageant, but it was nothing like this.

It started with the carnival grounds and the main tent filled with people. Townsfolk from surrounding villages, the people looked familiar to Anise. They were not very different from the neighbors they had in Hero. Elaine explained that, though it seemed to be in the middle of nowhere, the spot where the carnival was set up was carefully chosen. It was halfway between two villages, such that it wasn't a long walk from either.

There were some sideshows. The villagers milled about for a while, looking at the animals, playing games, buying food from booths, and enjoying the sights.

Once they all filed into the main tent, the ringmaster opened the show. Jugglers threw things through the air, and Acrobats walked wires and flew between trapezes. In addition to the exotic animals from the menagerie, there was a horse act and a dog act. When Rufus died at Baby's malevolent glance, Anise cheered. The people sitting near her gave her strange looks.

Anise was unused to being in such a crowded space. She was between Briac and Sebastian, but there were people in front of and behind her. The show was close to sold out. The seats around the ring at the center of the tent were almost all occupied.

The ringmaster *was* the man Anise had seen at the pub. His words filled the tent when he spoke, and there was some kind of magic in them. Anise found herself wanting some of the acts to end so she could hear him introduce the next one.

The thespian troupe came out and performed a

short piece about halfway through. Elaine had a female part. She was stunning. Anise observed the beautiful woman and wondered how they hadn't seen Alan for what he was from the beginning.

After the performance, they gathered at the pub again. Happy carnival performers filled the other tables. Rufus was nowhere to be seen, but Elaine got them all ales.

"There's a place for you to sleep," she said. "We've got bunks in our 'guest' wagon. There should be plenty of room."

Sebastian thought about Rufus's question from earlier.

"Thank you so much for your hospitality," he said, "are you sure we can't pay for the tickets for the show, at least?"

Elaine laughed. Briac had his elbow on the table, his chin in his hand, and gazed at her.

"Of course not," she said, "I'm enjoying seeing the carnival again for the first time through your eyes."

The ale kept flowing. Even watered down, it was more than Anise had drunk before. The evening faded into a series of images for her. Was there a time she stood on the strong shoulders of an acrobat, who himself was on top of several others? That image ended in the feeling of falling and strong arms catching her.

Another image was Briac and Elaine laughing at something that Anise didn't think was funny.

She remembered explaining to Betsy that she was very wise not to drink ale, as it made the world spin in an exceedingly awkward way.

One of the last images Anise remembered from that evening was her uncle tucking her into bed in an unfamiliar bunk.

# 12

When Anise awoke the following morning, she was alone in the 'guest' wagon. She got up and went out to find Sebastian loading Betsy with her saddlebags. He took stock of her, nodded, and asked how she felt.

"Where's Briac?" she asked.

"I don't know," said Sebastian, "I didn't see where he slept last night. I want to get an early start. We can break our fast later."

Briac came out from between two wagons.

"Where've you been?" said Anise, "we need to get going."

Briac shook his head. "I'm not going with you. I played some music for Elaine last night. She said the carnival always needs musicians. She offered me a job."

Anise felt like the ground was dropping out beneath her. She wasn't sure why she cared, but she did.

"Good for you, son," said Sebastian. "Gonna stay with the carnival for a bit, huh?"

"I thought you were traveling with us," said Anise. She tried to sound calm, but she worried she didn't.

"It's an opportunity for me," said Briac. "They have other musicians here, good ones. I'll learn and practice playing with other people." It sounded to Anise like he was rationalizing it to himself.

As they walked out onto the roadway, Briac walked with them for a bit, then stopped, and they paused a little before continuing.

"It's been good traveling with you," Briac said.

Anise felt a teardrop starting to form, so she looked away so he wouldn't see.

Sebastian nodded. They started down the road.

Briac looked sad as well as he watched them go.

Sebastian turned, fished a copper out of his change

purse, and flipped it to Briac. "Here you go, son," he said. "For that new lute string."

# ASHTON

# 1

L akeside, the town on the eastern side of the lake, was a little disappointing. So close to their destination, it seemed an utterly ordinary village, if a little wealthier than Anise was used to. Ashton and the Academy were on the western side. As they left Lakeside, walking along the road that someone from the town had pointed out, Anise was excited for her first glimpse of the lake.

The sun shone through trees onto the road in front of them. The path wound down a forested slope. They had been told there were two ways around the lake. The trail along the north shore was called 'The Wizard's Way' and was less traveled and a little longer than the main track along the southern side of the lake. The southern road was called 'The Peddler's Path.' They had been encouraged to go that way.

The path broke through the tree cover, and the lake was visible to the west. The intersection stood in front of them. It was clear the northern track was less frequently used.

The lake looked clear, cool, and inviting. Betsy immediately started putting pressure on the lead, pulling toward the lakeshore. There was a fourth path from the intersection, a narrow track that led down to the water.

Sebastian didn't see any reason to resist, so they walked down to the lake edge. Anise looked out over the water. The day was bright, the sun shone down, but the middle of the lake was obscured by mist. The other side was shrouded.

Betsy started slurping up the lake water like she had been parched for hours. Anise thought that the sounds that she was making weren't very ladylike.

"Which trail are we going to take, Uncle?" she asked.

"They made it sound like it was obvious that the

southern way was for us," said Sebastian with a frown. "It's as if; if you're not a wizard, you're a peddler. But, they did say that it was shorter, so I guess that way makes sense."

As they walked along the Peddler's Path, with the sun gradually lowering in the sky, Anise kept sneaking glances over the lake. The mist in the middle didn't burn off with the warmth.

The day settled, and their way started turning a little north of due west. Anise noticed several threads of thick black smoke rising into the sky. They looked like beacon fires. She pointed them out to Sebastian.

"Ash fires," said Sebastian. "They need ash for the soap. Those fires are probably going a lot."

"Soap?"

"They keep outside of town because of the smell, but Ashton is a major soap production center. Seeing those smoke plumes means we're close."

# 2

Ashton didn't have a town wall. The road they were on, along the shore, turned away from the lake, and houses and other buildings sprouted alongside it. Without a clear transition, they were in town. Ashton was not a city, but not the smallest town they had traveled through on their way, either. Even in the late afternoon, or perhaps early evening, people, animals, and carts were on the streets.

Anise noticed some individuals among the people making their way through the streets. Not merchants, not regular citizens, they were young and more prosperous than the rest of the populace. She pointed one out to Sebastian.

"A student, most likely," said Sebastian. "They have to have a bit of money, or their parents do, to afford to travel here and attend the Academy. Most of them probably came by coach." Sebastian's tone gave the impression that riding in a coach was an extravagance.

"Rose doesn't have any money," said Anise with concern.

"Lilith made arrangements," said Sebastian reassuringly.

They noticed street signs labeling the street they were walking down, "Main Street." It headed straight toward a hill. The road split into two and curved around the hill's base in both directions. A green, grassy, park-like area was between the street and the hillside. Trails climbed and wound through the park and up the slopes. On the peak of the hill was a crumbling stone tower. The last rays of the setting sun illuminated the stones and made the spire look very appealing.

A watchman carrying a lantern was among the people in the street. Sebastian approached him.

"Excuse me, sir," he said. "Is there an inn nearby?"

"New to town?" said the watchman. He looked Sebastian and Anise up and down. In a not wholly unfriendly tone, he continued, "You're probably looking for something inexpensive."

Sebastian considered taking offense, but instead, he just nodded.

"The Greedy Gull is just down Dead Man's Alley." The watchman pointed. "Don't mind the names; it's probably the best inexpensive inn in town."

"Sir," said Anise quickly, "What's that tower?"

"That's the Dragon Watchtower," the man said. He puffed up his chest to show off his uniform. "I'm part of the Dragon Watch."

The uniform was a leather jerkin and linen britches with a red tabard over the jerkin. In the corner of the front of the tabard, just over the watchman's heart, was a black silhouette of a dragon's head. The watchman was armed with a sword on his belt.

"But the tower's in ruins," said Anise.

"There aren't any dragons anymore," said the man, "if there ever were. Our order's charter specifies that we're supposed to keep a constant watch, but it was a long time ago if we ever did that."

He continued, "Nowadays, climbing that hill is mostly just the first thing that visitors do. There's a nice view of the whole town from up there."

The watchman smiled at them. "Welcome to Ashton," he said.

# 3

The dining hall of the Greedy Gull was warm and friendly. There was a roaring fire in the fireplace, and the flickering flames cast shadows throughout the room. Sebastian and Anise sat at a table eating stew, which they hadn't had to prepare themselves for the first time in a long time. It was delicious.

"Can we afford this, Uncle?" said Anise.

"Not really," said Sebastian. "Don't worry about it."

The young woman waiting tables in the room came over to them. "Can I get you anything else?" she said. She was just a few years older than Anise. She had tied her blonde hair back in an elaborate set of braids bundled on her head. Sebastian believed that he had figured out that she was the innkeeper's daughter.

Sebastian shook his head.

"Why doesn't Ashton have walls?" asked Anise. "We saw a town that was the same size as this, that had walls, on our way here."

The young woman tilted her head to one side and contemplated Anise. "What good are walls?" she said. "A dragon can just fly right over them."

Sebastian looked at her curiously. "I thought people didn't believe in dragons anymore."

"Well, still," she said.

Anise woke up later that evening. The beds in the inn were surprisingly comfortable. She sat up and looked around the room. There was moonlight shining through the window they had opened to get some air. Her uncle's bed was empty.

She got up, dressed quickly, and crept over to the door. She couldn't think of any good reason why she should keep quiet; it just seemed like the right thing to do.

Still trying to keep quiet, she opened the door and crept down the stairs. The room they had been given was on the second floor up the stairs from the dining hall.

Her uncle was down in the hall, talking to the innkeeper. There were still a few patrons at tables, though it was emptier than when they supped.

Anise crept closer until she found a spot where she could hear what they were saying.

"Is there a weekly rate?" said Sebastian, "I probably need to stay for a week."

"Of course," said the innkeeper.

"You don't, by any chance—" started Sebastian. He paused as if what he was about to say was embarrassing. "Have work available? I'd love to work off the cost of my lodgings."

"Well," the innkeeper started, then he paused also, "our stable boy just quit." His short, well-combed hair was blond, streaked with gray. The similar hair color was part of how Sebastian had recognized him as the waitress's father.

"Yes?" said Sebastian.

"But, you wouldn't want to do his job," said the innkeeper, "it was mostly mucking out the stables."

"I'm a farmer," said Sebastian. "Mucking things out is what I've been doing my whole life."

# 4

Sebastian and Anise climbed the hill in the park at the center of Ashton. The park's name, The Dragon's Eye, had been on a sign at the gate. The hill was a more strenuous climb than Anise expected. She huffed and puffed a bit. They had been walking every day on their way here, but most of that had been flat. She was glad that Betsy was safe back at the Greedy Gull's stables. They wouldn't have to hear her complain. The morning air felt fresh and clear.

The hillside was forested, and there wasn't a view as they hiked up the gravel pathway. The trees were a mix of pines and birch trees, with a few larches mixed in. To Sebastian, the trees felt different than the ones around Hero. Probably more because of the elevation than being further north. Ashton was in the foothills of the Etenies, and it felt higher and more chilly than Hero.

A few other people were walking in the park, especially closer to the bottom of the hill. Sebastian and Anise just smiled, nodded, and continued on their way.

They reached the top of the hill. There was a clearing around the base of the stone tower. The trees still obscured most of the view, but the trail led right to a dark stone opening that used to hold a wooden door in the tower.

There were ruins of other buildings around the tower's base, overgrown with weeds and vines. The tower still stood, but it had been a long time since it had been occupied or maintained.

Anise ran on ahead, charging into the dark opening. She liked heights, views, old ruins, and exploring, and, though she enjoyed climbing steep hills a little less, this morning's adventure was suiting her fine.

There was a crumbling spiral staircase in the round tower. It wound up the inside of the tower wall. A stone railing was between the edge of the stair and the open central space, but it also was weak in spots and didn't look very stable.

"Careful, Anise," said Sebastian. He had a love-hate relationship with heights. From the bottom, he loved them. From the top, he hated them. Sebastian had inched his way over the bridge at the Serpent's Gorge.

Anise raced up the stairs. The lighting was from narrow arrow slits, and the interior was dark. Sebastian made his way up the tower a bit slower because of the shadows and the crumbling stone.

When he reached the top, Anise was already at the edge taking in the view. There was a broad platform with stone parapets all around. The stonework here was also crumbling, though the town or perhaps the town guard had made some repairs with safety in mind.

"Anise," said Sebastian, "a little further from the edge, if you please."

Sebastian walked over to join her. They were now above the treetops with the tower's height added on, and the view was impressive.

The town of Ashton was spread out below them. Beyond the buildings, the lake was east, and the Etenies mountains, behind Anise and Sebastian, off to the west.

Anise shielded her eyes from the sun with one hand and pointed with the other. "Is that the Academy?" she asked.

A walled-off section with buildings, paths, and green areas was between one part of the town and the lake. The walled-off part and the rest of Ashton had separate waterfronts on the lakeshore.

Streets from town ended at the wall, but Sebastian could see gates.

"I think so," said Sebastian.

Both the town and the Academy felt huge to Anise from here, but she had never seen Hero from above.

Perhaps Hero would be even more impressive when seen from a high tower, though she doubted it.

They took in the view for a while, silently. Finally, Anise broke the stillness. "Do we go to the gates of the Academy? What's next?"

"Lilith gave me an address," said Sebastian. "An address and a name—Maeve."

## 5

After asking around, Sebastian and Anise tracked the address, 13 Leafdrop Lane, to a battered old oak door in an unassuming part of town. The house, one of a row of houses, was painted green.

They would have walked right by if there hadn't been a number on the door. Sebastian hesitated, then knocked firmly. The sun was setting, casting the last rays of its light onto the entryway. Their hike up the hill had taken a little longer than they expected.

The door opened. It took Sebastian a moment to adjust his gaze. The woman opening the door was the most petite person he had ever seen, small in stature but not in presence. Once Sebastian looked in the right direction, he was stunned by bright green eyes and hair so red that it was like a campfire's ruddy glow on a night when someone had pulled the moon out of the sky.

"Can I help you?" she said, looking at Anise, standing a step behind Sebastian. For a second, Sebastian thought that she hadn't seen him because he was too tall.

A sizable open space with brown wooden walls was behind her through the open doorway. The decor and layout of the room reminded Sebastian of a hunting lodge. A few people were in the room, looking with curiosity at the arrivals at the door.

"Um ..." Sebastian started.

"Can I help *you*?" the woman repeated, still looking through Sebastian at Anise. She smiled.

The smile was so warm and open that Anise thought of her mother. The thought made her sad. She squeezed her lips together and made an effort to return to the moment. "I'm supposed to be going to school," she offered.

Sebastian moved out of the way a bit. He felt like his feelings should be hurt, but for some reason, they weren't.

"Of course you are," said the woman. If possible,

her smile grew even warmer. She stepped to one side and opened the door wider. "You must be Anise. Come in. I'm Maeve."

# THE WAY-HOUSE

# 1

The room was a common area. There were tables set up for dining on one side next to a kitchen pass-through and an open door frame leading back to the kitchen. The other side of the room had comfortable chairs and benches near a large fireplace.

Two people in the room were watching Anise and Sebastian. One was a man who was probably a bit older than Sebastian, relaxing comfortably by the fireplace. The other was a young woman who ducked down a corridor across from the kitchen, like a startled rabbit, as they entered the room.

The man watched them with open curiosity. He wore a patchwork tunic of linen squares of brilliant colors. He must have had some reason to draw attention to himself, as the tunic did it without difficulty.

"I've been expecting you," said Maeve. "Lilith sent me a letter." She still spoke directly to Anise with a smile on her face. Sebastian wasn't used to feeling invisible.

Two young women came into the room from the hallway on the other side, chattering cheerfully. They were both a little taller than Anise, blonde, and fascinatingly for Anise, identical.

Anise had never seen identical twins before. She'd heard of them, and there were a pair of fraternal twins in Hero, but these two were dressed the same, and Anise was sure she wouldn't be able to tell them apart. They wore blue bodices with light pastel red skirts below. Anise thought they were beautiful.

"Ah, our twins," said Maeve. She raised her voice and called the girls, "Vin, Jord, come over here." She turned to Anise and said quietly, "You might as well start meeting people."

The girls, still chattering happily, started over toward Maeve.

"They're just starting, like you," whispered Maeve in Anise's ear. "Master Videmon will be ecstatic to have them in his class. He's written papers about his theories about twins."

"Girls," said Maeve, "I'd like you to meet Anise. Anise, this is Vin and Jord." Maeve gestured to one of the girls as she said each name. It seemed that she could tell them apart.

"Anise will be living with us," Maeve said to the twins.

# 2

T he twins appraised Anise. Maeve was waiting for her to say something. Anise turned to Sebastian. "I am?" she said. Sebastian hesitated. He hadn't thought this far ahead. The journey to get them here had filled his attention.

"Of course you are," said Maeve. She pulled Anise to her and tried to envelop her in a hug. It was a little tricky because Anise was taller than she was. "You're part of our family now."

The warmth in Maeve's voice did make Anise feel like part of the family. She didn't even know what the family was, but how Maeve spoke made her feel like she was part of it.

Maeve released Anise and asked, "Didn't Lilith tell you about us?"

Anise shook her head.

Maeve turned to the twins and said, "You'll have to wait a minute for the greetings, girls. We've got some orientation to get through."

For the first time, she acknowledged Sebastian. "What did Lilith tell you?" she asked, looking at him.

"Pretty much just your name and address. And that, we should get in touch with you about getting Anise into the Academy," said Sebastian.

"We'll have to start at the beginning then," said Maeve. She looked disappointed. Sebastian felt like he had let her down personally.

"This," said Maeve, sweeping her arm through the air to cover the room's interior, "is a cunning folk way-house."

Sebastian looked around the room again. The rough wood and simple construction struck him once more. The interior had the feel of a communal living space rather than a private dwelling. The benches, tables, and even the more comfortable chairs near the fireplace look rough and lived-in.

"The cunning folk have a network of way-houses across Liamec. Any cunning folk who need shelter or help can call on a way-house in their time of need."

From the way she was speaking, Sebastian couldn't tell if she included herself as a member of the cunning folk or not.

"Oscar over there—" Maeve gestured toward the man in the colored tunic, still lounging near the fire. "—is staying with us as he passes through."

Oscar gave a wave when Maeve gestured. His clean-shaven intelligent-looking face broke into a welcoming smile.

"This house, though," Maeve continued, "is a little different." She almost lit up as she filled with pride. "We have the additional honor and privilege of passing on students who need that something extra that only the Academy can provide.

"If a cunning person encounters a person with magical potential beyond what they can train, we recommend them to the Academy and, if they need it, house them while they study."

"Recommend?" said Sebastian. A sudden worry filled him.

"We have a relationship with the Academy. The disregard some graduates feel for the cunning folk is not shared by history or all the Academy administration members. In the years this arrangement has been ongoing, neither the Academy nor the cunning folk has had cause to regret it." Sebastian could hear the pride in her voice again as she said this.

# 3

One of the two blonde girls, impatiently waiting while Maeve spoke, broke in. "I'm Vin. This is Jord. We just got here last week." Maeve looked at her. The expression on her face spoke of patience, but there might have been a whisper of something else underneath.

Anise looked at her as well. Her voice was excited, and her face animated. Anise thought again about whether she could see any difference between the two that she could use to tell them apart. Was there something different in their complexions?

"I'm Anise, and this is my uncle, Sebastian," she said politely.

Maeve broke in. "Vin," she said, "why don't you and Jord show Anise and her uncle what you can do?"

She continued, "As I said, each person that we recommend for the academy has shown signs that they have some unusual degree of talent."

Vin didn't hesitate. She held out one arm and turned her palm upward. A column of flame shot out of her hand and rose toward the ceiling. Anise took a step back in reaction to the sudden heat. She looked with fascination. The flames came out of the air a short distance above Vin's skin. The flickering yellow and orange fire grew from her hand to just a few feet above it.

Lilith had shown Anise some simple elemental magic, but it wasn't Lilith's area of expertise. She was more familiar with alchemy and illusion.

The flames continued to crackle out of Vin's hand. The sound and smell were reminiscent of a campfire.

Maeve turned toward the other girl. "Jord?" she said, a little delicately. Jord stepped forward, more hesitantly than her sister. Anise thought that she might be able to tell them apart by behavior.

Jord lifted her hands and started moving them as if

she was forming a sphere. One to the left, a little below, the other above and to the right. Fluid flowed out of her palms. She was cradling a glistening ball of water in her hands in seconds. The campfire smell mixed with another scent that combined salt and a hint of sweat. The skin on Jord's forehead glistened, while Vin's looked dry.

The twins seemed comfortable with this. It was a show they had performed before.

Jord made a throwing motion with her hands, and the ball of fluid flew through the air and crashed into Vin's cylinder of flame. There was a loud sizzling sound, and both the watery sphere and the column of flame vanished, leaving a cloud of steam and a damp, musty smell.

# 4

Sebastian was still trying to absorb what he had just seen these two young girls do. "Stay here for a moment," Maeve said. "I've got something for you. Let me go get it." She spoke to Anise, "Why don't you girls get to know each other a bit."

"For me?" said Sebastian with surprise.

Maeve crossed the room and disappeared down the corridor across from the kitchen.

Vin turned to Anise and said, "What do you do?"

Anise was confused. "I don't have a job. My aunt's a baker," she started to say.

Vin held up one finger, and a little spurt of flame shot out of it. "No, I mean, what do you *do*!" she repeated.

Jord looked embarrassed.

"Oh," said Anise. She thought for a moment. "Well, I guess I'm a Channeler."

"That's just the one where you dream about things," said Vin. "That's boring."

Jord looked upset. "Vin," she said quietly, "don't be rude." She turned to Anise. "They sent us here when Vin set fire to Mr. Barlow's barn."

Sebastian stepped away from the girls. Perhaps Maeve was correct that they needed to get acquainted. Anise was a little younger than Vin and Jord, but Sebastian was sure she would be able to hold her own. He walked over toward the fireplace and the man Maeve had named Oscar.

"Sebastian," said Sebastian, holding out his right hand toward the man.

Oscar stood from where he had been lounging on one of the benches in front of the unlit fireplace. He held up both empty hands in front of himself. "Oscar," he said with a smile.

"You look a little old to be a student," said Sebastian.

"Well, actually," said Oscar, "the students come in all

ages, but I'm not one. Didn't Maeve tell you about this being a cunning folk safe house?"

"Oh. She did. Are you a cunning person?"

"I'm not sure how cunning I am, but I try," said Oscar with another smile. There was a bit of a self-deprecating slant to his smile. One might have called it a wry smile. "Actually, some of the more proper of the cunning folk might call me a hedgewitch, not a cunning person. Don't tell that to Maeve, or she might kick me out." He winked at Sebastian. "You must be new to Ashton."

"We just got in yesterday," said Sebastian. "Traveled all across Liamec. Outlaws, wolves, slavers. It was quite a trip."

"Sounds like it," said Oscar.

Maeve stepped back into the room. She came over to Sebastian and handed him a velum envelope. It had his name on it, and a wax seal sealed it shut.

"That's the seal of one of the masters at the Academy," said Maeve. "Apparently, you have friends in high places."

# 5

Anise took the bottom bunk of a bunk bed in the girls' dorm. Vin and Jord's bunk was on the opposite side of the room. Anise was used to sleeping alone in her room in the bakery back in Hero, and she selected her bed to have a little privacy.

There were ten rough wooden bunk beds in the girls' dorm room. Aside from Vin and Jord, there was only one other occupied bed. Maeve told Anise when she selected her bunk that, the occupancy went up and down. Still, during her time as the way-house manager, the girls' dorm had never been full.

There were several things about the dorms that Anise found noteworthy. There were wooden lockers at both ends of the bed-one for the top occupant and one for the bottom. Maeve explained to Anise that her locker would only open for her. "They're enchanted," she said. "They attune to the person who's sleeping in their bunk."

Earlier, when Maeve had shown her and Sebastian around the way-house, she had waved to the left side of the corridor they were walking down and said, "Boys' dorm room." And then to the right side, "Girls' dorm room."

Anise found herself looking at what seemed like a solid wall on the left-hand side of the corridor, while Sebastian had the same experience on the right. Both of them saw arched open doorways on the opposite side.

"Excuse me," said Sebastian politely. It turned out that Sebastian couldn't even see the girls' dorm room entrance, and Anise couldn't see the boys'.

"It's old magic," clarified Maeve. "This way-house has been here since before my time, and that's longer than you might think." She smiled. She stepped over to what appeared to Anise a blank section of wall and tapped on it. "The boys' dorm," she said. Sebastian was astonished to hear a rapping sound while she knocked on what seemed like an open door frame to him. "And the girls'." She waved toward where Anise saw an open doorway on the other side of the corridor. Sebastian saw a solid wall. "Every so often, we have a student who can enter into both," Maeve concluded.

Later, when Maeve led Anise into the girl's dorm to select her bed, Sebastian watched them walk through what looked to him like a solid wall. He shook his head as he wondered what world he had entered.

The fourth occupant of the girls' dorm was the young woman that Anise and Sebastian had seen briefly when they first arrived. She occupied a top bunk somewhere between Vin and Jord's bunk and Anise's chosen bed. The only way to tell that she had claimed her bed was that her bedding was on it. Anise still hadn't met her officially. She asked Maeve about her.

"Oh, that's my Cian," said Maeve. "She likes to keep to herself." She smiled a little sadly, it seemed to Anise. "You'll meet her when the time is right."

The first night Anise slept in the dorm, she explored the little world that her bunk made between the wood of the upper bed above her, the bed-frames, and the wooden wall of the way-house. The blankets and sheets were warm and soft. The wood of the wall and the bunk was worn down to a shiny polished texture that made it look ancient. There were some carvings and scrapes in the wood. Anise found several names carved into the wall, where she put her pillow. She put her hand on the old worn carved names and felt a connection to the other girls who had long ago slept in this bed.

# 6

The door was plain and unadorned and not particularly tall. If it hadn't been in the wall that separated Ashton from the Academy, there would have been nothing distinctive about it. Maeve approached it confidently.

"Are you sure this is the right door?" said Anise. She looked up and down the street to see if there was something she was missing. The wall towered overhead, tall and bold. The wall knew where it was and what it was. It was the kind of wall that Anise had been expecting. On the other hand, the door was too quiet and unassuming to be the door that would lead Anise into her new life.

The street also was not what Anise had been expecting. It was almost an alley. The houses on one side and the high wall on the other cut out the sunlight, so it was dark and dingy in the early morning shade. There was no one out this early, and perhaps no one out in this part of town, so it was quiet and empty as well as dim.

Maeve gave Anise a glance. She didn't say anything with her voice, but her eyes, bright green and glowing in the shade like emeralds, spoke to Anise clearly. "If I weren't so polite and nice," those eyes said, "the put down you would be receiving for that lack of faith would make you quake in your little girl boots."

Anise turned her eyes down to her boots. Made by Mr. Fletcher, the cobbler in Hero, they weren't anything to be terribly proud of. They were simple leather boots, worn and dusty from miles of walking. Still, she didn't feel they were anything to be ashamed of either.

Maeve turned her attention back to the door. "There's a whole test thing that the door does on new students," she said. "It checks to see if you're worthy or some such twaddle." She reached out toward the handle. "But, I have to get back in time to shop for the cook for dinner tonight, so we'll just skip that part."

Maeve opened the door, and she and Anise stepped over the threshold and into the Academy.

Anise held her breath. She had the feeling that a new chapter in her life was beginning.

# 7

Sebastian lifted the shovel load carefully. It was more manageable if you moved the whole load onto the wheelbarrow with one scoop. That way, you didn't have to do a second. The lovely smell of fresh horse manure filled the stall. Sebastian had grown used to the scent over the last few days, though he was more familiar with the perfume of the cow.

As he shoveled, he thought about what had happened since he had left Anise in Maeve's care. Walking away while she stayed behind at the way-house had already been hard. Of course, thought Sebastian, that's the most challenging part of the job for any parent. Sebastian wasn't really Anise's father, but he felt like he was nowadays.

Swen, the innkeeper, was paying Sebastian a bit extra in addition to covering his room and board. He appreciated having Sebastian helping out. His daughter, the waitress in the inn, refused to have anything to do with the stables. Swen had had to do double duty.

Sebastian had had a few interesting conversations with the innkeeper. Swen came from the north and told Sebastian a little about his past.

*I wonder how it'll feel when Twilight is old enough to go off on his own*, thought Sebastian. He felt a shiver run down his spine. For some reason, the idea gave him a chill.

The letter Sebastian had received was from Lorenzo. He was now a master at the Academy, leading the advanced studies in Channeling. Sebastian had met with him in a pub near the main gate to the Academy the previous evening.

Lorenzo had been pleased to see him. "There you are," he called out. Lorenzo laughed as he shook Sebastian's hand firmly. Sebastian was reminded of the hearty traveling tradesman he had first met on the road years ago.

"Enzo," he said more carefully.

They took a seat at a table in the corner of the dim torch-lit room. Sebastian inspected the man sitting across from him. Lorenzo looked fit. Life at the Academy was suiting him. He looked older than he was in Sebastian's memory. Still, his master's robes from the Academy were elegant and fine and made him seem like a man in charge of his destiny. He still had a broad handlebar mustache, but he had gotten rid of the magical spirals that Sebastian remembered. He was wearing a small jade pendant in the shape of a heart on a leather thong around his neck.

Sebastian had a flash of regret that he hadn't reclaimed that piece of jewelry. It was one of the few things left that had been his mother's. Then he thought about how vital the gem had been to Lorenzo's transformation into the amenable person in front of him.

"How was your journey to the Academy?" said Lorenzo. He had the demeanor of someone getting the pleasantries out of the way before addressing what he really wanted to talk about.

"A bit challenging," said Sebastian. "We barely made it in time for the end of registration."

"That's good. That's good," said Lorenzo distractedly. He leaned forward, looked around at the other tables in the pub without really seeing what he was looking at, and whispered conspiratorially, "I've studied the prophecies again. I think that this is the year. This is the year that the channeler who was predicted to change the world will come to the Academy!"

"That's very exciting," said Sebastian. "I've brought my ..." He hesitated before continuing, "... ward, Anise. She's just starting at the Academy, and she hasn't been away from home before."

"Of course. Of course," said Lorenzo. "I'm glad your niece will be joining us." He shook his head as if trying to clear it of other thoughts. He continued, "I've been looking at the incoming students, but it may be hard to identify this channeler. I've also been watching the other realms through my dreams. While I've felt something, it's annoyingly hard to pin down."

"I'm sure you'll figure out who it is eventually," said Sebastian.

# 8

T he room on the other side of the door was huge. As Anise followed Maeve over the threshold into the vast echoing chamber, she felt intimidated. There was a giant face covering the far wall of the room. Otherwise, it was unadorned and unfurnished. Anise first thought the face was a mural.

She thought it was a mural until the eyes turned to look at her, and the giant head leaned forward. The most forceful voice Anise had ever heard boomed, "Who dares enter the presence of the Registrar of the Academy!"

The visage was of a stern, older gray-haired man, and the sound made the air in the chamber vibrate. Anise tried to hide behind Maeve, which was difficult, as she was close to a head taller than the older woman.

Maeve stepped in front of Anise and called out, "Hey, Earl, it's just me, Maeve." She turned toward the face and continued, "You can stop the show."

The giant face vanished. At the base of the far wall was a modest desk with a young man sitting behind it. The desk was littered with an assortment of random papers. Maeve and Anise started across the floor of the large empty chamber toward him.

"What was that?" asked Anise. She tried to sound nonchalant.

"Illusion," said Maeve. "Earl's good at them."

As they approached the desk, Anise dropped into her best impression of a curtsy. She hadn't had to practice curtseys much in the town of Hero, but Isabel had taught her. "Just in case," she had said.

"My Lord Earl," said Anise carefully to the young man sitting behind the desk. He looked young, maybe a year or two older than Anise, and his acne-ridden face froze into an expression of surprise.

Maeve laughed. "Oh, dear," she said, "Earl's not really

an Earl. That's just his name."

Anise flushed. Earl's expression of surprise faded, and he looked pleased. "That's never happened before," he said. "I guess, even with the name, I don't look enough like an Earl for anyone to make that mistake." He smiled as he spoke, and the gentle expression warmed his face. Anise didn't quite know where to look. He had a sweet smile, but she didn't want to make him self-conscious about the acne.

"Did you talk to the master healer about that?" Maeve made a gesture toward her face. "As I told you?"

"I tried," said Earl, "but the masters are busy, and I felt there were more important things for the master healer to do."

"Nothing is more important than your health," said Maeve with a concerned frown.

# 9

Maeve drew Earl's attention to Anise by turning her own gaze at her. "Earl," she said, "This is Anise. She's here to register for the fall semester." Earl stood up from his chair behind the desk. He nodded his head politely to Anise.

"Pleased to meet you," he said. Standing on his feet, he could be seen to be tall, angular, and skinny as a stick. His smile persisted, however, and Anise felt an affinity for him.

"Make it green," she said.

"Huh?" said Earl.

"The face, the head," said Anise, "make it green. It'll scare people more." She met Earl's gaze. "That's what it's for, isn't it?"

"I guess so," said Earl. "Green, Huh? I'll take that under advisement for next year."

"Today's the last day of registration," said Maeve to Anise. She turned to Earl, "Let's get her set up."

"Of course," said Earl. He started digging through the papers that were scattered all over the desk. "She's on my list, right?"

"She should be," said Maeve. "I talked to the masters about her weeks ago."

"Here we go," said Earl as he pulled some papers from under the jumble. "I'm afraid you don't have any choice about your schedule." He looked sympathetically at Anise. "First years don't get much say, anyway, and it's the last day of registration." He handed her a small piece of paper.

Anise looked down at the square of parchment in her hand. Her breath caught in her throat. She nodded. It was just a simple piece of paper with some lines and words on it, but it felt to her like a golden ticket to a new life. She studied it carefully.

She looked up. She felt guilty complaining about something when she should feel nothing but gratitude. Still, the error was so egregious that she had to say something.

"I think that there's a mistake," she said. "Lilith says I need to study channeling, and this has something called clairvoyance on it instead."

Earl shook his head. "That's Master Lorenzo's doing," he said. "It's not a mistake. He's changed some things. Clairvoyance is a new class, and he's changed how you enroll in channeling. You have to find it yourself."

"Find it yourself?" repeated Anise.

"If you can figure out where and when the channeling class meets, you're enrolled," said Earl. "No rules about how except that the other students aren't supposed to tell you."

# 10

A nise was saying goodbye to Sebastian. It felt like she was dying. With tears streaming down her face, she said, "What if the Watcher finds me. What will I do without you?" She felt guilty about crying, but she couldn't make herself stop.

"The Watcher?" said Sebastian.

Anise sniffed. "Yes, the Watcher. I told you about him."

"Anise," said Sebastian, "you didn't. Someone is watching you?"

"In my dreams," said Anise. "For a while now. He's looking for me more than he's watching me, I guess." She frowned. "I thought I told you."

"In your dreams," said Sebastian. He felt relieved, though he tried not to show it to Anise. "Sometimes bad dreams are just bad dreams, Anise."

"Helios said he'd hide me from the Watcher." Anise smiled through her tears. "I think he likes me."

Sebastian reached out and pulled Anise to him in a tight hug. "Don't cry, Anise," he said. "You'll be fine here. I've asked Maeve to take care of you, and you're excited to start classes, aren't you?"

Anise sniffed again. "Yes," she said.

"You should feel sorry for me," said Sebastian. "I'm the one who has it hard." He looked thoughtful. "Well, Betsy and I. We're the ones who have to walk home."

# 11

Anise was lying in her bed. The wood of the top bunk was like an additional cover over her. The confinement gave her the sensation of being in a cocoon. Her blankets were warm enough, but she worried about her toes. She lifted her legs, reached down, and folded the bottom edge of the blanket under her feet to create a pouch or pocket for warmth.

She felt she should still be crying and wanted to, a little, but her eyes were all cried out.

It was dark in the dorm. Maeve had called for everyone to put their candles out when the curfew bell rang. There was a church not too far from the way-house, so they felt each peal of the hourly bells.

There was a noise by the door of the room. It was Maeve. Anise saw the candlelight come closer as Maeve walked between the bunks. She pulled her blankets up to her face and watched the glow approach her over the top edge.

Maeve sat down on the side of Anise's bed and put the candle down on the wooden locker at the head. There wasn't much in that locker. Just the clothes Rose had stuffed into one of Betsy's saddlebags as they left Hero, the little pouch of coins that Sebastian had given her, and the little wooden caged bird puzzle Isabel's mother had made.

Maeve reached out one hand and stroked Anise's hair out of her eyes. There was a dried salty tear streak on her face.

"Anise," said Maeve. She assessed Anise's face, licked her thumb, and wiped away a little of the salt with it.

Maeve was holding something tucked under her arm. Anise saw some small portraits or pictures on a folded bundle of fabric in the flickering light of the candle flame.

"I brought you this," said Maeve. She unfolded the piece of fabric and spread it out over Anise and the bunk bed. It was a quilt. As it settled over her blankets and especially over her feet, Anise felt her worries about her toes fading.

"Thank you, Maeve," Anise said. She looked more carefully at the quilt. It was beige. Each fabric square held embroidered images of dragons in different poses and colors. Anise reached out and felt it. It was soft and felt thick and comfy.

"It's beautiful," Anise said. "And so warm." She wiggled her toes. "What's it made of?"

Maeve looked thoughtful, like that wasn't the question she was expecting. "It's stuffed with thistledown," she said. "I make them for the first years." She frowned a little as she said, "For some reason, I picked this one out for you. Something to do with the pictures."

"Thistledown?" said Anise. "But it's so soft."

"My people have been using thistledown for a long time," Maeve said. "I mean, my family. We have a technique for softening it. It's good against dragons."

Maeve leaned over and kissed Anise on the forehead. She got to her feet and turned to go. "Sleep well, dear," she said.

Anise wiggled her feet again. Her toes were beginning to appreciate her pocket of warmth.

# THE ACADEMY

# 1

Anise, Vin, and Jord approached one of the main gates between the town and the Academy. Unlike the little door that led into the registrar's office, this double-doored gate was wide enough to admit two carts side by side when fully open. It wasn't fully open now. A smaller person-sized door was set into one of the gate doors.

A couple of guards were sitting on chairs on both sides of the open person-sized entry. One of them was leaning his chair back against the gate behind him. The other was staring idly at passersby on the street. The guards looked bored. This street was busier than the little alley outside the registrar's office; people passed the gate to the left and right. However, not many were going through the door between the two guards.

Like the watchmen in Ashton, the guards were dressed in leather jerkins and linen britches. The tabard that they wore over the leather was black. Also, like the watchmen, they had a silhouette stitched into the fabric just over their hearts. The symbol, shown in white to be visible on the black of the tabard, was an owl's head.

Vin, as she had all morning, took the lead. She strode decisively over toward the guards. Anise and Jord followed.

The guard who had been people-watching looked up at Vin, "Can we help you, ladies?" he said. The other guard leaned forward on his off-center chair. The back moved away from the gate wall, and he balanced on two chair legs for a moment before the front legs dropped to the ground with a thud.

Maeve had been the one who had suggested that Vin and Jord take Anise along with them into the Academy. It would be their second expedition. They had already toured the campus once, learning where their classrooms were and how to get around. Vin had not looked too happy at the suggestion.

"You're all first years," Maeve had said. "You're probably in most of the same classes, anyway."

The late morning sun shone down on Anise's back as she watched Vin talking to the guard. She felt like Helios had his arm around her shoulders.

The guards didn't seem surprised to see them. It was the last sun's day before classes started, and there had been lots of students going back and forth. The guards took a quick look at their schedule cards and waved them on.

As they stepped through the doorway onto the Academy grounds, Anise held her breath. She hadn't thought about this place much while growing up, but she'd certainly been thinking about it for most of the trip with her uncle to get here.

Her first impression didn't disappoint. The sun was shining down on an immaculate green crisscrossed with gravel walkways that cut across it at every conceivable angle. There were stone buildings on both sides of the broad green and another tall one at the far end. It had a tower that sported a clock and a belfry.

People walked on the paths across the green. Some were in groups, walking together, and some individuals were walking alone. Anise watched one man in a black robe, which she took to be master's garb, walking hurriedly across the green on one of the gravel paths. He was looking at the ground in front of himself, muttering distractedly. He hardly noticed others that crossed his path.

The bell in the tower rang right as they stepped off the cobbled road that ran between the wall and the green and walked onto one of the gravel trails.

"Sext," said Vin with satisfaction. "That gives us some time." She dismissed Jord and Anise with a glance. "You two try to find your classrooms." A slight smile crossed her lips. "I'm going to see if I can find someone interesting to talk to." She took off down one of the gravel ways, leaving Anise and Jord looking at each other.

Vin and Jord had dressed similarly again today, though Anise was starting to feel that telling them apart wouldn't be so hard after all. They wore blue linen smocks, but Vin had hers tightly belted at the waist, while Jord wasn't wearing a belt.

The main reason, though, that Anise thought she would be able to tell them apart was by their behavior. Vin radiated an intimidating, fiery self-confidence. Jord was more easygoing.

Jord sighed and looked down at her schedule, which she still held.

"Is your first class on Moon's day morning: alchemy?"

# 2

Anise awoke in her bed. She considered the wood of the top bunk above her and wondered what time it was. The dorm room had windows on the wall opposite the doorway into the hall, but they were north-facing, so they never got direct sunlight.

The lighting felt strange. Anise sat up and looked around. The room was dark, except for a slight warm glow that reminded her of late afternoon sunlight on a sleepy autumn day. Except for hers, the room was empty of bunk beds. The open space made her realize how large the dorm was.

A man stood a few paces away from her. He was the source of the gentle glow of sunlight. The light was coming from his body, clothes, and hands, but the brightest rays came from his face and the golden crown atop his curly blond locks. He wore a purple mantle draped over one shoulder and across his chest. It was belted at the waist by a broad silver band with glowing images depicting the zodiac signs.

"My lord Helios," said Anise. She knew enough to be respectful to certain people in her dreams. She could issue orders to some of them; for others, she felt the need to listen when they spoke. Helios was in his own class. Anise was careful to afford him every courtesy she knew.

"Anise," he said. "I've been keeping an eye on you."

"Don't you watch us all," said Anise, "from your place on high?"

The golden-haired god laughed. It made him look even younger than he had at first. The sound of his laugh was a merry ringing noise. The rays of light in the room shook and trembled with his glee.

"I suppose so," he said. "But," and here, a sober look shadowed his proud face, "I'm not the only one."

"I know," said Anise. She shivered a little. "The

Watcher."

"I can keep his gaze from you a bit," said the god. "I can distract him with other things to see. But, it would be better to avoid the places where he is focusing his attention."

Anise waited patiently. It was clear that Helios wasn't done, and with him, she had determined that it made him happy to know that he was being listened to and respected.

"He's watching the students at the Academy," continued Helios. "Especially in channeling classes." He looked thoughtful, in as much as his shining face was capable of looking thoughtful. "I was going to tell you where and when the first channeling class will be held, but I think I'll tell you about the second class instead. It'll help keep his gaze off of you."

"Thank you, My Lord," said Anise. "I appreciate the help. But, I wonder, why me? I didn't even try to dream of you tonight." Anise frowned. *I didn't try*, she thought, *but perhaps I did it by accident. Maybe I do need control.*

The god laughed again. The sound of his laughter made Anise feel like her ears were warm, as the rays of light emanating from him made her body warm. He turned his gaze fully upon her. Her forehead and cheeks felt flushed. His eyes weren't any color; they were just the warmth and fire of light.

"Anise," he said. "I know you can't see it yourself, but here in the dreaming realm, you glow and shine as I do. You remind me of myself."

## 3

T he skin on Anise's forehead felt tight. It itched and burned a little. Maeve had spread a little honey over Anise's brow and cheeks when she noticed the reddening in the morning. "How did you manage to get a sunburn since yesterday?" Maeve asked. She didn't wait for an answer. Anise's face still felt sticky.

She and Jord were sitting in chairs at the back of a classroom. Vin had strode in confidently and immediately found a seat toward the front next to a girl dressed elegantly in purple. They struck up a loud conversation. Anise and Jord drifted quietly toward the back row.

"I'm not sure how she does it," Jord whispered to Anise. "She just seems to know what to say and when to say it."

Anise nodded and pointed toward a door on one side of the front of the classroom. The master was arriving.

The classroom wasn't huge. There were rows of seats with desks for the students and a podium at the front for the master. The walls were lined with cabinets and bookshelves. Jars of interesting-looking and sometimes creepy things sat on the shelves. Herbs and spices hung on hooks from the ceiling. Anise wished she had more time to look around the room. Perhaps she would have some time after class.

The master stepped through the door. He was the oldest man Anise had ever seen. She got the sense that his body was skeletal under his black master's robes. Wisps of white hair stuck out from both sides of his head. He leaned against the door as he closed it, then shuffled slowly over to the podium.

"Greetings, class," he said from behind the podium. His voice seemed as old as the rest of him. High and reedy, it felt like it might blow away in the wind if a window were left open. There was a large slate fastened to the wall behind the podium. Anise had never seen such a thing before. Written in white on one side of the black surface of the slate was the name Master Ernst.

Jord leaned over to Anise. "You know what Vin heard?" she whispered conspiratorially, "She heard that he's older than the Academy. When they came here to break ground to start to build, he was waiting for them."

Master Ernst began, "Alchemy is sometimes dismissed. Not as flashy as elemental magic or illusion. No bolts of fire shooting from your fingertips. No images of dragons flying through the sky." His voice was reedy, but it fought a path through the room to the furthest chair.

"Look at me," said the old man. Delicate though it was, Anise felt his voice conveyed information that she wanted to hear. "How old do you think I am?"

Several hands in the class went up.

"That was a rhetorical question," said the master. "I don't care what you think. I'm three hundred and seven years old." There were gasps from some of the students.

Jord leaned over to Anise again. Anise struggled with her attention, as she was interested in what Master Ernst was saying, but she didn't want to be rude to Jord.

"Vin heard," Jord whispered, "that he's been asking the same question in each introductory class for twenty years, and he's said three hundred and seven each time."

# 4

The master continued, "Potions. They can have lasting permanent effects on the world. A bolt of fire or shifting of the earth can impact things. Channeling can erratically cause events. But, if you want a consistent, reliable way to make changes, particularly changes to people, give me alchemy every day. Don't even get me started on illusion; the definition of impermanence.

"I can brew an elixir that will cause you to grow a tail. I can concoct a draught that can make you fall in love. I can prepare a mixture that melts iron. Nothing in any other discipline you will study here at the Academy will be as permanent and lasting as what you learn in this class.

"Alchemy is disrespected in some ways, but it is respected in others. My potion of health, which has allowed me to live to my hale old age, is favored by the Kings of Liamec. Have none of you ever wondered how the reign of King Liam II could have lasted a hundred years?

"If you grasp what I teach and do well, you too will be able to change the world with your powerful brews and concoctions."

The Alchemy master removed a small vial from a pocket in his black master's robes. He held it up in the air. The glass of the vial, or perhaps the fluid inside it, was colored pink. The facets in the small bottle caught the morning sunlight and glittered prettily.

"You'll hear a lot about Keys here at the Academy if you haven't already," the aged master said. "A Key, as we use the word here, is a thing, a place, and an idea simultaneously." He made a small gesture with the vial to draw the student's eyes to it again. "This, the fluid in this vial, is the Key to Alchemy."

The master put the vial back in his pocket. "The Key to Alchemy is also, at the same time, a place and an idea, but we will cover those aspects of it another time."

Jord searched Anise's eyes. "Vin heard about the Key to Alchemy," she whispered. Anise looked at her and lifted her eyebrows. "No," Jord shook her head. "I'm not going to tell you; it's too gross."

"You'll all be getting vials like the one I just showed you," said Master Ernst, "next time." He shook his head as if the thought of the students all getting those vials was too much. "Be very careful with them. One drop is all you need for each potion."

"I suppose you're wondering why we have class so early in the morning," the master continued. "Alchemy is best and usually practiced during the daylight hours." The master looked thoughtful. "There are some exceptions. Some potions require moonlight, and some need an absence of light. Still, for the most part, sunlight is a cleansing agent, and the freshness of a morning yields an unsullied liquid and an alert alchemist."

# 5

The residents of the way-house ate dinner together. Not always, and not everyone sat at the table every time. Still, as a rule, when the town bells rang Vespers, there was food available, and Maeve's charges would be there to partake.

Since Sebastian had left on his return journey to Hero, Anise had met the other residents of the way-house. In addition to Vin, Jord, and Maeve herself, four other people lived there.

Anise, who was used to eating at the bakery with just Rose for company or eating with Aunt Isabel and Uncle Sebastian, found the crowded evening meals fascinating.

Oscar, of course, who Anise had been introduced to when she arrived, was one of the four. Cian, who Maeve had referred to as "her" Cian, was quiet and kept to herself, though she ate with gusto and relished her meals.

The cook, who they all called Cookie, didn't live in the way-house. He was a burly man with a large brown mustache that turned down at the corners. It looked a little sad to Anise. Not that it was a poorly maintained mustache. It was well-groomed and must be Cookie's pride. No, it was just that the downward turning corners made her think of a frown and reminded her of grief.

The cook's boy, who helped in the kitchen, lived in the way-house. Apparently, he had no other place to live. Maeve told Anise that Cookie had rescued him off the streets. Anise tried to find out his name, but no one knew it. "He's just the cook's boy," Maeve said. He seemed like he might be a few years younger than Anise. He was skittish and jumped when anyone moved too near him.

Both Cookie and the cook's boy would sit with them and eat after serving. There were two large wooden tables in the dining area of the common room. There was enough room at either of the tables for the whole group to sit at the same one. They spent some dinners that way, but sometimes, one diner would choose to sit alone at the other table. This was usually Cian, or Niall, the final resident of the boys' dorm.

Niall, like Cian, liked to keep to himself. The first time Anise saw him sitting at the dining table, she had difficulty breathing for a moment. He was tall, dressed simply in a green tunic, and strikingly handsome. He was an upperclassman. He was at least a few years older than Anise. He hardly said a word that first mealtime, but she covertly snuck glances at him several times.

# 6

A nise had found herself sitting next to Oscar during her first meal at the way-house. His patchwork tunic of brightly colored linen squares struck her again. The colors flickered and flamed in the setting sun's light pouring in through the windows.

"Anise, right?" he asked.

Anise nodded.

"Oscar," said Oscar. He held his right hand out briefly, palm outward, fingers pointed toward the ceiling.

"I know," said Anise, "Maeve told me." The house matron watched the conversation from the other side of the table.

"How're you settling in?" asked Oscar.

"I guess I'm a little homesick," said Anise. She considered Oscar and returned the question. "Are you a student? You look old."

Oscar laughed. "I wouldn't have them, and they wouldn't have me," he said. "I'm just passing through. Didn't Maeve tell you about the cunning folk safe-houses?"

"I guess she did," said Anise.

"Your uncle told me about your trip to Ashton," said Oscar. "It sounds like it was quite an adventure. He said something about wolves and outlaws."

"Oh, the wolves weren't anything," said Anise, "That was just a bad dream I had. The outlaws were a little scary. They shot arrows at us."

"They didn't try to hurt you, though, did they? Probably just looking for money."

"They said they weren't allowed," said Anise. "They said they were only allowed to take money from the Young Lion's tax collectors and rich people."

"Well," said Oscar with another smile, "Imagine that, outlaws, with a conscience."

## 7

Vin and Jord weren't in Anise's illusion class. Cian was, however. When Anise saw her seated in the classroom, she thought briefly about sitting next to her. But, she was almost sure that Cian had seen her walking across the green, and had avoided eye contact, so Anise wasn't sure she would be welcome.

Vin and Jord weren't in the illusion class because they were taking a required course on literacy. The town of Hero had a surprisingly advanced education system for Liamec. The most progressive part of the system was that it existed. The incoming class of students at the Academy were more educated than the vast majority of citizens, but only about half could read. Anise hadn't taken a test, so she wasn't sure how the registrar had known that she could.

The classroom was similar to her alchemy classroom. There was a podium in front, a desk beside it, and a black slate on the wall behind.

She found a seat in a back row, not next to anyone, and waited for the master to arrive. A person stepped up to the podium at the front. The name Master Devona was written on the black slate behind her. At first, Anise was a little confused as to what was happening. Was one of the students playing a prank before the master arrived? The person behind the podium looked more like a girl than a woman. Certainly, not like a master. She hardly looked older than Anise herself.

Anise studied her. She stood on a box, or perhaps two, raising herself to the level of the top of the podium. She was probably no taller than Cian, if not a little shorter. She had curly blond hair that fell in ringlets to her shoulders and a face that was as bright, sunny, and pretty as a porcelain doll.

The girl cleared her throat. The eyes of the students in the room turned to her, and some of the chattering stilled.

"Hello, class," she said, "I am Master Devona. Welcome to the world of illusion!" Her voice reminded Anise of a warm spring day and happy times from her childhood.

The master scanned a piece of paper on the podium. "Anise," she called out loudly, then looked up expectantly.

Anise's heart started beating strongly enough that she felt it would bounce out of her chest. *Could she have already done something wrong to be called out in front of the class in the first session?* The master was scanning the room as if looking for her.

Anise slunk down in her chair, trying to appear invisible while at the same time raising her hand. The master spotted Anise's hand and marked her parchment with a quill pen. She called out, equally loudly, "Cian?" and looked up again.

Anise's heart started beating again. She had missed the moment when it went from beating like a drum to stopping, but it started back to normal now. The master was taking attendance.

A young man sitting in the second row spoke up. Anise disliked him on sight. He slouched on his seat and had his legs draped over the chair in front of him. "My parents aren't paying good money to have little girls teach me," he said.

Almost nonchalantly, the master waved her hand in his direction. She hardly looked at him. Anise gasped, as did most of the people in the room. A lion appeared in front of the first row of chairs, charged forward, put its paws up on the desk the young man's legs were on, opened its jaws, and roared, shaking the room.

The young man fell off his chair and tried to hide under the desk. Anise looked again at the lion, who had started sniffing around the seat. It looked a little transparent at second glance, though it didn't look like the young man thought so.

Master Devona waved her hand again, and the lion disappeared. Anise thought she caught a whiff of its scent as it vanished.

"What I've just demonstrated," said Master Devona calmly, unfazed by the interruption, "is a targeted illusion. There's an aspect of illusion that allows a connection with the subject's mind."

The master finally met the eyes of the young man, and Anise thought she caught a hint of a smile. The young man climbed out from under his seat and sat back down. He was breathing as if he had just run a marathon.

"When a skillful illusionist targets an illusion," said Master Devona, "an image will be selected that comes from the target's fears and anxieties. The illusionist may not even know what image is being created."

The young man lifted his hand timidly. "Master Devona," he said, "Might I be permitted to visit the restroom?"

# 8

Anise was finding the solid wooden boards a little uncomfortable. She sat, cross-legged, on the polished oak common room floor. Around her were the other residents of the way-house. Many were fidgeting like Anise, trying to get comfortable.

They were seated in a circle, all on the floor, facing each other. At the head of the group was Maeve, practically glowing in anticipation. The afternoon sunlight was shining in through the windows. Bands of light dappled the oak floor.

The door to the outside opened, and someone started to walk in.

"Oscar," called out Maeve cheerfully, "Come and join us."

The door stopped, then moved back and forth as if whoever was on the other side was unsure which way to go. Finally, it opened further, and Oscar stepped into the room.

"It's Woden's day, isn't it," he said sadly.

"It is," said Maeve happily. Her smile widened.

Oscar resignedly came over to join the circle. Cian and Jord moved aside a little to give him room to settle on the floor between them.

"Now," said Maeve. "For the benefit of those new to the house," She eyed Anise as she spoke, "I'll explain what we are doing sitting here on the floor."

Anise looked around at the circle of faces. Looks varied, but they mostly seemed resigned. Vin and Jord were sitting next to each other. By now, Anise could tell them apart without difficulty when she saw them together.

Cian, Niall, and Oscar all shared the same expression. They were the prisoners who had accepted that there was no way to avoid their fate and went to the gallows, determined not to show weakness.

The cook's boy was sitting between Anise and

Maeve. He looked like Anise felt: worried and unsure. If Anise had known him better, she would have put her arm around his shoulders.

"On Woden's day," said Maeve, "we enjoy a moment of peace and companionship, where we share our feelings and talk about our lives. A little thing that I call the time of the circle."

Maeve grinned like a cat that just caught a bird. "Oscar," she said, "Seeing as you were so enthusiastic about joining us, maybe you can get us started." She turned to Anise and continued, "During the time of the circle, we take turns talking about things that we are grateful for."

"Well," began Oscar. The patches on his shirt caught the light streaming in through the windows. The bright colors of the linen squares glowed in the warm afternoon sun. Anise wondered if he had multiple shirts with the same design or always wore the same one.

"I'm beholden to Maeve for maintaining this wonderful house and giving me a place to stay," said Oscar. Maeve was shaking her head and frowning. "And, I know that's the same thing I said last week," he continued. He looked thoughtful.

"I'm grateful that the world affords a wandering man so many interesting possibilities. I'll be leaving you all soon to try to find my next adventure." Oscar smiled. "Maybe something political this time."

There were murmurs of regret at Oscar's announcement, but it didn't come as much of a surprise to the long-term residents. Oscar had been at the way-house for several weeks, but he had always said he was passing through.

Maeve pointed to each resident in turn after Oscar. Most shared some form of the same gratitude about the existence of the way-house. With the warm sunlight flooding the oak floorboards and warming her back, and with the presence of the circle of people around her, Anise started to feel closer to her fellow residents.

When it was her turn to speak, she overcame her nerves and talked a little about how excited she was to be at the Academy. About how much she was looking forward to learning. And, finally, about how welcome she felt at the way-house.

It turned out that the cook's boy was named Raphael. When he spoke, he quietly shared how grateful he was to have a place to sleep and enough to eat. He was thankful to Cookie for offering him employment and Maeve for the roof over his head.

# THE HALL OF ELEMENTS

# 1

J ord and Anise walked together to Elements class. Vin had started keeping company with some girls she had met, and neither Jord nor Anise felt welcome to join them. As they approached the stone-walled building that their class was in, Anise took a moment to look at it.

The building was huge; it towered over the adjacent structures. It was also broad as well as tall. Anise had seen it before when walking to her classes. It was impossible not to see it. The building occupied more than its fair share of the Academy grounds. She had had to trek around it several times over the last week.

"The Hall of Elements," said Jord quietly. She gazed at the stone wall looming above them with admiration and apprehension.

Anise had a flashback to climbing the tower in the Dragon's Eye park with her uncle. She remembered seeing a huge building in the center of the place they had identified as the Academy. Even though it seemed vast from the tower top, it looked even larger standing below it.

"This should be the classroom," said Jord, pointing to a door. The door was dwarfed by the height of the stone wall above it.

As they opened the door and stepped into the room, it struck Anise as different from her previous classes' rooms. There was still a Master's podium at one end of the room, with a slate board behind it. There were still rows of desks for the students. But, the room was narrow and long, with one side having windows opening out onto the green walkway outside the building and the other side a windowless inner wall. There was only one doorway other than the one that they were entering. It was as if the room was an afterthought in a building that was thinking about something else. Like the building's wall had been made a little wider here, and the classroom stuffed into it. The one other exit was a narrow door on the windowless inner wall. Made of solid metal, the door shone as if polished. There was a massive lock just below the door handle.

Anise glanced around the room. Though narrower than the other classrooms, the walls on both sides were still lined with bookshelves and cabinets. On one shelf, she saw a glass jar that contained a whirlwind. Small feathers were spinning around in the sealed jar, swirling continuously in a spiral.

Anise didn't have much time to think about it as the master of the class was leaning on his podium, intently watching the two of them walk through the door into the classroom.

"Vin and Jord?" he said.

# 2

J ord looked up, raised her hand, and walked carefully toward the master. Anise followed. Not in response to what he had said, but because she planned to sit beside Jord in the classroom. The master studied them as they walked toward him. The expression on his face changed from attentiveness and interest to disappointment as Jord, with Anise following, advanced down the central aisle between the rows of desks.

Anise looked back at him. With an effort, she kept her mouth from opening in shock. The master's skin was dark. Darker than anyone she had ever met before. She hadn't known that anyone's skin could be that dark.

"You were supposed to be identical twins," said the master sadly. He was about average height. His tightly curled dark hair peeked out from under the black master's cap he wore, matching his robes. "You don't even look alike." He spoke with a trace of an accent that Anise couldn't place. Though if the truth is told, she hadn't heard many accents until visiting the Carnival of Wonders.

"Oh," said Anise. "I'm not Vin." She looked around. "I guess she's not here yet."

The master looked relieved. "That's good then," he said. "Grab a seat, and we'll get started." He looked up and scanned the class. "Welcome to Elementary Elements," he said.

The door opened, and Vin entered the room. She was in the company of the girl wearing purple who she had met in alchemy class. The master glanced at them, paused while they found seats, and continued. "Some words of introduction are in order. I am Master Videmon," he gestured to his name on the slate.

"I hail originally from the empire of Mali in the African continent," the master went on. There was a bit of a murmur in the class at this. "I learned my knowledge of the elements in the libraries of Timbuktu."

One of the young men sitting toward the front of the class raised his hand. The master nodded at him in acknowledgment.

"Master," said the young man, "Did you ever meet Prester John?"

Master Videmon laughed. "Prester John?" he said with a smile. "Africa is big."

He continued, "And, after all, I'm not sure Prester John would want to meet someone whose only minor skill is being able to do things like this:"

The master lifted his hand in a gesture eerily similar to what Anise had seen Vin do what felt like a lifetime ago. A column of flame shot up out of his hand. He then moved his other hand in a spiraling motion around the column. A water trail formed a glistening spiral around the flame, flowing as if streaming through the air. All the air in the room was being sucked toward the fire and the water. Anise felt a wind flowing past her face.

Master Videmon snapped his fingers on his left hand. Several steel spheres, lying on his desk, leapt into the air and started circling the flame and water construction.

The master stared fiercely at his creation. In addition to the wind, Anise felt all the moisture being sucked out of the air.

Master Videmon relaxed, smiled at the class, and waved his hand. The structure vanished with a hissing sound, and the steel balls clattered to the floor.

# 3

**M**aeve was leading an expedition. Jord, Cian, and Anise followed her like ducklings following a mother duck. They walked down Leafdrop Lane away from the oak door of the way-house. The sun's light showed signs of starting to withdraw to the west.

Jord and Anise walked side by side, just a step behind Maeve. Cian was bringing up the rear. Vin had asked to be excused; she had a rendezvous scheduled with a friend.

Anise was excited. She hadn't been to the bathhouse yet. They each carried a linen towel and a canvas bag to keep their belongings in while they bathed. Maeve had a lantern to light for the walk home.

"Is it just people from the Academy who are allowed to use the bathhouse, or can people from town use it also?" she asked.

"Just the Academy," said Maeve casually.

Anise wondered again exactly what Maeve's relationship with the Academy was. She was afraid to ask.

As they approached the Academy gate, the two guards on duty stood up from their chairs beside the door. "Maeve," said one with a nod. The other opened and held the door for them. Though they had been relaxed in their chairs, their black tabards were clean and neat, and they seemed alert.

The bathhouse was down nearer to the lakeshore than Anise's classrooms. She wondered if the water for the baths came from the lake or some other source. They skirted around the Hall of Elements before approaching the front of the bathhouse building.

The entrance to the bathhouse was impressive in its way. Not as large as the Hall of Elements, not by half, it sported a broad marble staircase fronted by columns that supported an archway over wide double doors. Anise stopped to admire the columns. Maeve marched confidently up the stairs, followed by her ducklings.

"Come on, Anise," called out Jord.

Anise was a little uncomfortable at first getting undressed in the bathhouse. Maeve explained that there were many different pools and rooms. Some were just for the masters, some were for students, and some were for women only. They went to one of the rooms that was for women only. After pointing out the room for them, Maeve went off on her own. Anise wasn't sure where to.

The pool they were lying in was in that room. Anise lay back between Cian and Jord, soaking in the deliciously warm water. The pool was exactly the right temperature. Somewhere between hot and warm. Just the perfect somewhere. Maeve had told her that students were assigned to practice their elemental talents by producing fire to heat rocks in the water and maintain the ideal temperature.

They were alone in the small stone-lined room, except for a few other women on the other side of the pool. The warm water flowed into the room through a channel at the bottom of one wall. The warm water flowed in one channel, and cooler water flowed out another.

She was relaxed now. The warm water and her companion's company had removed her doubts.

"You know what the Key is, don't you?" said Jord.

Anise met her eyes. Jord had a bit of a crooked smile on her face.

"Relaxing?" Anise asked.

"No," said Jord, "I mean the Key to alchemy."

Cian looked up. She looked first at Anise, then at Jord. She made a shushing gesture with one finger on her lips to Jord. Jord ignored her.

"Well," Jord continued, "You remember how a Key is a thing, a place, and an idea simultaneously?"

"Yes," said Anise, "Master Ernst gave us those little

vials. The Key to Alchemy is the liquid in them."

Jord nodded. "That's the thing." She made a broad gesture that took in the walls of the room around them and the pool they were lying in. "The bathhouse is the place." She laughed. "Get the idea?"

Anise was confused. She turned her head toward Jord. "No," she said.

Cian looked down at the water they were soaking in. She had a melancholy expression on her face.

Jord laughed again. "I'm sure Master Ernst will talk about the mystical properties of bodily fluids. But, the reason that the academy bathhouse is the Place is that the masters-only baths have an outlet that leads to a room where they fill those little bottles. Apparently, the water the masters soak in is very potent."

Anise frowned. She looked searchingly at Jord with a shadow of distress on her face. "That's gross," she said.

# 4

A nise and Cian were both in the same clairvoyance class. Vin and Jord weren't in that class either. At first, Anise wasn't sure why. Cian and Anise still hadn't exchanged more than a few words, but the older girl had stopped shying away from Anise when she came close, so that was progress.

Anise guessed that Cian was a little older than her. Perhaps a year. She was shorter, though not anything like as small as Maeve. She had her mother's red hair and brilliant green eyes, though it was hard to see them as she avoided eye contact.

After noticing Anise looking back and forth between her and Cian, Maeve had commented one time, "Remind me to tell you about the birth sometime." Then she laughed and continued, "Or better, don't."

The clairvoyance class was in an undistinguished building on the edge of campus. The master was a middle-aged woman, though, to Anise, she seemed unutterably old. She was exceptionally unexceptional, dressed in her black master's robes with her straight brown hair hanging just to her shoulders.

"Now," she said, "those of you who are expecting to be able to forecast the future after your first class with me, I am afraid I have to disappoint you. This class is going to be more theoretical than practical." She looked down at her notes. "We're going to be doing a lot of reading."

Anise thought that perhaps she knew why Vin and Jord hadn't been assigned to the class.

"Clairvoyance is a lost art," continued the master. Anise read the slate behind the podium. "Master Huginn" was written there. "A long time ago, it was one of the disciplines here."

The master frowned and looked down at her notes again. "It's unclear what happened, but within a short period, two hundred years ago, the Academy curriculum went from having five disciplines to having just four."

Master Huginn shuffled her papers. "I am a researcher here at the Academy. When Master Lorenzo approached the Academy council with his proposal that the study of clairvoyance should be re-added to the curriculum, he encountered skepticism."

Master Huginn shook her head. "I'm giving you too much politics," she said. "Let me start again."

Anise thought she could see why the master was a researcher rather than a lecturer.

Master Huginn lifted her head from her notes and looked out at the class. "That same two hundred years ago, the Academy library was intentionally stripped of books on, and references to, the discipline of clairvoyance. Finding that shocked me as a researcher. It brought me firmly to the opinion that Master Lorenzo was right. We need to bring clairvoyance back to this school."

The master shook her head again as if she was still having trouble deciding what information she should be giving the class.

"This class is an experiment," she said. "We don't know how to teach clairvoyance. We have no books, no method, and no equipment. We're starting with first-years, as you won't have any preconceptions about what is or isn't possible. Your assignments will be finding and researching references to clairvoyance in the library. You will be helping the Academy regain lost knowledge."

The master pointed to the door in the back of the room. "Anyone who isn't interested in this curriculum is welcome to drop the class. Just speak to the registrar."

Master Huginn lifted a paper. "This is a list of books in the library that still contain some reference to clairvoyance. Your first assignment will be to go to the library and locate and familiarize yourself with one of the books on this list.

"Even though the registrar's process puts those with gaps in their education into an appropriate class, sometimes people who have trouble reading slip through the cracks. Please familiarize yourself with the library's reading alcoves if you have trouble reading. The reading aids from last year had overstayed their welcome. I believe Master Lorenzo channeled a new set just last weekend, so there should be a fresh reading aid in each alcove."

# 5

**A**nise stepped up onto the stairs at the front of the library building. Marble columns supported a triangular pediment above the entrance. There were four alcoves, each containing a black stone gargoyle, in the pediment. They all glared down at Anise as she started climbing.

She hesitated at the top of the stairs. A shimmering transparent glow hovered across the wide-open double doors leading into the library interior. A friendly-looking young man was seated behind a high counter in the entrance hallway just beyond the glow.

"Can I help you?" he called out to Anise as she stood there.

Anise braced herself and stepped through the glow and up to the desk, trying to seem confident and unafraid. She felt a bit of a tingle as the glimmer surrounded her, but nothing else happened.

"I'm looking for a friend," she said to the young man. "She said she was going to be in a reading alcove."

The young man smiled at her and pointed to an opening on the right-hand side of the entrance hall. The words 'Reading rooms' were written on a sign over the archway.

Beyond the doorway was a corridor that went on a long way. Both sides were lined with cubicles. Each alcove contained two chairs, a desk, a lantern, and a cage hanging over the back of the desk.

Anise looked into the nearby cubicles. Several of them had people sitting at the cubicle's desks. They each seemed to be listening intently to something, but the corridor was as silent as the grave.

Relieved that she wasn't going to have to spend a lot of time hunting down the corridor of alcoves, Anise spotted the back of Jord's head in one of the nearer nooks.

As soon as she crossed from the corridor into the alcove's entry, Anise heard a low, raspy voice. It was reciting something. Jord turned as she noticed Anise.

"Anise," she called out. They had just seen each other that morning, but Jord still sounded excited. The raspy voice stopped immediately.

Anise looked around for Jord's books. There was nothing on the desk. The cage behind the desk had a built-in book rack made of the same metal as the enclosure's bars. A book was resting on the shelf. Anise moved closer to see a shape in the cage more clearly.

A bit bigger than a large cat, a small gray creature crouched in the enclosure. It stood on its hind legs, forelimbs held in front of it. The forelimbs ended in sharp-looking claws of black material hard as stone. It had a round head with two small horns of the same black substance. Leathery dark gray wings flapped idly behind its back. Crinkled skin textured between rough leather and tree bark covered the creature's body. It had a tail with the same leathery texture. The appendage wrapped prehensily around its legs.

As Anise stepped nearer to the desk where Jord was sitting, the creature turned to look at her. If it hadn't been for the expression of singleness of purpose and focus on its face, the face might have seemed almost childlike and human.

She shuddered and stopped. "What's that?" she asked nervously.

Jord smiled. "That's my reading aid," she said cheerfully. "I call him Iggy." The creature turned its gaze toward her as she spoke. "Iggy, say hi to Anise," she said.

The creature turned back to Anise. "Burn," it said in the same low, raspy voice Anise had heard when she stepped into the alcove.

"Doesn't Iggy have a sexy voice?" said Jord.

"Uh-huh," said Anise carefully. "He has a name?"

"I think he's a fire imp," said Jord. "I don't know if he has a name. I just started calling him that. Let me show you how it works," she continued enthusiastically. "Iggy, read page three."

There was a faint rustling noise, and some of the pages in the open book turned over by themselves. The raspy voice resumed. Anise thought she heard a smoky quality in the sound that she hadn't noticed before. It was talking about potions, ingredients, and volumes of liquids.

"Is that our alchemy textbook?" said Anise.

"Iggy, stop," said Jord. The voice stopped immediately. Jord continued, "Yes, it is. Iggy's not much of a conversationalist, but he reads a treat. I tried talking to him, but it didn't work too well. Iggy, tell Anise about your interests."

The creature turned toward Anise. A wistful expression crossed its face. Anise tried to determine if she saw innocence or an absence of understanding in that expression.

"Burn?" said Iggy hopefully.

# 6

The second class in alchemy convinced Anise that Master Ernst wasn't only the oldest human being she had ever seen; he was also the dullest. The master droned on through the first half of the class. Somehow he managed to make the fact that one of the ingredients in their potions was used bathwater, dull, in addition to being disgusting.

"The Key to alchemy is the concept that the fluids of the human body hold power," said the master. His high, reedy voice pierced through to all the classroom seats, but the shrill sound sucked the life out of his words.

"Of course, there are other ingredients in alchemical potions," the master continued, "but a classic recipe will always contain some essence of liquid from a person."

Master Ernst lifted his eyes and gazed out over the students. His piercing gaze cut right into Anise as it passed over her. His eyes were a bright blue, though they were fogged just a bit by cataracts.

"Sometimes from the potion brewer. Sometimes a drop from the Key," he held up a small pink crystal vial, similar to the ones passed out to each student before class. "Sometimes, a potion calls for some bodily fluid from the person who is to be targeted by it.

"An elixir of mind control, for example, is more effective (some would argue only effective) if it contains a drop of blood from the person who is to be controlled."

The master frowned as he continued, "There are those, in these debased times, who argue that potions can be brewed without employing bodily fluids."

He concluded dramatically. "Until you show me a tincture of terror that manages to frighten a mouse without a drop of human spit in it, my faith will not be shaken."

Jord turned to Anise and whispered quietly, "Do you

think when he was young, he bored the other Romans as much as he's boring us now?"

# 7

Anise and Jord were sitting in the reading alcove in the library again. This alcove had become Jord's favorite spot to study. Iggy watched the two of them from the safety of his iron-barred cage. Anise had gotten used to the intensity of his gaze.

"Why weren't you at our first channeling class?" said Jord. "I thought you came here planning to study channeling."

"Did you have a dream telling you where it was?" asked Anise.

"I did," said Jord. She smiled proudly. "Vin heard that they did something to make it more likely that students with channeling ability would have those dreams. She didn't have one herself." Jord's smile drifted a little toward self-satisfaction. "She asked me where it was, but I wouldn't tell her."

Iggy stuck one of his obsidian claws between the iron bars of his cage. He focused on Jord with a yearning expression on his face and said, "Burn?"

"No, of course, you can't burn her," said Jord to the imp. "I don't know what you're thinking." She frowned at the fire imp. "Sometimes, Iggy," she said. She stopped and looked thoughtful, "Anyway, she likes fire."

"What was the dream like?" asked Anise. She was genuinely curious, as she wanted to compare it to her own.

"Dreamy," said Jord. "It was like I woke up in the wayhouse dorm, but all the bunks except mine were gone. No one else was there. Vin's bed was empty. I don't know where you were."

Jord looked thoughtful. "I've never had a dream like that before. It felt both more and less real than my usual dreams." She hesitated, then continued. "More real, in that it felt powerful, like things were really happening. Less real in that I knew that I was dreaming."

Jord took a breath and leaned toward Anise excitedly. "There was a spirit there, a Daemon. She was beautiful, though her skin was green. She said her name was Fyki, and she was there to help me." Jord looked confused. "She said she was the spirit of kelp or something like that. She told me where the class was going to be."

Anise looked away from Jord. Her gaze crossed Iggy's. He seemed to be staring at her. His pupils were fully dilated like a cat's in a dark room. Anise dropped her gaze to the ground.

"Did it feel like someone was watching you?" she said carefully.

Jord looked surprised. "No, I told you there was no one there in the room but me and the Daemon." She shook her head, "Who would have been watching me?"

Anise looked thoughtfully at the ground, remembering Helios's warning that she should keep a low profile. She didn't reply.

Jord looked sternly at Anise. "Promise me that you won't miss the next class," she said. "I don't want to have to go alone again."

"Wouldn't dream of it," said Anise.

# 8

Anise and Cian walked together to illusion class. When Anise had suggested that they walk together, Cian favored her with a shy smile. The smile, and a pair of bright green eyes, glowing like emeralds, peeked out at Anise from under an unruly mop of red hair. Anise took the smile as assent, and they made their way to the classroom together in companionable silence.

Anise and Cian found seats toward the back of the classroom. Master Devona stepped up to the podium.

One of the students in the front row held up a hand. The master acknowledged him with a nod.

"Master Devona," he said, "They've been talking about the Keys to the disciplines in our other classes. Could you tell us about the Key to illusion?"

"I guess you've heard something about Keys," she said. "Otherwise, you wouldn't be asking the question." She looked around the class, seemingly trying to meet each student's gaze one by one. "Well, as you know, the Key to a magical discipline is, at one and the same time, a place, an idea, and a thing.

"I won't talk about the place and idea of the Key to illusion just yet, but the thing that is Key to Illusion is the absence of a thing that is Key to Illusion. The physical Key to the discipline of illusion is that there is no physical Key."

# 9

Anise spent an uncomfortable amount of time at meals at the way-house looking at Niall. She tried to be careful. She tried to avoid looking when anyone else might see, but he was just so pretty. He was tall, like her uncle, and had straight brown hair that might feel soft and warm to the touch, like a loaf of bread fresh out of the oven.

She was careful to make sure that no one saw her looking, especially Jord and Vin. Jord would tease her in a friendly way if she knew. Vin's teasing would probably not be so kind.

One time Anise thought she saw Maeve noticing her looking. She just smiled at Anise and passed the peas.

The cook's boy, Raphael, served food to the table before he sat down to join the group and eat himself. Several times, Anise found her view of Niall interrupted by Raphael putting something on the table or asking her if she needed something. A slight boy, Raphael was probably not much younger than Anise but seemed younger due to his size. He had red hair. His hair color made her think of Rufus from the Caravan of Wonders.

Anise hadn't spoken much to Niall. He was an upperclassman, and she worried he wouldn't have time for a first-year like herself. Vin seemed comfortable chatting away with him. Anise found herself envious when Vin sat next to Niall at mealtimes.

# 10

J ord and Anise barely had time to sit down in elements class before Master Videmon bid all the students rise. The master smiled. "We're going on a field trip today," he said. Seeing some of the class looking around them to grab their books and bags, he continued, "Don't worry, it's not a very long trip." The master pulled a bulky ornate key from his belt and approached the solid metal door on the narrow classroom's inner wall.

The key was large, crafted of metal, like the polished door, and was painted in forceful colors. Anise saw red, brown, blue, and white bands around the shaft. Master Videmon handled it reverently.

The master unlocked the door and swung it open; it swung open silently. Master Videmon stood beside the open door and gestured to the interior.

"This way, please," he said amiably. The students started filing through the door.

When it was Anise's turn to step past the master and into the corridor on the other side, she had to overcome a moment of claustrophobia. The passageway on the other side of the metal door was not much broader than the doorway itself. It was low, dark, and led straight as an arrow into the blackness away from the classroom.

Master Videmon stepped into the corridor after the last of the students, turned behind himself, swung the heavy door closed, and locked it. The darkness and stillness were absolute. Anise felt she couldn't breathe.

A light appeared through the darkness. Master Videmon held up his hand, and a glowing sphere appeared above it. Anise examined the sphere curiously. She was close enough that she would have felt the heat from a ball of fire, and this globe didn't feel warm. It also was more yellow and white than red. For an instant, she wondered if it could be that light was its own element and if there might be more than four elements.

Then Master Videmon set off down the corridor, gesturing for the class to follow him. Such heretical thoughts were driven from her head.

They reached a staircase after a shuffle along the narrow corridor. It was probably shorter than it felt. The flights of stairs wound down for a long time. It was hard to judge both time and distance in the dim space.

The stairs ended, and after another short corridor, they approached another door-a twin to the one from the classroom. The master opened this one with the key as well. He repeated his gesture of standing by the door and letting the class file by him. All Anise could see was a red glow coming through the doorway.

As Anise, the last of the students, walked by the master, he called out in a theatrically loud voice, "Welcome to the Key to the discipline of the Elements!"

Anise milled through the group of her fellow students and wasn't able to see much. The floor of the space beyond the door was cobbled stone. Anise was a little confused. Had they come back outside? Everything looked red, and the air felt warm.

Anise reached the edge of the group of students and the cobbled area, grasped a stone railing, and looked up.

Her mouth dropped open. The space above and before her felt as vast as the outside. Everything was suffused with a red glow, but it was the source of that glow that loosened her jaw. Below the railing she held, and her grip on the stone tightened as she looked, was a drop to a body of water wide enough to be called a river. Beyond that was a mountain of rough black stone rising to an open peak flowing red with lava streams. The whole thing was contained within the building. The far walls were visible at the limits of Anise's vision (though the smoke and steam from the water and heat reduced that limit).

There was a spiraling vortex of clouds around the

peak of the mountain. Below the clouds, the top of the stone summit was open in a fuming crater. Anise felt she could barely make out the ceiling high above the spire and the clouds. There was a hint of an opening in the roof. A trace of blue sky peeked in just over the volcano's crater. The spiraling winds funneled and conveyed the smoke and fumes through the hole.

"It's a small volcano," said Master Videmon to the group, "as such things usually go." He spoke forcefully to be heard over the rumble of the distant lava and the murmuring bluster of the winds.

"Of course," continued the master, "Volcanoes inside buildings isn't how such things usually go." The master laughed. If he hadn't amused any of his students, at least he had amused himself.

Master Videmon lifted both arms above his head. "Do you feel it, my students?" he said. "Do you feel the power, the elements?"

Anise did. There was a strong odor of sulfur in the air. She felt the hot wind on her face and the swirling mist rising from the distant river below. They filled her with a feeling of strength. She felt that capturing and controlling these elements would be easy to learn.

"Of course," said Videmon, laughing again. He was amusing himself today. "If you don't feel it here, you're probably in the wrong class."

# THE ISLE OF THE WISE

# 1

T heir channeling class was in a stone building on the lakefront. Since coming to Ashton and the Academy, Anise hadn't been down to the lake. Jord made her lead the way, as she wanted to be very careful to make sure she wasn't being tricked into giving away where the class was being held.

"If I wouldn't tell my sister, who I have trouble hiding things from," she said, "I don't think I should be telling you."

Helios had told Anise where to go, so she didn't have a problem.

It was late afternoon. As Anise and Jord walked through the Academy toward the class, the afternoon sun was cut off by a forceful mist that reached out from the lake. The entrance to the classroom was on the side of the building. Some wharves stretched out into the water from the structure's lakeward face.

The wharves were shrouded in the mist. Anise thought she saw several large rowboats tied up by the docks.

The classroom was similar to the rooms for Anise's other classes. The now-familiar black slate was behind the master's podium. The master wasn't there yet; Cian was, however. She was sitting in the last row away from the master's desk. Behind the last row of seats were open windows looking out over the lake. Cian nodded to Anise and Jord when they sat down next to her.

A cold, clammy breeze was coming in through the windows behind them. Anise turned and looked out over the water and the wharves. The mist was thick enough that there wasn't much to be seen beyond the docks and the nearby waters. The quiet sound of gentle lake waves knocking the tied-up boats against the wood filled the air.

Anise turned back around. Jord and Cian were discussing something from the last class, perhaps. The master entered the classroom, and Anise shushed them.

The master stepped up to the podium. Anise noticed that Jord and Cian were looking at her, not the man in front of the class. She gasped as she looked at the master's face. Or perhaps, better said, at where his face should be. A massive scar ran diagonally across his face from his forehead's left-hand side, across the center, to the right-hand side of his chin. There was little left of his nose, and it left one not knowing where to look. Bright, intelligent brown eyes peered out through the ruin beneath a youthful-looking head of brown hair.

Jord reached out and touched Anise's hand. "Vin heard that it was a mountain reaver raid when he was a child. The raiders left him for dead, but he didn't die."

Anise had heard of the mountain reavers. A tribe of savages that supposedly lived in the Etenies just past the borders of Liamec in the northwest. She had thought them a myth.

"Welcome class; to our second session," said the master. "Or, for some of you, our first." His clear eyes scanned the classroom. Anise thought that they rested on her for a moment. The name Master Callum was written on the slate behind him. His voice was clear and vigorous, though there was a bit of a strange sound to it, which Anise attributed to the damage to his jaw and lips.

"As I mentioned in our last class," continued the master, "today we will begin some practical exercises." He opened a leather satchel and brought out several candles.

"If those of you sitting in the back could close the windows," the master said, "I'm going to try to lead you all through a controlled channeling session." He set the candles down on the desk in front of him and lit them. A sage-like scent started to fill the air. "Mugwort," he said with satisfaction.

"As I mentioned in our last class, a good part of this year will be dedicated to acquiring control. You need to control when you travel to dream and, perhaps more importantly: when you don't. If everyone could look next to your desks," the master continued, "you should find a rolled-up sleeping pad there. We're going to journey together to the realm of dreams." The master laughed, "It's nap time."

# 2

Anise opened her eyes and sat up. The classroom looked the same, though there were fewer desks, and she was the only one there. The familiar feeling of dream flooded into her. She stood and looked around. Was Helios coming to see her?

The door to the classroom opened, and a young man entered. Anise didn't feel that she had ever seen him before. Though he seemed familiar in the way you know someone in a dream.

She thought of Briac. She still thought of Briac on occasion, though the time they had shared on her journey to the Academy seemed like a lifetime ago.

She thought of Briac because she had thought Briac handsome. Next to this young man, her memories of the lines of Briac's hardy face felt like a fountain by a waterfall. His face shone in her dream, like Helios's, though with beauty rather than light.

The young man walked over to her. His bright brown eyes captivated her. "Anise," he said. Anise waited for him to continue, a little lost.

"Seeing as you missed our first class," the man continued matter-of-factly, "I'll start with some basics."

"Master Callum?" said Anise.

The young man frowned. "Of course," he said.

"But your face?" Anise stammered. Then she blushed and turned her gaze to the ground.

The master gazed at her calmly. "Who would dream that they had a face like that?" he asked.

When Anise didn't reply, Master Callum continued, "Anyway, basics, as I said."

"How are you here, sir?" said Anise. "In my dream?"

"That's a bit beyond the basics," said Master Callum. He laughed. Anise watched with fascination as the laugh made his face friendlier and more handsome. "But we must encourage inquiry.

"I am what's called a dream-walker," said the master. "This is your dream, certainly, but at the same time, I am making it mine as well. I will be visiting the dreams of each of your classmates in turn. A bit of personalized instruction."

"How do you do that? Can I do that? Can any channeler do that? Can you do that, even if I don't want you to? Can you go anywhere you want in the dream world?"

The master laughed again. Anise felt like making him laugh was probably a goal she might want to strive for in and of itself.

"So many questions. Like I said, basics. First off, you are here and not off gibbering quietly to yourself in some madhouse somewhere because you know the answer to your last question instinctively." The master gestured around them at the classroom they were standing in. "This is what is called the 'circle of light.' Your channeling dreams always have a circle of light. A channeler summons forces, or creatures, into the 'circle of light' but doesn't leave it."

"I saw you come in through that door," said Anise.

"I'm sure it looked that way," the master replied. "I made your dream into a common dream with my own. If we were to open that door and look out, I don't know what we'd see. I know what would happen if we were to step out. Madness, and probably death. The lesson I stressed beyond all others in the first class, which you missed, was: never leave the circle of light. Here be dragons."

# 3

Anise was sitting next to Maeve at dinner. Maeve had her claimed spot at her selected table, and woe betide anyone who thought about sitting there. The other seats were available for anyone, and Anise sometimes sat next to Maeve.

Rafael stood behind Anise, holding a soup pot almost as big as he was. "Anise," he said, "do you want some soup?"

"Put that on the table, Raffy," said Anise. "You'll drop it." She moved to clear some space on the table next to her bowl.

"I can hold it," said Rafael. He huffed a bit as he moved the pot closer to the table's edge.

Anise reached for the ladle that was sticking out of the pot. She spooned some of the soup into her bowl. Rafael turned to Jord, who was sitting on the other side of Anise.

Anise looked around the table. She missed Oscar. He had talked about things that weren't about Ashton, the Academy, or the weather. He spoke of his travels, conditions in other parts of Liamec, and places and things he'd seen. He even talked about politics.

One of Oscar's frequent topics of conversation was how the prince regent, the young lion as he was called, was taxing the people of Liamec to excess.

"He's making the poor poorer and the rich richer," he had said. "It's wrong, and something needs to be done."

No one else really disagreed when Oscar talked like this. In fact, no one really replied. The affairs of the regent and the king's court in the distant King's Seat in the city of Capitol seemed very far away to them all. It didn't have much to do with the food on the table or what classes they had tomorrow.

Anise looked around again. Vin was quiet. Sometimes Anise got the impression that she didn't feel like any of them were worth talking to. Her new friends at the Academy were not the poor that Oscar had been defending. Anise thought she had seen Vin frowning at some of Oscar's comments.

Niall was carefully spooning his soup into his mouth. Anise studied his face like one might appreciate a work of art. There was something about his nose; it was a straight Greek nose. It gave his profile a strength that she found appealing.

Jord and Cian were talking loudly about something. Anise listened in. They were talking about something that Master Callum had said in channeling class. Cian had started talking to Anise and Jord now. In fact, sometimes, it was hard to get her to stop talking.

Maeve leaned over toward Anise. "A penny for your thoughts, my dear," she said.

"Maeve," said Anise. Tears started to well up in the corners of her eyes. "I would have been so homesick without you."

# 4

**M**aster Ernst was slow and careful with the instruction of the alchemy class. Like his shuffling walk had implied he might be each time he approached his podium. Jord kept talking about how boring the master was. Still, Anise found the idea that he'd been here since the Academy's founding quite fascinating. She kept wondering about what he must have seen, what he must know about things at the Academy, and how they worked. The thought that a drop of his essence was in each potion the students made since he bathed at the bathhouse was also interesting in its own way.

For the first three classes, the master did nothing but talk. He spoke of the theory and practice of alchemy. What kind of flasks to use, how ingredients were prepared, and how they interacted with each other. He tried to instill some feeling of the science's greater purpose and responsibility. Reagents, reasons, and retorts. Jord just wanted to make a potion that would turn someone into a frog. Not that she had anyone she wanted to turn into a frog, just as an academic exercise.

By the fourth class, they finally got to go to the lab. The lab was next door to the classroom. It was divided up into stations. The master instructed them to split up into teams, with each team taking a station. Jord and Anise immediately claimed one of the stations toward the middle of the room. Vin and her friend, who still usually wore purple, took one toward the back.

The station was a little raised counter area above the floor. There was a sink, a bucket with clean water, and a set of glass tubes, vials, and retorts. Anise had never seen so much glass in one place at the same time before. Glass was expensive and, therefore, a bit uncommon.

The walls were lined with cabinets and shelves filled with exotic plants and jars containing strange substances.

Anise quickly gave up trying to make sense of the bewildering array of smells that assailed her nose.

The master made an announcement from the front of the room. He was trying to look stern, but the effect was spoiled when his voice broke partway through and became even more reedy and high-pitched. "Be careful with the glass," he said, "whatever pieces you break will be taken out of your hides." After that warning, he described the morning's assignment in excruciating detail.

Brewing the potion was easy. Anise was relieved when she and Jord finished the assignment without a problem. It made her feel good when Master Ernst praised their work. He held up the vial they had produced, examined the liquid through the light, and sniffed it. He said, "Excellent work, you two. This has a fine bouquet," he paused and took a delicate sip of the brew, "and an excellent body."

He picked up a seedling in a small pot from the central table. "Now, for the real test," he said. The master poured about half the liquid in the vial into the earth around the small plant. There was an audible crackling sound as the sprout shot up to twice its height in a flash. The ceramic side of the pot cracked, and a small root thrust its way out into the open air.

"Well done," said Master Ernst with a smile.

# 5

Anise woke up. She sat up in her bunk bed. The feeling of being in a dream washed over her. Her bed was alone in the dorm room again. Her forehead felt flushed as if there was some light or warmth in the air. Her first thought was that Helios was visiting her in the dream realm again.

She recognized the circle of light that Master Callum had spoken of. The room was lit by simple candlelight, but it felt like a friendly ring of warmth and safety. She shivered when she tried to imagine what was outside the wooden walls. She realized now that she had always known to stay in the circle, though until the master had said it, she hadn't been conscious of her knowledge.

It wasn't Helios. Iggy was hovering in the air just a few feet from her bunk. His little leathery wings, flapping fiercely to keep him immobile, stretched and gloried in the freedom of flight. The warmth seemed to be coming from him.

"Iggy," said Anise. "What are you doing here?"

Iggy's catlike eyes pondered her. His face, hard to read at the best of times, seemed to be showing a quizzical expression as he said, "Burn?"

All at once, Anise knew why Iggy was there; she had summoned him. She hadn't done it consciously. Her thoughts and speculations had been of Iggy, channeling, and the world of dreams. She was disappointed in herself and knew that Master Callum would also be disappointed in her. He had talked about focusing on control and discipline.

Anise felt a surge of panic. She was in a channeling dream, without Helios to hide her from the watcher. Then she realized that she didn't feel the watcher's presence. *It makes sense*, she thought. *He can't watch all the time.*

Anise stood up and stepped toward Iggy. She wasn't

afraid of him. For one thing, she didn't feel a sense of menace, and for another, she thought he knew that she had been the one who had gotten him out of his cage, though she had no idea how that had happened.

"Do you want to go back, Iggy?" she asked.

Iggy fixed his gaze on her. His pupils had gotten even wider in the dim candlelight; His eyes looked almost wholly black. "Burn!" he said defiantly, shaking his head.

Iggy turned from Anise and flew rapidly over toward the outside wall of the dorm room. He briefly paused in front of the wall, then sped directly toward the wood. There was a crashing sound, and a cloud of smoke and steam obscured the area.

"Iggy!" called out Anise as she ran after him. She reached the wall as the smoke and steam faded. There was an Iggy-shaped hole in the wood of the wall. The edges were smoldering, though the wood looked thin and hazy. Anise considered looking through the hole. Then she shivered and thought better of it. Iggy was gone.

# 6

Anise didn't take to illusion. At least not the big impressive illusions Master Devona demonstrated for the class and that her fellow students were eager to emulate. She wasn't sure she wanted to make an illusionary dragon soar through the sky or conjure an insubstantial castle from mist and cobwebs.

"They're not really there, are they," she complained to the master as the class worked on conjuring an image of a coin as an exercise. "It's like lying."

"I suppose that's true," said Master Devona thoughtfully. Then she laughed and lifted her hands into the air. Shining gold coins dropped from her fingertips and vanished after hitting the floor with a distinctive sound. Anise had never heard it before, but she still recognized the thud of a heavy piece of gold hitting a hard surface. "But, I'm not sure I care," continued the master. The bright shining gold disks falling from her hands were like the ringlets in her hair.

Master Devona continued. "If you remember, the physical key to illusion is that there is no physical key to illusion." Her smile warmed Anise.

Anise couldn't help it, but whenever she saw Master Devona, she never failed to remember a poppet that her mother had made for her. It had yellow yarn for hair and a permanent smile on its cloth face. It made her sad to remember her mother.

"And the targeted ones," said Anise sadly, "They're worse. You don't even get to control what they look like. That's up to the target."

Master Devona smiled again, or perhaps still. "I'm not sure they would say that it's up to them. They don't have a conscious choice about what appears. It's a weave between the desires of the illusionist and the target's mind. They often don't appreciate the image."

"Still," said Anise stubbornly, "If that's what illusion is, I don't like it."

Master Devona looked serious. The change of expression made her look even more doll-like and charming. Like when your dog tilts his head to look at you as if he was trying to understand the secret mysteries of the universe.

"Well, Anise," she said, "though we usually emphasize two forms of illusion: display and targeted, there is a third."

Anise waited patiently for the master to continue.

"Transformative. Most people prefer the flashier ones. Transformative illusion is the illusionary transformation of a thing that really exists into another form of itself. Making a bridge appear to have collapsed or hiding a doorway or gap in a wall. It's useful for hiding, traps, and changing one's appearance. It's sometimes called glamour. I have to confess, I'm a little older than I look." The master's smile grew a little rueful with this last comment.

Anise almost laughed with relief. "I like that," she said. "That's what I'll do."

# 7

Anise had gotten quite tired of digging through old books in the library for her clairvoyance class. There was usually just one small reference to clairvoyance or the teaching of clairvoyance. Master Huginn greeted each discovery with an excitement that was contagious, however. She would smile and light up. It made her look a little less unexceptional.

Anise was sitting in what had been Iggy's reading alcove. He had been replaced with a water imp. She was trying to ignore the sad look on the imp's face. There was a bit of a sloshing noise when he moved around in his enclosure. The bottom of the pen had a waterproof lining and was filled with a murky liquid. Anise hoped it was water. The imp had bluish moist-looking skin with a texture that reminded Anise of fish scales.

She had taken to thinking of him as Drippy. Anise had been unable to get him to say anything except while reading. There was a small pile of books on the desk, and one was open in the book slot beside the imp's enclosure.

Drippy was reading to her from the book. Anise was tired and had thought that having Drippy read the book would be less tiring than reading it herself. She wasn't sure that it had been a good idea. Drippy's voice was smooth and rhythmic, like water flowing over river rocks. It had a certain wet quality to it. She started to think of it as a squishy voice. It was putting her to sleep.

Anise dozed off briefly, then woke with a start. She had a momentary vision of a bonfire. Why had she been dreaming of a bonfire? Drippy had stopped talking. Anise looked up toward his enclosure.

Iggy was hovering outside the enclosure, his wings flapping busily. Drippy was crouched on the bottom of the cage, looking up at the fire imp. After glaring momentarily at Drippy, Iggy peered at Anise, his black pupils feeling like they burned through her. He pointed the tip of his prehensile tail at the book that Drippy had been reading. He said, conversationally, "Burn."

Anise sat up and looked from side to side. "Iggy?" she said. "How did you get in here?"

Iggy picked up the book Drippy had been reading in his scaled claws, brought it over to her, and dropped it open on the desk. "Burn," he said forcefully.

Drippy watched Iggy. Anise wondered if there was a hierarchy in the imp world. It seemed Drippy was deferring to Iggy, though that may have had to do with who was in the cage and who was outside it.

She inspected the book. It was a journal from one of the masters at the Academy from a long time ago. The master's personal book collections were usually donated to the Academy library upon their passing. She scanned the open section. It was a report of a book burning. The master whose journal it was described stumbling across a group of fire imps burning a pile of books. *I'll have to take this to Master Huginn*, thought Anise. "Iggy?" she asked.

"Burn," said Iggy affirmatively.

# 8

Vin and Jord respectively took to elements class like a phoenix and a mermaid to fire and water. At their first class, Vin was already able to produce a burst of flame from her hand. Still, after Master Videmon showed her some techniques, she achieved a measure of power and control by the third class that he said rivaled some Academy graduates. Jord's mastery of the element of water wasn't far behind.

Anise didn't have such an easy time of it. She was able to get a feel for the elements of air, water, and earth. She could make the little fan on the lab counter spin with gusts of air. She could make water flow through the piping and tubes into the sink provided for the purpose. She could even make the steel spheres the master supplied them with clatter and clank together. But, no matter what she did, she couldn't produce a flame. When she snapped her fingers together in one of the gestures Master Videmon taught them, she was lucky if her fingertips felt a little warm.

The lab was in the Hall of Elements, like their classroom. As they worked at their lab station, Anise could feel the presence of the Key, the volcano, through the stone wall on the inside of the narrow, long chamber. The elemental forces flowed through the ether, through the wall, into her, and into the power she was summoning. Until she tried to conjure fire. She could feel the flames, but something was blocking them from flowing through her.

"Of primary concern," said Master Videmon, "is the source of the potential you draw from. Near the Key, the volcano and its effects will help you. It's the biggest and strongest power source near here, so it will be hard to draw from anywhere else."

Videmon showed particular interest in Jord and Vin's progress in class. He praised them for their work and native aptitude. Anise remembered what Maeve had said about his interest in twins and wondered what his theories were.

"If you're summoning forces in a place where the wellspring of the element is not so obvious, you need to choose it, rather than just drawing on the nearest source." Videmon shook his head. "The nearest source is probably your own body."

Videmon clicked his tongue. "We've had students lose fingers from frostbite after sucking all the heat out of their bodies with a flame blast. Desiccation with water. Pulling the moisture from the air is harder but won't leave you in the infirmary."

# 9

**M**aster Callum was excited. "We'll be having an adventure this afternoon," he said. He instructed the class to stand, form into lines, and follow him out of the classroom. The perpetual mist that shrouded the docks made it a little chilly as they all trouped out through a door they hadn't used before that led directly onto the docks.

"The first time is always the most interesting," said Master Callum. He had half the class sit in the first of two long oared boats tied up by the wharf. He instructed the rest to sit in the second. "Anise," he said, "Why don't you sit in the front of the second boat."

The master looked up, standing on the dock, and called out to all the students at once. "The Isle of the Wise is the Key to channeling. We will be making a trip to the heart of dreaming."

He untied the boats and lashed them together. He told the students in the first boat to take the oars. The second would just be towed. The master lit lanterns in the front of each rowboat, then took up a position in the stern of the first boat, his hand on the tiller.

Anise went and sat in the front seat of the second boat. Jord sat beside her. The light from the lantern cut through the mist, forming a circle of visible space around them. Anise smelled the now familiar smell of mugwort. The oil in the lamp must be mugwort infused, she thought.

Master Callum turned to Anise from the stern of the front boat. Anise had almost gotten used to seeing his ruin of a face, though seeing it over the lantern light, through the mist, was still startling. "Try to make sure the rope stays tied," he said. It was hard to see if he was smiling or not. "Sometimes, the second boat doesn't come back."

Jord gasped.

"I'm kidding," the master continued, "It usually

comes back, eventually." The master used his steering oar to push off from the dock. The first boat drifted slowly away from the wharf. The second, pulled by the attached line, followed.

"Oars in the water," called out the master. "Row, my neophyte dreamers, row!"

Many of the students had never been in a boat before. There was a clattering and clunking sound as they tried to figure out how to use their oars. The sound echoed through the fog and disturbed the stillness of the misty waters.

Eventually, they formed some semblance of order and moved off into the mist. Master Callum used the tiller to guide the boats straight away from the dock toward the lake's center.

Anise tried to think inconsequential thoughts to conceal herself from the watcher. If this boat trip had something to do with channeling, he would be keeping an eye on them.

She watched the dock vanish into the mist with a shiver.

# 10

Anise walked along a gravel pathway. The gravel crunched beneath her feet with a satisfying sound. There was nothing to be seen except a thick mist around her. She felt like she was following a path through a grove of trees, but the thick fog obscured everything except the trail.

Anise thought she was walking alone, then she realized, with a start, that Master Callum was walking beside her.

"Master Callum?" she said. "Where are we? Where are the boats? Where's Jord?" She took him in more carefully. "What happened to your face?" The master was again the youthful, handsome young man she had seen in her first channeling class dream.

The master smiled and laughed. Anise was a little worried that he was laughing at her, then the infectious sound touched her, and she smiled back.

"Anise," Master Callum said, "Welcome to the Isle of the Wise, the Key to channeling." He flourished his arm in a gesture that would have been much more effective if there was anything to see but mist.

"Did we dock?" asked Anise.

The master's smile grew a little thoughtful. "You think it's a simple question, but it's really rather existential," he said.

Anise was a little annoyed. "Why won't you ever give me straight answers," she complained.

"Ask me some more questions, Anise," said the master, "I promise to answer them as straight as I can. That's what we're here for, after all."

"Who's the Watcher? What did you mean by 'Here be dragons.'? How do I get to be a dream-walker? How come I can sometimes channel a bit while awake?"

"All right," said the master. He lost his smile.

"There's a lot to unpack there." He looked down at the gravel beneath their feet, then looked up and met Anise's eyes. His good looks took her breath away.

"I'll answer the easy one first. You can't channel while awake. That's not something that's ever been done, and I don't believe it ever will be." He frowned. "Then, moving on, I'll return with my own question. What do you mean by 'The Watcher.'?"

It was Anise's turn to look down at the gravel beneath their feet. "The Watcher," she said. "The man who watches our dreams here at the Academy." She wasn't comfortable mentioning that she had felt the Watcher in her dreams before coming to the Academy.

Master Callum looked relieved. "Oh, that's just Master Lorenzo." He smiled again. "He's just concerned for the students. As the head of the department here, he tries to keep track of the channeling to protect and safeguard the student body. You wouldn't believe what damage a bunch of untrained out-of-control young channelers can do. I suppose it's a form of dream-walking, what he does." As he said this last sentence, his expression changed to a more contemplative one.

"That's not it," said Anise. "The Watcher is looking for someone. He wants something. He's scared, and he's mean." She pointed to a spot in the mist-obscured sky as if the Watcher was behind the fog.

"I assure you," said Master Callum earnestly. "Master Lorenzo has the best interests of both the Academy and Liamec at heart. If he's watching us, it's for our protection and safety."

"How about 'Here be dragons'?" said Anise.

"Well," said Master Callum, "That's just a thing you say, isn't it? Here be dragons. It just means that there are monsters and dangers beyond the edge of the map. It's just to make you scared to even think about leaving the circle of light."

The master hesitated. "Though," he said, "There are old stories. People used to think that dragons lived both in this world and in another. That the world outside the circle of light is more than just death and insanity. They even say that people used to know how to travel there. Not just hop from one person's dream to another's, like I can, but explore outside the circle. They say that's where the truth lies." Master Callum shook his head as if shaking off a bad dream. "But, no one's seen a dragon in hundreds of years, and I sincerely advise you, Anise, not ever to leave the circle of light."

A few days later, in her next alchemy class, Anise asked Master Ernst about the Isle of the Wise. She figured that if he was older than the Academy, he must know if there really was an island out in the lake or if the mist was just a portal to the world of dreams.

"That's channeling stuff," said the master in his creaky old voice, "I don't bother with that. They all sniff too much mugwort if you ask me."

# THE HALL OF THE HOLLY KING

# 1

The post came to the way-house once a week. There was usually something for Maeve. It was a big event whenever anyone else got a letter or a package. The rest of the residents of the way-house would crowd around asking what it was or who it was from.

When Anise took her letter from Aunt Rose back to her bunk and opened it alone, everyone was disappointed.

She started crying before she got through the greeting in the letter. Aunt Rose had addressed it to 'My darling Anise," and Anise felt her eyes begin to well up.

There wasn't much news in the letter. Things in the small town of Hero didn't change very fast or very often. Everyone in the village must have told Aunt Rose to send their love and greetings, and it seemed she had taken it literally. There were greetings from everyone Anise knew. Even some from villagers who she didn't really know that well.

Aunt Isabel shared something else with her greeting. "Tell Anise that we really miss her as a keeper for Twilight. No one else seems to be able to stop him from wandering off. Her Uncle Sebastian and I have spent hours hunting through the village for him."

There was a little news; of the small village sort. Uncle Sebastian and Aunt Isabel's farm was doing well. The crop was growing as it should, and the cows were content. Anise had one particular cow, who she called Buttercup. Sebastian and Isabel said that Buttercup's lowing was particularly plaintive because she missed Anise.

Anise started crying again as she reached the end of the letter. Uncle Sebastian wasn't coming to get her to take her home for the summer. It made sense, and through her tears, she understood, but the trip took too long. The time it took to travel from Ashton to Hero and back would take up most of the time that the Academy was out of session. Apparently, Lilith had already communicated with Maeve about Anise staying at the way-house over the summer.

It made sense, and Anise understood, but understanding comes in many forms. She was still crying when she put down the letter. Home felt very far away.

# 2

A nise's first year at the Academy rolled to a close. Jord and Cian were hesitant about the testing that the masters put the students through at the end of the school year, but Anise was confident in her abilities.

She passed her exams with flying colors. Master Devona was a little disappointed that she refused to embrace the more spectacular aspects of illusion. Still, her understanding of the concepts and her skillful application of transformative illusions put her in the ranks of the better students. Master Videmon assured her that her blockage with the element of fire would go away with time, and her grasp of the other elements was more than adequate.

Master Erst had taken a liking to Anise. As the master shuffled among the workstations watching the students work on the final assignment he had given them, he just nodded appreciatively when he saw Jord and Anise's work.

Master Callum was also pleased with Anise's progress. The primary focus of the first year of channeling training had been on learning how not to channel. Learning how to decide if a night's sleep would be broken by a channeling dream or not. In the last session, Master Callum told the class that Anise's ability to not channel was superior to any first-year student he had ever had.

Master Huginn from the clairvoyance class was happy with the progress that they had made as a group. "I will compile and study all the references you have found," she said. "Perhaps next year we will have a class where we actually try to learn something about the application of clairvoyance, instead of just trying to find out if it exists."

In some ways, Anise was worried about what the

summer would bring. The break between academy sessions wasn't very long, as such things go, but it was long enough for her to wonder what she would do. The hot weeks of summer stretched in front of her like a desert.

The day when Vin, Jord, and Niall packed up and left the Way-house felt like an ending to her.

# 3

**M**aeve apologized to Anise about the way-house. "I'm afraid it will be boring this summer," she said. "It'll be just you, I, and Cian." She hesitated, "And, of course, Cookie and the cook's boy." She laughed. "I didn't mean to neglect them."

Anise shook her head. "Maeve," she said, "I am so grateful to you for letting me stay here."

Maeve looked thoughtful. "I hope you don't mind if Cian and I have some family things to do in the next few weeks." She paused before continuing, "we have some obligations we've neglected."

The following days were quiet. The Academy grounds were still open, and the guards would let Anise in. Still, no students wandered around campus, and most buildings were locked. Ashton itself was also quieter. Without the students occupying inns and guesthouses and traveling the streets, the town seemed a shadow of its former self.

One day Cian and Anise decided to go on an outing. They talked to the cook's boy, Raphael, about food for an excursion, and not only did he make it for them, but he also eagerly offered to help carry the basket. Anise looked skeptically at his skinny arms but couldn't find it in her heart to refuse.

As they walked through town to the park called the Dragon's Eye, Anise felt bad about the huffing and puffing coming from behind them, but Raphael refused any offers of help. He was following along behind her and Cian, still dressed in his cook's apron.

Anise wondered how Raphael could be so frail. As Cookie's helper, he should be moving big things and working hard in the kitchen. Maybe Cookie took it easy on him and did the heavy stuff himself.

It got worse as they climbed the curving gravel path that spiraled around the hill up to the Dragon's Watchtower. Anise wished she had one of the potions they had brewed in her alchemy class. One session had been devoted to brewing a draught that refreshed the body and restored strength. If she'd had such a brew on her, she would have offered it to Raphael.

They reached the hilltop and found a spot to lay their blanket with a view of the town spread below them. Raphael stood gawkily beside the spread blanket until Anise insisted he sit and join them.

Raphael had packed an excellent meal. He sat awkwardly, cross-legged, on the edge of the blanket. Anise kept trying to get him to relax, join the conversation, or eat something. Still, he refused to soften, and he insisted that he had only packed enough food for her and Cian.

"So, Cian," said Anise, "what did your mother mean about family obligations?"

Cian looked leery as if trying to decide how much she could share. "My mother's family is," she paused, "complicated." She looked shyly down at the blanket, her coppery hair falling over her eyes.

"She made it sound like it would affect me," said Anise carefully.

"I think she was mostly thinking of the Litha," said Cian, "the solstice celebration." Cian looked up and met Anise's eyes. "You can hide in the dorm if you want, but it'll be hard to avoid it completely. The family can get a little rowdy."

Cian blinked, glanced over at Raphael, and continued, "We've been hosting it at the way-house for the last few years. Last summer, Cookie went home, and Raphael just hid in the dorm."

Raphael nodded, then looked down at the blanket himself, ashamed at his eruption of expression.

"The Litha?" said Anise.

"The battle between the Holly King and the Oak King," said Cian, as if that made it perfectly clear. "It's the day the days start getting shorter again, instead of longer. It's the longest day of the year. It's the day the sun goddess Sulevia spits on the solar usurper Helios. But, for my mother's family, it's mostly a chance to party."

It was Anise's turn to look down at the blanket. Partying hadn't been a big part of her life so far.

# 4

The days got longer. One day, that was almost as long as a day could be, Anise was sitting in the way-house common room. She was trying not to be affected by the heat. She was trying not to be affected by boredom. Her trying was interrupted by a knock on the door.

Anise jumped up. Visitors to the way-house had been few. She hoped for relief from the boredom. She opened the door.

She found herself face to face with a round ball of scarlet hair. So red, as to not look human, it was perched on the head of a man dressed in rough linen britches, without a tunic. His bare chest was covered in wiry, coppery hair and beautiful, colorful patterns, pictures, and images.

Anise had never seen a tattoo before, and she found herself fascinated by the colors, markings, and designs. Most of the tattoos were blue, but there were figures, lines, and parts of images in reds and yellows also.

The man had an iron link chain around his neck. It dangled down his bare chest. Anise wondered if the links ever caught in his chest hair. It was matched by a similar iron link belt that supported his britches. A wicked-looking sword hung from the belt on his left side.

The red ball on the top of his head was a bundle of braided hair. It was at Anise's eye level because the man was shorter than her. Just a little taller than Maeve, he was the smallest full-grown man Anise had ever seen.

Her eyes turned finally to his face. A big smile was spreading across the tanned features under a bristly mustache that matched the hair color of the bundle of hair atop his head. He started speaking. His voice was deep, melodic, and friendly, but Anise couldn't understand a word.

Anise turned and practically bolted for the corridor

into the backrooms of the way-house. "Maeve!" she called out urgently.

Anise hid in the library. It was quiet there, and the massive stone building stayed cool inside, even on hot summer days. Maeve and Cian's family had been arriving for the evening's celebrations all day, and she didn't feel like she could help, so she wanted to stay out of the way.

The reading alcoves were a nice place to relax and be alone with her thoughts. Still, eventually, Drippy's forlorn expression got to be too much for her. Anise left the library and started on her way back to the way-house. As she walked through the tranquil Academy grounds, the late afternoon sun started considering whether or not it should begin its withdrawal from the sky.

Anise reached the now-familiar green building, number 13 Leafdrop Lane, and opened the door. Maeve locked up at night, but the door was never locked during the day. A man was standing just on the other side. Anise was startled. She had hoped to sneak through the common room and hide in her dorm room before the party started.

He was dressed, or not dressed, similarly to the man she had seen before. His upper body, bare from the waist, was covered with tattoos. Anise found her eyes caught again by the patterns and pictures.

He was startled, as well. He had been stationed or had stationed himself at the door as a greeter or guard. The door opening without a knock must have surprised him.

He recovered quickly. More quickly than Anise. He bowed deeply from the waist, then took her hand, looked up into her eyes, and said, "Welcome, my lady." He hesitated before continuing, "You must be the Lady Anise. Welcome to the hall of the Oak King." He spoke with an accent, as if English wasn't his first language, but clearly, and with a lilt in his voice that Anise found charming.

The small man stepped aside and swept his arm across the common room with a welcoming gesture.

Anise gasped. The room had been transformed; she felt in another world. The walls had been covered with tree boughs, so none of the wall's wood showed through. The floor had been littered with flower petals. It felt more like a forest glade than a room in a house.

All the tables had been cleared from the open area, leaving a wide-open expanse crisscrossed by people. It was more people than she felt like she could count, certainly more people than she wanted to count. Everyone was dressed in various colors and fabrics, but the tattoos were a commonality. Anise was relieved to see that the women wore strips of cloth across their chests. Most of the men were bare-chested. The tattoos covered much of the exposed skin.

A stack of cut wood set up as a small bonfire was at one side of the room. Anise thought it was lit for a second, as it glowed as if burning. Then she saw that someone had arranged reflective surfaces in the windows that shone the setting sun's light into the room. Coming from multiple angles onto the woodpile, the orange and red glow of the setting sun was making Helios blush.

"Anise!" came a call from across the room. Cian charged across the floor to the door. Flower petals skittered away from her feet. She was taller than anyone in the room but Anise.

# 5

Cian grabbed Anise's arm and pulled her into the room. Cian was wearing an outfit like the rest of the women. She didn't have tattoos, but she wore a strip of cloth across her chest instead of a tunic. She pulled Anise over to the other side of the room. Anise looked down at the flower petals as they walked.

Two tables were set up there. One had a lavish spread of foodstuffs on it. Anise glanced at the dishes, but she had trouble recognizing what things were.

The other table was set up as a bar. Stools were lining one side of the table, piles of earthenware mugs on top, and several oaken casks were underneath. Maeve stood behind the table. She was also dressed like the other women in the room: colorful linen skirt and just a fabric bound around her chest in a matching pattern. Anise gaped a little as she regarded her housemistress. Maeve did have the colorful tattoos that the other people in the room wore. Anise realized that she hadn't seen Maeve without a full sleeve tunic before. When they had gone to the bathhouse, she had left to bathe in a different room.

"Close your talkbox," said Maeve. "You're gathering flies." She smiled to lessen the bite of her words. It seemed Maeve was tending bar. She put mugs in front of Cian and Anise and said, "What're you having?"

Anise just looked confused. Cian leaned over toward her and said, "There's mead and chouchen." She leaned even closer and whispered, "It's better if you drink chouchen. Some of them think of mead as a drink of the móra."

"What's chouchen?" asked Anise. "And móra?"

Maeve glanced at Cian. There was a bit of weight behind the glance, but Anise had no idea what it meant. "Well," Maeve said, "mead is honey wine. Chouchen is the nectar produced when you lead the work of nature's chosen insects, the bees, through the apple tree's fruit and into a blissful union with the sunlight of a glorious summer day. And móra? Well, you're móra, Anise." She smiled again.

"Oh," said Anise. "I guess I'll have some chouchen, then." She looked hesitantly over at the table with the enticing food and then at the amber fluid that Maeve was pouring into her mug. "I won't be in trouble if I eat this stuff, will I?"

"You mean, will you be trapped in faerie if you eat or drink the fae food?" Maeve laughed. "Look around, Anise. You know where we are. We're not in faerie; we're in my way-house. And, you're trapped here already, aren't you?"

Maeve slapped the mug down in front of Anise. It hit the wooden tabletop with a thud. It seemed to be something you did, as she did the same with the mug she put in front of Cian. Cian glanced sidelong at Anise and said, "Just take sips. There's bee's venom in the brewing, and it's strong."

Anise took a sip. The flavor was sweet but heady. It felt like she was taking a sip of a summer day. It was delicious.

"I was going to hide in the room," she said hesitantly to Cian.

"Too late, now," replied Cian.

A group of musicians had been tuning up in the corner, and they started playing. There was someone with a harp that was bigger than he was. There were two pipers and another person on a fiddle. The music was fast, tuneful, and infectious. Quickly many of the people in the room started dancing. The flower petals on the floor swirled around their feet.

A man walked over to Anise and Cian, sitting at the bar. Anise was about at his height, sitting on her chair, and their eyes met. It was the man she had opened the door to earlier.

"Anise," said Cian, "meet my uncle, Drest." She turned to the man standing before them and made an openhanded gesture toward Anise. "Uncle," she said, "meet Anise."

The man bowed, grasped her hand, and raised it to his lips. He said something in the same language he had used when she opened the door for him. There was a lyrical, musical quality to the sound, but she couldn't understand a word. Anise appealed to Cian for help with her eyes.

"He wants to know if you would like to dance," said Cian. She smiled. "Drest doesn't come to the móra towns much. He doesn't speak much English."

Drest started pulling on Anise's hand. He was surprisingly strong.

"I don't ... I can't ..." said Anise as she rose to her feet. The town of Hero had a weekly dance. It was held in the town square each Frigg's day evening. Anise had often gone with her friend Mary to watch the couples dancing. They hadn't danced themselves, however.

"Don't worry, you'll be fine," Cian called out to her as Drest pulled her out to where the couples were dancing.

# 6

T he dances weren't that different from those she and Mary watched in the Hero town square. At first, Anise spent all her time looking at other people to see what they were doing and how they were moving, then she started to get the rhythm and began enjoying herself.

She warmed up. She had taken a second little sip of the chouchen in her mug before putting it down, and it left a pleasant feeling in her stomach. Drest smiled at her and encouraged her when she made a misstep in the dance. The other dancers gave her curious looks, but they also were very tolerant of her newness. She felt welcome.

Drest's iron chain and belt rattled as he moved. The sound was enough in rhythm with the dance that it sounded like part of the music.

The music stopped. One of the musicians produced a horn from somewhere and blew a blast on it. He tried to keep the sound down because he was indoors, but it was still distressingly loud. Drest walked Anise back over to the bar where Cian and Maeve were waiting, kissed her hand, and headed hurriedly down the hallway leading to Maeve's rooms.

"Where's he going?" asked Anise.

"You'll see," said Cian.

The dance floor cleared. The former dancers and those who hadn't taken part in the dancing formed a circle around the central space. The sun had set, and the reflected sunlight no longer lit the stack of wood. Some of the partygoers held lanterns. A dusky light cast shadows throughout the room. There were gaps in the circle of onlookers on both sides, one near the front door and the other near the corridor that led to Maeve's quarters.

A drumbeat started slowly, building steadily. It felt like it was beating in time with Anise's heart. The crowd of people with their tattoos and strange clothing, the green leaves covering the walls, the dusky light, and the beating drum left Anise feeling like she had stepped into another world.

The door to the outside opened, and a man stepped in. He was dressed mainly like the rest of the crowd—bare-chested, tattooed, and with a sword strapped to his belt, but he wore a mask. He moved oddly as he stepped through the doorway and into the hall. He moved slowly, hesitantly. He moved how Anise might have imagined a tree would move if she had ever imagined a tree moving.

Two curled antlers rose out of the mask covering his whole head. The face was a grinning green visage of leaves and bark. It was expressive, that face; it gave a feeling of strength and life.

As the man in the mask moved slowly and with halting steps toward the middle of the room, the crowd started a low chant. It met and joined with the drumbeat, but the chant made Anise's heart feel like it was beating faster, whereas the drumbeat matched her heartbeat.

Cian leaned over and whispered in Anise's ear, "The Oak King. It's his hall now."

# 7

A horn blast blew. Similar to the horn blast that had halted the dancing but with a different tone. This sounded a call of warning. The Oak King lifted his head, his antlers raised toward what Anise knew must be the ceiling but felt like the night sky, and turned toward the sound.

The crowd, and Anise, turned to look where he was looking. Across the clearing, over the flower petals littering the wooden floor, down the hallway that led to Maeve's chambers. Slowly, carefully, another figure emerged from the shadows. Discreetly at first, but with increasing speed, a second man moved forward into the lamplight.

Anise thought she recognized the pattern of tattoos on the body of Cian's Uncle Drest, but this man moved similarly to the first. Hesitantly, and initially, slowly. He moved from the shadows into the circle of onlookers.

He was also masked. This mask was a face of brown bark crowned by a wreath of green holly leaves. Bright red berries were sprinkled throughout the green leaves in the crown.

Cian whispered to Anise again, "The Holly King."

The Holly King moved slowly forward, bent over, to present less of a threat. The leaves of his holly crown were fresh and green, while the leaves on the Oak King's face were starting to show signs of turning to autumn. The Oak King looked around curiously as if he wasn't aware of the presence of the other.

The Holly King rose fully upright and leapt forward to stand in front of the Oak King. Both men drew their swords. The metal of the blades glittered in the glimmering light from the lanterns. Anise gasped. The edges looked deadly sharp.

The drumbeat accelerated. Anise worried whether her heart could keep up with the speed of the drum. The two men clashed together, and the clang of the swords filled the room.

Anise couldn't watch for a moment. Then she did look and saw that what had seemed a deadly fight could also be seen as a dance. The ringing of the blades touching each other kept time with the beat of the drum and the crowd's chanting. Each man moved back as the other moved forward, like the couples on the dance floor had done only minutes before.

The dance continued for a little until the Holly King, with a roar, the first sound either man had made, made an overhand cut through the air above the Oak King's head. There was a thud as the ends of the Oak King's antlers fell to the wooden floor.

The Oak King turned and fled out the door.

Cian whispered to Anise again, "And so, the hall of the Oak King becomes the hall of the Holly King, once more."

# 8

A nise felt like things were returning to normal when the summer drew to a close and the fall classes approached. Even though she'd been at the Academy for only one year, it felt like the stars were starting to align again when Vin, Jord, and Niall came back to the way-house.

Niall had reached the exalted rank of senior. This year would be his last. Vin and Jord, of course, like Anise, were returning for their second year. There were two new students at the way-house, a girl and a boy. Anise had the haughty feeling of superiority that came with having a full year of knowledge and experience under her belt.

When they checked in at registration, Anise was gratified to see that Earl had taken up her suggestion. The massive illusory head displayed in the registration hall had an eerie green cast to its complexion.

The masters took up where they had left off in the previous semester, including Master Huginn in clairvoyance. She started with a comment of appreciation for the students who had helped her collect information the last year and said she had been compiling it over the summer.

# THE HALLS OF LEARNING

# 1

**M**aster Huginn lifted her gaze from the paper in front of her. "As I was saying," she continued, "the information collected last year has helped us put together a picture of what happened two hundred years ago." She frowned. "Though, we still don't know why."

She brightened as she carried on. "We have learned a lot, however. This year we will be able to teach a little about the theory of clairvoyance. And, hopefully, we will also be able to begin to make a start into real-world applications."

Anise looked up at that comment. Master Huginn's unexceptionalness hadn't changed over the summer. She still made eye contact with her papers rather than with the students. Still, the prospect of learning something practical in the class caught her attention.

"So," the master continued, "there are several things for you to think about." She took a breath.

"We will be reading a book usually assigned by the channeling masters. In fact, you may be asked to read it by your channeling master. But, it turns out that it's relevant for us. How relevant we had forgotten until now.

"*The Archipelago of Dream* is assigned by channeling masters as a cautionary tale. What not to do, and why not to do it. However, with our newfound knowledge of clairvoyance, or perhaps better put, refound knowledge, we now know that clairvoyance and channeling are closely connected. The realm of dream that the channelers visit is the same realm that clairvoyants search for prophecy and truth.

"Two hundred years ago, for some reason, the masters at this academy decided to remove clairvoyance from the curriculum. They collected books from the library that referenced clairvoyance and burned them with the aid of some channeled fire imps."

"The motivation behind this extraordinary act

seems to have been intentionally hidden. It seems like the masters intended for the study and practice of clairvoyance to be lost. This effort succeeded remarkably well."

Master Huginn lifted her eyes to the class. "But, now, with Master Lorenzo's encouragement, and your help, we shall make a start on restoring clairvoyance to its rightful place in the Academy."

## 2

A nise was lying in her bunk, reading. She had opened *The Archipelago of Dream* just before Maeve came into the dorm room. The book's first paragraph was something wholly fantastic about flying on the back of a dragon through an unfamiliar night sky over the sea of truth, looking at the shoals of dream below. Anise understood why people usually dismissed it as the writings of a crazy man.

"Anise," said Maeve, smiling, "you have a visitor."

Anise dropped the book onto her bunk and hopped to her feet. For a moment, she had the hopeful thought that someone had made the voyage across the country from Hero to see her. Then she dropped that thought as impossible and simply wondered who it could be.

This time, Maeve's smile was more private as she said, "A most handsome young man if I say so myself."

Anise gawked at her. *A handsome young man?* She wondered.

When she reached the common room, a man was there talking to Niall. Niall must have run into him while leaving to go to class. She hesitated, then ran across the room toward them.

It was Briac. He had gotten taller in the year since she had seen him last. He was dressed more respectably in refined, though still travel-worn, clothes. A lute was strapped to his back. Anise wasn't sure if it was the same lute, cleaned up, or if he had gotten a new one. There was a traveler's backpack on the ground near his feet.

His mustache had filled in. Anise thought that Uncle Sebastian wouldn't be able to say it was a little patch of dirt now. Briac's face was a little older but otherwise the same as she remembered.

She raced across the room toward him, then stopped abruptly, just a little short of where he was talking to Niall.

She was overcome with shyness.

Briac stopped talking to Niall, stepped forward, and pulled her into a strong bear-hug.

"Anise!" he called out. He lifted her off the floor and spun her around in a twirl. As her feet left the ground, she wondered when he had gotten so strong.

## 3

Briac and Anise sat at one of the tables in the common room. They got curious looks as people came and went from the way-house, but they were reluctantly left their privacy. Briac looked more like a man and less like a boy to Anise, but she was hesitant to say so. He had no such hesitancy.

"I can't believe what a young lady you've grown into," he said admiringly. "All confident and grown-up."

"Not always so confident," said Anise, looking down at the tabletop.

"Tell me about going to school here," said Briac. He looked around the room as he spoke.

"You don't want to hear about that," said Anise, "It's just classrooms and lecturing professors. Anyway, this is just the way-house, not the Academy." She nodded at him. "I'm much more interested to hear what you've been up to. Lots of adventures, I'm sure. Where've you been? What happened to the Carnival of Wonders? Where's Elaine? Did you come all the way here just to see me?"

Briac smiled. "Well," he said, "there are some stories there. And, from all your questions, I guess you do want to hear them."

"I believe I'll answer your last question first," he said, "As the answer to that one is sort of the answer to all of them." He looked a little rueful as he continued, "I'm afraid I didn't come here just to see you. I was excited when asked to come to the Academy because I hoped I would see you here, but I'm here on an errand."

"An errand?" said Anise. "For who?"

Briac looked proud. Anise had been missing the brash boy, Briac the Magnificent. She felt like she saw him again under the thin veneer of adulthood this new Briac was wearing.

"I'm a bard!" he announced. A smile grew across

his face until it stretched from ear to ear. "I sang at the Eisteddfod in Taliesin, and they picked me to join the order."

Anise was a little familiar with the order of bards. A bard was assigned to the castle of each noble or ruler in Liamec, and others wandered the roads of the land singing and telling stories. Still, she had never met anyone who had even been to their legendary city of Taliesin and had thought it just a story. The festival and musical competitions of the Eisteddfod were also fabled. The mayor of Hero had tried to call the summer market fair an Eisteddfod, but he had been laughed at.

The expression on Anise's face must have shown skepticism because the smile on Briac's broke like a wave crashing onto gray rocks on the shore.

"Well," he said quietly, "I guess I'm still just a student minstrel, but my master says I'm learning fast."

# 4

**M**aeve walked over to the table. Anise tried to hide her disappointment at the interruption. She felt like she wanted Briac all to herself, for the moment. Everyone else could talk to him later.

"Anise," said Maeve, smiling, "I hope you don't mind. I've offered that Briac can stay here for a while. Until he's done with his charge for the bardic council, at least."

Anise felt herself glowing. Then, she recognized the glow, and it turned into a flush on her cheeks.

Maeve laughed. "I guess you don't mind," she said. She turned to Briac. "And, Briac, I hope you will sing a song or two for us in the evenings. It'd be a fair way to pay for your lodgings with us."

Maeve winked at the two of them. "Well, then, I'll leave you to it." She turned and walked towards the backrooms.

There was an awkward silence. Then Briac said apologetically, "I hope I'm not intruding." He cleared his throat and continued, "The Bards and the Cunning Folk have an understanding. In fact, there's a bit of an overlap." He picked up his lute, sitting next to his backpack under the table.

"Let me show you something I'm learning how to do," he said. He started strumming the lute. The sound was soft and sweet, and she watched his fingers as he played. She wasn't sure if it was a new lute, but certainly, it had new strings and wasn't missing any, and it seemed that he had gotten better at playing since she last heard him. "Look," said Briac.

"Don't you mean, listen?" said Anise.

"I mean what I say, and I say what I mean," said Briac, while his fingers were moving smoothly on the lute strings.

Briac started singing quietly. It was a song Anise knew. The lay of the mother. It was rumored that it had been written by Liam I himself or, perhaps, by a bard at his castle. It was about his love for his mother. It always made Anise cry when she heard it. This time, though, her tears were stilled when she saw little people appearing on the tabletop. Briac's voice grew slightly strained. The tiny people, ghostly and translucent like they weren't solid, started acting out parts of the story. Anise watched in fascination as a miniature Liam cried when he said goodbye to his mother for the last time.

Briac stopped playing and rested the lute on the edge of the table. There was a bead of sweat on his forehead.

"It's still hard for me," he said. "My master says I'll get better at it."

# 5

A nise stared at Briac in astonishment. "It's an illusion. You're doing illusions. I felt it. I heard it in your voice. Can all bards create illusions? Is that why there's a connection between the bards and the cunning folk? What else can you do?"

Briac laughed. "Well, I'm supposed to be able to make suggestions that influence people's emotions, but I'm not very good at that one yet. It all comes out of the playing and singing."

Anise nodded. "You didn't tell me about the Carnival of Wonders and what happened with Elaine."

Briac gazed at Anise thoughtfully. "There will be time for that later," he said. "Right now, I have a favor to ask you."

Anise nodded again eagerly. "Of course," she said.

Briac hesitated like he was considering his words carefully. "Well, like I said, I am a student minstrel. There are levels and promotions within the bardic order."

Anise watched Briac's face as he spoke. His presence filled her with a feeling of calm.

"I've been given an assignment. If I complete my other training and do the assignment to my master's satisfaction, I will be promoted to the next rank." Briac pulled aside the fabric of his cloak and showed Anise a pin he wore under it. It was a tree branch cleverly crafted out of bronze. There were little bells attached to it. The bells tinkled as the fabric pulled away from the pin. They had been muffled by the cloak.

"My master asked me to travel here and do some research in the Academy library. He wants to know more about the history of a man who left the bardic order and became a master at the Academy. This was two hundred years ago. I'm not sure if they really need the information or it's just a test for me, but they want me to write a report on what happened to him here at the Academy. His books and journals are supposed to be in the library."

Anise studied Briac. "So, how can I help?" she asked.

Briac looked down at the tabletop. He flushed as he said, "I haven't told them I can't read. I've been hiding it."

Anise scrutinized Briac. She wondered how delicate she needed to be about this topic. "Is there a deadline for when you need to report back? How much time do you have to do your research?"

"Not really a deadline, no," said Briac. "I just report back when I'm done." He frowned. "Of course, I don't get promoted until I finish the report."

Anise smiled. A realization had been growing in her. This was how she could give something to Briac. "I'm going to teach you how to read!" she said excitedly. He needed more than just help on this one report; he would need this knowledge if he wanted to become a bard.

Briac's frown deepened. "I was hoping you could read the books to me," he said. "I'm not sure I can learn that."

"Of course you can," said Anise confidently. "Briac the Brilliant can learn anything!"

Soon it seemed like Briac had been in the way-house forever. Everyone liked him; everyone, except perhaps for one person. For some reason, Raphael, the cook's boy, didn't take to Briac, but no one really noticed.

Anise took Briac with her to the Academy library. Maeve had given them a pass. When they showed it to the guards at the Academy gate, they waved them on through without hesitation.

Briac stopped at the base of the stairs leading up to the library doors. "I'm not sure," he said hesitantly to Anise. "I'm not sure I should be here."

Anise snorted. "Nonsense," she said. "For one thing, Maeve said it was all right and gave you that pass. For another, if it's all right for me to be here, it's all right for you to be." She marched confidently up the stairs, and Briac hesitantly followed her.

At the wide double doors, Briac paused once more but followed Anise when she stepped assuredly through the shimmering glow across the doorway. She hardly noticed the glimmer anymore.

There was a thud, and Anise turned to see Briac on the ground on the other side of the doorway, clutching his nose.

"Ow," he said.

He rose to his feet, and he and Anise inspected the shimmering barrier across the doorway. It felt as insubstantial as ever to Anise, but to Briac, it felt solid, though transparent. The student working at the library front desk was watching them with amusement. He came over and asked for Briac's pass.

He took the pass back to the desk and did something to the pass or the barrier. After he was done, when holding the pass, Briac could enter and exit the doorway as easily as Anise.

They stepped together into the entrance hallway of the library. Briac took in the marble columns, the high vaulted ceilings, the corridors stretching off in all directions, and the students bustling to and fro. Anise marveled again at the majestic building. There was nothing like this in Hero.

Briac's journey to the land of the literate had begun.

# 6

J ord and Anise moved to the second row in Master
Callum's channeling class. They weren't brave enough
for the front row yet, but they wanted to be closer.
When the master was done taking roll. Anise raised her
hand.

The master looked up from his papers. He saw
her raised hand and said, "Anise?" Anise felt like she
was familiar enough with his damaged face by now to
recognize a smile.

"Master Callum?" said Anise. The master made eye
contact with her and nodded. Anise took a deep breath. She
began, "Where do we go when we dream? What determines
what spirits we meet in our dreams? Where are the spirits
when we're not dreaming about them? Is the dream world
we visit in our dreams the same as non-channelers visit in
theirs? Why do some people channel gods and others just
spirits? What's outside the circle of light?"

Master Callum's smile, insofar as it was recognizable
as such, broadened. "Well, Anise," he said. "First off, did you
have a nice summer?" He didn't wait for her to reply but
continued, "Obviously, you spent quite a bit of it thinking
about channeling."

Master Callum drew a breath himself. "Well," he said
again, "I guess I'll be throwing away the lesson plan I had
prepared for today."

He laughed. It was a pleasant sound. The contrast
between how his laugh sounded and his face looked struck
Anise again.

The master looked around at the class. "Some of
the questions Anise has just asked have probably occurred
to most of you," he said. "I haven't tried to answer them
before now because we don't know the answers to many
of them. Channeling as a discipline has evolved over time
through trial and error. The trials sometimes succeed, and

sometimes not, and the errors sometimes cause death or madness."

Master Callum lifted his head again and looked directly at Anise. "Gods, huh?" he said. "Ambitious, aren't we." He smiled again, "Most channeling will be affecting the spirits of people or animals. A powerful channeler will be able to speak to daemons. The most capable channelers of history were said to be able to get the attention of the gods. They don't usually listen to the likes of you or me.

"With regard to the realm of dream, most channelers believe that the place we travel to when channeling is not the same as where the non-channelers go. The dreamland that we can visit has continuity and reality. If you and I both channel the same Daemon, the description and characteristics of that Daemon will match.

"Some channelers even go as far as to speculate that the realm of dream is a real place, and it might be possible to physically travel there."

# 7

**B**riac glared at Anise indignantly. "Do you think I'm stupid?" he said. "Of course, I know that those are letters. He looked more carefully at the row of characters on the parchment in front of him. "That one's a 'z,' right?" he said.

Anise and Briac were in one of the reading alcoves in the library. Drippy was sitting in his enclosure, observing them carefully. He seemed to be hoping they wouldn't ask him to read something. A sour, moist resentment furrowed his scaly brow.

"Of course, I don't think you're stupid," said Anise. "I just need to find out what you already know so I know where to start."

"All right," said Briac. He accepted that explanation. He pointed at one of the letters on the parchment. He said eagerly, "That one's an 'x.'"

Drippy, showing a little more interest now, looked over at the parchment. The water imp shook his soggy head sadly.

Anise wasn't really sure how to go about this. She thought that maybe learning the names of the letters in the alphabet, how to recognize them, and what sounds they made would be a good beginning. She had asked if Briac would allow her to go to one of her masters for help, but he insisted that no one but her should know what they were doing in the library.

They had found a few books that might be good sources for Briac's research, but the plan for the day wasn't to do much reading. Anise wanted to start teaching Briac, and they mainly had brought the books for cover. Drippy had looked very relieved when they put the books in the reading rack but hadn't asked him to read them.

"Let's start," said Anise, "by learning to say the letters of the alphabet in order. There's a song I can teach you that helps you remember."

# 8

**M**aster Videmon had them all playing with fire. Anise and Jord had taken up the same station they had last year. It felt familiar and comfortable to be back in the elemental lab. Anise felt the forces of the Key surging around inside her head as they flowed through the stone walls from the volcano. What didn't feel familiar and comfortable was the assignment that the master had given them.

"A bolt of fire or a surge of flame from a fingertip is one of the more effective tricks that an elemental mage can employ," he said. "It impresses and can be a useful weapon in times of need." He paused before continuing, "Of course, more commonly, lighting a campfire or fireplace in a house is also a useful application."

He demonstrated, producing a quick, brilliant surge of fire from his fingertips. Anise thought she could feel the heat of his flame from her station at the back of the room.

Soon there were bright flashes of light from every side. Anise noticed some particularly bright flares from the station where Vin and Orlaith were in the front. Orlaith, who Anise had thought of as the girl in purple last year, was dressed in her familiar color. She had immediately reconnected with Vin when this new year started. She hardly glanced at Anise or Jord.

Jord had no trouble with the creation of flames. She wasn't exceedingly strong in her use of fire, as she was in the control of water. Still, she could produce an adequate blaze without much difficulty.

On the other hand, Anise was struggling, as she had all of the previous year. She could feel the heat and power of the molten rock in the volcano not very far away. She could sense what the others were doing; it felt like a compelling tickle in her mind. But, all that was happening at her fingers was a little warmth.

"Close your eyes, Anise," said Jord. "Close your eyes, and let the heat flow through you. Let the fire flow from the Key, through your mind, and out your fingertips."

Anise obediently closed her eyes. She waved her fingers around a little for effect. Nothing changed.

Anise felt a weight on her shoulder. She felt something wrap around her neck. Not tightly, not threateningly, but lovingly, like a caress. She opened her eyes and scanned her own shoulder. There was nothing to be seen except for a little spiraling smoke trace. She smelled an acrid smell.

There was a touch of warmth on Anise's temple. A voice that she recognized as Iggy whispered urgently, compellingly into her ear, "Burn!"

Massive flames started shooting out of Anise's fingertips. The heat was searing, demanding, though Anise could tell that she wasn't being burned.

The flames knocked everything on the lab counter off onto the floor. The wood of the counter below the stone top started smoldering. Jord jumped back. Everyone in the lab turned to look.

Master Videmon raced over to Anise and Jord's station. He waved his hands and gestured as if pulling something down from above. A wave of water came crashing down from the ceiling dousing Jord, Anise, and everything on their workstation with an icy rain.

"There's one in every class," the master commented dryly as the water extinguished the flames.

## 9

Briac inspected the book in Anise's hand. "That's a kid's book." He frowned. "I may not know how to read, but I'm not a kid." Briac glanced suspiciously over at Drippy to ensure he wasn't smiling.

Anise was a little frustrated. She picked up one of the books they had brought to the reading alcove for cover. She opened it to a random page. "Well, if you're ready to read the other books, what's that word?" she asked, pointing at the page.

"Well," said Briac, "That's a 't.'" He opened his lips a little. "Tuh…"

"No," said Anise, "that's the sound that a 't' makes by itself. When it's followed by an 'h,' it sounds more like thuh." She continued, "Try reading the whole word."

Briac checked where her finger was pointing in the book. "It's too long. I can't," he said.

"It's the word thistledown," said Anise.

She picked up the beginning reader book that she had been showing Briac. "That's why we are using this book. It's not that you're a kid. It's just that it has simpler words and a less complicated structure." She smiled at Briac. "When you learned to play the lute, you didn't start with the most complicated songs? Did you?"

# 10

Master Devona was addressing the illusion class. Anise marveled again at how much she resembled the blonde poppet her mother had made for her when she was a child. Then she blinked. Was Master Devona letting a bit of gray show at her temples? It couldn't be her glamour slipping. She was too skilled at illusion for that. Perhaps she was trying to show her age a little to get more respect from the students.

"The trick to defeating an illusion," the master said, "is disbelief."

Cian shifted a little in her seat next to Anise.

Master Devona continued, "If you believe an illusion is real, it will influence your behavior. It can safely be ignored if you don't believe it or disbelieve it. As long as you are correct."

Anise looked around the classroom. Vin's friend Orlaith was sitting by herself at a desk in the front row. She was dressed in her usual purple. Anise wondered why Orlaith didn't like her. She didn't feel like she had done anything to make the other girl feel that way. Perhaps it was a carryover from Vin's dismissal of her sister and friends.

"The debate is strong among illusionists as to whether disbelief is a real thing or not," continued Master Devona. "Do we have a sense as to the reality of an illusion? Or, is it just a matter of convincing oneself that the thing you are perceiving isn't real."

The master frowned and looked thoughtful. "I believe, personally, that I am sensing something when I look at an illusion and believe that it is an illusion and not a real thing. Still, an argument could certainly be made that what I am sensing is simply my confidence that the perceived thing is not real.

The master laughed. The gleeful tinkling sound

made Anise smile. "That said, if you disbelieve the wolf charging at you in a magical duel and ignore it to continue with your own castings, you had better be right. If it turns out that your opponent has a pet wolf or is a channeler who had a dream the night before that allowed them to control a wolf, you could be in serious trouble."

# 11

All the residents of the way-house were gathered in the common room. All the residents except one. Raphael was nowhere to be found. They were there to hear Briac sing a song. There was an early fall chill in the air, so a fire roared in the fireplace. The fire and lantern light in the room cast shadows over the wooden walls, the rough tables, and Briac, seated near the fire, lute on his lap.

"This one's an oldie," said the young bard. "It's called the Ill-formed Knight and the Wyvern."

His fingers moved smoothly over the strings. Gentle notes filled the air.

Leander stood before the beast,
The object of his quest.
The creature dark and serpentine,
slithered forth from its nest.

His armor shone with golden light,
His heart replete with strength,
The Ill-formed knight, the hero, born,
faced down the serpent's length.

Anise noticed tiny figures forming on the floor near the fire. She was expecting it, but she heard a gasp from one of the new students. A little knight clad in golden armor stepped forward toward the hearth. A dark scaly creature crawled from the fire, seeming to come out of it. Anise remembered the sense of intelligence she had gotten from Flambé, the dragon she had seen at the Carnival of Wonders. This creature seemed more animal-like. It felt like a snake, though it had a dragon-like head, wings, and scaled legs ending in razor claws.

The tiny knight straightened as the beast emerged from the flames. Anise felt her heart go out to the brave champion. She had always been fond of the legends of the Ill-formed Knight. Her father had told her the stories in the evenings when she was little.

A viper's hiss, a burning glare,
The wyvern seethed its wrath.
His secret doubt behind him then,
Leander saw his path.

The little golden knight braced itself on the wooden floor of the way-house.

His sword held firm, Leander's heart
was beating like a drum,
the creature leapt, its claws outstretched,
he thought his time had come.

The sword struck true, the golden suit
was drenched in serpent gore,
The cruel beast, its heart pricked through,
would plague the land no more.

Once more, the knight, Ill-formed though he was,
had managed to prevail,
The golden knight, though drenched with doubt,
was never going to fail.

# 12

M aster Ernst wasn't any more interesting than he had been last year. But, today's alchemy class might be. They were in the lab, getting ready to work on a potion that was supposed to be able to turn someone into a frog. Jord was very excited. This was what she had been hoping to get out of Alchemy class all along.

"Why do you want to be able to turn someone into a frog?" asked Anise. She scrutinized her friend curiously. Perhaps she was about to hear something from an unexpected dark side of Jord.

"Well," said Jord, "I've always liked frogs. Maybe, if the potion is safe and temporary, I could try it on myself."

Master Ernst stressed the importance of the temporary nature of the potion. "When you make a potion," he said, "the ingredients determine the duration of the effects." He grunted a little as he looked up as if the process of raising his gray head to meet the students' eyes was an effort. "The ingredients and your inherent ability. Someone with a knack and instinct for alchemy will produce a potion with a longer-lasting and more robust effect.

"I don't want to be spending as much time as I have had to in previous classes cleaning up your mistakes."

The croaking from unhappy students and the muttered curses from the master were still ongoing when Anise got ready to leave for her next class. She left Jord at the station, cleaning mucus out of her hair. Anise thought she might not be so eager to test a potion next time.

She saw Orlaith a little ahead as she walked out the classroom door. Orlaith's purple smock was elegantly tailored and belted at the waist. Anise hurried a bit to catch up with her. It was a rare opportunity to talk to Orlaith without Vin around. Perhaps Vin had already left.

"Orlaith," began Anise. She was a little out of breath. The taller girl turned to look at her. She looked very regal in her purple. "Why don't you like me?" Anise continued.

Orlaith's refined face looked surprised. The expression was like what you might see on a farmer if one of his pigs started speaking to him.

"Anise," she said calmly, "You're nobody. Nothing. I am Orlaith Fisher, of the North-gate Fishers."

"Fisher," said Anise excitedly, "My aunt's name was Fisher!"

"No," said Orlaith dismissively, and she turned and walked out of the lab.

## 13

B riac put the book down with a sigh. Anise smiled at him and said, "That's amazing! You just finished that whole book!" Even Drippy looked proud. He flapped his scaly wings in his enclosure. Anise reached up to wipe a drop of Drippy slime off her cheek.

"It's just a kid's book," said Briac.

"Well," said Anise, "every journey begins with a first step, and every book reading begins with the first page."

The rest of the school year flew by for Anise. She enjoyed her lessons with Briac but realized that she was teaching him the skill he would need to leave. Once he could puzzle through the books he needed to finish his assignment, he would head back to his bardic master to continue his training.

As finals started creeping up on her, she was torn. Sebastian had promised that he would make the journey to escort her back to Hero for the summer this year. Even if it wasn't practical, she would be able to spend some amount of time at home. Anise was excited to see her Aunts, Rose and Isabel.

On the other hand, that would mean leaving while Briac was still laboring his way through his task. She wanted to be able to help him complete the job.

Briac was working on reading the journals and other books that referenced his subject. Anise was still standing by, ready to help when needed. Still, he was getting better and better at pushing through the material. The key, he had learned, was to be patient when he was having difficulty with a word and stop and work on it until he was ready to go on.

A picture was forming of who the man Briac was studying had been. His name was Drun Coeloc, and as Briac had told Anise, he had left the bardic order to become a master at the Academy. Interestingly enough, he was listed on the Academy rolls as a master of Musicology. A subject of which he was the first and only master that Anise and Briac could find in the Academy's history.

The source material in the library that referenced him was intermittent and spotty. His personal journals were there, though some pages had been removed.

His journals referenced his reasons for coming to the Academy. However, the missing pages were frequent throughout this section of the book. He felt that there was some clear danger to the land of Liamec, or perhaps to the whole world, though he used the word creation. From reading what was left of the journals, one got the impression that he felt he was the only one who could save the world from this danger. He thought his coming to the Academy would be part of that help.

That was when the letter from Uncle Sebastian came.

# UNDER THE EARTH

# 1

T he first thing that Anise understood from the letter was that her uncle wasn't coming to take her home. Her initial reaction was a feeling of disappointment. *How could he? He'd promised.* Then she read further and understood why he wasn't coming.

Twilight was missing. Aunt Isabel and Uncle Sebastian had taken him on a luncheon in a field by a forest. It wasn't clear from the letter if they had fallen asleep or if he had just snuck off while they were momentarily unaware. But, either way, the baby had wandered off into the woods.

This happened a week ago. The rest of the searchers had given up, but Sebastian wasn't going to. He sounded like he would be out there every day throughout the summer, searching.

Uncle Sebastian asked Anise to understand why he wouldn't be able to meet her. He hoped there might be something the masters at the Academy could do, some magic they might be able to apply, to help find their baby.

Anise was in tears before she finished the letter. She thought about her willful, difficult charge and couldn't imagine how lonely and terrified he must feel.

After her alchemy final, Anise approached Master Ernst. "I'm sorry for your loss," he said gruffly in his scratchy voice. "I'm afraid I'm not much of a hand at finding."

"Finding?" asked Anise.

"It falls under clairvoyance," said the master, "I took a class in it long ago. I never got the hang of it."

Master Videmon wasn't much help either. "Elemental magic is pretty much here and now," he said.

"You need something a little more mystical. It sounds more like clairvoyance to me, as well." He frowned sympathetically, "It's too bad it happened now. We might have relearned how to do it in a few years."

Master Huginn agreed. "The science of clairvoyance and the specific application of finding would be the right thing to apply to this question. Unfortunately, as you know, they're lost." She met Anise's eyes sorrowfully, "I'm afraid I have no idea how to help you."

# 2

Anise woke from a deep sleep in her dorm room. She had the sad thought that this room was starting to feel more familiar than her bedroom in Aunt Rose's house in Hero. Then she noticed that the other bunks were missing and that she was in the circle of light of a channeling dream.

She sat up and looked around the room. The walls blocked the edges of the circle, and the light flickered like candlelight. Now though, she knew that if the walls hadn't been there, there would still have been a barrier of darkness at her dream's boundary.

Anise felt the distant presence of the Watcher, but something was blocking his attention. She knew that he couldn't tell what was happening in her dream.

Helios stood in the center of the room. His crown, and his youthful, proud face beneath it, shone with a warm, bright light.

"Anise," he said. "You're sad. How can I help?"

"Lord Helios," said Anise. She paused, trying not to cry. The sympathy he was showing her made it harder, not easier.

"It's my ..." She hesitated, "... brother, Twilight."

Lord Helios stood calmly, gazing at her, waiting for her to continue.

"He's missing."

Helios blinked. Part of the light shining from him that flooded the room was coming from his eyes. When he blinked, the lighting in the room changed a little.

"Seeing as you see everything under the sun," Anise continued. "I was hoping you could look for him."

"Of course," said the god quietly. He closed his eyes again. His handsome shut-eyed face looked still, then thoughtful, then he reopened his eyes.

"I'm sorry, Anise," he said, "I wish I had better news

for you." He frowned. "As you said, as you know, I see everything under the sun, everything under the light of day."

The god stepped forward and put his hand on Anise's shoulder. The featherweight touch felt warm, like the light of a spring day.

"He hasn't been under the light of day since he was lost. He hasn't been under the sun since then. Since he isn't under the sun, he must be under the earth."

# 3

Since hearing the sad news that Twilight was gone, Anise had had difficulty feeling anything. Seeing as Sebastian wasn't coming to take her home, she could help Briac complete his project. She felt like she should be happy about this. The emotion wouldn't come.

Niall was leaving after completing his final year at the Academy. Anise had never formed the connection with him that she had wanted. It didn't matter. She felt like the presence of his handsome face had been like a painting on the wall. Something she had been able to admire from a distance.

Jord tried to cheer her up before she and her sister left for the summer. Anise appreciated the effort, but the reality left her cold.

Anise couldn't bring herself to write Uncle Sebastian what Helios had said. She just wrote to him that the magic of the Academy had been unable to locate Twilight.

It wasn't until the Midsummer festival, the Litha, came again to the way-house that Anise started to recover. She hid at the library with Briac as Maeve and Cian's relatives again prepared the event. When they came back to the way-house, Maeve served them chouchen.

They danced with the revelers, watched the battle between the Holly King and the Oak King, and had perhaps one drink more than they should have.

Later, when Briac was escorting Anise back to her dorm room down the wooden corridor, he turned and kissed her gently on the lips.

Raphael's head of tousled red hair disappeared back into the doorway just as Briac turned toward it.

"Goodnight, Anise," said Briac quietly as he crossed the hall to the boy's dorm.

As the students were all off for the summer, Anise and Briac had the library almost to themselves. They spent more time than perhaps they should have in their favorite reading alcove with Drippy the water imp.

Anise felt Drippy had started to recognize them, though he never said a word unless they asked him to read. When they came into his alcove, his moist leathery wings would flap in what she thought of as a friendly manner.

Anise didn't mention anything about the summer solstice kiss to Briac, though she did spend quite a bit of time thinking about it. However, in a momentary break from poring over the journals of Drun Coeloc, she did ask him about his time with the Carnival of Wonders and how it had ended.

"Oh," said Briac, "that's not much of a story. Did I ever tell you what happened with Flambé, the Carnival's dragon?"

"No," said Anise hesitantly.

"She kept getting bigger," said Briac cheerfully. "Eventually, the folk of the Carnival weren't sure what to do with her." He looked thoughtful. "She might have really been a dragon. In the end, she was growing lumps between her shoulder blades that could have been the starts of wings."

"What did they do?"

"She took it out of their hands. One morning Elaine came out to Flambé's cage, and she was gone. She'd broken the bars like they were twigs. She must have been growing stronger even faster than she was growing bigger."

"But you and Elaine?" insisted Anise.

"Like I said, not very interesting. I think Elaine just got tired of me. We were in Taliesin for the Eisteddfod, so it worked out well for me."

Anise regarded Briac a little skeptically. She was sure there was more to the story that he wasn't telling her. She thought about pressing the issue, but it was clear that he didn't want to talk about it. Reluctantly, she dropped the question.

## 4

Briac finished his report on the mysterious Drun Coeloc. There were gaps in their understanding of what had happened and his motives, but the basics were there. Anise helped him write the final version. His reading had gotten passable, and he was working on writing, but his handwriting was not yet a thing of beauty.

Two hundred years ago, Drun had thought that something catastrophic was happening at the Academy. And that he was the only one who could solve the problem. He had acquired this idea while engaged as a bard in Taliesin. Briac was initially confused about this. "There's not really a connection between things at Taliesin and the Academy. At least there isn't now," he said.

Drun had, apparently with the bardic council's blessing, traveled to the Academy and petitioned for a master's position. Somehow he had been successful at this. He had been the only professor of musicology the Academy had ever had.

There were missing pages and inked-out paragraphs in the records from before Drun became a master, but they increased after. It was hard to form a picture of his career after he had become a master. There was an impression that he had been respected and listened to but no clear indication of why.

One thing that Anise found strange was frequent references to something called dragonfell. It seemed Drun had some process for turning this material into cloth and made his clothes out of it. It seemed odd how much this was emphasized in his journals, so Anise did some research. In an old herbology reference work, she found that dragonfell was a word for thistledown.

The timing of when Drun came to the Academy struck Anise as curious. He had arrived at the Academy not long before the time Master Huginn had been researching for Clairvoyance class. Anise kept an early draft of Briac's report to show to her when the school year started.

Once Briac finished his report, nothing was keeping him in Ashton. When they said goodbye, Anise and Briac pretended that they would see each other soon. They seemed to be pretending further, or perhaps it was part of the same pretense, that parting wasn't a serious thing.

However, as Briac stepped out the door of the way-house, he kissed Anise lightly on the lips. His lips felt warm. Then he turned and headed down the street, his lute and his travel backpack on his back.

Anise stood in the doorway, watching him walk away. Maeve stepped up behind her and put her hand on Anise's back. When Briac went out of view, Anise turned to Maeve, buried her head in the older woman's shoulder from above, and started crying.

# 5

Anise and Jord were third-years. They knew the superiority of the upperclassman. They looked around the green the first day they walked to classes and marveled at how young the first-years looked. Jord felt wise. Anise felt old.

"They look like little kids," said Jord. "Look, they don't even know where their classes are."

"We don't know where all of ours are either," said Anise. Her class list looked the same as last year, except for an optional class that she had added at Maeve's suggestion. It was a training class for students to learn to be able to physically defend themselves. Jord had signed up with her.

"You mean the fighting class?" said Jord. "I don't know why Maeve made us take that. We're going to be mages, not brawlers. We don't need that stuff."

"It might be useful," said Anise.

At dinner that evening, Anise looked around at her fellow way-house residents. She, Cian, Vin, and Jord, were now the elders. Except for Maeve, of course. The new students were chattering excitedly among themselves. Anise sighed to herself; she felt the weight of her years.

Raphael stepped up next to her and put a plate down in front of her. Her eyes caught on his arm in its white cotton cook's tunic. Had he been putting on a little muscle?

She looked back at him and met his eye. He'd been getting taller as well. He'd been in the way-house with her all summer, but she hadn't noticed. His unruly mop of red hair was a little long. As he straightened up from putting the plate down, she resisted the urge to reach out and either muss it up further or smooth it flatter.

"How are you doing, Raffy?" she asked.

Raphael glanced sideways at her, smiled shyly, and nodded his head. Then he moved on to put a plate in front of Jord.

# 6

A nise stood at the end of a line of girls. Some were giggling, though Anise didn't see how they could be. She was dressed in a cotton blouse and a skirt that was the lightest she had in her small collection of clothes. Jord was down at the other end of the line. As they had come into the room, talking, the woman now standing in front of them had separated them. She made Jord move across the room to the other side. She had done the same with other girls who had come in together.

It was a woman, though Anise hadn't been sure at first. She was wearing strange clothes. Red from head to toe. She wore a red cloth top, loosely belted at the waist by a strip of fabric, and red cotton leggings. Anise had rarely seen a woman out in public in leggings. Though, when she had visited the Carnival of Wonders, some people were dressed very unusually.

But it wasn't just the clothes that had made Anise unsure if she was a woman. Her head was shaved, and Anise had also rarely seen a woman without long hair. At first, she had confused Anise, but her face was beautiful and a little exotic. Her features were delicate, and she had charming brown eyes and long lashes. The shaved head made the delicacy of her features stand out.

She was a little loud, however. Barking out orders, she strode down the line of girls, poking at dresses, commenting on shoes, and, in general, making people uncomfortable.

The room was high-ceilinged, and the floor was smooth and polished. It didn't look polished with age; it had been buffed and waxed until it shone.

The woman stopped examining people and stepped to the front, turning to face the line of girls.

"I am not a master at this Academy," she announced. Proudly, it seemed. "I am your trainer, instructor in the physical arts, worst enemy, and best friend." She looked over the line of girls. "You will call me teacher or Sifu."

The teacher pointed to a pile of folded red clothes. "Next time, we will dress more appropriately. For now, however, I will make you sweat in what you are wearing."

# 7

**M**aster Huginn was as interested as Anise had thought she would be in Briac's report. "We didn't find this information because it doesn't mention clairvoyance," she said. "But what if all those references were in the missing pages and inked-out areas? The timing's very interesting."

"I have a theory," said Anise.

The master glanced up from the report and looked expectantly at her.

"I think Master Coeloc was the one who started the Academy down the path of eliminating clairvoyance. He brought them some news or information that made them feel like they needed to do it. The timing's just right. There was enough time between when he arrived and when they burned the books for them to have confirmed something he told them."

Anise started to feel powerful. She had confidence that she could decide whether or not she would have a channeling dream. Although she got into the habit of suppressing channeling dreams to avoid the gaze of the Watcher. She had the knowledge to produce illusions that could deceive and confuse, though she had worries about whether or not this was a form of lying.

In alchemy class, the potions they were producing were more effective and powerful than ever before. Though, they were also harder to concoct. Master Ernst encouraged them to use their elemental skills to help brew potions. Fire to heat. Air and wind to desiccate, and so forth. "It's the only thing elemental magic is good for," he said.

Anise wasn't so sure. Her burgeoning elemental skills were a big part of what made her feel powerful. Now that Iggy had helped her free herself from her fire blockage, the ability to shoot forth a bolt of flame from her fingertip was exciting. Not to mention controlling the flow of water, earth, or wind. Being able to manipulate the elements made her feel like she could influence the world around her.

That's when the next letter from home arrived.

# UNDER THE SUN

# 1

T he letter was written by Uncle Sebastian. He told Anise that he had some good news to share. Her Aunt Isabel had given birth to a baby girl. Her name was Sunshine, but they were calling her Sunny for short.

Uncle Sebastian went on to say that Sunshine would never replace Twilight. Not in the world or in their hearts. Still, he was pleased to see a smile on Isabel's face again.

Anise did a quick calculation and figured out that Isabel must have been pregnant on the outing where Twilight was lost.

With the letter came a small wooden box. It was beautifully inlaid with different woods, and Anise was sure that Isabel's mother, Mrs. Fisher, had made it. She took a moment to open it and remove a small sealed vial before reading on.

"The vial in the box we sent you along with this letter is a gift from Lilith. She suggests you drink it after you finish reading."

Anise inspected the vial and held it up to the afternoon sunlight streaming through the window. The liquid inside was clear and looked slightly thicker than water when she tilted the vial.

Sebastian went on to provide some more news. Aunt Rose, he wrote, had been courting or perhaps was being courted. Anise stopped reading again. She took a moment to wrap her head around this concept.

"Mr. Shepherd, the miller, and Rose have been seen about town together," the letter continued. "At first, I was surprised, but Rose says he has an inner sweetness that he hides behind a gruff exterior."

The letter ended with expressions of how much everyone was missing her. Isabel and Rose sent their love. Anise put down the paper.

She picked up the vial and pulled out the cork; it

came off with a light "pop." The liquid inside smelled like nutmeg. She drank it down.

Anise's vision grew cloudy. She blinked her eyes, trying to see. Then she could again. What she saw was the smiling image of a young baby. The baby's face was close: as if she was holding it in her arms. Bright blue eyes, traces of thin blond hair, and a clear light complexion surrounded that sunny smile. She heard a cooing sound, the baby reached up a tiny hand, and Anise felt a warm grip on her thumb. She gazed into those bright blue eyes for a moment. Then she blinked again, her vision cleared, and the baby was gone.

# 2

Anise awoke in a sun-dappled meadow in a clearing in the woods. The clearing reminded her of places she had explored in the forests outside the little town of Hero. In fact, she supposed, in some ways, it *was* a clearing in the woods outside of her hometown.

She rose from the soft bed of grass she had been lying on and looked around, satisfied at her success. Master Callum had instructed the channeling class with more details about how the circle of light worked.

"I have already warned you never to leave your circle," he had said, "but that doesn't mean you can't have some control over it. The instinct to not even approach the edge is strong in every channeler I have ever worked with, but it is, after all, still a dream. By default, your circle of light, your safe haven in the dreaming realm, resembles where you went to sleep, but it doesn't have to. You can control how your circle appears. It's related to dream-walking. When I want to dream-walk, I manipulate my circle of light to be yours, which brings me to you."

Anise looked across the sun and shadow dappled grass at an approaching figure. It was Helios. For the first time, the brightness of his crown didn't outshine everything. The light streaming down from above the trees lining the edges of her circle was as bright.

As usual, the presence of Helios made her feel safe from the attention of the Watcher.

"Anise," said Helios, "what do you need?"

"Lord Helios," said Anise, "I have a new ..." She hesitated. "... sister."

"I know," said the sun god with a smile. His smile brightened the sunlight in the clearing. "Her name pleases me."

"I want to give her something. I want to protect her, to love her. I was hoping you could help me with a gift for her worthy of her name." Anise glanced down at the grass. "I know that I have a limit on the number of times I can beg your favor, but this is important to me."

"Anise," said the sun god, "you have just begun your account with me." He gazed at her and continued. "Look to the sun for a gift for your sister."

# 3

A nise was leaving the way-house the following morning when something made her stop. She was supposed to be meeting Jord at Alchemy class, and she was running a little late. Still, something about how the morning sunlight shone through the front windows drew her attention.

The sunlight streaming through the windows at an angle onto the wooden floor looked solid. It seemed almost like it might be firm enough to touch.

Anise stepped over nearer the window. Dust motes floated in the golden light that pressed its way across the floor. She looked down at the floorboards. One knot in one of the boards shone with reflected light like it was made of something other than wood.

Anise reached down and felt the surface of the knot. It was raised a little above the rest of the floorboard wood. She touched the edge, lifted, and picked up a circular object that shone as she raised it.

It was a golden medallion. Shaped like a coin, one side had a wood grain pattern, as if from the knot in the floorboard, and the other showed the face of Helios in profile. A smooth link-less golden chain was attached to one edge.

It was beautiful. Small enough that it might be worn by a young child, the patterned surface glinted in the light. As Anise moved her hands, the golden chain flowed like water through her fingers.

Anise felt the attention of the sun god and knew what the medallion would do and how it would help the wearer.

The medallion would draw just enough of the sun god's attention to the wearer that his sight of everything that happened under the sun would warn them of danger. Any threat that was under the light of day would sound an alarm.

Anise felt that it was a very fitting gift for her new relative.

# 4

Anise looked down the line of red-clad girls. *Not girls*, she thought. *We're all away from home studying to be mages. I should be thinking of us as women.* She felt a surge of pride gazing at the group of women.

"Sifu," said Anise, raising her hand carefully. "When are you going to teach us how to use weapons?"

The teacher turned to Anise, her delicate features flashing briefly through a smile before firming up into a look that was supposed to be stern. She stood in front of the line of women.

"In this world, and especially as women in this world, we are not always armed. You will, on occasion, have to face someone with bad intent who has a weapon when you don't."

She softened her tone. "That said, I will be teaching you the use of some common weapons once I feel like you all have a basic idea of how to respond to an attack. This class aims to teach you to be able to defend yourselves against attack, not to attack others."

Jord was lined up next to Anise. Their teacher had softened her stance on girls who knew each other standing near one another once they had learned to respect her rules.

The two of them paired up as often as they could on the bout mat, though that was a little frowned upon.

"You need to learn to face different opponents. It will most likely be against someone unfamiliar that you find these skills called upon in the real world. It's best to have a different opponent for each match."

For the first several classes, Sifu had been asked why they should learn to fight physically when they could just use magic to defend themselves.

"As you have all learned from your classes, your

masters, and your own experiences, casting illusions and focusing elemental forces drain stamina. There may come a time when you have no more energy for magic, and yet you are still in a position where you need to defend yourself." She blinked her long lashes. "Also, those who are stronger as alchemists and channelers have skills that don't lend themselves directly to fights."

# 5

That spring, Anise's feeling of increasing power grew. But, along with it came the idea that the abilities she was acquiring could be used for everyday things as well. When she was asked to light the fireplace in the common room on a chilly evening, she didn't think to try and reach for the tinderbox. Instead, she made contact with the element of fire. A blazing flame shooting from the tip of her finger made the old box feel obsolete.

When Cookie complained about an invasion of mice in the kitchen, Anise dreamt her way into their furry little minds and cleared the problem that way. She convinced the little mouse clan's leader that life would be better somewhere else, and the rest followed.

Anise's feeling of power and control grew in all of her classes but one. In Master Huginn's clairvoyance class, the master and students started approaching an understanding of clairvoyance techniques. However, none of them became very proficient at the practice.

The clairvoyants of old had methods of trancing themselves into states where their perception left their bodies. Meditation and the judicious use of certain herbs allowed them to sit in a room, take a spiritual journey to another plane, and return with insights and visions.

Anise couldn't help but detect a similarity to the journey into the world of dreams that channelers took. One difference, however, was that the clairvoyants described their trips as journeys along paths. They talked about these routes as clear, well-marked, and well-trodden. Like channelers with their circle of light, the clairvoyants warned against leaving the marked paths until you reached the end.

The path of life, the path of family, and of death. There were many paths, each with its own method of trancing, its own herbs, and incense. And, importantly, its own truths to be learned.

But as spring started to turn into summer, Anise's thoughts weren't on either her growing powers or the upcoming exams. Sebastian had promised to come to get her and escort her home for the break. She would get to see Aunt Rose, Aunt Isabel, her friend Mary, and she would get to meet Sunshine for real.

# 6

Anise packed. She didn't own much and couldn't carry much with her anyway. But there were things she wanted to take and things she felt she had to. Helios's amulet: her gift for Sunshine, was placed in a position of honor and safety at the bottom of her pack.

She had little gifts as well for Rose and Isabel. She didn't have any money. It had been a source of embarrassment when Vin and her friend Orlaith went on their frequent shopping expeditions to Ashton's market. She had never felt comfortable joining them. Though they knew that she didn't have any money, showing it by being on a shopping trip without buying anything was more than she was comfortable with. Jord went with them sometimes.

She had done odd jobs for Maeve, sometimes for small change. That's how she had saved up enough to buy her presents.

It didn't matter. Uncle Sebastian was coming; she was going home. Her heart started beating faster when she thought about seeing Aunt Rose again for the first time in almost three years.

Anise thought that she would miss Maeve and Cian this summer, and maybe Cookie and Rafael, but that thought paled next to the excitement she felt.

Finals and the departures of the other students blew past. Everything faded into a blur that ended the afternoon when Maeve called her to the front door. A dusty Sebastian stood there, holding the lead of an even dustier Betsy.

Anise had prepared by loading a couple of carrots into her belt. Still, when the reality of standing in front of her uncle hit, she was suddenly shy. He looked older. He looked older, a little tired, and a little sad. Though, his face lit up when he saw her.

Betsy called out, "Heee Awwww," her familiar mule

bray, and started pushing at Anise's smock near the carrots in her belt. Sebastian dropped the lead, stepped forward, and enfolded Anise in his strong arms.

# 7

The journey to Hero flew by. Anise remembered the trip out to Ashton three years ago as an odyssey. A hazardous, dangerous trek. It was almost disappointing how smoothly the return trip went. It took time, of course. She had plenty of time to reconnect with her uncle and her favorite mule.

Sebastian was very interested in what she had learned at the Academy. She described channeling class, alchemy, what they had learned about clairvoyance, and showed him a few simple illusions. Sebastian was most impressed, however, with her elemental mastery of fire. He assigned her the task of lighting the campfires in the evenings. Every time he watched a little burst of flame shoot out of her fingertip, he would say, "Now, *that's* useful."

Betsy was initially pleased to see Anise as well. Though, once she ran out of fresh carrots, their relationship returned to pretty much what it was before. Anise sized up both Sebastian and Betsy and felt that it might have been the man that had aged more in the last years.

One evening as they sat around the campfire, Sebastian asked Anise a question that it seemed had been on his mind.

"Why'd I have to come to get you, Anise?" he asked.

Anise felt sad. "Because I wanted to come home, and I thought you wanted me home," she said.

"No," said Sebastian, with a shake of his head, "that's not what I meant. Of course, we want you home." He put his hand on top of hers. "No, what I meant was, why didn't you fly home, ride home on a dragon, or vanish in one place and reappear in another?"

Anise was relieved at his explanation. "Well," she said, "no one knows how to fly, though there are air elementalists who have been working on it." She shook her own head. "I'm not sure what discipline would lead to the disappearing thing, and no one's seen a dragon for two hundred years."

Anise stopped short. Suddenly a thought occurred to her. Her own words echoed in her mind. *Two hundred years. That couldn't be a coincidence.*

Sebastian didn't notice her momentary distraction. "Well," he said, "we'll just have to learn how to ride horses."

# 8

After they set up their camp the night before they were due to arrive in Hero, Sebastian pulled a little vial out of his pocket. There were two liquids in the vial, one colored blue and one colored yellow, separated by a thin barrier. The vial was cleverly constructed. There was a catch on the side that, if loosened, would allow the fluids to mix.

"What's that?" asked Anise.

"It's a potion that Lilith gave me," said Sebastian. "Although, she said it wasn't really a potion cause a potion is usually something you drink." He released the catch on the side and shook the little vial. The yellow and blue fluids mixed together, making a clear fluid with an emerald green color. Betsy observed the transformation carefully, wondering if the green liquid might not be a new kind of grass.

"She said that if I do this, a little bottle of similar stuff on one of her shelves will turn the same color," said Sebastian. "She will be watching it and should know that we're almost home. That way, they can meet us." He shook his head. "I made the mistake of asking her how it worked. When she said something about spooky action at a distance, I stopped listening."

Anise thought that she'd be able to talk about some trade secrets with Lilith. It seemed that maybe the cunning folk did have some knowledge that the mages of the academy didn't share.

People were waiting to meet them when they got to the town gates. Anise felt like the whole town was there. She looked around to see who had come. Her vision was obscured by a vast sweep of pink linen.

"Anise," cried Aunt Rose as she hugged her niece so tightly that Anise had trouble breathing. "You're home."

When her breathing resumed, Anise found herself held out at arm's length by her aunt. With a shock, she noticed that they were the same height.

"Let me look at you," said Rose. Teardrops were hiding in the corners of her eyes, and her voice was a little shaky. "My, how you've grown." Anise took in her aunt as her aunt scrutinized her. She wondered how someone could change so much in such a short time and yet still be exactly the same.

A man stood behind Rose, seeming to Anise like he wanted to have his hand on her aunt's shoulder. It was the miller, Mr. Shepherd. Anise wondered why he looked different to her. Then she realized that he was smiling.

The rest of Anise's welcome went by in a blur. Of course, they hadn't been able to get through the event without a speech from the mayor. He had had banners made up. He must have asked someone how to spell her name because they read simply and surprisingly tastefully, "Welcome home, Anise!"

"Our brave town of Hero," said the mayor, "having already acquired a champion for the ages." He swept his hand in front of Sebastian. "Now boasts an Academy-trained mage among its ranks as well."

Even more than when she left to go to the Academy, Anise wondered who he thought he was talking to. Half the town was there, but half the town was still less than half the crowd at one of the Carnival of Wonder's performances.

Of course, Isabel, Lilith, Mary, and Isabel's mother, Mrs. Fisher, were there. Still, Anise felt a unique rush of excitement when she met Sunshine for the first time. Isabel was holding her in her arms. The little baby tugged at Anise's attention with her wispy blond hair and bright blue eyes.

"Wait a minute, Aunt Isabel," said Anise. She opened her backpack and pulled out the amulet. It had been moved to the top to be easy to find. The metal glinted in the sunlight as she put the chain carefully over the baby's neck. Sunny cooed and reached out a hand toward the shiny thing as it was lowered toward her. "May it always keep you safe," Anise whispered.

Aunt Rose called for Anise's attention once more. She stood beside Mr. Shepherd, with his hand on her shoulder this time.

"Anise," she said, "we have something to tell you."

# 9

Sebastian told Anise a little about how Rose and Mr. Shepherd had gotten together. It had started with a feud over who would be making the baked goods for the little town of Hero. Mr. Shepherd had been baking bread with the flour from his mill until Rose came to town. It started with the feud and ended with Rose's rhubarb pie. Once Rose got Mr. Shepherd hooked on her rhubarb pie, the battle was as good as won.

The wedding was a bright, sunny, happy affair. Mr. Shepherd and his daughter Mary had become Rose's assistants at the bakery instead of the competition, so the cakes, pastries, and other foodstuffs were plentiful and delicious.

Anise got to escort her aunt down the aisle. It was a little unconventional, but both Anise and Rose wanted it that way. So, Mr. Shepherd, or Byram as he now insisted Anise call him, didn't dream of fighting it.

As soon as she noticed that she was missing, Anise asked Mr. Shepherd (Byram) about his older daughter, Anne. The smile that was a permanent part of his face nowadays wavered. He mumbled that he didn't want to talk about it.

Mary tried to fill Anise in. "Anne ran off with an outlaw," she said excitedly. Mr. Shepherd's smile, which had been starting to come back, wavered. He scowled at Mary. She glanced down at the ground. "Papa doesn't like to talk about it. I worry about her."

Aunt Rose moved into the mill house, Byram Shepherd's home. It was a large stone house attached to the mill. It was one of the grandest homes in Hero, but since Mr. Shepherd's first wife, Anne and Mary's mother, died, it had become a little neglected.

They found a little room for Anise to stay in while she was there for the break. Anise found it strange at first. The room shuddered and shook with the grinding of the mill and the turning of the wheel. She could also hear the water running outside her window. It became a lullaby after a few days, and she slept better than she had in years.

There was a small mossy spot between the bottom of the mill wheel and the mill's stone wall, just above the smaller pond where the water flowing over the wheel started its journey toward the river. It wasn't visible from the lane that crossed the stream a little below. You had to clamber down a slope and duck under the moving axle of the mill wheel to get there. Still, it was dry unless the stream was flowing more than usual. And the luxurious green moss made a soft cushion on which to sit if you were so inclined.

It was Mary's particular spot to hide from her father and spend time alone. Of course, now that her best friend was also her sister, she sat there with Anise with the afternoon sun shining down on them.

"Tell me about Anne," said Anise. "Did she really run off with an outlaw?"

Mary shook her head. "I want to hear about the Academy," she said. "Show me some magic."

Anise reached over towards Mary's ear and pantomimed pulling something out of it. A large gold coin dropped through the air and fell to the mossy ground. It looked like it indented the moss.

Mary gasped. "Is it real?" she said as she reached out toward the coin.

"Of course not," said Anise. She waved her hand, and the coin disappeared.

Mary looked disappointed. "Why not?" she said.

"Well," said Anise, "it has to do with the littlest bits

of stuff. You can move them around and change them a bit, but making new ones out of nothing isn't something we can do."

She smiled at her new sister. "I'll tell you more later if you want to know. I really need to hear about Anne."

# 10

Sebastian and Anise spent part of that summer learning how to ride. Sebastian didn't own any horses, but the mayor generously offered to share some town resources to help out. He asked Mr. Thatcher, the farrier, to provide Anise and Sebastian with the loan of a pair of horses for learning and the trip back to school.

Betsy was not happy with the newcomers in Sebastian's barn. She reluctantly put up with the cows, but these newcomers, snorting and neighing, were more than she could bear. She went on a food strike initially, but then she got hungry, and that ended.

Anise adored riding. She felt a bond with her horse and loved spending time with her uncle. She named her horse Quickly because she enjoyed saying things like, "Let's go, Quickly," or, "I'm going to ride Quickly."

Anise and Sebastian learned to ride. Anise learned to ride Quickly. By the time the break was rolling to an end, they were riding well enough that they would be able to make the trip on horseback.

Betsy wasn't going to be able to come. She wouldn't be able to keep up with the horses. Anise dreaded the day that she had to say goodbye.

Saying goodbye to everyone was hard. Sunny grabbed Anise's finger, as she had in the vision from Lilith's potion, and wouldn't let go. Rose cried again. Anise cried too.

The trip back to school went even quicker than the trip to Hero. Soon enough, Anise was back at the way-house saying goodbye to her uncle. Quickly turned around to look at her inquiringly as Sebastian rode off, holding on to his lead. If Anise hadn't known better, she might have thought that he had tears in his eyes, like she did in hers.

# DRAGON'S GULLET AUDITORIUM

# 1

A nise and Jord discussed their final projects. As part of your last year at the Academy, you submitted a final project in your chosen field of study. Jord and Vin were working together with Master Videmon. Anise was planning her project with Master Callum.

Jord and Vin kept their project secret. This was the first time she told Anise anything about it. "You have to promise not to tell anyone, Anise," she said. "Vin and Master Videmon want it to be a secret until we demonstrate it to the other masters."

Master Videmon's theories about twins had a lot to do with how they interacted with magic. He had been fascinated with Jord's abilities with water and Vin's with fire. His belief in the connection between the twins and his knowledge of elemental magic had led to Vin and Jord's final project.

"We've invented a new element," said Jord. "We call it firter." She looked shyly at the floor. "You know, for fire and water put together. I came up with that." She got excited. She hadn't liked keeping her work from Anise, and she was eager to share her knowledge.

"It turns out that water is made up of parts. Too small to see. But, when you take the tiny parts of water apart, both sides of it want to burn." She lifted her hand and drew a little spiraling line in the air. A string of water rippled in the air behind her finger. Then she concentrated, holding her other hand out and spreading the fingers around the floating stream of water. The water sprang into flame but kept flowing.

It was like a gleaming, burning snake writhing above Jord's hand in the air. They were far enough away from the Key to the elements that Jord was drawing the moisture and heat from the air. Anise could feel the air drying out. She shivered.

"You take the parts of each little bit of water apart, burn its parts, then put it back together again," said Jord. "It took both Vin and me to figure out how to do it, but I can do it a bit by myself now." Jord stopped concentrating and dropped her hands to her sides. The fiery writhing snake fizzled a bit as it disappeared.

"Master Videmon is trying to figure out if there's a use for it. Still, he was very excited that we figured out how to do it," said Jord.

# 2

Channeling class had become a bit boring. Master Callum spent most of his time warning the class about things they shouldn't do and things they should be wary of. "The spirits and souls you encounter in the dreaming are not your friends and will not always be under your control," he said.

"For example," Master Callum's face took on a severe look, though, as always, it was a little hard to distinguish expressions on his damaged face. "The spirits of the dead and the daemons of death are dark and dangerous. Even if you are powerful enough to channel them, you probably shouldn't. Interaction with the daemons of death can leave a shadow on your soul."

Master Callum's voice took on a somber tone. "I had personal experience with this when I was a student like you. I had a friend. A young man; friendly, charming. Generally a happy sort. He specialized in channeling the darker spirits. Over the time I knew him, he changed from a cheerful young man into a bitter unfriendly soul. I'm not sure if it was entirely the channeling of death spirits that led him down this path, but it certainly felt like it."

Master Callum proceeded, "There are some that can do it. Our own Master Lorenzo, the head of the channeling department, has power over the darker spirits. As we all know and trust, his soul is still free of darkness and taint."

"Anyway," the master concluded, "Though it has its uses, the channeling of the daemons of death is probably best left to those with the propensity for it."

Later, Anise spoke to Master Callum about her idea for a final project.

"That's very ambitious, Anise," he said. "As we've discussed in class, conjuring an artifact from a channeling dream is quite possible."

He continued, "It's said that the spirits don't like leaving items behind when their channeling missions are done. They think of it as messy. As unfinished business." Master Callum frowned, "Though, even that may be dependent on the power and presence of the channeler."

Anise had been inspired by her gift for Sunshine. When thinking about what to do for her own final project, the shiny golden amulet she had given her sister kept coming to mind.

Somehow, though, she couldn't bring herself to talk to Master Callum about Helios. She spoke of a sun daemon. She knew that the power of the spirit you conjured in your channeling dreams reflected your own ability. She wasn't comfortable with Callum knowing she could commune with Helios.

"If you do manage to conjure an artifact," said Callum, "Please let me see it as soon as possible. I am sure the other channeling masters will be impressed."

# 3

Anise awoke on a soft surface and sat up. She was on a cushioned couch in a glorious room. The sun was shining in through stained glass windows. She felt the presence of her circle of light, her little bubble of safety in the realm of dream. Though, if she hadn't, she might have thought that she was in the prince regent's room in the King's Seat in the city of Capitol.

Helios stood beside the couch, smiling indulgently down at her.

"Welcome to my home," he said. "You've dreamed yourself to me, this time."

Anise looked around some more. The place was worthy of being the home of a god. The fabric on the couch she had been lying on was cloth-of-gold. Everything was marble and stained glass.

An archway behind Helios led to a balcony above a courtyard. Below the balcony, standing in the yard, Anise could see a parked chariot. Beyond that was a field with horses running about. They looked a most unusual color. A bright orange or yellow, like they were made of flame.

Anise wondered if what she was seeing was from her imagination, her dream, or really from the dwelling place of Helios.

An elegant lady stepped into view. Her bearing felt as strong and proud to Anise as Helios', but she glowed with an inner calm where he radiated youth, energy, and intensity. There was a bright light coming from Helios and his crown, but this lady cast the soft glow of a full moon in her elegant flowing gown.

Helios swept his arm in front of the lady in a gesture of introduction. "I believe you know my sister, Selene," he said.

"Mistress Luna," said Anise. Shyly she stepped closer

to the woman, who enfolded her in an embrace. Anise felt a calm comfort flowing from the woman's arms.

"Anise," said Luna, "It's been a while."

# 4

A nise looked for the siblings' gift from the morning of the next day, even though Luna had said to look at twilight. "Look for a moment when the moon and sun are simultaneously in the sky."

She felt the warming presence of Helios on her shoulders when she walked to class in the morning, but Luna's company was mainly of the night.

After the evening meal, as Anise left the table to head back to the dorm room, her eye was caught by a glint of light. Something was shining in the afternoon sun on one of the windowsills of the common room.

Glancing around to make sure no one was watching her, Anise moved over to the window sill to see what had captured her attention. The light of the setting sun was cascading in through the window. It cast a warm glow over the sill and the wooden floor below.

Anise felt another presence as she looked at the window. There was a crescent moon in the sky, and its cooler glow mixed with the fading blush of the sun's light.

What had drawn her eye was something on the sill. Like before, with Sunshine's amulet, it was a raised knot in the wood at first. Anise touched the edge with her finger and lifted. Again, as her finger caught on the knot's edge, the sunshine mixing with the moonlight flowing through the window formed a metal shape.

It was a medallion, formed from sunshine, twin to the one she had conjured for Sunny. Twin, that is, until she saw the backside. Where Sunny's medallion had the impression of the knot in the wood on the back, this one had a back seemingly made of silver. An image of Luna's calming face showed on the silvery metal.

Anise lifted the amulet. A chain followed. Smooth and link-less, it had a pattern of gold woven with silver. It wove itself from the light streaming through the window as she raised it.

She placed the amulet over her neck. It settled into place and immediately made her feel safe. If she was in the sight of the sun or the moon, she knew that Helios or Luna would warn her of dangers.

# 5

**M**aster Huginn was quite interested in Anise's speculations about the clairvoyance mystery. "It's certainly true, Anise," she said, "that it does feel like a big coincidence." She looked down at the speaking podium in front of her. Anise approached her after class as the other students left.

"The fading of the dragons is another mystery, and, as you say, the timing is suspicious." She waved with her hand in the general direction of the town. "Here in Ashton, the town guard is called the dragon's watch. That's not a fanciful name. They did fight off dragon attacks.

"That said," the master continued, "I'm hard-pressed to see the connection. Sometimes a coincidence really is a coincidence."

Anise shook her head. "I feel it," she said. "There is a connection. Maybe this Drun Coeloc person talked to the dragons and learned something from them. Maybe he stopped them from attacking."

Master Huginn considered Anise. She shook her head as well. "One thing I do remember from my own studies. Zoology. Dragons don't speak. They were thought to have intelligence. A certain malevolent intelligence, but they didn't speak."

"Not at all?" said Anise. She remembered Flambé at the Carnival of Wonders and her feeling that she could reach Flambé with her mind.

"Well," said Master Huginn, "there are stories of an ability called dragon-speak. It was apparently something some Academy mages could do. I think it was a rare talent. I'm not even sure what discipline it falls under.

"You know what, Anise," concluded the master, "I'll do some research. I'll let you know if I find any connection or useful information."

# 6

When Anise told Master Callum she had finished her project, he called her into his office. The masters mostly had offices in the same building on campus. The building was a large hexagonal marble structure called the Well. No one was sure why it was called that; it just was.

Anise hadn't been to the Well very often. It made her feel a little nervous. Like she might meet someone, or something, scary in the halls. But she braved it to talk to Master Callum about her project.

Master Callum pointed to the amulet on her neck. "Is that it?" he said. "Can I see it?" He held out his hand.

Anise hesitated. It was a very reasonable request, but the thought of taking off the medallion and putting it in Master Callum's outstretched hand felt wrong.

"I'll need to show it to the other channeling masters," said Callum. "We'll need to see it to grade it. They were very impressed when I told them what you planned. Master Lorenzo, especially, was quite curious."

Anise slowly took the amulet off. She hadn't had it very long, but she already felt naked and unprotected without it. It wasn't Master Callum. She trusted him. It was the idea of removing the medallion and especially the thought of leaving the master's office without it on.

She had gotten a sense of how it worked. She, Jord, Raphael, and Cian had had a snowball fight one afternoon after classes. Though the sun was beginning to set, she had felt the delicate touch of Helios's attention. Someone let fly with a snowball from behind her at one point. Usually, she would have been hit and might have complained about the sneak attack. But instead, she felt alert to the presence of the flying snowball in a way she didn't fully understand. It was like she could see the flight, even though it was directly behind her. She dodged it and acquired a reputation for having eyes in the back of her head.

Anise dropped the amulet into Master Callum's outstretched hand with a shiver.

# 7

The graduation ceremony was held in the auditorium. The auditorium was called the Dragon's Gullet Auditorium by the students. However, its official name was "The William Smith Memorial Auditorium." No one called it that because it was boring.

William Smith had been one of the founding members of the Academy. But, the students called the auditorium the Dragon's Gullet because what he was known for was crafting the bridge over the Serpent's Gorge.

The students who graduated from the Academy specializing in the element of earth often went into construction. Using one's control of the element of earth to construct large rock and earthen structures was an ancient art. Some among the masters argued that it was a bit of a lost art. Certainly, you would find few among the modern mages who would be able to make structures like the bridge over the Serpent's gorge or the Dragon's Gullet Auditorium.

The Dragon's Gullet Auditorium (Or, if you prefer, The William Smith Memorial Auditorium) was a miracle of construction. The outside walls were seamless sheets of polished granite. They towered over the neighboring buildings. You entered through doors at the base, and climbed, again seamless, spiral stone stairs to the top of the outside wall. A sweeping succession of benches arched into the distance, curving around the auditorium. The structure's interior was designed to carry voices from the central stage to all the seats.

The auditorium was used for events where the entire student body needed to hear things. There weren't very many of those. Even when all the staff, faculty, and students were sitting in the auditorium, it wasn't nearly filled. William Smith had had ambitions for the Academy.

The only other time Anise had been in the Dragon's

Gullet was when she had attended Niall's graduation.

The graduation ceremony for Anise, and her class, was short and sweet. The faculty stood on the boards and called each student's name. The student called, stood, and walked a long and lonely walk up the stairs and across the stage. Then the headmaster of their discipline presented them with their Academy ring, followed by a kiss on the cheek.

It was the first time Anise had been so close to Master Lorenzo in her time at the Academy. She had seen him from a distance but hadn't spoken to him. He gave her an inquiring glance as he handed her her ring and kissed her cheek. But, he didn't say anything more than the congratulations he was offering to each student.

# DREAM

# 1

A nise woke once again into a state of dream. She recognized it immediately, though she was a little confused, as she hadn't tried to enter the dream realm. Her control over her dreams recently was such that she didn't enter channeling dreams unless she chose.

She was lying in her own bunk in the dorm room. As usual in her channeling dreams in the dorm, the bunkbeds other than her own were gone. The room was filled with flickering candlelight. Anise sat up and looked around. It was darker than usual. At first, she didn't see anyone else there, then she noticed a shadowy figure standing against the wall on the far side of the room.

"Lord Helios?" Anise called out. "Where's your crown? Why's it so dark?"

The figure stepped a little closer, not quite into the light. Anise still couldn't make out who it was.

"You're not Lord Helios," she said. "Who are you? What do you want?"

The figure took another step closer. A voice Anise didn't recognize sounded out; quietly, calmly.

"Hello, Anise," it said, "don't worry, I just want to talk."

"How are you in my dream?" said Anise. "Who are you?"

The figure took another step forward, moving at last into the flickering light of the candle flames. It was Master Lorenzo.

## 2

**M**aster Lorenzo stepped fully into the light of the candles. He smiled. A warmhearted, charming smile, full of good cheer and friendliness. He had a broad handlebar mustache. He looked younger and more robust here in the dreaming realm than in the waking world. He had seemed old and frail at the graduation ceremony.

"Anise," he said, "I didn't mean to startle you." He stepped forward, grabbed her hand, and pressed it to his lips. Even in the dream, the hairs of his mustache tickled her hand.

He continued, "I just wanted to congratulate you again on your graduation. I am proud of all the students who graduate from the Academy and my own channeling department. But, you, you seem to be something special."

"Master Lorenzo," said Anise, a little hesitantly. "How are you here? In my dream? Is this my dream? Are you a dream-walker like Master Callum?"

"Like Master Callum?" said Lorenzo. He laughed. "I suppose I am something of a dream-walker. And, as to whether this is your dream or not, I guess you could say it's both of ours. We're sharing this dream between us."

"But I didn't try to dream tonight," said Anise.

"I just want to say again how proud of you I am," said the master. "Your final project. That's something the likes of which we haven't seen in the years I've been teaching here. It's really something special. You can feel the power glowing from it. In fact, I found it a little familiar."

"Thanks ..." said Anise. She opened her mouth to continue, but the master kept talking.

"You aren't going to stick to the story you told Master Callum, are you?" Lorenzo smiled again. His smile had the comfort of an old tale told around a crackling campfire. "There's more to that object than just a sun spirit or a moon spirit. You're talking to someone higher up, aren't you?"

# 3

M aster Lorenzo nodded thoughtfully. "It's you," he said quietly to himself. "It's always been you." He reached down to his chest and fidgeted absentmindedly with the jade heart-shaped medallion he wore.

"Master Lorenzo," said Anise, "Are you the Watcher?"

"The Watcher?" said Master Lorenzo. "Do you mean do I watch my students, especially the channelers, in dreams to make sure they stay out of trouble? Of course I do."

"But, I felt the Watcher," said Anise, "He was angry, scared. He was worried about something."

"Anise," said the master, "I assure you. I have only the best interests of the Academy, the students, and Liamec at heart." Distractedly he clutched the jade medallion as he said this as if *it* was his heart.

"That's what Master Callum said," said Anise.

"And right he was, too," said Lorenzo.

"That medallion," said Anise. "I recognize it. It was Sebastian's. It belonged to the Knight of Moon & Shadow."

"Of course," said the master. "I kept it." He smiled again, somewhat ruefully this time. "I'm sure your uncle thought I kept it as a sign of contentment or satisfaction with what it had done to me. When, in fact, I kept it to remember what I could overcome."

Anise frowned.

"You know what time it is? In the waking world, I mean," said Lorenzo.

"Not really," said Anise.

"It's after the sun has set and before the moon has risen," said the master. It seemed like he came to a determination. He held out his hand toward Anise. "Come with me," he said, "I want to show you something."

# 4

Anise took Master Lorenzo's hand. He started to lead her toward the door of the dorm room. She hesitated and pulled back. "Master Callum says we should stay away from the edges of our circle of light."

Lorenzo laughed. "Master Callum doesn't know everything," he said. "You know the secret, don't you? The realm of dream is the same place where the clairvoyants go. They travel their paths of truth through this same realm. The truth is out there. There is something you need to see."

They reached the door, and the master pulled it open. At first, there was nothing but blackness outside. They stood side by side, looking out.

"Look closely, Anise," said the master, "Look closely; you'll see it."

Anise peered into the dark. After a bit, she did feel like she was starting to see something.

"You know," said Lorenzo, "Years ago, I tried to help a clairvoyant." He sounded angry. "I almost didn't know what a clairvoyant was. I tried to help her, and I failed." He had one hand in a firm grip on the wooden frame of the door and the other on Anise's shoulder.

"There were two things that I promised myself that I would do in her memory. First, I would bring back the study of clairvoyance so people like her could find help, and second, I would follow her teachings, her prophecies."

Anise shivered. The intensity in the master's voice was starting to scare her.

"Her prophecy told of a dark channeler. A powerful channeler. A channeler who would endanger the world, open the cracks of truth, and fracture the cosmos."

Master Lorenzo was almost yelling. His grip on Anise's shoulder got tighter. "I'm the only one who knows what's wrong! I'm the only one who can fix it!"

"Master," said Anise, "You're scaring me."

Master Lorenzo grew noticeably calmer. "I'm sorry, Anise," he said. "I'm sorry for everything. There hasn't been a channeler as powerful as you born in two hundred years. You're the powerful channeler in the prophecy." His grip on her shoulder tightened. "As soon as I touched your medallion, I knew you were the one I had been looking for. You hid well, but that was your one mistake."

Anise tried to break free from his grip. "I haven't done anything," she yelled.

"But, you will," said Master Lorenzo. "Sometimes hard things have to be done for the good of everyone else." He shoved her in the back, directly toward the looming dark.

Anise teetered on the edge of the door frame. *It's only a dream*, she thought desperately. *I can wake up whenever I want.* She tumbled into the yawning blackness.

Anise's arms flailed as she fell. She opened her mouth to scream, but there was no air left for her lungs. The darkness of the dream swallowed her.

# DEATH & DRAGON

## The Channeler Trilogy Book Three

J. Steven Lamperti

*Dedicated to Sebastian,*
*who was the first,*
*and started it all for me.*

# PROLOGUE

She was falling, falling through a dream. Anise still felt the pressure on her back where master Lorenzo had shoved her. She was confused. *Why had he pushed her?* Then she felt hurt. *I trusted him.* Then she felt anger. *Never again. From now on, people will have to earn my trust.*

She wasn't falling fast. It was somewhere between a float and a fall. She could look around her as she dropped. *Am I falling asleep or falling awake?* She wondered.

She was falling through some sort of vertical tunnel. Rough earthen walls surrounded her on all sides. It wasn't uniform, though; side channels and chambers opened up around her. Some of them might lead outside the tunnel.

Scenes floated by in the side chambers. An armored figure led a line of red-clad women through exercise drills. A dragon flew above an inky, black night sky. *Was that a person riding on the dragon's back?* A blacksmith pounded on his anvil. An open green field of grass surrounded a bright red barn. It was too much to take in.

Anise wasn't sure how long she'd been falling. She wasn't sure if she'd been falling for a minute, an hour, or a day. As sometimes happens in a dream, her sense of time abandoned her.

Another thing. *Had she been pushed, or had she fallen off a horse or some other animal she had been riding?* Both felt right. Anise was confused.

She didn't have time to think about it. A surface was coming up below. Anise tried to twist and turn so that she could land on her feet.

# DREAM

# 1

I t was a small village of perhaps fifteen to twenty houses. Nestled among the trees of the green forest, under the clear blue sky, you might have thought it a romantic, picturesque sight. Until that is, you saw the villagers being led, manacled in chains, in a column into the central town square.

Groups of armed men dressed in chain mail were escorting the line of bound people. Some of the villagers in the column were weeping, some complained, and others just sullenly and grimly accepted their lot.

In addition to those escorting the villagers, other armed men moved about in the village. All were dressed in purple tabards over their chain mail. The bright purple color of the tabard was broken by a black silhouette of a coiled serpent about to strike.

The men who weren't escorting the column were ducking into houses, overturning haystacks, and breaking open barrels. Looking to see if they had missed any villagers.

It took a moment for the men in their purple to notice the lone figure standing at the forest's edge. The sunlight shone down on the figure, dressed head to toe in black. The sunlight shone down, but somehow, it failed to illuminate the shape. The black clothing, of some indeterminate material, not linen, metal, leather, but something other, absorbed the light. It sucked the light rays into it, not reflecting, not brightening, and not allowing any of it to escape.

It took a moment for the men in purple to notice the figure, but once they noticed, it didn't take them long to react. The first one to see the shape let loose with a cry, almost like a scream. Then, as if embarrassed at his initial reaction, he stopped what he was doing, pointed at the figure, and bellowed, "There!"

Another of the men, startled, gawked at the figure and called out loudly, "It's Death's Daughter; sound the signal!"

The figure reacted for the first time. It moved, taking a step forward into the light. The sunbeams, who had been so reluctant to illuminate the shape, relented a little. The black silhouette of the figure resolved itself into a woman's form. A woman stood on the clearing's edge, clad in tight, inky material that flowed over her. Her head was enclosed in a black helmet. Dark like her clothing, the helmet was made of similar material. It showed a white outline of a skull embossed into the front.

One of the men pulled out a horn and blew a shrill blast. The rest stopped and stood expectantly as if waiting for something.

Armed guards started pouring out of the houses. It was evident that the earlier action had been a bit of an act, as, with all these armed men inside the buildings, the searching hadn't been necessary. Many of the men were bowmen. The bowmen formed up into ranks and readied their weapons.

The woman hardly seemed to notice the archers preparing to fire. There was a wisp of smoke curling around her left shoulder. At times the smoky tendrils looked like they formed a shape.

The archery captain stepped forward. "Nock!" he called out, followed quickly by "Mark!" and then, "Draw!" The archers pulled back on their bowstrings. The woman hardly moved.

"Loose!" called out the captain. A volley of arrows arched through the air toward the dark figure at the edge of the clearing.

## 2

The woman responded to the flight of arrows. Lifting her right arm, she splayed the fingers of her hand out toward the sky. The quantity of smoke on her shoulder solidified into some sort of creature, perhaps the size of a large cat, before turning back into vapor. A tendril of the smoke crept out from the mass and wound around the woman's neck.

A sheet of flame surged forth from her fingertips. Several archers recoiled from the heat, even standing on the other side of the open space. The fire rose, crackling into the sky. The arrows weren't just singed and seared but were also pushed back, tumbling from the sky as if the flames were more solid than simply heat and fire.

As the flames burst among the arrows and they burned, the air grew chill. Some of the archers shivered. Frost started forming on the leaves of the trees edging the clearing. The chill of death was in the air. Persephone, mother winter, was kissing Hades, father death, in that green space.

One archer crossed himself and cried out, "Spawn of Thanatos!" He broke from the end of the line and ran for the woods. The others looked after him like they wished they could do the same.

As the archery captain began readying his men for another volley, soldiers armed with weapons other than bows formed into a line. Their captain drew his sword, raised it above his head, and called out, "Charge!" The row of men, clad in their chain mail and purple tabards and armed with shields and swords, began racing across the clearing.

The woman readied a short spear she had strapped to her back. The weapon lengthened as she drew it from a sheath across her shoulder until it was a bit longer than half her height. Holding the spear in her right hand, she reached out with her left hand, splayed the fingers on her hand again, and raised it, palm upward towards the sky.

Stones burst forth from the ground, shooting into the air with great force. The men standing above where the rocks sprang from were brushed aside like flies. The rest, with some hesitation, kept charging forward.

The archery captain recited his litany of "Nock! Mark!" and then "Loose!" again. Another rain of arrows came arching through the sky.

The woman crouched, lifting her left arm above her head to guard herself. A black shield appeared on the raised arm as the arrows pelted down. Black, except for the golden outline of an owl's face embossed on the surface. The arrows splintered on the shield or were knocked aside.

The woman rose, facing the men almost upon her, her spear in her right hand. The shield vanished from her left arm. In a voice hardly recognizable as human, amplified by something, perhaps the helmet, she said, "You sold your souls for profit, safety, and money. I hope the judges of the underworld will have mercy on you when you reach the other side because I will not." With a quick motion, almost too quick, she hurled the spear. It flew across the distance and struck the captain of the charging soldiers square in the chest. Somehow it pierced through him, kept on moving, and inscribed a great arc through the sky above the clearing until it returned with a small clank into her gloved hand.

The troop captain crumpled to the green grass, surprised to find himself lifeless. The men, clad in their purple, almost as one, broke and fled the clearing. Many dropped their shields and weapons on the grass as they ran.

# 3

Anise twisted and just managed to get her feet under her as she landed on a narrow path's rough dirt and stones. She caught her balance. The trail wound its way through a valley between some hills. The trees lining both sides of the track looked stunted, scraggly, and barren. Everything was dry and brown. A chill, stale breeze blew by her.

Anise started walking. A dreamy confusion overtook her. She lost track of whether she had just gotten here or if she had been walking for a long while. The trail led onward through the dry forest toward a mountain pass in the distance. A shudder of panic went through her. Anise didn't remember when she had started walking; she didn't remember where she was going.

She swallowed. Her throat felt dry, parched. The dry air felt hostile, unwelcoming, inhospitable to life. She looked again at the brown hills, the barren trees, and the mountains in the distance. Everything looked dry. The sky loomed gray overhead, cloudless but still not clear.

Anise felt a little cold; it wasn't just the cool, dry air. She felt the chill of loneliness and uncertainty. She pulled the sides of her cloak tighter around her. It was the warm red cloak Maeve had given her when it got frosty last winter. Anise didn't remember putting it on.

Anise frowned. *What did she remember?* She didn't know where she was or why she was here. The last thing she remembered was her graduation ceremony and the celebration with her friends afterward. After four years of study at the academy, she had graduated. Her friends had been discussing what they would do next. What she had been looking forward to most was traveling home and seeing her Aunts Rose and Isabel and her Uncle Sebastian.

She almost teared up when she thought about Aunt Rose. Rose had been her only living blood relative since the death of her parents. Sebastian and Isabel were like family, but Rose was family. Anise had already been missing Rose even before whatever was happening to her now had happened.

Suddenly she was overcome with relief; this was just a dream. She was still asleep. She was sleeping in, in the morning. Soon she would wake up in the way-house, where she had been living for the last years while going to school.

Gradually the relief turned back to unease. This wasn't just a dream; it was a dream of power, a channeling dream. It was a channeling dream, and Anise couldn't feel her circle of safety, her circle of light. *What would master Callum say?* She thought.

The memory came unbidden of a section in the book she had read for master Huginn in clairvoyance class. The *Archipelago of Dream* had a part where the unnamed writer described a place called the Dry Lands. The land between Death and Dream, he'd called it. The book had been long on ornate description and philosophy but short on down-to-earth details. Her recollection was that he had only been able to leave the Dry Lands with the help of his dragon guide. In fact, most things the writer had escaped or survived had been through the agency of his escort.

Anise looked around her. *Where was her dragon guide?*

Anise started. There was a man next to her, walking beside her. Had he been there the whole time? She looked more carefully. It was master Lorenzo. "Master Lorenzo," said Anise. "How are you here? Where are we?" She frowned. "Wait," she said, "you pushed me! Why did you push me?"

# 4

Anise turned and glared at master Lorenzo, waiting for a response. She shook her head in surprise. It wasn't master Lorenzo. How had she ever thought it was? It was Uncle Sebastian. Anise opened her mouth, excited, and began rattling out some words for her beloved uncle.

"Uncle Sebastian," she said, "I'm so glad to see you. I don't know where I am. It's so dry here." Her uncle's steady, calm presence encouraged her, and she continued. "I'm so sorry about Twilight. I wish I could have protected him. He was so young."

"Don't worry about your young charge, Anise," said the figure beside her. "His time is not over, and his story is just beginning. It'll turn out to be quite a story."

Anise turned to look. The voice had calm, reassuring tones, like her uncle, but it didn't sound like him. Anyway, what did it mean about Twilight's story not being over?

It wasn't Uncle Sebastian, after all. The man walking beside her was a tall, pale man dressed in flowing black robes. A group of tiny, winged men and women flapped around him like a flock of birds. The wings on these little people looked bat-like. The man himself looked bemused.

Distractedly he turned to Anise and said, "You know, Anise, your soul, life, and sanity should be forfeit to me, lord Morpheus." The bemused look changed to a slightly more attentive smile with a smooth transition. "But, someone higher up wants you alive and relatively sane." He laughed, "We all have higher powers to whom we have to attend." Anise remembered that Lord Morpheus was the king and lord of the realm of dream. The little creatures fluttering around him must be the Oneiroi.

A little man no taller than a mouse, one of the tiny people, flitted over to Anise. Its little bat wings blew the dusty air into her face. She flinched a little as it flew toward her.

The little creature silently landed on Anise's shoulder, then stretched and morphed into something else. Its wings changed shape; it grew. Anise recoiled but was too scared to try to brush it off. As the creature changed shape, it began turning into something more familiar. After a moment, it was Iggy riding on her shoulder.

"Iggy," called out Anise happily. Anything familiar was comfort. The fire imp who had started as a reading aid in the Academy library and escaped through Anise's channeling met her gaze with his cat-like eyes. He settled in. His tail crept around Anise's neck lovingly. He touched her forehead lightly with one of his talons. "Burn," he said reassuringly.

Morpheus watched this with patience and calm that felt somewhat abstract. "Do you have any questions for me?" he said. "Time and night are wasting."

Anise turned her attention back to the pale man. "You said someone wants me safe? Who? Is it Lord Helios?"

Lord Morpheus shifted back to his inattentive smile. Anise felt she preferred the calm. "I didn't exactly say safe," he said. "The sun's rays do not reach into the Dry Lands, the realm of Dream, or the underworld, so, no, not the god of the sun."

The lord got a slightly more attentive look on his face. "I must be off. I don't have time to spend with every lost soul with a bad dream." He lifted his arms. The little bat-winged men and women flew up into the sky. The black robes fluttered and wavered, and then there was nothing but a cloud of little winged men and women flitting off in a flock into the dry breeze.

## 5

Iggy stayed, reassuringly, on Anise's shoulder. He uncoiled the end of his tail from her neck and pointed it along the path. "Burn," he said persuasively. With nowhere else to go, and nothing else to do, Anise resumed her walk up the trail toward the distant, dry mountain pass.

With Iggy on her shoulder, Anise moved forward with renewed confidence, though she still had no idea where she was going. Looking ahead up the path toward the mountains in the distance, she had the feeling that everywhere in this dry, forsaken land would be the same. Still, a trail had to go somewhere, and she couldn't help but think that anywhere would be better than whatever or wherever here was.

Anise thought about trying to wake up. She knew how to wake herself from a channeling dream. She always had. Though, until her channeling classes at the Academy, she hadn't known why or what she knew.

What you did was you thought of your circle of light, the safe space within your dream, as a loop that you could jump through or move through. It wasn't a physical thing, more of a mental exercise. Without her circle, and the absence was almost painful, Anise had no idea what to do.

She felt a momentary sensation, almost as if a door was opening. A ghostly figure appeared in front of her, beside the track. Iggy looked up expectantly, "Burn?" he said.

The figure stepped forward. Shadowy and transparent, it gestured to Anise urgently.

"Master Callum?" she asked.

It was the master. At least it looked like him. Like he looked in Dream. Handsome and young, his semitransparent brown hair waving in the dry wind. She remembered how her channeling master's face looked in the waking world, with the massive scarring from a childhood injury.

"Anise," he said, "You have to come with me. You have to wake up."

"You're just another dream," said Anise. She felt angry. As if someone was playing a trick on her.

"No," said the master sadly, "I'm really here. You have to wake up, Anise."

He did something then. He grabbed her somehow. Not physically, but with his will, with his spirit. Anise had the feeling that he was trying to pull her through his circle of light. It hurt. It felt wrong. Somehow she knew that he was trying to help, that he thought he might be able to wake her this way. Somehow she also knew that it wouldn't work. It would kill her or rend her soul.

Iggy opened his mouth and blew a blast of fire at the ghostly master. The flames passed through the figure without effect.

"Master Callum," she cried, "No, it won't work." She fought back. She resisted.

Something ripped. Something tore. Anise saw master Callum's figure recede toward his vanishing circle of light. At the same time, the brown hills, the gray sky, and the dirt trail shredded apart into a haze of dust, and she was falling again.

# 6

A nise shifted her weight. She felt off-kilter, as if she had just landed after a fall. She adjusted her balance and felt more stable. She looked around. The sky felt familiar, gray and brooding, dry like an old bone, but unexpressive.

Nothing else did, however. *Where was she?* She was standing at the top of a hill. A green grassy slope stretched before her down the hill toward a split rail fence at the bottom. Both sides of the grassy slope were lined with trees. The brilliant green grass and the trees were so lush and inviting that they felt surreal. When she took in the sky and its expanse of dry gray, her throat felt parched as if she hadn't had a drop in a week. When she gazed at the green grass and the leaves of the trees, she felt the opposite. It felt so lush, fertile, and pregnant with life that she wanted to spend time rolling in it.

Beyond the fence was a further field of rich green grass, and beyond that was a large building that she assumed must be a barn from its appearance. It was bigger than her uncle's barn. Much bigger. It was also bright red. The fiery bright red color made any red dye or paint she had ever seen feel pale. The red hue of the cloak Maeve had given her was nothing to that color. Next to the barn was a cylindrical tower with a domed roof. It also was painted the same bright red.

Between the fence and the barn was a broad field. There was a herd of something roaming the grass. From her height, she couldn't make out what kind of animals they were, but she could recognize the patterns of herding and the motions of a herd. She felt she could almost make out the herder, though something looked a little peculiar about that also.

Anise felt a weight on her left shoulder. She looked and saw Iggy looking back at her implacably. The tip of his tail unwound itself from her neck and pointed down the hill. "Burn," said Iggy conversationally. As she met his gaze, the fire imp faded from a solid creature resting on her shoulder into a nebulous column of smoke. There was still a wisp of sooty vapor pointing toward the barn.

"Iggy?" said Anise.

"Burn," a calm voice whispered in her ear.

Anise started down the hill toward the fence, as she had nothing better to do.

# 7

Halfway down the hill, Anise saw something on the grassy slope ahead of her. As she approached the fence and beyond it, the field and barn, a sense of dread fell upon her. She pulled the hood of her cloak up over her head. It made her feel a little safer. Whatever this shape was, investigating it would delay her reaching the pasture, which was welcome.

It was a sundial. A few years ago, Brone, the town scribe of Hero, had gotten hold of a translated Persian scroll that detailed this marvelous time engine. He had persuaded Victor Potter, the tombstone maker, to make him one. The mayor had initially been quite impressed. He had set up a place on the edge of the cobbled town square for the sundial. He was sure that this unique device would encourage the tourist trade he knew was soon and inevitably coming to Hero.

When this failed to happen, and when the villagers commented that they knew perfectly well what time it was by looking at the sun's position in the sky, he became disillusioned with the technology.

This sundial looked similar to the one that still graced the town square of Hero. Built of stone, it had a column, which was topped with a circular platform marked with lines and words. It was crowned by a triangular wedge meant to catch the sun's rays and cast a shadow on the lines below. It stood on a level place in the grass of the slope. The dazzling green continued above and below it.

Anise realized two things as she looked more closely at the device. The first was that she had seen no trace of the sun on her descent down the hill. The gray sky was uniform, cloudless and sunless. She hesitated; hadn't someone told her that the sun didn't shine here?

The other thing was that the sundial's circular piece

was draped or stretched over the top of the stone column like a wad of pastry dough. It reminded Anise of her aunt kneading bread in her bakery. The triangular stone wedge still stood on top, but the stone circle flowed and drooped down the sides of the column.

Anise shivered. The sheer pointlessness of this bothered her.

Perhaps sensing her distress, Iggy stroked her shoulder with the tip of his tail.

"Burn," he said convincingly.

# 8

A nise drew nearer to the fence. The herd was moving her way. She was interested to see what manner of animals they were. Sebastian kept cows, but other farmers in Hero raised pigs, sheep, and goats. There were, of course, also geese and chickens, though you wouldn't keep them in a field such as this. She marveled again at the size and bright color of the barn. It must be a wealthy farm she was approaching.

She heard the crack of a distant whip, and the herd wheeled in her direction. A thin cloud of dust was in the air around the animals, obscuring her view. The pasture grass inside the fence was less lush than the hillside. Patches of dirt and dust showed through between the stretches of green. The lead animals pulled toward her, breaking through the dust.

Anise gasped. The herd wasn't animals at all; it was people. The herd leaders raced toward her, veering off to one side at the last minute to avoid the fence. They were men and women in various stages of dress and of different ages.

A middle-aged woman charged by Anise bellowing. She wore what might once have been an elegant dress, but it was torn and ragged. Her face was a mask of non-focused rage. Following her was a young man. He looked panicked but, at the same time, focused, like there was someplace he needed to be so urgently that he wouldn't let anything stand in his way. He was bare-chested and had on ratty linen britches. Next was an older man, then a young girl. Each was as focused as the last.

The herd thundered by. Anise tried to get the attention of some of the runners, but they ignored her. Each was absolutely fixated on following the person in front of them.

She was standing just on the other side of the fence.

As the last of the herd rumbled by, the herder came into view. Curious at first who could be herding such a mob, Anise regretted her curiosity when the herder turned to look at her.

It was a woman. Or was it? Naked from the waist up, the herder had the body of a young woman. Still, Anise had never seen a young woman with either a pair of wings that should be on a giant eagle or the head of a wrinkled crone.

Flying low so that the tips of her eagle wings just brushed the ground, the herder cracked a leather whip at her charges whenever one strayed from the herd. She wore black leather pants and boots. Her gray hair was cut short, and wrinkles and other age marks painted her face.

The winged woman met Anise's gaze as she flew by the fence. Anise had never seen such a look of anger. The raw scorn coming from the woman made Anise feel guilty about things she hadn't even done yet.

The whip arm drew back. Anise braced for the blow. Just then, one of the herd bellowed and broke from the pack. A boy. He couldn't have been more than fifteen. He split from the herd and started away from the fence, in the direction of the barn.

The herder woman halted her whip swing, wheeled her flight off toward the boy's path, and moved away from the fence.

"That was a close one, wasn't it?" said a voice.

## 9

Anise looked to her right as the herd thundered off toward her left on the other side of the fence. A young woman walked toward her, her mouth stretched wide in a big toothy grin. She wore cloth britches with a partial leather covering over them. The leather was more on the inside of her legs than the outside. *Maybe for riding?* Thought Anise. She had on a loose gray top and a broad-rimmed hat. Her smile was so infectious that Anise immediately felt an affinity for her.

"Anise," she said. "Welcome to the farm. Let me help you over the fence." She stepped forward, put her foot on the first rail, and held out her hand.

Anise hesitated. She heard a low hiss near her ear from Iggy.

"How come everyone knows my name?" she complained. "I don't know yours."

"We don't get many visitors," said the young woman cheerfully, "Especially not ones that drop in the way you did."

Iggy turned to smoke again. The sounds in Anise's ear were like a hissing, sizzling campfire as it's being put out. Anise moved forward and climbed over the fence, taking the young woman's hand as she reached the top. Her grip felt firm and warm.

"Let's go up to the barn for a bite," the woman said when Anise's feet were on the ground on the other side of the fence. "Some breakfast?"

Anise thought about it. "What time is it?" she said. "Is it breakfast time?"

The woman laughed. Her smile broadened as she laughed. "Does it matter?" she asked. "It's always time to break one's fast for someone, somewhere."

They started walking toward the red barn. The shorter grass and dusty dirt felt reassuring under Anise's feet. A momentary breeze blew, and she pulled the sides of her cloak a little tighter against the chill.

"So, who are you?" said Anise, "What's your name?"

"Lyssa," said the woman. Her smile grew even broader. Anise wasn't sure the smile was so charming anymore. There were a few too many teeth showing. She thought about the name. It was familiar. She should remember something about it, but at the moment, she didn't.

The group of people running along the fence turned toward them. Anise noticed two other herds in the field. They had been too distant to be seen from above, but they were coming closer now. Each of the others was being driven by a woman like the first. They looked enough alike to be sisters.

"Should we get out of the way?" said Anise. "They're coming this way."

"It's alright," said Lyssa. "It's not a problem."

The herds closed in on them. The herders stopped their flocks just short of running over Anise and Lyssa. Soon they were enclosed in a circle of the herded people. Anise tried to meet the gaze of one young woman wearing the tatters of a yellow smock. All she saw was a disturbing, unfocused stare.

Iggy was hissing like a teakettle about to burst. Anise thought about preparing her elemental abilities to defend herself, but she was in Dream. There was no connection with the elemental forces in the dream realm.

Lyssa turned to Anise. Her smile broadened even more. It was wider than should have been feasible. Sharp teeth were showing at the corners of her mouth. Anise thought she saw flecks of foam there as well.

Anise shied back. "Why are your teeth so sharp?" she whispered.

"The better to eat you with, my dear," said Lyssa. She moved toward Anise. Her mouth opened wider than humanly possible. A row of razor-sharp teeth, dripping with foam, gleamed pearly white.

# 10

Iggy tensed on Anise's shoulder. It was surprising that she could even tell because he was still just a curling wisp of smoke, but something about the curl seemed tense, and she heard a low growl in her ear. The three herders readied their whips, and Lyssa moved toward her.

A sound arose at the back of the milling crowd of humans. The herd stirred and grew disquieted. This clearly wasn't something Lyssa was expecting. She stopped her advance toward Anise to look.

Cries of "Pardon me," "excuse me," and "sorry" were heard as a man made his way through the crowd. The herd gave way to him surprisingly freely. Even one of the herders stepped out of his way as he emerged from the mob.

The smile that had never left Lyssa's face, even when that face hadn't looked human, left it now.

"Koalemos," she said. "What is it? It's not a good time. I'm in the middle of something."

Anise scanned the man. He was big. Dressed in a dark blue tunic and brown britches, he was taller than many in the mob he had made his way through. A little bit of a belly pushed out the blue fabric of his tunic. He had a smile on his face. Though she had begun to doubt her ability to judge, Anise thought it was a more genuine smile than Lyssa's. He didn't seem to have a weapon on him.

"So sorry, Lyssa," said the big man. He was panting a bit as if the exertion of pushing his way through the herd had tired him. "I don't mean to interrupt; it's just that my cousin asked me to do him a favor."

Lyssa looked annoyed. "Your cousin," she said, "Which cousin? You have so many. I'm one of your cousins."

Koalemos just stared at her. His face seemed to imply that she should know the answer to her question.

"Oh," Lyssa said.

Anise wasn't sure what to do. Should she be irritated or relieved that they were just ignoring her?

"She is not yours," the big man said. "Our cousin just wanted you to know that she is under his protection."

Anise stamped her foot. "Why does everybody keep talking about whose I am. I'm not any of yours. I'm not yours," looking at Lyssa, "I'm not his," with a wave in a direction that might have been toward Morpheus if she had any idea where he was. "I'm not your cousin's," glancing at Koalemos. "I'm my own. You all may be gods, or whatever you are, but that still doesn't mean you own me."

Koalemos sadly met Anise's eyes. "That's one of those things we keep telling ourselves, isn't it?" he said. Lyssa looked angry. The smile that had faded from her face a while ago didn't look like it was coming back soon. The three furious herder sisters were standing by for a cue from her. The human herds were waiting for a whip to crack.

Koalemos reached out and took Anise's hand. "My lady," he said, "If I may, I would like to take you from this place. It's not a good place for the likes of you."

Anise looked down at her hand lying in Koalemos's larger, slightly beefy one. "Can I trust you?"

"Well," said Koalemos, "Trust." He hesitated. "That's a difficult thing to come by." He indicated the human herds, the three herders, and Lyssa with his eyes and a head motion. "I would like to think that you can trust me more than you can trust them."

Koalemos smiled. "Let's take a little leap of faith together." He made a motion as if preparing to hop up into the air.

Anise followed, and the two of them, hand in hand, made a slight jump up and down on the dusty ground.

Lyssa howled. The sky, ground, and everything else fractured into brown dust. The last thing Anise saw was Lyssa's mouth opening again, showing her gleaming foam splattered teeth.

The world splintered into fragments, and Anise was falling again.

# KOALEMOS

# 1

The landing was a little smoother this time. Koalemos held her hand, which made the twisting turn to get her feet beneath her a little easier. She still staggered a bit on the impact, however. Anise tried to look around herself. It was hard, as there wasn't anything to focus on. She was surrounded by a borderless expanse of white. Iggy made a puzzled fizzling sound in her ear. Koalemos stood next to her.

"Welcome to my home. My safe place," he said.

"There's nothing here," said Anise.

"I haven't had time to decorate," said Koalemos. He sounded a little sad.

"Shouldn't there at least be some walls or something?" said Anise.

"Oh," said Koalemos, "That's clever. Why didn't I think of that." He made a gesture with his hands, both palms facing outward. Stone walls appeared around them, a stone floor below and a recessed ceiling above. It made Anise think of a monk's cell in a monastery. There were no openings in the uniform surfaces of paved stone.

"It's a little claustrophobic," said Anise.

"Right," said Koalemos. He made little twisting gestures with his fingers. Two windows and a wooden door appeared in the walls. The windows looked out onto the same white expanse as before.

"So," said Anise, "it's time for some answers," she gestured behind herself as if that was the direction where Lyssa was, "Who was that? And, who are you?"

Koalemos looked flustered. "I'm Koalemos," he said, "but please call me Cole. Not everyone does, but I'd like it if they did." He hesitated. "I guess I'm in charge of those people who know less about the world than they should or than the world knows about them." He hesitated again. "Some of my relatives think that I am one of those."

"And," said Anise, "who was that?" She pointed again.

"Lyssa?" said Cole, "She's my cousin. She's in charge of those people who know too much about the world and for whom the world is too much." He looked down at the stone floor. "She doesn't treat them very well." He glanced up at Anise. "She's usually the one who gets the ones who come here the way you did."

"All right," said Anise slowly. "And who did you say it was who asked you to help me?"

Cole looked a little nervous. "I'd rather not say," he said.

## 2

Anise looked out the window at the borderless white expanse. She had suggested some furniture to Cole and was sitting comfortably in a high wooden rocking chair. It had a pleasantly soft embroidered cushion on it. It was embroidered with the words, "Home, sweet home." She rocked gently back and forth.

"Some flowers might look nice out there," she said. Instantly a row of bright purple blooms appeared, bordering one edge of the expanse. "They shouldn't all look exactly the same," she continued.

"Sorry," said Cole. He sounded embarrassed. He waved his hand, and the heights of some of the flowers varied a little bit. Anise decided to let it go.

"Can you help me get out of here?" she asked. "Can you help me leave the world of dream?"

"I'm sorry, Anise," said Cole. "There are rules."

"Rules?" said Anise. "Whose rules! What rules?"

"Sorry," said Cole. "That's one of the rules. I can't tell you."

Anise sighed. "Well, maybe some of Aunt Rose's raisin pastries, then," she said.

A table appeared between her and Cole, loaded down with baked goods. Anise smelled the delicious odor of her aunt's work.

Cole picked up one of the raisin pastries and took a bite. His face lit up in pleasure.

"Theesh aar guud," he said through a mouthful of cake and raisins.

Anise picked one up and took a bite herself.

Cole looked sadly down at the ground. There was a woolen carpet covering the cold stone floor. "I'm sorry, Anise, it's time we said goodbye."

"Said goodbye?" said Anise, "Where are you going?"

"I'm not going anywhere," said Cole, "you are."

"I have nowhere to go," said Anise sadly.

"Even so, you still have a long journey in front of you," said Cole. He waved his hand. The chair, stone walls, raisin pastries, even Cole himself started dissolving, and Anise was falling again.

## 3

Anise landed on her rear on a dirt trail. "Ow," she said bitterly. Fortunately, she wasn't falling fast enough to hurt herself. She looked up. Both sides of the path were lined with scraggly dry leafless trees. Brown hills stood beyond them.

"Burn," said Iggy sympathetically.

Anise picked herself up, brushed off the dust, and tried to figure out where she was. *Dream, of course, but which part of Dream?*

The brown hills, gray sky, and dry air made her remember the Dry Lands from the book *The Archipelago of Dream*. Between Death and Dream, the author had said.

Anise tried to remember what else he had said about the Dry Lands in the book. He had described the place as a crossroads, where he stopped between visits to other parts of Dream and other places. She hadn't really been paying too much attention, as she had thought the book the ramblings of a madman. She regretted that now.

There was only one trail. Anise started walking forward. The brown hills on both sides were featureless. There was a mountain in the distance in front of her, and somehow the air looked clearer there. *Is that a spot of green on the mountainside?* She thought. Anything would be better than the unrelenting dryness and brownness of the trees lining the trail.

Iggy flapped above her. Around a turn in the trail, they came to a fork. Anise gazed at the fire imp. "Burn," said Iggy doubtfully. He seemed like he shrugged his shoulders, though he had such a thick neck that the motion was almost imperceptible.

Anise inspected the trails. The left branch might be headed more toward the distant mountain. She went that way.

There was no way to judge time with no sun in the

sky and the uniform light. The mountain didn't seem to get any closer.

"Iggy," said Anise, "You don't remember any of the chapters from that book, do you?"

"Burn," said Iggy with a firm shake of his head.

# 4

Anise twisted her falling body to try to land smoothly on the rough warm stone floor beneath her. She caught her balance. It was starting to feel normal to rise into consciousness as if she had just recovered from a fall. In front of her was an archway. A flow of warm air blew through the opening. The stones that made up the arch were old, ancient. They were covered with lingering traces of soot. They'd been burned or exposed to fire at some point. Behind her ..., but she couldn't look behind herself for some reason. She didn't want to; she didn't need to; she couldn't.

Iggy chirped excitedly on Anise's shoulder. It was a sound she'd never heard him make before. It was almost as if he felt some welcoming presence or familiarity with where they were. She stepped forward through the archway.

The warm air flowed past her as she moved down the stone passage. It felt more like a tunnel than a corridor. The walls were natural rock, though there were signs that they had been widened. The sooty look continued. The air smelled a little smoky as well. It smelled a little like the smell you got when you put a piece of metal into a campfire. The tunnel was broad and high.

As Anise moved down the warm tunnel, a sound that she had heard with the tail end of her attention started getting louder and louder. It was a metallic rhythmic ringing sound. She turned a corner in the tunnel, the sound grew loud enough to become unpleasant, and she recognized it. It was the rhythm of a blacksmith's hammer. A little further, the corridor opened out into a large rocky chamber, and she saw the smith.

His forge was against the far wall, the massive anvil beside it. Waves of heat surged into the room from the open flames of the forge. There was a rough wooden workspace to one side covered with iron tools. A trough of water stood on the other side.

The smith himself had his back to her. His arm was lifted, holding a hammer whose head had to be as big as Anise's, if not larger. The hammer was moving up and down steadily, faster than seemed possible. He wore a gray woolen skullcap. Strands of unruly brown and gray hair poked their way out from under the cap in all directions. A leather smith's apron partially covered the sleeveless linen tunic he wore. His arms, massive as small tree trunks, overpowered the edges of the tunic. From the waist down, he wore short leather pants and simple sandals. The back of his right leg was covered with scar tissue.

The forge's fire was being maintained by a fire imp; twin, to Anise's eyes, to Iggy. As they walked into the chamber, the creature was breathing flames onto the coals. Iggy launched himself off Anise's shoulder with another chirp and flew across the room.

# 5

Iggy chirped several more times as he flew across the broad cavern. The smith didn't notice. He just kept pounding his hammer into the iron on his anvil. The other fire imp did, however. It launched itself into the air also and streaked out to meet Iggy. The bright fire of the forge immediately dimmed.

The two imps met in mid-air. Anise wasn't sure at first what she was seeing as she watched them start to spiral around each other. An intricate aerial dance that could have been fighting, love, or just excitement formed. First, one imp, then the other, flipped, dove, and spun around.

The smith hadn't noticed the chirping or the fire imp leaving the forge. What he did notice, however, was the cooling of the forge fires. He went to reheat his workings, found the fire dimmed, and looked up to see the dance that Anise was watching in fascination.

"Magnus T. Fire Imp," he bellowed.

The dance stopped. One of the fire imps flew, apologetically, over toward the smith. Anise couldn't tell them apart. She felt like her inability to recognize Iggy was some kind of betrayal. Iggy stayed in the middle of the room, flapping his wings.

Anise stepped forward to stand just behind the flapping fire imp. The smith took notice of her for the first time. The other fire imp, Magnus, Anise concluded, landed on the smith's shoulder. "Scorch," said Magnus.

Iggy shook his head. "Burn," he said definitively.

The smith frowned. He looked Anise up and down. "And, who," he said, "might you be?"

"My name is Anise, sir," said Anise.

"Oh, right," said the smith. His annoyance faded. He smiled at Anise. "You're here to pick up your order."

"My order, Sir?" said Anise. "I'm pretty sure I didn't place an order with you."

The smith frowned. "I remember the name," he said. "That's not the sort of thing I forget." He turned and started toward the workbench against one wall. He walked with a pronounced limp. "Let's check the paperwork."

Anise followed.

Magnus, from the smith's shoulder, gave Iggy a once-over. "Burn," said Iggy.

"Scorch?" said Magnus.

The smith started moving iron tools and other things around on the top of the workbench. "Where is it?" he muttered. Some of the things he picked up and tossed casually aside looked intriguing to Anise. There was a glowing two-handed sword, a shield with the face of a bull that winced as it fell to the tabletop, and various things that looked golden or jeweled.

"Aha," said the smith as he pulled a brown leather-bound book from the jumble, "here we are." He opened the book and ran his finger down the open page. "Right," he said. "Your order is not to be picked up; it's for a later delivery." He read a little further. "And I guess you're right. You didn't order the armor; it was ordered for you."

The smith put down the book. He questioned Anise with his eyes. "So why are you here?" he asked.

"I'm afraid I have no idea," said Anise sadly. "Armor, Sir?"

The smith put a kindly, brawny hand on Anise's shoulder. "Well," he said, "I guess you'd best be on your way, then." He snapped his fingers, the cave walls started dissolving, and Anise felt the stone floor begin to fragment beneath her feet.

"Scorch," said Magnus in farewell.

# 6

Anise wasn't able to get her feet beneath her smoothly. She slipped and fell backward. A surge of anger went through her. *I'm getting tired of all this falling*, she thought. She was sprawled on a perfectly flat green grassy lawn. Beside her was a row of purple flowers, almost identical. The green grass stretched off to the horizon. The horizon was a green wooded hillside. It looked like a painting. Anise rose to her feet.

She strode forward and knocked on the wooden door of the little stone-walled cottage that was the only thing there except for the flowers. She caught a glimpse of Cole's head peeking out of the window. After a moment, the door opened, and he stood there smiling at her.

"Anise," he said cheerily. "I'm so happy to see you. I'm so glad you could drop by. Would you like some tea?"

Anise frowned. "I'd like some answers," she said.

Cole didn't seem to notice her frown or her tone. He dropped his head and whispered quietly, "What did you think of the grass and the hills?" He lifted his head again and continued in a louder voice, "and, do you know how to make tea?"

Anise pushed past Cole into the cabin. It looked the same as it had, except there was a kettle of boiling water and a tea service on the table between the two chairs in the center of the room. She stepped over to the table and poured the hot water from the kettle into the teapot.

"Can you tell me why I keep falling and can't remember anything from before I land?"

"Well," said Cole, "The distances between the way-stops in the dream realm are sleep. You're falling asleep, and when you're sleeping, you don't remember anything except your dreams, isn't that right?"

The hot water started seeping into the herbs in the teapot. The smell of warm chamomile filled the room.

Anise felt it relaxing her. Chamomile was her favorite.

"Who's deciding where I go?" she asked. "Can I do anything about it?"

Cole looked thoughtful. He reached up and started playing with his short curly brown hair. "Well," he said, "I think you were ready to drop before you fell asleep." He started winding the hair above his forehead around his index finger. "Also, I don't think you can swim against the dream." He shook his head. "No, that one's not right. What I meant to say was, you're getting a lot of beauty sleep, so you're going to be even prettier when you wake up."

Anise poured the tea into cups, settled back in the rocking chair, and took a slow sip. "You're not being very helpful," she said.

"No?" said Cole. "I'm not?"

The tea was very soothing. Anise struggled to keep her eyes open. "I can't be falling asleep in a dream," she muttered.

Cole winked at her. "You've been doing nothing else," he said.

The rocking chair, the room, and Cole broke into a myriad of shattered dreams, and Anise felt herself falling once more.

# HADES

# 1

Anise landed with a thunk on an inlaid marble floor. She was in an ornate throne room. Rows of people lined both sides of the vast chamber, each of their heads turned toward her. There were entrances on all four walls, including an immense closed double door behind her. There were no windows in the walls, though they were covered with detailed engravings of fields, mountains, and hills.

A raised dais was at the far end of the room with a large ebony throne. In front of the throne stood a man. He had his hand on the collar of a dog. After the crowds turned their heads toward Anise, they turned toward the man. He met Anise's eyes and made a beckoning gesture with his free hand.

Anise walked cautiously down the center of the hall toward the dais. She didn't see that she had any other choice. She looked from side to side as she made her way. Many of the people in the room had an unusual blue pallor on their faces. They were watching her walk with varying degrees of interest.

Anise gasped when she recognized several faces among the crowd. Lyssa and her herders were there. The herders stared at Anise. The anger on their faces felt almost like hunger. Lyssa grinned widely enough that it seemed her face might snap in two. Anise wondered again how she had ever mistaken that look for friendliness.

Anise reached the base of the dais. The man standing there was, of course, Lord Hades. Cerberus was the dog holding under his hand. Each of her three heads was gazing at Anise. One was panting a little, one was tilted a bit to one side, and the third was staring at her intently.

Anise bowed deeply. She knew that you weren't supposed to say Hades' name so as not to draw his attention, though, considering the situation, she thought that maybe that ship had sailed. "My Lord, keeper of the underworld, I crave your indulgence," she said.

Hades towered over her. In addition to being on the dais, he was larger than he had any right to be. Though, as a god, perhaps he had some rights that others didn't have. He was dressed in a gray mantle. His head was covered in thick curly black hair streaked with silver. Leaning against the dark wooden throne behind him was a bident scepter.

Anise glanced past the tall god and spotted a hand waving among the crowd below the dais. It was Cole. He waved a friendly greeting with a smile on his face.

"Anise," said Lord Hades conversationally. "Is it that time already?"

# 2

**L**ord Hades and Anise walked side by side through an orchard. He had motioned the throne room crowds to silence and had taken her through a small door behind the throne with hardly a word. After walking down a few marble-floored hallways, they had emerged into a vast open space lined with seemingly endless rows of fruit trees.

Cerberus padded silently beside them. One of her heads sniffed at Anise for a pocket with a treat. Another looked watchfully down the long rows of trees, and the third gazed faithfully at her master.

The sky overhead was a uniform gray, without a cloud or a sun. Anise saw a flock of some distant flying creatures winging by far overhead. They didn't look like birds; they looked more angular and less feathered.

When they first stepped out into the orchard, she had looked carefully at the trees. Though she couldn't imagine the amount of labor it would take to maintain an orchard of this size, they were well looked after. Ripe pomegranates hung low from the branches.

Finally, Hades spoke. Anise gazed up at him, hopeful that he would tell her something to help her understand what was happening to her.

"Anise," said Poseidon's brother, the lord of the underworld, the eldest son of Cronus and Rhea. "I've been expecting you." He held his bident scepter in his right hand. He leaned on it as he walked. He frowned a little, "Though I have to say, I don't enjoy seeing the living down here. There's been a little too much of that going on lately."

"My lord," said Anise, "am I in Hades, or am I in the realm of dream, dreaming I'm in Hades?"

"Yes," said Hades, "you are." The keeper of souls wrinkled his nose. "There's something about the smell you people have while you're still alive." He sneezed.

Anise sniffed. She could smell nothing but the fruit on the pomegranate trees.

"Anyway, Anise," said the brother of Zeus, "We'll talk more later." They approached a small ramshackle wooden hut under one of the trees. "There's someone here who's desperate to meet you." The grim lord of the dead frowned. "I could almost say she's been dying to meet you if I wanted to be funny, which of course, I don't."

Lord Hades opened the door of the small hut.

Anise hesitated before stepping through the door. She firmed up her resolve. "My lord," she said almost angrily. "How could you take Twilight? He was so young."

"Twilight has not been here yet," said the unseen god. "Though some around him have. Now, go on in. She's been waiting. She refuses to visit the judges until she gets something off her chest."

Anise stepped through the door. One of Cerberus's heads gave her pocket one last disappointed sniff as she walked inside.

# 3

The interior of the hut was dark and dingy. The rickety wooden door thudded against the frame as Lord Hades closed it from the outside. Anise jumped. The darkness felt complete until her eyes adjusted to it a little bit, then she saw slivers of light filtering in through cracks in the walls. They cast lines of vision across the contents of the room. A slight creaking sound eased into Anise's attention.

She looked around the small space. A bed was against one wall, and a table was against another. An old woman in a rocking chair sat in front of her. The creaking sound was the woman rocking gently back and forth.

"Hello?" said Anise. She didn't dare speak loudly, so she said the word in a whisper. The old woman was looking down at the floor. She wore a shawl around her shoulders and didn't turn to look at Anise. As far as Anise could tell in the dim light, her face was the same bluish color as some of the people's faces in the throne room had been. It was both blue and blotchy. The pallor wasn't uniform.

"Anise?" the woman asked. Anise revised her opinion of her age. Her voice had an air of distraction, but it didn't sound like an old woman's voice.

"Do I know you?" asked Anise.

"No," said the old woman, "though I know you." She shook her head, still gazing fixedly at a spot on the floor. "I see you clearly. Even more clearly now that I am here in the netherworld." She turned her face toward Anise. Her gaze was focused somewhere outside the hut. Milky white clouds of cataracts marred her eyes.

Anise got a little irritated. "Look," she said. "if you have something to tell me, just tell me. I'm getting tired of all this mystery. So, who are you?"

"My name doesn't matter," said the woman. "I was a student at the Academy, like you. Some number of years ago."

Anise revised her estimate of the woman's age down again. The rocking chair and the woman's manner had fooled her. Without the blue pallor and the dark room, she might have looked not much older than Anise herself.

"I was a student at the Academy," continued the woman. "I was trying to learn to walk the paths. The Path of Life, the Path of Death, the Path of the Truth."

Anise scrutinized the woman. She suddenly was full of sympathy for her. Her voice sounded strained. It was like she felt all the world's pain and was trying to bear it for everyone.

The woman continued. "No one knew how to do it. I could find the paths, but no one knew how to help me walk them. But, there was one man who tried to help. One master who thought what I was doing was important."

It suddenly dawned on Anise, who she was talking to.

"Master Lorenzo tried to help me, but he didn't understand. Anise, he got them all wrong. He got my visions, my truths, all wrong."

# 4

The dead woman gazed through Anise with her sightless eyes. "Master Lorenzo tried to help me while I was alive. But then, after I was gone, he became obsessed with what I had seen, with what I had prophesied." She turned her blind gaze away from Anise and back toward the floor. "I didn't see how he was reading my words until after I had left the world above."

Anise thought for a second about Master Lorenzo. He was the one who had pushed her. The headmaster of the channeling department at the academy, he was supposed to help the students. A wave of bitter anger flooded her. Her Uncle Sebastian had given him a piece of his heart back when he was the Knight of Moon & Shadow. He should have been reformed, but he was the one who had trapped her in this nightmare of dream. "What did your prophecies say?" she asked. "And, what does it have to do with me?"

"I foretold the coming of a powerful channeler. I foretold the existence of a dark channeler, a channeler of death and doom." Her voice grew louder as she spoke. It developed a pitch and timber that made it feel like it was cutting through the gloom in the hut and shaking the walls. "I foretold that the dark channeler would bring doom upon the world. A doom that threatens to shatter and crack existence itself into fragments." She rose to her feet and turned her blind gaze upward as if she could see through the hut's roof. "I foretold that our world would end in a cataclysm of dragon fire, wizard battles, and splintered reality if something wasn't done."

Anise gazed at her. "What does that mean? And, again, what does that have to do with me?"

The woman turned at the sound of Anise's voice. She moved hesitantly toward where Anise was standing. "I tried to get him to listen. I tried from here. I tried to get him to channel me into his dreams, so I could tell him he was wrong. To tell him how he was wrong. But he wouldn't listen. He wouldn't talk to me."

The blind woman was moving too close to Anise. Anise put out her hand toward the woman to hold her at a distance.

"You," she said. "You are the powerful channeler from my prophecy." She reached out her bony finger toward Anise. Her hand was blue and blotchy, like her face. The finger touched Anise on the forehead. Her touch felt cold, clammy, and forceful. "You are the one marked by the silver of the moon and the gold of the sun." Anise felt a force fly from the bony finger on her forehead, into her scalp, and across to the back of her head. She fell back and scrambled toward the door.

The woman stopped, stepped backward, and reached out for her rocking chair. Her voice returned to something approaching normal. "Master Lorenzo read it wrong; he heard it wrong. There were two channelers in my prophecy. The dark channeler and the powerful channeler. He thought there was only one who was both dark and powerful. He's been looking for the powerful channeler, you, because he thinks he will save the world by stopping you."

Anise stood and shook herself. Her scalp tingled. "So, if he's wrong and I'm not the dark channeler who's endangering the world," she said. "Who is?"

The woman looked sad. "I am afraid that master Lorenzo has taken on that role," she said. "Anise, you have to stop him."

# 5

The woman, subdued now, started rocking again in her chair. "Anise," she said. "I'm tired. I wonder if you could help me." Once again, she turned her sightless eyes in Anise's direction. "I've been waiting for you. I put off going to the underworld judges because I needed to talk to you first. Now I'm done." She held out her arm.

Hesitantly, Anise reached out to help her stand. She waited to feel the same force when she touched the woman's arm, but it didn't come. "How am I supposed to stop Lorenzo?" she asked. "And, what is he doing that could destroy the world?" The woman rose, with Anise's help, to her feet.

"I don't know," she said. "He's doing something or going to do something that is cracking reality. He's fracturing creation." She frowned. "The only other thing I can tell you is that it has something to do with the dragons."

They shuffled together to the door of the little hut. The woman breathed a sigh. "It's been hard," she said, "waiting. But, now, at last, I'm free to go."

Anise opened the door. Hades and Cerberus were still standing outside. Or, perhaps they were standing there again. Anise didn't know. She and the woman, arm in arm, moved across the threshold.

Cerberus bounded forward. She seemed conflicted. Her central head started barking fiercely at Anise. The one on the left dropped toward the ground and whined apologetically. The head on the right tried to lick her.

"Cerberus," called out Hades. All three heads turned, and the dog started walking back toward her master. Hades stepped forward. He held out an arm toward the woman. "Thank you, Anise," he said. "I'll take it from here." The woman took his arm and released Anise's.

Hades turned his eyes to the dog, then back to Anise. "Her job is keeping the dead in and the living out, except those with a reason to be here." He nodded apologetically. "I think she likes you, but she knows you shouldn't be here anymore.

"We'll talk again, Anise," he said, "though, not here." He made a small gesture with his bident scepter. The unwelcome sensation of dream fracturing surrounded Anise, and she was falling again.

# 6

Anise landed off-balance. She almost fell backward before righting herself. She was standing in the line of red-clad women that she immediately recognized as her Academy physical arts class. She hadn't wanted to take the course at first, but it had evolved into one of her favorites. Her Sifu, their teacher, was standing in front of the line of women. Anise was disoriented.

She shook her head. The rest of the red-clad women disappeared. It wasn't her Sifu; it was a woman Anise had never seen before.

Anise looked around. She was wearing the red linen tunic and leggings that had been the required training gear for her physical arts class. However, the rest of what she had thought she had seen was gone. There was no one there except her and the woman, and her Sifu was nowhere in sight. The only other thing that matched Anise's initial impression was that they were in a training hall.

"We'll have to do something about that," said the woman, referring to Anise's lack of balance. "When you fall, no matter how much time you have or don't have, you need to tuck and roll with the fall to keep your equilibrium."

She was tall, helmed, clad in armor, and held a spear and shield. The armor was a combination of metal, leather, and thick cloth. It seemed like it was designed to balance movement and protection. The spear was short, made of some black material, and looked lethal. The shield was golden in color and bore the image of a woman's head with snakes instead of hair on it. Anise tried not to look directly at the shield, as the snakes gave the impression they were writhing and alive.

The armored woman walked over and tapped the side of her spear against Anise's back leg. "Straighten that one up," she said. "Otherwise, the stance isn't too bad.

You've had some training?" She turned her gaze to Anise's face for the first time. Her stormy gray eyes made Anise look away.

"A little," Anise mumbled to the floor.

"Well," said the woman, "You'll have had more than just a little when I'm done with you."

"My lady," said Anise, still looking at the floor, "Are you the goddess Athena?"

"My name doesn't matter," said the woman. "Who I am to you is the person who will get your flabby spirit into shape."

Anise glanced up at the woman's helmeted face. She thought she caught a hint of a smile on the lips just visible under the helmet's edge.

# 7

**A**nise didn't quite manage to stick the landing. Athena had emphasized dropping and rolling to recover quickly after a fall in their training sessions. It allowed you to keep your momentum and maintain your defense if an opponent was present. *I'll get it next time*, she thought.

She was on a trail between dry hills in the Dry Lands again. *I've been here before.* Anise was confused. *I've been here before*, she remembered, *But how many times and for how long?* The times all blurred together. Anise started off down the trail.

A mountain ahead was taller than the hills on the sides of the trail. Anise felt like she recognized it. *I've been trying to get to that mountain*, she recalled. She felt like she saw a spot of green on the distant slopes.

"Burn," said Iggy wearily. He started flapping off along the trail toward the mountain.

"Wait for me, Iggy," said Anise. She ran after him.

Anise hoped that if she reached the mountain and started to climb it, she might get an overview of the brown hills. She thought she'd be able to see if there were other destinations or places to head towards in this dry landscape.

After walking a while, they came to a junction in the trail. Anise stopped. *I've been that way already;* she thought about the left path. She set off along the right one.

The path wound through the trees. Anise wasn't thirsty, although she thought that she should be.

"Have we been here before, Iggy?" Anise asked.

"Burn," said Iggy in confirmation.

# 8

Anise dropped and rolled as Pallas Athena had taught her. The gravel of the pathway felt rough on her shoulder as the roll carried her into a fighter's crouch. A fighter's crouch, but with no opponent and no weapons. Anise straightened and looked around her.

Her sleeping fall through the Dream realm had brought her, this time, to a fog-shrouded gravel pathway in a barren landscape. The lighting was a uniform gray. She felt like there would be things to see off the sides of the path if the fog wasn't so dense. The place felt a little familiar, though she couldn't precisely place it.

The pathway went two directions, the way she was facing and behind her. Anise started walking carefully forward.

After a few minutes of walking, she spotted two shapes coming toward her through the fog. One was the shape of a tall man, the other a smaller creature walking beside him. She stopped and waited a moment, unsure what to expect.

The man stepped out of the fog, the murky shape resolving into the gray mantle, silver-streaked black hair, and bident scepter of Hades, the lord of the underworld. He wore a golden belt, with a massive key ring covered with keys hung on it. Cerberus bounded into sight beside him. She charged over to Anise, and one of her heads started licking Anise's face. Another kept a watchful eye on Hades to see if he would call her back. The third sniffed Anise for a treat.

"Anise," said Lord Hades, "I said we would talk again. So, here we are."

Anise patted Cerberus on a head. "Where is here?" she said with a glance into the fog.

Lord Hades frowned. "I selected this as a place to meet because I thought it might be more comfortable for you. This is the Isle of the Wise." He gestured to one side as if there was something to see.

Anise looked around again. "The Isle of the Wise." *No wonder it had looked a little familiar to her.* The little island in the lake off the shores of the Academy had always been a place of mystery. Still, she had visited it a few times with Master Callum during her channeling classes. "I can't say that I've been here that often," she said.

One of Cerberus's heads found a stick on the side of the path. The other two immediately grabbed at it with their mouths, and a three-way wrestling match started.

"Maybe you know," Anise continued. "We never got a straight answer out of master Callum. What is this place? And, how does it connect with the realm of Dream?"

Lord Hades looked thoughtful. "The Isle of the Wise is a thin spot, a fragile patch, in the fabric that separates dream from waking." He nodded sagely. "The isle itself is actually in the realm of Dreaming."

Cerberus fell to the ground, her three necks writhing as her heads battled over possession of the stick.

"But, you can see it from the shores of the lake," said Anise.

"As I said, it's a thin spot. Thin enough that you can see through it. It's old. Older than the Academy." Hades continued, "In fact, the Academy's founders recognized its power. That's why they built the Academy here."

# 9

L ord Hades gazed at Anise thoughtfully. "But," he said, "that's not what I'm here to talk to you about." He hesitated a moment. The look of hesitation didn't seem to fit on his forceful face. "I need your help, Anise."

Cerberus was still rolling on the ground beside the gravel path. One of her heads yipped, another growled.

"My help?" said Anise. "How could I possibly help the lord of the underworld?"

"Well," said the ruler of the dead, "There are rules. I am limited in some ways as to what I can do directly in the waking world. An agent, or intermediary, can sometimes be necessary."

Anise looked skeptical. "You want me to kill for you? To bring more souls to the nether world?"

Lord Hades looked hurt. "Why does everyone always assume that. I'm not all about killing." He looked contemplative. "You're all coming down to me sooner or later, anyway."

"Then, what?"

One of Cerberus's heads had won the battle for the stick. She stood, and that head shook it forcefully from side to side. The other two looked jealous.

"The clairvoyant you spoke with," said Lord Hades, "I've confirmed what she predicted with other sources. There is a doom coming to the world above. Cracks are forming. Something needs to be done."

"And if the world shatters, your supply of new souls will be cut off," said Anise quietly.

Lord Hades looked a little taken aback. "Well, yes," he said, "But, there are other reasons."

"Uh-huh," said Anise.

"Anyway," continued Lord Hades, "They will call you the Daughter of Death. They will fear you. I will give you a symbol to bring fear to your enemies." He reached out and touched Anise on the forehead. The graveled roadway beneath her feet started to crack.

Cerberus held up her stick for Anise to admire as she began to fall.

# 10

A nise caught herself, though she didn't do the roll Athena had taught her. She caught herself as she landed astride an animal. She recalled learning to ride with her Uncle Sebastian, then she flailed wildly not to lose her grip. There were no saddle, no reins, and the creature felt wider than a horse. She grabbed the nearest thing she could find to hold onto and breathed a sigh of relief as she got a firm grip with both hands on something rough, scaly, and moving.

She was sitting astride a large reptilian winged creature. She was perched just behind the wings and had a grip on the junction where the wings joined the body. The wings were flapping up and down, and Anise felt a night breeze blowing past her face.

She was riding a dragon. Anise felt a surge of adrenaline. She remembered the chapters in the *Archipelago of Dream*, the book she had read for master Huginn back at the Academy during her clairvoyance classes. The author had described riding on a dragon. Then she realized that this memory was even more appropriate than she had thought. Not only was she riding on a dragon's back, as he had described, but the setting was exactly the same.

The dragon wheeled a bit to the right. Anise clamped down her grip on her hold on the dragon's wings and took in the view.

The sky overhead was similar to the dry gray sky of the Dry Lands but darker. Anise wasn't sure how night could fall in a land without a sun or moon, but it had. The surface far below was a uniform black, marked here and there by white points of light. It was almost like the sky and ground were reversed. Like they were flying over a field of stars. Except for the randomness of the lights, it all looked the same until she looked forward in the direction they were flying. There was something there, on the ground, something more complex and patterned than the simple points of light.

Anise wondered how she could be on the dragon's back without it knowing she was there. She only wondered briefly because as soon as she had the thought, the dragon turned its long serpentine neck, twisted back towards her, and fixed her with its gaze. *It has something in common with Iggy*, Anise thought; *it has cat's eyes.* Then she noticed the expression in those eyes and on that face. It reminded her of Lyssa's herders; it was pure and simple fury.

# 11

T he fury in the creature's eyes stopped Anise's heart. First, she was scared, then she was shamed, then she got angry herself. She met the dragon's gaze head-on. The creature kept flying straight forward with its neck turned towards her. *What have I ever done to you?* she thought.

*What haven't you done?* The thought entered Anise's head as if she had thought it herself, but she hadn't.

*What was that?* Anise thought.

*You and your kind have broken the pact. You're breaking the world. You've restarted the war.* The dragon's eyes burned into Anise's. The intelligence behind those eyes fed the anger.

*I haven't done any of those things*, thought Anise. *What is this? Who are you?*

*You knew me as Flambé*, came the voice in Anise's head. *You could not say my real name; you could not understand my real name; I do not want you to know my real name.*

Anise tried to recall where she might know the name Flambé from. At first, nothing came, then she remembered a visit to a carnival when she, Sebastian, and Briac were traveling together years ago.

*I haven't done anything to you,* she thought.

*Look upon the works of your kind and despair.* The dragon dove, giving Anise a view of the structure or pattern she had glimpsed in front of them. She held tight to the dragon's wings and looked. It was a vast, roughly round spider web of lines or scratches in the dark surface below. They were all gravitating out from a central point. The lines were colored bright white as the dots or points she had noticed before. There were dots of white scattered between the lines.

At first, it looked like a spider's web to Anise. Some of

the lines were brighter, some dimmer, but all glowed white. Then her perception of the pattern changed. Not a spider's web, but instead the pattern of cracks that would show on a frozen lake in winter when someone stepped in the wrong place, and the ice started to fracture. She saw the pattern as the cracks in the clear surface just before the ice expanse shattered, and the walker fell into the frigid water.

*It's always been a weak spot,* came the voice in her head again. *The holes don't cause too much damage, but the lines, the paths, they score, they splinter.*

The dragon started bucking like a horse trying to throw its rider.

Anise held on for a moment, but the force was too great, and she was thrown. As she plummeted toward the spider web of cracks far below, she felt one more thought intrude into her mind.

*If I meet you again in the waking world,* came the thought, *I will kill you.*

# 12

Anise was falling again, but it was different this time. She remembered why she was falling. She remembered what had happened right before her fall. She remembered everything: Master Lorenzo had pushed her. *No, that wasn't right.* She had been riding a dragon, and it had bucked her off.

The dry air rushed up past her. She looked down at the spider's web of cracks and dots looming quickly closer. There wasn't much time before she hit something. She wasn't sure what she was going to hit, but she didn't think it would be pleasant, whatever it was.

Anise focused on one of the bright white dots. She recognized it. It was a circle of light. It was a channeler's circle of light seen from above. They all were. She felt them with her mind. She reached out to them. She knew that she could grab one of them and pull herself through into the waking world.

Anise remembered when master Callum had tried to rescue her by pulling her through his circle of light. She remembered how it had hurt and how she knew it would kill her. She wasn't sure she had much choice.

Thinking her goodbyes to her Aunt Rose, Aunt Isabel, and Uncle Sebastian, Anise prepared to try to pull herself through the nearest circle of light. She hesitated. There was another one. Not the closest, but it was calling to her.

Anise reached out to this new circle of light. It felt welcoming; it felt like home. She caught a whiff of the scent of herbs. The glow of light was coming from a group of clay lamps. Anise grasped this new circle of light like a drowning man clutching for a floating branch. She pulled herself through.

The sight of a room in an infirmary greeted her as she fell asleep and finally woke up.

# THE ACADEMY

# 1

Anise thought about opening her eyes. Then she thought about thinking about opening her eyes. She shifted her body. Was that the feeling of lying between clean sheets in a bed? She felt like she'd forgotten that feeling. She heard a gasp. Then she did open her eyes. A young blond woman was leaning over her. Maybe in her early twenties. Not much older than Anise herself.

"Anise?" said the woman cautiously.

Anise opened her mouth. She licked her lips; her mouth felt dry as dust. *Of course,* she thought, *I've been in the Dry Lands.*

The blonde woman hurriedly grabbed a clay cup of water and held it toward Anise.

Anise attempted to sit up. She felt weak and struggled a bit. Holding the cup awkwardly in one hand, the woman tried to help her with the other.

"Are you Aphrodite?" said Anise.

The woman laughed. She arranged a pillow behind Anise so she could sit up more comfortably. "I wish," she said. "Thank you, Anise." She shook her head. "My name is Aela."

The process of sitting up and leaning against the pillow took all of Anise's concentration. Her body didn't seem to be responding to her thoughts the way it should. She felt heavier and weaker than she remembered. She looked around the room when she was situated relatively comfortably.

There was sunlight streaming into the room from a row of high open windows on the far wall. The sunlight stretched into the room across the tiled floor but didn't quite reach the bed where Anise was lying. Her bed was one of six beds with clean linen sheets and covers in the room. The other beds were empty.

There were lit clay lamps arranged on side tables

around her bed. The room smelt like herbs. It smelled a little bit like Lilith's house back in Hero had always smelled to Anise. She took a deep sniff of the fragrant scents. It felt like she hadn't smelled anything in years.

"Where am I?" said Anise. She lifted the clay cup to her lips. The cup felt heavier than it looked. Her arm and hand as she lifted the cup looked different. The cool water felt like heaven as it moistened her mouth and flowed down her throat.

"We're in the infirmary at the Academy," said Aela. "They've been taking care of you here."

"Am I sick?" said Anise. She looked down at her body under the linen bed covers. She didn't feel sick, though something felt wrong or different.

"You're not sick," said Aela. She frowned, "I'm not sure I should be telling you this so soon, but you've been asleep for fifteen years."

*I've been falling asleep for fifteen years?* Thought Anise.

# 2

Aela leaned back in her chair and allowed herself a little bit of a self-satisfied smile. "We did it," she said. She smiled at Anise. Anise looked over the circle of little clay lamps, then looked again at Aela.

"What did you do?" she asked. "And who are we?"

"We woke you, of course," said Aela. "Vix and I, we …" She stopped speaking and blushed. Her flushed cheek showed through the wave of blonde hair hiding the side of her face. "I mean the queen. The queen and I came up with a plan to wake you. We heard about The Girl Who Dreamed, and we came up with a treatment plan." She smiled a sort of secret smile. "We will be arguing forever about whether her magic lamps or my herbs did it, but it doesn't matter; it worked."

"The queen?" said Anise. "There isn't a queen. The prince regent isn't married, and if he got married, wouldn't she be a princess regent or something?"

"I'm sorry, Anise," said Aela. "I'm not doing this very well. You have been asleep for a long time. There have been some changes. The prince regent was deposed several years ago. He's locked up in the White Tower."

"So who's the king? Or is there just a queen?"

Aela smiled proudly. "Our good king Twilight. He's the great-grandson of Liam III. People are already saying that they think he's the best king ever."

"Twilight?" said Anise. "The king is named Twilight?"

Aela stood. "I should let you get some rest. Also, I need to tell everyone that you're awake. I'll make sure they don't come in more than one at a time for a while." She frowned. "We'll have to send a message off to Hero as soon as possible, but in the meantime, there are many people around here who will want to see you."

"Who's been coming to see me?" asked Anise.

"Well," said Aela, "I've only been coming here for the last few months, but I heard that some villagers from Hero have made the long trip pretty often. The head of the healing department has been helping with our treatment ideas. Some of your former classmates have visited, I think. A kitchen boy from town has been here a lot." She smiled. "And, of course, master Lorenzo will be excited to hear that you're awake. He's been very interested in the treatment plan, and he's stopped in to see you every few days while I've been here."

If Aela had been looking more closely at her patient as she said this last name, she might have noticed the blood draining from Anise's face.

# 3

Anise acted quickly after Aela left the room. She wasn't sure how much time she had, but it wouldn't be much. She started by assessing herself, her clothes, and her belongings. She was wearing a simple nightgown, her amulet, and nothing else. There were no clothes near the bed. Other than the beds and the end tables with the clay lamps, the only other furniture in the room was a closed cabinet.

Anise tried to move to the edge of the bed. Her body felt weak and heavy. When she swung her legs over the side, she felt a rush of blood to her head, and she almost fainted. She sat for a moment, breathing heavily.

She considered trying to stand, then decided against it. A more practical means of motion, if less dignified, would be a crawl.

The cabinet was her first target. Painfully, slowly, Anise crawled over to it. She felt old and heavy. She hadn't been in peak physical condition before, though her Sifu, her physical arts teacher, had tried. Now, though, she felt like she hadn't moved in years. For a moment, Anise considered that if she'd really been asleep for fifteen years, the fact that she was moving as well as she was was a minor miracle. She breathed a silent thank-you to the staff of the infirmary.

The cabinet door swung open. It was stuffed with supplies. Anise didn't recognize everything. During her Academy time, there had been a debate about whether or not they should accept healing as a separate discipline. Looking at the unexpected things in this cabinet, Anise thought the healers might have won. There were potions with labels she didn't recognize and devices that looked unfamiliar to her.

One shelf, however, contained herbs and infusions that looked more recognizable. Anise scrambled out some staunchweed, ginseng, mistletoe, and other things. She took a small bit of each herb in her mouth and chewed them to a paste. As she chewed, she thought of Master Ernst and his instructions to carefully measure how much of each ingredient you added to a potion. If he could see her now.

Anise bit her cheek, hard enough to draw blood. The Key to alchemy was, of course, bodily fluids. She sloshed together the ingredient paste she had made with the blood from her bit cheek in her mouth and swallowed.

Anise felt strength flow into her joints. She might feel the repercussions later, but her makeshift concoction was working for now. She stood and looked out the window. It was late afternoon. The sun was lowering toward the horizon. The window was on the first floor and low enough to the ground that she could climb out. There was even a hedge there for concealment.

Anise scrambled out the window and into the shadows behind the hedge. The cool early evening breeze ruffled the bottom edge of her nightgown around her legs.

# 4

T he gray stone outer wall of the Academy rose in front of Anise. It felt like the wall of a cage or a prison for the first time. She had made her way here, her nightgown flapping around her, skulking through the setting sun's shadows. However, the wall was a more formidable barrier than those shadows had been.

Working with the element earth was different than working with fire, water, or air. With fire, you drew on a heat source from somewhere close. If there wasn't a fire to hand, body heat, or the ambient temperature of the air. Water involved pulling moisture from some nearby source. Air was always moving somewhere, and you stilled it in one place with your mind to cause it to move elsewhere.

Earth was different. With earth, you had to dig deep. You had to feel the forces moving beneath your feet to get them to move the way you wanted. Earth work was usually slow. Fortunately for Anise, she was still on Academy grounds. She could still feel the presence of the volcano: the Key to the Elements, roaring and belching fire and lava. The volcano that lived inside the vast Hall of Elements on the Academy grounds flooded her mind with elemental force.

She moved close to the wall and put her hand on the smooth stone. The wall was a seamless expanse of rock above her, formed by some long-ago mage. She let the power of the streaming molten lava of the Key flow through her hand. The smooth stonework started to move and surge under her touch.

Anise shaped a round rabbit hole of an escape tunnel into the stone. She had to reform it a second time to make it a little bigger, as her hips were just a little wider than she remembered. She scampered through and looked to see where she was when she reached the other side.

Her tunnel had opened up into a place just on the outskirts of Ashton. Just between the edge of the town and the beginnings of the soap workings. The soap-makers kept their fires and ash pyres outside of town to keep the smoke and the smells away from citizens who might complain.

The last rays of the setting sun were leaving. Sunset was transiting to twilight. An almost full moon was rising in the sky. Anise felt the warmth of the sunny side of her amulet start to dim and noticed a cool touch on her skin from the silver side.

With the sun leaving the sky, she felt Helios' attention leaving her. Her amulet connected her to the sun god during the day, and his sister, Luna, at night. She didn't hear them speak, but instead, she felt aware of what they could see from the sky above. It had proved helpful during snowball fights with her fellow students back at the Academy. She had acquired the reputation for having eyes in the back of her head. It might prove even more helpful when things got more serious.

She looked toward Ashton. The town felt like home to her. She had lived in Maeve's way-house in Ashton the whole time she was a student at the Academy. She couldn't see much of the town from here. The hill and watchtower of the Dragon's Eye were silhouetted against the sky. The tower on the top of the rise, a familiar sight to her, was surrounded by scaffolding. The Dragon Watchtower was being rebuilt.

Anise shivered a little and pulled her nightgown more tightly around her. She turned away from the Academy and away from Ashton, into the soap works, and toward whatever lay beyond.

# 5

The air started to grow cold as twilight faded into the night. The glow of the nearly full moon was enough so that Anise didn't have to summon light. In the last year at the Academy, master Videmon had taught his students how to conjure his shining sphere of white and yellow. Anise still wondered if it was somehow a mixture of fire and other elements. Summoning it felt different than producing fire, and it didn't consume wood or other materials like flame did.

Anise shivered as the breeze pressed her nightgown against her body. Soon she was going to need something to keep her warm, as well as something to see by.

She crept through the fields, sheds, and buildings of the soap works. Several competing families had run the town's soap production. After a while, they had seen the value of working together. They had formed a guild and located their businesses in the same vicinity.

Anise avoided guards and lit areas. The businesses mostly ran during the daytime, but they kept the facilities guarded at night. She saw a massive mound of charcoal and wood ash ahead of her. The piles or hearths were kept smoldering to produce the wood ash needed for soap production. The radiant heat from deep inside the mountain of gray and black material warmed her as she started past it.

It was more than just the heat warming her. Anise felt drawn to the black and gray of the smoldering mound. She stopped, rose to her full height from her crouch, and turned to face the ash and charcoal mountain. Anise lost herself for a moment. Something about the pile was drawing her toward it.

She took a step toward the ash and charcoal. The mound's edge pushed aside and around her foot as it approached. She moved a little further. More of the pile shifted around her other foot as it moved into the sooty charcoal. Another step, and then another, and she was waist-deep in the ash. The ash and coal flowed around her body. She encountered no more resistance than a person wading through water.

Anise walked further into the charcoal hearth. After a moment, her head disappeared into the mound. The surface of the ash stirred for a second, then settled.

An owl flew overhead over the undisturbed mountain of charcoal and hooted as it made its way on its nightly hunt.

# 6

The nearly full moon shone down on the charcoal pile. A passing hedgehog startled and fled into the underbrush as the ash and charcoal on the edge of the heap started shaking and moving. Anise pulled herself out of the black and gray mound. She was covered from head to toe in the product of the charcoal maker's work.

She stepped away from the pile and coughed. She reached up and wiped her face. A smear of gray ash dropped off. As if waking from sleep, Anise looked around herself. There was no one in sight, but she hurried away from the charcoal pile and into the woods. The mound had been at the edge of the soapmaker's workings, and the woods beyond were blessedly free of any signs of people or town.

More gray ash fell off her body as she fled into the woods through the underbrush. The ash fell off, but the black that she had thought was from the charcoal remained. Anise broke through the low growth into a clearing in the forest. She stopped to examine herself by the light of the gibbous moon.

Her nightgown was gone, lost somewhere in the depths of the charcoal pile. She stamped her foot. The last of the gray ash fell off her body. She was clothed from neck to foot in some black material. It felt light. Light enough that she could move freely but strong enough to have protected her from the brambles and branches of the underbrush she had pushed her way through.

There were separate boots, leggings, tunic, and gloves, but they all fit together like tongue and groove fittings in fine carpentry. Clever little snaps and clasps kept the fit tight but could be unfastened to take the suit off. The clothing wasn't just strong; it was warm as well. Anise no longer felt the bite of the crisp night air.

She unclipped the clasps that held on one glove. She tried to stretch the material. She examined it as well as she could by the moon's light. It wasn't linen, it wasn't leather, it wasn't metal, as best as she could tell. She formed a pretty good idea of what it wasn't, which didn't help her much with what it was. She wondered if this might be the armor delivery from the blacksmith in her dreams.

*First things first*, thought Anise. She snapped the glove back on and oriented herself by the north star through the clear sky over the clearing. She headed off through the woods to the northeast, away from Ashton and away from the Academy.

# 7

Anise was growing tired of pushing her way through the underbrush. Her miraculous new armor helped with the cold. Still, her makeshift restoration potion was starting to wear off, and she felt tired and weak. She had been walking as directly northeast as she could, orienting herself by the north star whenever she caught a glimpse of the sky through a break in the trees.

The way had been mostly downhill. Ashton, the Academy, and the lake were higher in altitude than the lowlands to the east. Walking to the northeast, Anise was headed toward the sea and the Dragon River. She would somehow have to cross the river if she kept going east. Or else her path would eventually be blocked by the sea.

She broke through the underbrush into a clearing. A stream cut through the clearing, heading down the slope to the northeast, as she was. Anise stumbled to the bank of the stream, fell to her knees, and lowered her face to the cold mountain water. The water was icy and refreshing and brought her back a whiff of alertness.

The gibbous moon lit the clearing enough that she caught a glimpse of herself reflected in a pool of still water at the side of the stream. She didn't recognize her face at first. *An Old woman* was the first thought that reflection brought to mind. *What by god's bones did they do to my hair* was the second. The people taking care of her body at the Academy infirmary hadn't taken too much care of her hair. It was cropped relatively short and straight across, without attention to style. But that wasn't the main thing she noticed. There was something wrong with the color.

Anise held out her hand, palm upward, and conjured a tiny point of master Videmon's light. She got a better look at herself in the reflection on the water's surface. Her face looked older, but she could still see herself in there. Her hair, though, had changed. The color was mostly the same, but a gray or silver streak ran right through the center, from her forehead through to the back. She reached up to touch it. The silver part didn't feel any different than the rest.

Anise shook her head. She was too tired to worry about this right now. The light flickered out, and she looked around the glade. A spot under a bush would be out of sight if anyone entered the clearing. It would be a good place to hide.

Anise blessed the armor keeping her warm and cushioning her body from the hard ground as she curled up into a ball under the bush and dropped off to sleep.

# 8

The familiar feeling of waking into a dream overtook Anise as she opened her eyes. At first, it was familiar, but then it wasn't. *Wait*, thought Anise, *I'm not falling*. She looked around her. A moonlit clearing next to a rushing stream met her inspection. She reached out with her mind and felt the reassuring presence of her circle of light. She had almost forgotten what a regular channeling dream felt like.

Anise crawled out from beneath the bush she had been sleeping under. She looked around the clearing. The moonlight and the trees circling her defined the edges of her circle of light. She pushed and pulled at it with her mind, ensuring that she had control and could end this dream when she chose. The relief she felt when she was sure she did was almost palpable.

A flapping noise wafted across the space. Anise turned and saw Iggy winging his way across the clearing toward her. She choked up.

"Ig … Iggy, ….," Anise sputtered.

Iggy flew over to Anise, hovered in front of her, then landed on her shoulder. His tail wrapped lovingly around her neck.

Anise reached up and squeezed Iggy's tail. "Where've you been?" she asked.

"Burn," said Iggy calmly, by way of explanation.

# 9

A nise awoke. Something was different. She didn't have the sensation of falling. She rested, her eyes comfortably closed, and reveled in the feeling of lying on a flat surface. She was comfortable. Her body felt warm and relaxed, and her head felt warm too. In fact, her head felt a little too warm.

She opened her eyes then and shifted her body. Iggy, who had been settled on the ground pillowing Anise's head, sleepily muttered, "Burn?"

Anise sat up and looked around. She was in the clearing by the rushing stream. The sky overhead started shifting from the starry black of night to early morning gray. Iggy blinked. His eyes had vertical slits for pupils, like a cat.

While sleeping, her armor had cushioned her from the hard ground and kept her body warm. Iggy, who burned a small furnace inside himself, had kept her head warm.

She stood and took in the heavens. Iggy flew up and landed on her shoulder. The moon wasn't up, and though the sun's light was just beginning to creep its way into the sky, she could still make out the north star.

An owl called. Instead of thinking that it was just the owl's last call before he settled in to sleep the day away, Anise had the feeling that he was calling to her.

Anise was overcome with a rush of happiness. She was back; she was back in the real world. She had left the world of dreams behind and could continue her life. There might be trials and challenges ahead, but she would face them awake and on her feet. Now, though, it was time to see what that owl wanted.

Anise picked up a short stick from the ground and started beating her way through the underbrush toward where the owl call had come from. It called out again as she made her way. She corrected her path and continued.

The sky she spotted overhead through the trees started to grow lighter still. Anise broke through the underbrush to a spot under a large oak that was a little clearer. There, hanging from a low branch of the tree, was a round black shield with an owl's face outlined in gold on the surface. Anise looked down at the stick she had been using to beat back the underbrush. It was a short sharp spear made of some dark metal.

"Burn," said Iggy with satisfaction.

## 10

S	till using her new spear to clear the underbrush from her path, Anise made her way through the forest. The sun had risen, and she used the occasional glimpses she got of it through the trees for orientation. She kept to her northeast course directly away from the Academy as best she could.

Iggy was planted on her shoulder. Her relief at having a companion in the waking world and, she hoped, a friend was fading as he grew heavier through the morning. He was snoring. The sound was a little like a cross between a car's purr and the rumble of the water mill back in Hero.

The shield with the golden owl on its face gave her a surprise. She had strapped it onto her arm, and it had flickered a bit and then disappeared. With a bit of practice, she had found that she could make it appear and disappear at will.

Anise spent most of that day trekking cross country, using the sun as her guide. She found some berries at one point and nibbled away a little bit of her hunger. She re-encountered the steam she had seen the day before and slaked her thirst. At one point, she made her way across a road. She wasn't sure why, but she carefully waited until she was sure no one was coming before she crossed.

As the sun got to a place in the sky where Anise thought it might be afternoon, she came to a broad river. Anise wasn't that familiar with the geography of this part of Liamec, but from what she did know, this had to be the Dragon River.

The Dragon river wound its way from the mountains to the south and west, cutting the Serpent's Gorge into the rocks. After coming down from the mountains, it turned to the north and flattened out a bit as it made its way toward the ocean. Anise was relieved to see that the river was smooth and calm here, though wide. She had heard that it got rough and wild as it got closer to the coast.

She made her way down to a river-pebble-covered bank. The far side of the river was forested, but a grassy slope led down to the water's edge. Her thirst had returned. Anise got down on her knees and leaned over the still water to take a sip. Iggy flapped off her shoulder as she approached the river as if he was reluctant to be so close.

Anise caught a glimpse of her reflection as she hovered over the water. She gasped and pulled back. Her body looked right in the reflected image. She saw the black material of her armor and even glimpsed the spear she still held in her right hand. But, her face had been replaced with a skull.

Anise reached up to her face and felt her cheeks. She felt flesh under her fingertips. She looked again into the reflective water. The empty eye sockets of a skull looked back at her.

Anise reached out and carefully put her fingertips into the water. She felt the edges of something solid. She lifted and pulled a solid head-sized object out of the water with a grinning skull's face on the front. It was a helmet.

# DEATH'S DAUGHTER

# 1

T he river stretched in front of Anise, wide and deep. She wondered if her new armor was flexible enough to swim in. Then she thought that it didn't matter. Her idea of swimming had been splashing around in the millpond with her friend Mary back in Hero. She wouldn't have ever tried to swim something this wide, even without the armor.

Anise kicked at the smooth river pebbles that covered the beach. She thought about ways she could get across the river. She needed to cross to get further away from the Academy to make it harder for Lorenzo to find her. Then she thought about where she might be going in the longer term. Anise shook her head. That thought was for another time.

"Burn," said Iggy thoughtfully.

"Well, Iggy," said Anise, "that's a good suggestion." She shook her head again. In fact, Iggy's suggestion had given her an idea.

Anise stepped to the river's edge. She held out her hands, palms downward, and drew on the elements. She pulled heat away from the water's surface.

The water on the surface of the river froze almost immediately. The ripples and tiny waves froze in place. It wasn't totally smooth, but it was smooth enough. Anise expanded the scope of her action and started crafting a path of ice away from the pebble beach.

"Burn," said Iggy resentfully when he felt the cold. He flapped off her shoulder and took off into the air above her.

Anise took her first step onto her ice pathway. The ice shifted a bit under her weight, so she directed a bit more heat away from under the top layer. She kept one hand palm down toward the ice and faced the other upward toward where Iggy was flying. She conducted the heat she was pulling away from the water up in Iggy's direction.

"Burn," said Iggy gratefully. He started doing flips and aerial maneuvers in the warm updraft.

Anise froze the water in front of her for her next step. She felt grateful for the boots in her armor, as they were insulated well enough that her feet didn't feel the cold. She thought about the water flow, the depth of the river, and how much water she would have to freeze.

It didn't matter. Anise let the ice behind her warm and kept the ice under her feet cold enough and frozen enough so that it didn't shift when she stepped on it. When she needed to freeze it more, the additional blast of heat that she released into the air sent Iggy into spasms of joy.

Anise crossed the river. When she reached the other side, she stopped, took a deep breath, and flopped down on the grassy bank for a rest. Iggy flew down and landed on the grass beside her.

The fire imp looked behind them, across the river, over the bits of drifting ice. Iggy launched himself urgently back into the air, his wings flapping hard. He coughed out a quick burst of flame, turned his catlike eyes to Anise, and called down to her in warning, "Burn!"

# 2

There was something large and dark standing on the other side of the river. Standing on the river pebble beach that Anise and Iggy had come from. The sun was setting behind the shape, and the river was wide, so Anise had difficulty making out exactly what it was. She could tell it was big, however. It was probably about twice the height of a man.

Iggy started hissing and spitting like a kettle that needed to be taken off the stove. Anise watched the shape, unsure what it was or what it was doing there. At first, it just stood there. It was facing toward where Anise and Iggy were. Anise tried to look at the shape carefully through the bright light of the setting sun. There was something familiar about it.

The shape moved. It took a step forward toward Anise's side of the river. It didn't take precautions or make any preparations; it just started walking into the water. Anise started. She had felt relatively safe with the broad expanse of water between her and whatever it was. She wasn't so sure anymore.

The shape waded into the water like a child wading into a puddle. The slow water near the pebble beach didn't slow it down, and the faster water further away from the shore didn't affect it either.

Anise had hopes for the depths near the center of the river, and in fact, as the shape approached that point, the creature slowed a bit. Anise felt relieved when it totally disappeared under the fast-flowing river water.

Her relief faded when the setting sun's light reflected off of an unwavering moving arrow of v-shaped ripples that advanced right toward her.

Iggy hissed the entire time. The sound grew steadily louder. Anise worried that he might hurt himself.

"Enough of this, Iggy," said Anise urgently, "Come

on." She stood, turned, and started scrambling up the grassy wooded slope behind her. She thought, *there is no reason to just stand and wait for it, whatever it is.*

# 3

Anise fought her way up the forested slope. At the top, there was a clear space. She stopped for a second to catch her breath. Iggy flapped off above her and turned to look behind them. The open space was the cleared area at the side of a road. Some major thoroughfares in Liamec were kept clear on both sides to make it harder for bandits to surprise travelers and prevent the routes from being overgrown.

This roadway was such a thoroughfare, though there was no traffic right now. It ran north/south, paralleling the river.

"Burn," said Iggy sadly.

Anise turned to look back in the direction he was looking. She couldn't see anything, not having Iggy's high vantage point, but she heard a loud crashing sound. It sounded like a tree falling. *Is it strong enough to just knock the trees over?* She thought.

*If it's already at the bottom of the wooded slope, then it's gaining on us, even with having to ford the river.*

She darted across the road, then crossed the cleared area on the other side. She found a spot behind some bushes where she could hide. The thundering sound of trees falling continued from the other side of the roadway. It seemed like it was knocking over everything in its way as it crashed up the wooded slope.

In less time than she would have thought possible, the creature, whatever it was, knocked over another tree and stepped out onto the space beside the road. It was close enough now that she could see it plainly, though, in some ways, its appearance was still confusing.

Anise recognized it. It was her worst fear; it was a nightmare brought to life. It was death and destruction, walking on two feet. It was at least ten feet tall and an indeterminate gray color.

Anise recognized it and felt a rush of despair. From what felt like an eternity ago, she remembered how her uncle had become the Knight of Moon & Shadow and defeated an identical monster. The creature had been summoned by Lorenzo to attack their village. Her uncle had fought the beast using the magical gifts he had borrowed from his fellow villagers and his father's sword. It was a nightmare, a dream beast, twin to the one that had killed her parents.

# 4

The beast stepped out onto the roadway and then stopped. It was facing right toward where Anise was behind a bush at the far edge of the cleared ground. It stopped and waited for something. Anise remembered when she saw a creature like this step into the Hero town square and stand precisely this way.

Tears came to her eyes. At that time, she had been sure, confident that her Knight of Moon & Shadow, her Uncle Sebastian, would defeat the beast, as he had. There was no one here but her this time, and she was hiding behind a bush.

The tears weren't just for her, however. She remembered how that creature had left her an orphan. She remembered who had summoned that beast and who had most likely channeled this one as well.

The tears stopped flowing. Anise took a firm grip on her spear. She let her shield flicker in and out of existence to ensure it was still there. She checked the buckles on her boots and gloves. The fading tears turned to anger, then the fading anger turned to rage.

It must have been Lorenzo that had summoned this beast. He had pushed her into the nightmare of fifteen years of Dream. He had bragged about overcoming her uncle's attempt to give him a piece of his heart. And now, he was going back to his old tactics and summoning death dreams to attack her. She had had enough.

Anise conjured a bright ball of master Videmon's light, gripped her spear more tightly, stepped out from behind her bush, and strode toward the creature.

The light drifted up and to one side, illuminating the clearing alongside the roadway and overpowering the last rays of the setting sun.

Anise reached up to her head and pulled the visor of her death's visage helmet down over her face. The ghostly image of a skull on the front of the helmet almost glowed in the white light.

Iggy flew alongside Anise. "Burn," he said eagerly.

# 5

As Anise stepped into the cleared space, the beast responded. It moved forward, reared back its head, and roared. The sound was loud. The leaves on the trees lining the sides of the roadway trembled as if in a strong wind.

Anise trembled a bit, too, though her armor hid it. The sound was fear. It fed fear through your ears, across your soul, and into your heart. She trembled, but her rage held firm. With a smooth motion, she lifted her spear above her head, cocked her arm back, made a short approach run, and launched the razor-sharp weapon at the beast.

The creature looked startled as if it had expected its challenge roar to have at least delayed its opponent's attack. Still, with a preternaturally quick motion, it knocked the flying spear to one side. Any human-forged weapon would have shattered with the force of that blow, but the spear was a gift from Athena, goddess of wisdom and war, and it would take more than this to break it. However, the weapon's course was changed, and instead of flying back to Anise's hand, it struck the trunk of a tree behind the beast. The tree trunk shattered, and the spear fell to the ground.

Anise stood, momentarily disarmed. She called her shield into appearance with her thoughts and raised it toward the creature.

Iggy flitted over to where the spear had landed and picked it from the ground. He started flapping back toward Anise with the weapon clutched in his talons.

The beast moved forward. For something so huge, it moved surprisingly quickly.

The formerly empty roadway wasn't empty anymore. Out of the corner of Anise's eye, she noticed that several carts and other travelers had gathered from both directions. They were stopped, watching her face off with the beast. No one dared approach, but they couldn't tear themselves away from the spectacle.

"What is that thing?" Anise heard someone ask in terrified, hushed tones.

"Do you mean the monster or the woman who looks like she's related to Death?" someone else responded.

Slowed by carrying the spear, Iggy got too close to the creature. It lashed out with one of its limbs. Somehow even this close to the beast, it wasn't clear if it had hands, claws, or tentacles. The limb struck the fire imp, and he crashed to the ground. The spear clattered down beside him.

"Iggy!" called out Anise. She raced forward.

# 6

The creature stepped over Iggy's crumpled form. Anise realized there was nothing she could do for the fire imp until she had done something about the beast. She dove toward the fallen spear, dropping and rolling in a move Athena had taught her, which should leave her armed and ready at the end of it.

Once again, the creature moved preternaturally quickly. It seemed to know where Anise was moving to before she moved there. Anise could see the blow coming but couldn't shift her momentum fast enough.

"Burn," came a weak voice from below the creature. A blast of fire shot upward from the ground, bathing the beast's legs in flames. It wasn't clear if the fire damaged the beast, but it did distract it. The blow it had been aiming for Anise missed. Her roll completed as planned, with her alert, armed with her spear, and facing the creature.

Anise thought about what to do next. She would have to keep the beast's speed in mind. She couldn't afford to underestimate it again.

A particular smell filled the air. It smelled like something burning. Perhaps Iggy's fire had done some damage. Anise remembered one time when Aunt Rose had left her in charge of the bakery ovens while she ran an errand. Anise had gotten distracted by something, and a day's worth of goods had been burnt to a crisp, leaving their little house smelling like burnt bread. This smell didn't remind her exactly of burnt bread. It reminded her more of seared, rotting meat.

The creature hesitated as if waiting to see what Anise would do next. Anise felt slow. She hadn't regained whatever fitness she had had before her sojourn into Dream. Still, she felt like she knew something about fighting this beast from watching her uncle long ago. And she had confidence in her armor, weapons, and abilities.

The armor supported her uncertain muscles, and the shield and spear gave her courage.

Anise was now on the other side of the wide road. The moon showed itself over the horizon behind the creature, and the last rays of the setting sun were bathing its gray front in a ruddy glow. *At least it's got the sun in its eyes*, she thought.

The creature grew tired of waiting. It charged at Anise, lifting one of its limbs over its head in preparation for a devastating blow.

# 7

B oth the moon and sun were in the sky. Anise felt a shift in the knowledge coming to her from her amulet. She could feel the direction and location of the blows the beast was delivering. The source of the awareness was drifting from Helios and the sun to Luna and the moon.

Of course, in this case, she could see the blow, as well as sense it with her amulet. She brought up her buckler and moved to the side as quickly as she could. The beast drove its limb down toward her. The tentacle struck her shield with a glancing blow. Even through the magical protection of the owl's head buckler, Anise could feel the force of the impact. The limb continued downward, smashing into the rocks and gravel of the roadway with a thunderous crash.

Anise heard the people watching gasp. They moved backward to give the combatants more space as the gravel shot out from the impact.

Anise thrust with her spear, holding it near the end to give herself as much length as possible. The creature had a greater reach than her, though, for that purpose, a spear was a better weapon than a sword might have been. She thrust at the nearer of the creature's legs while it was still recovering from its blow. The tip of the spear connected, and a drop of blue blood oozed from the gray skin.

The beast roared again and delivered a furious backhanded swing toward Anise.

Anise thanked her amulet and Helios and Luna for the little bit of foreknowledge the medallion gave her. It gave her a reaction edge that let her compensate for the creature's speed. She ducked just under the swing. She felt the creature's tentacle whistle through the air just above her head.

Reaching her arms outward, Anise conjured flame darts from the air alongside the beast. As the darting fingers of fire smashed into the creature from both sides, she heard the growing crowd reacting to the cold that surged outward in every direction. Anise had to concentrate on drawing the heat for the flame from the air and not from the crowd's bodies.

The smell of burning rotting flesh grew slightly, and the creature slowed a bit. It took another swing. Anise stepped back and jabbed her spear at the creature's limb as it whistled past. She was rewarded with another drop of blue ichor.

As the creature swung its tentacle backward to prepare another mighty blow, Anise launched her spear at it again. This time the beast was slowed enough that it didn't have time to knock the spear to one side.

In a spurt of blue fluid, the spear struck the center of the creature's chest, buried half its length into its body, and stuck there. The beast stopped and showed an expression that might have passed for surprise on a more expressive face. It started to topple over in Anise's direction, making her worry about whether or not it would hit her. Then, it faded into nothingness, leaving Anise's spear clattering to the roadway in a puddle of the creature's blue blood.

# 8

The crowd didn't quite know how to react to the beast's defeat. There was a smattering of applause like they had just seen the end of a show, but it was clear that some weren't sure if they had seen a monster defeated or a monster victorious. They didn't know if they should be relieved or scared.

Anise picked up her spear and wiped the blue ichor off it on the grass on the side of the roadway. Some of the crowd, the ones who clapped, started shuffling forward. She turned to face them, stood straight, and spoke. She hadn't spoken with her helmet on before. The mask amplified and changed her voice so much that she almost didn't recognize the loud and powerful sound. She heard gasps from the crowd as they saw the skull on her face, and they heard her augmented voice.

"I am the Daughter of Death," Anise thundered out. "Stay back if you value your lives."

Having hopefully bought a little time before she was interrupted, Anise turned to Iggy.

It almost made her cry to see him. Iggy was lying in a crumpled heap on the gravel of the roadway, his wings twisted beneath him. Like where the beast had fallen, there was a thin puddle of blood beneath him, though the fluid that flowed in his veins was a bright orange color.

Anise leaned over the fire imp. She felt a rush of heat coming from the puddle and the fire imp's body. At first, she thought his spirit was gone, perhaps departed back to wherever he had been channeled from. Then, Iggy opened his eyes and looked up at her. His cat-eye pupils were dilated to almost fully open, perhaps from shock.

Iggy moaned when Anise tried to straighten out his twisted wings. She mumbled, "What am I going to do with you." She shook her head. "What am I going to do for you?"

Iggy opened his mouth. A trickle of the orange ichor

ran from a cut on his lip down his chin.

"Burn," he said weakly.

Anise's eye's widened. "Of course," she said. She held her hands over the fire imp's prone body and conjured a searing surge of fire downward. The flames crackled over Iggy's gray leathery skin.

As Anise watched, the wounds and cuts on the creature's body healed. His eyes closed, and he began making a soft sound. Anise didn't recognize the sound until she stopped the crackling flames. It was somewhere between a purr and a snuffle. Iggy had fallen asleep and was snoring.

Marveling at the healing that the flames had done, Anise picked up the slumbering fire imp and slung him over her shoulder. She tried to ignore the crowd of people, still watching her fearfully.

Anise crossed the roadway and disappeared into the trees on the far side without another word.

# 9

The young king woke from a restless night. He reached out his hand for his queen, his Vix, lying next to him in bed. She wasn't there. He sat up and looked around the room, confused. *Had she gone off on an expedition herb hunting with Aela?*

At first, their bedchamber looked normal, but then he realized that the furniture in the room was missing except for the bed and the night table. There was something wrong with the lighting as well. He couldn't tell if it was night or day.

Twilight rose from his bed in his nightshirt and picked up his dagger from the nightstand. He kept it there mainly for sentimental reasons. He didn't feel the need to keep a weapon around while he slept. Capitol, the capital city of Liamec, had been peaceful and calm since the end of Taedum's Revolt. The smooth wooden handle of the knife felt comfortable in his hand.

The door opened, and a woman stepped through. She was a bit older than the king, perhaps a dozen years. She was dressed in ordinary clothes. He might not have noticed her on the street, except for one thing. Her hair, mainly brown, had a streak of silver that ran down the middle. It drew the eye.

"Excuse me?" said Twilight.

"Twilight," said the woman. "Is it really you?"

"Of course I'm me," said the young king. "More importantly, who are you, and what are you doing in my bed-chamber?" Twilight was a bit surprised to see tears in the corners of the woman's eyes. He wouldn't have expected to see such sentiment from an assassin, even a non-threatening one such as this.

"Twilight," said the woman, the tears flowing more freely, "I'm so happy to see you." She stopped, peering at him through the tears in her eyes, and continued, "You've grown into such a fine, strong-looking young man."

"Do I know you?" asked the king. He lowered the dagger he was holding a little.

The woman shook her head. "There's a lot to tell." She looked thoughtful. "First off, this is a dream."

Twilight shook his head in denial. Then he paused, looked around the room, and said, "Strange kind of dream."

She frowned. "I trained at the Academy as a channeler. I guess I can dream-walk as well. Dream-walking is something that some channelers can do. You channel yourself into another channeler's dream." She smiled. The expression lit up her face and made her look very friendly. Twilight found himself liking her, even under the strange circumstances. "Master Callum never said anything about walking into the dreams of non-channelers, but I seem to have done it."

# 10

T he woman continued, speaking eagerly to show him how much she wanted him to believe her. "I'm your sister," she hesitated, "Or maybe your aunt or something. I used to watch you when you were a baby."

"You're not helping your cause much," said the young king. He lifted his dagger again a little. "No one watched me as a baby. I grew up in the woods." He glanced at the carved wolf's head on the hilt of his dagger. "Tell me your name and why you are here. I've never heard of dream-walking. I know a little bit about channeling."

"You must have survived in the woods when they lost you!" she exclaimed. "Did you do that by yourself? You were only two!"

Twilight looked a little unsure. Regardless he repeated, "Your name."

The woman took a breath. "My name is Anise. As I said, I trained at the Academy. ..."

The king interrupted. "Anise. I know that name. Aren't you the one Vix was talking about? The sleeper, the patient at the Academy, The Girl Who Dreamed?"

"I guess so," said Anise. "I guess I must be." She reached out her hand as if to touch Twilight's arm. "But, listen, I may not have much more time. I'm not sure how long I can keep this going. I haven't tried it before."

The young king took a step backward to avoid Anise's touch. "All right," he said. "Let's get back to my question. Why are you here?"

Anise looked sad at his withdrawal. "I wanted to see you. I wanted to see if you were still alive. I thought for so long that you were dead."

"Lots of people have thought that I was dead at various times. But, so far ... Not so far," said the young king.

"One thing puzzles me, though," said Anise. "How are you, the king?"

"That puzzles me too," said Twilight wistfully.

Anise perked up. "I can take you to meet your parents, Twi," she said.

The young king darted a suspicious glance at Anise. "No one calls me that, except for Vix and a couple of old friends." He changed his tone and said, "I haven't got any parents, except maybe for ..." he looked again at the carved wolf's head on the hilt of his dagger.

"Of course, you have parents," said Anise. The tears that had dried on her cheeks started flowing again. "They'll be so happy to see you."

# 11

Anise woke up. The birds were just starting their morning chorus. Iggy made a fine pillow in some ways; the warmth of his body kept her head warm, but the rumbling snore was sometimes a distraction, and he wasn't as soft as he could be. She moved her head, and he grumbled in his sleep.

She had made a campfire last night. The remnants still smoldered in her improvised fire pit. After waking from his recuperative rest, Iggy had proven very good at gathering firewood. Her elemental skills had taken care of the fire-starting.

Food had been a little more challenging, but she had remembered some of Lilith's teachings. The cunning woman who helped the mayor run her home village of Hero had taught her before she came to the Academy. The herbal skills Lilith had passed on had been helpful. Anise had found some berries and mushrooms and stumbled across a modest growth of wild parsnip in a stroke of luck. She carefully avoided touching the leaves or stems of the parsnips, remembering Lilith's warnings. Her boots helped knock the plants to the ground, and after hesitation, she used her spear to dig the roots up. She checked the edge afterward and was relieved to see not a scratch on it.

Master Ernst at the Academy had been knowledgeable about the benefit of herbs for brewing potions. Still, Anise went back to Lilith's teachings for foraging. Master Ernst had expected the plants to already be packaged, bottled, or dried.

Anise knew that if she stayed in the wild for long, she would have to do some hunting. For some reason, she felt reluctant to use her Academy skills to trap animals for the hunt. It felt like cheating. Of course, when she got a little more hungry, her reservations would almost certainly fade.

Iggy woke and launched himself into the air. For some reason, the bird song seemed to annoy him. He blew a thin stream of fire in the direction the sound was coming from. The blast of flame made a crackling noise in the air. Even though the fire didn't reach them, the noise and heat made the closer birds stop singing.

"Iggy," said Anise. "What are we going to do now?"

"Burn," said Iggy sagely.

Anise didn't need Iggy's answer; she already knew her own. *What did you do when you were lost, unsure of yourself, and didn't know what to do next? You went home.*

# HERO

# 1

T he horses raced up to the town gate. William, who was on guard duty this afternoon, hopped off his chair, ran over to the gate, and started trying to pull it closed. If he remembered it right, the protocol was that you were supposed to challenge people if they came in groups of more than two or three. It was harder to challenge people with the gates wide open.

"I'm getting too old for this," William muttered to himself as he struggled with the heavy wooden gate.

He was relieved when the riders stopped in front of the open gate rather than riding through. There were six of them. Five were men at arms in the blue tabards and chain mail of the king's guard. The other was a young blond woman. The tabards bore the black silhouette of a wolf's head that king Twilight had adopted as his symbol when he took the throne.

The five guardsmen stopped their horses smoothly, with the practiced skill of people who had been riding since they were young. The woman's horse took several extra steps as if she hadn't communicated the message to the animal well enough.

"Hello," she called out to William. She looked from left to right at the men riding with her as her horse continued to take mincing steps over the cobbles.

Several of the men dismounted smoothly and came over to her to help. One took her horse's head, and another helped her dismount. She sighed and sagged against the horse's side when she reached the ground. Then she straightened and knocked some of the dust from the road off her clothes.

William gave up on the gate and walked over to where they were.

"Can I help you?" he said. He tried to hide his excitement. This was the most action he'd seen on gate duty in years.

The blond woman smiled at him. It was a sweet smile that immediately made him like her. "Sorry," she said. "I've just been learning to ride. I've gotten pretty good at the part where the horse just gallops on, following the other horses, but getting on and off is still a challenge. And, I get a lot more tired than they do." She glanced at the guardsmen.

She looked dressed in elegant finery to William, though her clothes were simple by court standards. Made of fine material, the cut of the blue tunic seemed customary. Still, the unusual thing about her outfit was her leggings. Aside from whether or not William had ever seen a woman in leggings at all, they were made of softened leather and seemed to have multiple pockets. There was a little road dust on her clothes, but it didn't detract from their grace.

She continued, "Anyway. What I'm here for is to deliver some news. Can you get the family of Anise, The Girl Who Dreamed, for me?"

## 2

T he afternoon sun was a little warm. The blond woman and the five guardsmen moved into the shade under the gatehouse to wait. Though summery, it was a pleasant day. The village was quiet, at least where they were, and the wait was restful.

The quiet was interrupted by the rapid patter of bare feet on cobbles. A young girl came racing through the gate into the cobbled area outside it. She stopped immediately upon seeing the guardsmen and tried to act like she hadn't been running. Her charade was marred by her being out of breath.

The blond woman rose and stepped over to the girl. "Hail, and well met," she said.

The girl was just a little shorter than the woman, but, like her, she was blond. Her hair hung to her shoulders in gentle curls. Her hair color was lighter than the woman's. It was a yellow that almost looked white. She was dressed in a simple beige linen smock. Her eyes shone bright blue. She was just old enough to be somewhere between a girl and a young woman, though you couldn't tell it by how she was acting.

She breathed heavily, looked the woman up and down, and blurted out excitedly, "Are you the queen?" Then she looked down at the ground, crossed one leg in front of the other, and scraped her bare dirty big toe across the cobbles. "Sorry, your ladyship," she said.

The woman laughed. "Of course not. My name is Aela. I'm very pleased to meet you."

The girl remembered something. She executed a successful but clearly unfamiliar curtsy. "I'm Sunny," she said.

"You certainly are," said Aela. "Are you related to Anise?"

"You mean The Girl Who Dreamed?" said Sunny.

"I think so. They tell me she's my aunt or cousin or something."

Aela scanned the girl again. In addition to the beige smock, she had a chain around her neck, with a shiny golden amulet hanging on it. It glinted in the afternoon sun. Aela recognized it as matching the medallion she had seen around Anise's neck.

A murmur of voices came through the gate, and a group of people walked out into the sunlight.

## 3

T hree people walked into the cobbled square in front of the gatehouse. The bouncy young girl Aela had spoken with transformed in front of her eyes. Sunny straightened her back and moved up to the incoming trio. She nodded almost regally to Aela. "Aela," she said, "I'd like you to meet my Aunt Rose and my parents, Sebastian and Isabel." She turned to the three newcomers and nodded to them as well. Her words started speeding up as she continued, "Aunt Rose, Mama, and Papa, I'd like you to meet Aela. She has something to tell us about The Girl Who Dreamed."

The woman who Sunny had introduced as Isabel gazed at Sunny. "Thank you for that excellent introduction, Sunshine," she said and smiled.

The other two turned to Aela. "Greetings," said the man, while the woman said at the same time, urgently, "What can you tell us about Anise?"

"Thank you for coming to talk to me," said Aela. "Are you all of Anise's family, or are more coming?"

"This is everyone," said Sebastian. Aela glanced at him. He was dressed in plain yet comfortable-looking farmer's clothes, a bit worn but patched lovingly. Aela might have thought of him as old if she had met him before she came to start living at the King's Seat in Capitol. Now, though, she encountered people older than herself more often than not.

"I have mixed tidings," said Aela. "And, I am sad to say I feel somewhat responsible for both pieces of news."

"Please," said Rose, "We've been betwixt and between so long that any tidings will be welcome."

"Of course," said Aela, "I'm sorry. Well, the good tidings are that Anise is awake and seems to be of not completely unsound mind."

Again, simultaneously, Sebastian and Rose spoke.

"Awake!" said Rose, and "And, the unfavorable?" said Sebastian.

"The unfavorable," continued Aela, "is that she's run away, and we can't find her."

# 4

At first, Anise stayed off the road and traveled through the trees, paralleling it. Then pushing through the bushes got annoyingly difficult, so she walked along the road, sneaking off into the underbrush when she saw anyone coming. Then even that became too much, and she walked along the side of the road, avoiding eye contact with other travelers.

While she fought her way through the woods, Iggy flew above her. Once she started walking along the road, it seemed he understood that it wouldn't help if he were seen. He faded into a wisp of smoke and settled on her shoulder. Anise noticed that she hardly felt his weight when he was in his smoke aspect.

She got some looks, though she wasn't sure if they were for her clothes or because she was a woman traveling alone. She dreaded the moment when someone would confront her for whatever reason, but she prepared herself mentally for it.

The road headed almost due south. For the moment, it was paralleling the Dragon River on the eastern side. Anise knew that Hero was in the southeastern corner of Liamec, and the Academy was in the northwest. She would have to travel through almost the entire kingdom to get home.

She pushed her helmet back on her head and carried her gloves to make herself look less conspicuous. She wasn't sure how well it worked. The helmet with the skull face was cunningly designed. It was almost as unobtrusive as a hat when the visor was up. Still, her clothes were unusual looking.

After an encounter with a farmer driving his cart north, who looked suspiciously like he was thinking about saying something to her, Anise was on the verge of reconsidering walking along the road. She was looking at the underbrush to see if it was any thinner here when a crossroads came into view around a bend in the way.

A man sat on a rock by the intersection, next to the marker stones which told the travel directions. He had the expectant air of someone who was waiting for something. Anise was trying to avoid attention, but he didn't look threatening, and she needed to read the stones to know which road she should take.

As she got a little closer to the man, she observed him. He looked very relaxed as he sat on his rock, though alert at the same time. She wondered how one combined being relaxed and alert, but he was doing it. He wore a worn traveler's cloak with a golden clasp holding the front together. A backpack was sitting on the ground at his feet, with a well-handled lute beside it.

Anise gasped when he turned to face her. It was Briac.

## 5

B riac looked older. A little grizzled, a little taller. He had filled out from a young man to an adult. It took him a moment to recognize her, then it was his turn to gasp. "Anise?" he said. Then, "Anise!" He jumped up, ran over to her, and squeezed her into an embrace that took away the little breath she had left.

Anise remembered the last time she had seen Briac. He had been walking away from her after they had shared their goodbye kiss. She had thought about the young, handsome bard often since then but hadn't imagined seeing him again in a place like this.

When she could breathe again, she said, "Briac, What are you doing here?"

He met her eyes and laughed. "What am I doing here? Last I knew, you were snoring your life away in a bed in the Academy infirmary." His face adopted a more thoughtful expression. "I visited you," he said. "I tried to wake you." He shook his head. "I even yelled at you to wake up, but you weren't having any of it."

"Sorry," said Anise.

"So, when did you wake up? Where are you going? Why are you by yourself? And where did you get that outfit?" Briac gazed admiringly at the black armor, boots, and helmet Anise wore.

Iggy faded into view on Anise's shoulder, hissed at Briac, and then diffused into smoke again.

Briac started. "What was that!" he exclaimed.

"Oh," said Anise. "That's just Iggy." She flapped her hand at the smoke trail on her shoulder. "Iggy, come out and say hi."

Iggy faded halfway into view. His head and upper body were visible, but his lower body was still smoke. He gazed at Briac suspiciously. Briac reached out his hand toward Iggy. The fire imp's suspicious look grew more intense.

Anise shook her head at Briac. "You might want to give him a little time," she said. Briac dropped his hand to his side.

She saw the golden brooch that held Briac's cloak together. It was a tree branch crafted out of gold or gold gilded. Little bells attached to the bottom of the clasp tinkled when Briac moved. She remembered the similar bronze pin he had shown her when he visited her at the Academy.

"Gold," said Anise. "You've moved up in the world."

"You'd think so, wouldn't you," said Briac, glancing down at the golden pin himself. "Sometimes, it feels like the errands, lessons, and ranks never end. There's a long way to go after gold." He gazed at her curiously. "In fact, I'm here because I'm on an assignment right now."

# 6

Anise smiled at Briac. "So," she said. "What's your assignment?" She looked for the young man she had known in that face. Then she looked for the kiss they had shared, what felt like an eternity ago. She thought she saw both, but she wasn't sure.

"Well," said Briac, "One thing about bards, especially bards in the bardic council, is they don't say anything straightforwardly if they can say it in a more convoluted way."

Briac shook his head woefully. "They told me to meet Death's Daughter at the Brierstock Kreuzung. The first thing I had to do was find Brierstock. It's a little town not far from here." He waved down the road to the west. "Then I had to figure out what a Kreuzung was."

Anise waited expectantly. She was a little reluctant to tell Briac that she thought she knew who Death's Daughter was. At least not yet.

Briac continued, "It turns out that some of the families that settled Brierstock were from Almany. Kreuzung means crossroads in Almains." He glanced at the inscribed marker stones next to the rock he was sitting on. "So I'm waiting here for Death's Daughter. I had thought that she might be a woman who is dying or almost dead? But that was just a conjecture. I have no idea." He patted the knife on his belt. "I hope she's not something really scary."

Iggy faded from smoke into solidity and hopped off Anise's shoulder. Briac watched him carefully and somewhat warily. The fire imp walked over where Briac's pack and lute leaned against a rock. He waddled a little bit as he walked. Like a goose, he moved more freely when flying than when walking.

Briac gazed at Anise to see if he should do anything about what the fire imp was doing. She shook her head.

Iggy pointedly ignored Briac. He sniffed a few times

at the backpack, then plucked a string on the lute with a talon. The sound of the lute string rang out clearly.

"What did they tell you you should do when you meet Death's Daughter?" said Anise.

# 7

Sebastian gave Aela a look. Though he looked like a small-town farmer, which she believed him to be, something about his manner made him seem like more. He carried himself like the people she had been dealing with in the King's Seat in Capitol, like a noble or a gentleman. There was a confidence there that seemed out of place.

"What do you mean, she's run off, and you can't find her?" he said. "Why would she run off?"

Aela shook her head. "I was there when she woke. I spoke to her. She seemed in her right head. She understood where she was and what had happened. I left her for just a moment to try to get the healers, and when we returned, she was gone."

"You left her alone?" said Rose.

"We had no idea that she might run away. In fact, we still don't know why she did. I was hoping you might have some idea," said Aela. "She definitely ran from something, though. We found the spot where she made her way through the wall around the Academy."

Sebastian turned away from the group toward the gate back into town.

"Where do you think you're going?" said Isabel.

"I've got to get ready," said Sebastian. "I've got to go find her."

Two more people walked through the gate. The mayor of Hero had gained a bit of weight in the last few years. He walked with a cane and leaned somewhat heavily on Lilith, the town's cunning woman, who walked at his side.

They were followed a moment later by William.

"What tidings," called out the mayor heartily. His voice didn't need a cane. "What news of our Girl Who Dreams?"

"You're not going anywhere," said Isabel to Sebastian, "Not until we've talked about this." Sebastian's face acquired a stubborn look.

"Anise is awake, and she's run away," said Rose to the mayor and Lilith.

# 8

M r. Thatcher, the farrier, was leading Sebastian through the stables. Mr. Thatcher's son, Brian, had been running the business of late, but Mr. Thatcher said he was in charge when it came time to equip the Knight of Moon & Shadow with steeds. He wheezed a bit as he showed Sebastian the horses.

"How about that one?" asked Sebastian. He gestured toward one of the stalls. A young-looking horse was peering over the stall door at them.

"She's a three-year-old mare," said Mr. Thatcher. "She'd be a good choice for you. She's calm and social."

Sebastian reached over and rubbed the mare's neck. She pushed her head against his arm. She had an intelligent look in her eyes and a light, bright yellow coloring that reminded him of the color of Sunshine's hair. "What's her name?" said Sebastian.

"Most horses don't know their names; they mostly recognize their owner's voices," said Mr. Thatcher. "Why don't you come up with what you want to call her."

"Hay-bale," said Sebastian immediately.

"Why can't I come with you?" pouted Sunny.

"We've been over this, Sunshine," said Sebastian. They were in their barn. Sebastian was grooming Hay-bale with a curry comb. "It could be dangerous, and I don't know how long I'll be gone. And, if I even thought about letting you come, I'd have to find myself a new wife."

"But, I could be helpful," said Sunny. "You've been teaching me how to sword fight, and you said I have eyes in the back of my head."

Sebastian turned and looked his daughter in the eye. "I'm sure you would be, Sunny, but I'm afraid it won't happen."

Aela and her guardsmen left the village. As they

prepared to ride out the gate, Aela pressed something like a coin into Sebastian's hand.

"What's this?" he asked.

"It's a King's Favor," said Aela. Sebastian studied the token in his hand. It had an engraving of a wolf's head on one side and on the other a tower. Aela continued, "It's a symbol that you have some connection to someone close to the king. It might be useful in your search." She smiled at him. "Come to the King's Seat, and show it to the guards. I'll notify them to admit you. You can check to see if we've had any luck in our own search."

## 9

Lilith insisted on giving Sebastian potions and magical aid on his journey. Her one regret from when he had traveled as the Knight of Moon & Shadow was that she hadn't been ready to provide him with more help. Though, at the time, she had felt a little outclassed by the magic he had been bearing.

She gave him her signaling potion. The same one he had used when he brought Anise home from the Academy one summer. This time, she told him that if he released the catch, mixed the yellow and blue fluids, and signaled her, she would take it to mean that he had found Anise, and she would tell Rose and Isabel.

She gave him several potions that promoted healing and increased strength. There were a few others as well. She instructed him what each one did and when to use it. Then they packed them carefully into one of Hay-bale's saddlebags. Sebastian had the mental image of opening the saddlebag and finding nothing but a stew of frothing fluids and broken glass. Still, they were wrapped and padded so thoroughly that, hopefully, that wouldn't happen.

The mayor planned a big farewell gathering for Sebastian's departure. He might be having trouble walking without his cane, but that didn't mean that city affairs were any less important. Sebastian derailed the effort by sneaking out of the village at night with just a goodbye kiss for his wife and daughter.

Sebastian sat by his campfire. He had found a good spot for it inside one of the circles of stones found near the roads and by-ways of Liamec. Hay-bale was tethered on the other side of the firepit. He had tied her so she had enough lead to graze but couldn't go too far.

"It's a beautiful night, isn't it, girl?" he said.

She nodded. Though, some might have thought she was just lifting and lowering her head as she grazed.

Sebastian was enjoying his first night of camping since leaving Hero. It was cold, and there were hardships, but it reminded him of other times, which wasn't totally amiss.

"It's too bad you never got to meet Betsy," Sebastian said. "You would have liked her."

Hay-bale lifted her head, met Sebastian's eyes, and nickered.

"She would have liked you too," he said. He hesitated, then continued reluctantly, "Well, she probably wouldn't have liked you, but she might have tolerated you, for my sake."

# 10

Briac gazed at Anise curiously. "Why would you wonder what I'm supposed to do when I meet Death's Daughter before you wonder who she might be?" he said. He shook his head again. "Anyway," he continued, "what they told me to do was to escort Death's Daughter to her destination."

"I think I might be Death's Daughter," said Anise. "That's what they might be calling me, anyway."

Iggy kept staring at Briac's lute. He seemed to be fascinated by it.

"Why would anyone call you that?" asked Briac.

Anise reached up and flipped down the visor on her helmet. She pulled her spear from its sheath and summoned her shield from wherever it was when she didn't need it. Briac gasped.

"All right," he said. "I see it. Christ's ear lobes, that's scary. Please take that mask off."

Anise flipped the visor back up. The shield disappeared with a thought.

"Where did they tell you to take Death's Daughter? What's my destination?" asked Anise.

"What happened to you, Anise?" asked Briac. "We all thought you were just sleeping, but it seems like something happened, didn't it?"

Anise frowned. "I think my question is more urgent," she said.

Briac looked thoughtful. "All right," he said, "I wish I had a better answer for you. I wasn't told a destination. They just told me to escort Death's Daughter, you, to your destination. Damnable bards. Never a straight answer to a question."

"Aren't you a bard?" said Anise.

"That doesn't mean I can't curse the rest of them."

"Well, if you and the bards aren't going to provide

me with a destination, I'll have to just stick to the one I was already heading for," said Anise.

"Where was that?" asked Briac.

"I was going to go home. I would like to go back to Hero to see my uncle and aunts."

Briac smiled. "That's fine. I've always wanted to see Hero. It's supposed to be a special town," he said.

"It is?" asked Anise. "What's supposed to be special about it?"

"Well," said Briac, "you and your uncle come from there, don't you?"

# 11

Briac and Anise set up camp for the evening. Briac had all the things Anise had been missing in his backpack. A pot for cooking, utensils, two cups, a waterskin, and some spices. He even had a little packet that he proudly showed her containing some salt.

They set up away from the road to avoid curious or prying eyes. Briac started getting used to Iggy flapping around and quickly appreciated his firewood gathering prowess. Once they had a fire going, Briac started adding ingredients for a traveler's soup. He had some leftover rabbit meat from a successful hunt the day before. Briac had become a decent shot with a sling and had had some luck with it.

Anise added what little she had gathered during the day. She was greatly looking forward to eating something more substantial than roots and berries. The smell of the simmering soup pot was making her water at the mouth.

Briac turned to her from where he was tending the soup to make sure it didn't overcook. He reached into his backpack and pulled out something else.

"Hey, Anise," he said, "Remember this?" He held it up in the air. It was a single withered turnip. "I bought it back at the market at Brierstock. I wasn't sure why." He flourished it over the pot before dropping it in. "For the soup," he said.

Later, after they had eaten and the stars were trying to peek through the graying sky, Anise asked, "Did the bards say anything else useful?"

"Well," said Briac, "I suppose that depends on what you think is useful."

"Was there more in this prophecy about Death's Daughter?"

"There was," said Briac thoughtfully. "It didn't make

much sense to me at the time. I'm not sure if it makes any more sense now that I know that you're Death's Daughter." He placed his fingertips together with his fingers arched. His face acquired a slightly emotionless expression, and he started to intone the words of the prophecy. Anise guessed that this was how a bard recited a spoken piece.

"The byways of the soothsayers have gouged cracks through Dream and into reality. Existence will fracture, and the waking world will fall into ruin if Death's Daughter is not there to hold the pieces together." Briac took a breath and continued. "The storms will shatter the planes into fragments until all that remains is Death and Dream."

He relaxed his pose and smiled at Anise. It was a bit of a crooked smile. "It's all a bit depressing if you ask me."

Briac only had one bedroll. He kept it lashed to the bottom of his pack. It was getting toward the end of summer, and though the days were still warm, the evenings were getting cold. They spent the evening reminiscing about times past. Briac filled in Anise as much as he could about what had happened in Liamec while she was asleep. When they said all there was to say, there was an awkward moment where they both stared at the bedroll.

"I'll just sleep over there by the fire," said Briac.

"Don't be silly," said Anise. "It's your bedroll."

In the end, a compromise was reached where they both squeezed as best they could into the bedroll with Anise's spear between them.

# THE KING'S SEAT

# 1

T he first dream storm hit the land of Liamec that night. It was a little one, just a foreshadowing of things to come. Most of the kingdom was asleep. Only the night owls, moonlight thieves, and insomniacs were stirring.

Both Anise and Briac slept through it, though Anise stirred fitfully and restlessly.

Vix woke and put out her hand to make sure her husband, the king, was still sleeping soundly beside her.

Hay-bale nickered fearfully but not loudly enough to wake Sebastian.

Near the Academy and the town of Ashton, there was a cracking and crackling sound, which the night-pads and other moonlight dwellers who were awake and busy at their work heard. It didn't seem to come from anywhere in particular but rather from everywhere at once. The thieves paused, waited a moment to see if the sound had any meaning for them, and then went about their business.

The people most affected by that first storm, the ones who would remember it, were those who had gotten up to get a sip of water or use the privy. Walking through a darkened house or a dim yard, with nothing but a flickering candle flame or perhaps a trace of moonlight to light their way, they already were prone to glimpse things out of the corners of their eyes. They would always look to see if the thing seen was really there. The confirmation that it was just a shadow or a trick of the light, or lack of light, brought back the comfort of the distance between reality and dream.

That night, that storm, that moment, brought

something different. When those moonlight candlelight walkers turned and looked to see if their imagination was playing tricks on them, for a moment, they saw whatever nightmare or bad dream they had known was there.

Just for a moment, for each of them, that nightmare *was* there.

# 2

**B**riac and Anise were standing on a grassy hillside looking out at the city walls of Capitol, and beyond them, the towers, spires, and battlements of the castle called the King's Seat. "I'd like to see it," said Anise. The keeps, walls, and fortifications of the Seat stretched to the horizon beyond the city walls.

"We are seeing it," said Briac with a smile.

"It's just," said Anise, "You hear so much about Capitol, the King's Seat, and the court. I never thought I would ever see it. Now, though, I feel like I will."

"Of course you will," said Briac. "We could go down now and try to get past the guards at the gate?"

"No," Anise shivered, though the morning sun was warm. "I want to find some friends, some family. I don't know what Lorenzo is up to or how far his reach extends."

"You have some friends," said Briac. "Or, at least one." He reached out his hand and rested it on her shoulder. The black material of her armor felt tough yet pliable under his hand.

"Of course," said Anise, "Sorry." Iggy faded into view on her shoulder. His hissing at Briac had gotten a little quieter, but that was his only concession to friendliness so far.

They found a spot to camp that evening where they felt comfortable lighting a fire. It was wooded enough that the light wouldn't show very far, and they tried to keep the smoke down.

After they had eaten, Briac brought out his lute and started tuning the strings. It was the first time he had played since they had met at the crossroads outside Brierstock. Iggy, relaxing in the campfire, lifted his head and stared fixedly at the lute.

"Play me something," said Anise.

Briac smiled at her. "Not a problem," he said.

He started into the instrumental part of a song. The notes floated through the air like moths above the campfire flames. Anise felt like she could see them.

Iggy leaned back into the burning brands and coals of the fire, his eyes lost focus, and he started making a noise that sounded like a cat purring. "Burn," he said languidly.

# 3

The moon shone down on the Lion's tawny mane.
He stalked the night through the wind and icy rain.
He'd left his Seat, his lair, perched high on its hill,
to hunt the night for the thrill of the kill.

A wolf cub, weak and small, young, newly born,
stood in a clearing, exposed, alone, forlorn,
The Lion saw his meal; he sensed his prey,
but after the fray, it was he who lost his way.

For the cub, not yet fully grown,
was Twilight, the young king coming to his own.
The Lion's dream of victory, a kingdom in thrall,
was soon to fail, and all would see his fall.

The cub was young, but he was the true heir,
And with his friends, the Fox, Falcon, and Bear,
He fought until the Lion was laid low.
The beast fell; the final blow brought his woe.

With the battle won, the Lion's hope was gone,
He'd shown his weakness, the wolf his brawn,
Those watching, those in Liamec far and near,
saw the wolf, our new king, without peer or fear.

# 4

B riac and Anise walked down the road away from Capitol and the King's Seat. Iggy was just a trace of smoke on Anise's shoulder. Since listening to Briac play, he had stopped hissing at him. Instead, he just stared at the bard with a confused expression.

"You remember Drun Coeloc," said Briac.

"Of course," said Anise, "The bard who left the bardic order and became a master at the Academy. You read his papers."

"Yes," said Briac, "well, a couple of years ago, the master scribe of the council found a damaged journal of master Coeloc's from his time after he left the Academy. He returned to the bards and lived the remainder of his days in Taliesin. The scribe knew I had looked into Drun's past at the Academy, and he showed the journal to me."

"What did it say?" said Anise curiously.

"Well, you know how the dragons are coming back?" asked Briac.

"They are?"

Briac frowned. "I thought I told you about that. Ashton has been attacked several times. There have been numerous sightings in the northwest of Liamec."

Anise remembered looking back at Ashton as she was leaving and seeing the scaffolding on the Dragon Watchtower. Now it was clear why it was being rebuilt.

Briac continued, "I mentioned that because the journal pages told how Coeloc knew something about dragons. Apparently, the bards got along with them better than the Academy ever managed to. Coeloc himself said he could talk to them. He called himself a Dragon Speaker. He said that he had gotten his calling to go to the Academy and get them to stop studying clairvoyance from something he'd heard from a dragon."

Anise got excited. "That's what I told master

Huginn," she said.

"Anyway," said Briac, "I just thought you'd find that interesting."

## 5

Hay-bale whinnied nervously as Sebastian led her into the line of people awaiting entrance to the King's Seat. There was a small group of guardsmen in the blue tabards of the king's men asking questions of people trying to enter. Most people were either admitted to the castle or turned away quickly, so the line moved swiftly.

Hay-bale was a small-town horse. She wasn't used to big cities. The walls loomed overhead, and the other horses and numerous people made her nervous. Sebastian patted her on the neck to try to calm her.

While they waited, Sebastian checked out the walls and what they saw through the gates. He was from the same small town as Hay-bale and understood her nerves.

The King's Seat was the biggest castle Sebastian had ever seen. It was larger than any castle he could even imagine. The Young Lion, the prince regent who King Twilight had deposed, had devoted the construction efforts of Liamec for years to expanding and enhancing the hereditary seat of the Kings of Liamec. Like the Egyptian Pharaohs, he had wanted his legacy to live on after him.

The Seat sprawled, rambled, and stretched its way throughout the capital city of Liamec, Capitol. It had grown until it was larger than many towns in the country. The Seat's outer walls met with the city's exterior walls in places. If the Prince Regent had succeeded in his efforts to become king, he might have expanded the Seat until it reached the city walls all around. Then the Seat and the city might have become synonymous.

Sebastian felt a little teary-eyed. He remembered when he had first started hearing the stories about the new king, Twilight, and how he had unseated the cruel prince regent. It had hurt that this new young king, so healthy and mighty, had the same name as his innocent long-dead son.

He and Isabel had never spoken of it, but he thought he had seen the same hurt in her eyes.

Sebastian reached the front of the line. He wore the purple jacket, thick white dyed linen britches, and black boots that Isabel and Anise had made him long ago. The thistledown that stuffed the quilted pockets of the jacket had gotten a little crushed, but it was still warm and tough. He had thought about leaving Hero without the outfit, but it had felt wrong to go on a quest without his armor. So, he had pulled the clothes out of their closet, dusted them off, and now felt like a proper fool as the guardsmen looked him over.

The guardsmen laughed. One of them turned to the others and said, "Look at this one. He thinks he's the Knight of Moon & Shadow."

Sebastian stepped forward, held Hay-bale's lead tightly so she wouldn't shy, and pulled the token Aela had given him out of his belt pouch.

## 6

Sebastian walked down the red carpet that led from the large double doors of the king's vast throne room toward the raised dais where the throne stood. The throne was partially hidden behind the king and his group of advisers. Sebastian was being escorted by one of the king's guardsmen.

The hall was wide and long, though it was longer than it was wide. Both sides were lined with high windows and crowds of people present for the day's court proceedings. Sebastian could hear some of them murmuring about him. His clothing and the road dust covering him were drawing attention.

The late morning sunlight flooded into the room through the windows on one side. Behind the dais that the throne and the king's retinue stood on were several tall stained glass windows depicting scenes from the history of Liamec.

The guardsman halted at the dais's foot and gestured for Sebastian to do the same. There was a little bit of whispering between some of the king's attendants, and one of them stepped forward. In a voice that was clearly intended to, and trained to, fill the room, he called out, "Sebastian of Hero, with a petition for the king!"

A young man stepped forward from the crowd in front of the throne. Though he wore no crown and was dressed in fine but unpretentious clothes, Sebastian thought he must be the king by his bearing. He walked a few steps down the dais and asked Sebastian, "How can I help you, friend?"

Sebastian performed a half bow. He surprised himself with his graceful execution of the move. A half-memory of his father and mother drilling him in things like that came to mind. He'd never had a call to use the knowledge before.

"Your Majesty," he said. "I am seeking the one who has become known as The Girl Who Dreamed. She's my niece. The Lady Aela advised me to ask here if there had been any word, or news, of her."

"Of course," said the young king sympathetically, "both my queen and the lady Aela have been talking of nothing else." He shook his head. "I'm afraid we have no new tidings."

Sebastian assessed the young king in front of him. For a moment, buried grief surfaced. This young man, strong and handsome, was just about the same age his own son, Twilight, would have been if he had lived.

The king continued. "This search for your missing relative strikes me as a noble quest. I will help you in whatever way I can. Can I provide you with some guardsmen to accompany you and help you on your journey?"

Sebastian met the young king's eyes. "Your majesty," he said, "I wouldn't know what to do with guardsmen. I am not a leader of men, and I am used to traveling alone. I merely hoped that there might be some word or news. The Lady Aela was very helpful when she visited us in Hero."

"Of course," said the king. "I am sorry that we don't have any tidings. I would like to provide you with supplies and other equipment to help you on your way." He focused on the man in the blue tabard standing next to Sebastian. "Guardsman," he said, "Please escort our guest to Smithy and see that he is provided with everything he needs."

# 7

Smithy was a big man. He greeted Sebastian with a hearty laugh. "There's something special about you, my good man," he said. "I've got orders from the king to treat you almost like you were one of the family."

They were standing in the Smith's Yard. Sebastian's guardian guardsman had led him here. The clatter of hammers and the creaking of bellows from all the various forges made a mighty din. It didn't seem to make a difference to Smithy's voice. He spoke strongly enough that he could be heard even over the clamor.

"What that mostly means is this," the smith continued. His sooty leather smith's apron was worn with use. He held out a silvery piece of fabric. With his big meaty hands, he spread it out. It was a tunic made of some shiny material. The way the big smith held it made it look almost weightless.

"What is that?" said Sebastian.

"It's armor," said the smith. "We call it attercop armor. It's something special that the queen and I work on. Like I said, you're unusual." He shook the tunic a little. It shimmered in the sunlight that was slanting into the yard. "It's lightweight, and yet it can stop a longbow arrow. Put it on." He handed the metal shirt to Sebastian.

The shirt was light. The material slid smoothly over Sebastian's hands. He pulled and prodded at it a little. It seemed to be all that Smithy had said it was. He removed his purple thistledown jerkin and put the tunic on.

Smithy took in Sebastian's faded jacket as he started putting it back on over the lightweight chain mail. "Would you like a nice new leather jerkin to replace that?" he asked.

Sebastian shook his head. "No, thank you," he said. "this has sentimental value for me."

Smithy inspected Sebastian when he was done putting the shirt on. "Do you need a weapon?" he asked. He focused on Sebastian's sword, which had been returned to him as he left the throne room.

Sebastian pulled the weapon partway out of its sheath. "I'm all right," he said, "I've got my father's sword."

The brawny smith stared at the blade and hilt in Sebastian's hand. "Wait a minute," he said, "I recognize that. Isn't that …"

Sebastian thrust the sword back into the sheath. "It's my father's sword, and that's all it is," he said.

"Oh, yes. Of course it is," said the smith. He glanced up and met Sebastian's eyes with a smile.

# 8

A nise sat quietly by the fire, cross-legged. Briac was out searching for more firewood. She had given him strict orders not to disturb her when he returned. He had told her that the Academy had been graduating clairvoyants at a pretty good rate. They had been doing so for the last ten years.

As part of the class's research in Anise's clairvoyance class, they learned theoretical techniques. However, they hadn't done any practical work. Anise thought that if there was ever a time when it would be helpful to know the truth or get a glimpse of the future, it would be now.

They were a little far from the Academy for Anise's taste. One of the things they had learned in class and that Briac had confirmed was that, unlike the other disciplines, clairvoyance was more potent the closer you were to the Academy. Briac told her that most of the graduating clairvoyants settled in Ashton, Lakeside, or nearby towns.

The process, which Anise had learned theoretically, was in several steps. The first was entering a meditative trance. Anise had started working on that as soon as Briac left the firepit they had set up for the evening. The next step was establishing a mental connection to the staging area, or the Room of Doors, as the references from her class had called it. To Anise's understanding, this was a place that was almost like a dream that the clairvoyants shared in common.

You entered the room of doors, and there was debate whether this was through a dream or astral projection. Then you picked your door and followed the path behind it. What happened next was different depending on who the clairvoyant was and which pathway they traveled.

The little Anise had been able to read about the paths was confusing. One clairvoyant had described traveling down the Path of Flowers when clients asked her about their wedding. She spoke about looking through seas of roses, violets, and other blossoms, looking for a glimpse of a groom or a bride.

Another told of traveling the Path of Death when he tried to find out how long someone had to live. That story hadn't ended well, with the clairvoyant ending the journey early in fear for their own life.

Anise focused on her breathing and her thoughts. Finding the room of doors felt like a different thing than entering into a channeling dream. Some images came from her subconscious mind when she entered a channeling dream. In this case, she was trying to find a shared creation, something that was in some ways more real, perhaps, than the realms visited in dreams.

Anise had tried to connect to the room of doors several times during her clairvoyance class without success. This time, even with the Academy as distant as it was, it felt easier.

Anise felt herself stepping into a huge chamber filled with doors of every shape and size.

# 9

The room of doors was vast. There were archways, entryways, openings, and doorways on every side. There were even hatchways and trapdoors on the floor. Some of the doors were dust-covered and looked like they hadn't been accessed in eons; others appeared like someone might have stepped through them just moments ago. The stone walls looked worn and ancient. The ceiling, somewhere high above, was an indeterminate gray color. Anise wasn't sure if there was a ceiling or the gray was swirling fog.

There was no one but Anise there. It came to her that perhaps it was easier for her to access this place now because it was being used more. Maybe the clairvoyants from the Academy were beating a path through the realms to these doors.

The center of the room was taken up by a large fixed stone basin. The stone bowl looked as ancient as the walls and floor. It might be a pool or bath, but it was sealed with a locked iron cover.

She thought about how she was going to choose which door to open. They all looked different. Each had its own unique character. A large black door set in a heavy frame near her had a skull engraved into its surface. Looking at it, Anise felt a shiver that reminded her of how she had felt the first time she saw Lord Hades. She thought she knew how the paths got their names. This door had to lead to the Path of Death.

Anise thought. What did she want to know? She wanted to know where to go next, how to stop Lorenzo, and how to save the world. She inspected the nearby doors.

Some pathway portals were easy to recognize. Anise saw the Path of Life with green curling plant fronds almost obscuring the entranceway. Some were more difficult. A small barred hatchway chained and padlocked gave her a deep feeling of mystery.

Anise wandered for a bit through the chamber, looking at the doors. She saw the Door of Truth. It was a blue door with daffodils carved into the wooden frame. The stylized head of an owl adorned the center. One of her texts had described the daffodils, owl's head, and blue color. It looked heavily traveled.

The truth was what she was looking for, wasn't it? Maybe this was the door she should open.

Anise's gaze was caught by another door. It was a massive steel construction with a sculpted dragon's head built into the top of the frame. The eyes, glowing like rubies, cut angrily into her heart. Almost involuntarily, she walked over to it and reached out for the handle, shaped like a dragon's claw.

# 10

A nise opened the door. The iron dragon's claw handle felt cold in her hand. The door swung open with a creak and thudded against the stone wall. It was easier to open than it should have been for such a massive piece of metal. She stepped through the door frame.

Anise was confused and couldn't understand what she was looking at. There was a gravel path on the ground leading away from the door frame, but there was no stone wall around it on the other side of the doorway. The door frame stood by itself, rising from the ground.

The pathway led into a mist that reminded Anise of the fog surrounding the Isle of the Wise. In fact, it felt like that same mist. Anise was almost disappointed. She had been expecting something more dramatic. Perhaps the other paths were different? She took a step out onto the pathway and away from the door.

As soon as Anise put her feet on the gravel, she felt the pathway draw her feet down it. It wasn't like she was walking down a path, but more like sliding along a grooved track. The mist continued on both sides. Without knowing how she knew it, she knew that she wouldn't be able to step off the way.

The path started to curve around a bend, and Anise thought she saw a little clearing of the mist ahead. Some color was leaching into the world, and she would be able to see something other than gray fog.

A sound broke through the stillness, the beating of heavy wings. Even though the mist obscured the light, so there was no apparent source, a shadow cast itself over the path ahead of Anise. A massive creature landed with a thud on the track before her.

It was Flambé, the dragon. Her black scaly face turned to Anise; she opened her mouth and roared. A thought intruded into Anise's mind. *Your kind are not welcome here.*

*I want to help*, thought Anise. *I can do something to help if you trust me. If you let me in.*

*Trust? You?* Came the thought. *Your kind are nothing but betrayal and ill faith. Look at what he is doing. He has found his way to the Keep and is searching for the keys to the Scrying Pool.*

*Who?* thought Anise. *The Keep? The Scrying Pool?*

*Your clairvoyants, they don't know what they are doing! These aren't paths; they are cracks in the fabric separating reality from dream. Every time a clairvoyant walks a track, they gouge the fracture deeper. And now, with the dark one trying to open the Scrying Pool, it will just worsen.*

*I will talk no more. Your wards may keep us from stopping your kind from using the other paths, the other cracks, but this one leads out of your territory. This one leads to our home. This one I can protect.*

The dragon reared back and loosed a blast of fiery breath at Anise. The flames washed over her. She felt the heat and the pressure of the dragon's breath. She felt her spirit forced off the path and back into her meditating body.

When she opened her eyes, Iggy flapped in the air above her. He waved his talons excitedly above her head. "Burn," he exclaimed.

## 11

Hay-bale was enormously relieved to be riding away from the gates of Capitol. She was a small-town horse. The ways of the big city were not for her. Sebastian reached out and stroked her neck. "How was it in those crowded stables?" he asked.

Hay-bale nickered. Perhaps she was responding to his question. Maybe she was complaining about the additional weight in her saddlebags from the supplies the king's guardsmen had loaded into them.

Sebastian shifted in the saddle. He felt the presence of the extra layer of armor on his shoulders, though he hardly felt the weight. The additional armor felt good, however. When he was younger, he had felt invincible on his quest as the Knight of Moon & Shadow. He hadn't worried about whether or not something would happen to him. Now, he just wanted to make sure that he made it back to Isabel and Sunshine safely.

"Where are we going to go next?" he asked. The question stumped Hay-bale.

With Hay-bale not providing any answers, Sebastian thought about the question himself. He realized why Isabel might have thought him ill-advised to venture forth on this quest. As the Knight of Moon & Shadow, he'd had supernatural guidance. Luna had been with him every step of the way. Liamec might be a small land by most standards, but it was a pretty extensive territory for one man and one horse to search for one missing person.

*Well*, he thought, *where do I start looking when I lose something at home?*

The answer was obvious; you started looking in the last place you had the thing you lost.

They needed to go to the Academy.

# 12

The second dream storm struck in the early evening. Unlike the first storm, this one happened when most of the land of Liamec was awake. The cracking sound that preceded the disturbance was louder this time. For those near Ashton, the first crack was an almost deafening boom.

People's dreams came to life.

Briac was out gathering firewood. The last traces of the setting sun still lit the sky, making it that part of an evening where the lighting was called twilight. He heard the barrage of the nascent storm. He dropped the wood he was carrying. The initial booming crack was replaced by a crackling sound.

Briac looked around himself, trying to see if he could see anything that could cause such a sound. Then he started through the trees back towards where he and Anise had set up camp. She might still be meditating and could be vulnerable.

There was a rustling in the gray shadows in the underbrush on both sides of Briac. He wasn't sure at first what was making the noise. Then he knew or thought he knew, though he didn't know how he knew.

It was spiders. Lots of spiders. Briac shivered; he'd never liked spiders. He started to run. The gray lighting made it hard to see his footing. The rustling sound grew louder, then louder still. He scrambled his way through the underbrush.

Briac tripped, or perhaps something tripped him. He stumbled and fell. The brush near him started stirring. Multiple hairy legs thrust themselves out of the foliage. Briac gasped and crawled back, away from the wall of leaves.

A spider came scuttling out of the bush. It leered at

Briac, making a chittering noise. Where arachnid features should have been was a human face. It started advancing toward where Briac was lying awkwardly on the ground. Its face was the face of his master in the council of Bards. A scowl of deep disapproval was manifest on that face.

The crackling that had pervaded the background sounds slowed and stopped. Briac blinked, rubbed his eyes, and the spider was gone.

Those who were asleep were lucky if they were between dreams. Some of the people who were having very bad dreams didn't wake up. Some of the people who were having very good dreams didn't want to wake up.

Those who were awake had run-ins with their dreams. Brief. Brief enough to survive for most of those who encountered their nightmares.

# GRISPUT

# 1

Anise woke slowly in the morning. Her trials with clairvoyance had worn her out. Briac was leaning over the campfire cooking the last of the eggs he had bought at the Brierstock market. "Should we talk about what happened last night?" he said.

"What happened last night?" asked Anise.

Briac put the pot with the eggs onto a boulder by the edge of the firepit and handed Anise a wooden spoon. "The crackling, crunching noises, and the spiders." He shivered.

Anise shook her head. "I'm not sure what you're talking about."

Briac frowned. "Maybe you were still meditating," he said slowly.

Later, after they had walked for most of the day, Briac started checking the oncoming travelers carefully as soon as they came into sight.

"We have to take a little care for the next bit," he said. "We don't want to run into the Grisput guards."

"Can't we just avoid the city?" said Anise.

"We'd have to go quite a bit out of our way to avoid it completely," said Briac. "The main road runs right through Grisput, and there aren't too many other choices." He frowned. "We should be all right if we're just a bit careful."

It was Anise's turn to frown when they were crouching in the brush off the side of the road, watching a troop of guardsmen marching by. They were wearing purple tabards with a black silhouette of a coiled serpent on the front. "I don't like this," she said. "We shouldn't have to hide."

"Better to be safe than sorry," said Briac, "We don't want to run afoul of the guard."

"What could they do?" said Anise, "We haven't done anything wrong."

"That doesn't really matter to them," said Briac,

"they don't need much excuse. They're always looking for new bondsmen and women to sell at the bond market."

"They'd sell us?" asked Anise indignantly. Iggy hissed on her shoulder. "They can't do that! That's not right."

Briac just shook his head sadly. He held a finger in front of his lips and glanced through the underbrush at the marching troop.

# 2

Sebastian was riding Hay-bale into the town of Brierstock. Brierstock was mainly known for its market. The settlers of Brierstock were from Almany, and they were famous for their woodworking and craftsmanship. The market also sold food and other goods. It was open every day except sun's day.

They rode into the marketplace. The market, bustling each of the other times Sebastian had passed through town, was quiet, and many of the booths were shuttered. Hay-bale looked disappointed. She had been anticipating a treat.

Sebastian called out to a man walking through the mostly empty marketplace, "Why are all the shops and carts shuttered?"

"The dreams from yesterday," the man answered, "Everyone's trying to recover."

"The dreams?" said Sebastian.

The man stared at Sebastian. The expression on his face made Sebastian think of how one might look at a slow child.

"Yesterday, when all our dreams came to life," he said, "Everyone felt it."

Sebastian shook his head. The man stared for a second in disbelief, then walked on.

They rode on a bit through the empty streets. The sun was shining on the cobbles of the road. Hay-bale was in a good mood and listened attentively to Sebastian's musings.

"You know," he said, "I did have something like a dream coming to life yesterday." Hay-bale nickered encouragingly. "Remember?" he continued. "I was almost falling asleep in the saddle, there was that strange sound, and then I felt like I was talking to Isabel and Sunshine?" He pressed his finger to his lips thoughtfully. "It felt like they were really there." He shook his head. "Why would everyone be upset about something like that?"

## 3

S ebastian tied Hay-bale to a hitching post outside a pub with Der Bunte Hund written on the sign. Above the words was a wooden dog with faded rainbow-colored paint on it. The dog stood unsteadily on its back legs and held an ale mug in its forepaws. Hay-bale gave Sebastian a resentful look as he finished with the reins.

"I know," he said, "But I don't think you'd be welcome inside."

Inside it was small and close, with wooden beams hanging low overhead. It reminded Sebastian of the pub back in Hero. Sebastian didn't spend too much time there, but he did stop in every now and then. He took a seat at the bar and flagged down the pub-keeper for an ale.

As he usually did when he went to the pub in Hero, Sebastian sat on his barstool and looked around the pub's interior. He found that listening and keeping quiet was often an excellent way to learn.

Several conversations were going on. Though the streets outside were empty, many of the people who weren't out there were here.

Two men sitting near Sebastian discussed what had happened with their dreams the day before.

One of them had been chased through the village streets by some mysterious unseen figure, and the other had been trapped in his own home, unable to get out. The second man had opened door after door, trying to exit his home, only to find them leading to unfamiliar rooms. The mysterious unseen figure the first one had seen had chased him for the duration of the dream time, vanishing just as he fled down a dark alley that ended in a dead-end.

Sebastian switched his attention to the conversation on the other side of himself. These people were discussing someone called "Death's Daughter."

"I saw her," said one of them to the other. "Just a little north of here. Before everyone was talking about her."

His companion made appropriately interested noises, and the first man continued, "It was after the Scute Bridge. You know, the one that crosses over the Dragon River toward Ashton. I was on my way to Meara with my crop of cabbage."

The second man frowned. "You've got to stop going up there. Sooner or later, they're just going to cut your throat and rob you. They're pirates; they can't be trusted."

"They pay really well for my cabbages," the first one continued, "Apparently, it's good for sea voyages. Stops some kind of disease." He shook his head, "Anyway, I saw Death's Daughter like I was saying. She had a face like a skull. She was fighting against a strange creature." He shivered. "It was a nightmare. I practically pissed myself looking at it. It looked like a bad dream."

## 4

A nise was sound asleep. She felt a presence intrude itself into her slumber. "Anise, dear," said a quiet, calm woman's voice, "I think it would be a good idea for you to wake up now." She opened her eyes to see moonlight streaming into the clearing where she and Briac were sleeping. It shone down onto their bedroll and the embers of the fire they had laid the night before.

Her medallion felt warm on her chest. She sat up and started quietly fastening the clasps on her armor. Briac snuffled a slight snore into the night air.

Iggy stirred as well. He looked up at Anise from where he lay beside the bedroll. In the beginning, Iggy tried to sleep next to her under the blanket. But, he generated too much heat, and she kicked him out. He still slept as close to her as he could. The feeling of his small body pressed against hers, even from outside the bedroll, was reassuring.

Anise heard some scuffling sounds under the trees outside the clearing in the brush. She stood, pulled on her gloves, put her helmet on her head, and took her spear into her right hand. There was a trace of torchlight glimmering through the trees.

Anise dropped the visor of her helmet over her face. "Who's there?" she called out. The helmet deepened and changed her voice. Iggy flapped his wings and took up a position over her head. Briac started and sat upright, wiping the sleep out of his eyes.

Four men charged into the clearing. They were dressed in the purple tabards and chain mail Anise had seen earlier. Another one stepped in a little after the first four. "Submit to the Grisput guard," he called out, "You're under arrest for vagrancy."

Briac scrambled to his feet, feeling around the bedroll for his knife. Iggy flapped his wings menacingly at the men and hissed.

Anise lifted her arms, shield on one, spear held in the other. She felt the moonlight on her face, even through the visor of her helmet. She knew that the skull contour was glowing with the luminescence of the heavenly body. "You've picked the wrong victims this night," she bellowed.

Anise disregarded the shield on one arm, and the spear clutched in her other hand. She brought her arms together in a sweeping motion and conjured a surge of wind toward the men. Iggy flapped desperately to stay in the air, even though he was out of the main path of the windstorm. All five men were blown backward towards the trees, their weapons and shields clattering to the earth.

From the ground, one of the men sputtered, "Death's Daughter ... ." Three of them took off running through the underbrush, leaving their equipment lying there. The leader and the one who had spoken started reaching to pick up their weapons.

Iggy swooped forward and blasted the area with his fiery breath. The remaining men abandoned their gear and took off after their companions.

## 5

Briac and Anise were talking while breaking their fast. Breakfast this morning was some hard bread and cheese. Anise had thought about warming her cheese in the fire-pit embers, like her uncle used to, but decided it was too much work. Instead, she was chewing on the hard cheese and regretting her decision.

Briac had suggested that they move on in case the guards came back, but Anise had gotten a look on her face and just said, "Let them come." Briac had never seen a look like that on Anise's face before. He wasn't sure what to make of it.

"Once we're the rest of the way past Grisput," he said, "We don't have too far to get to Hero. Just through the southeastern forest and past the towns of the Crossroads."

Anise knew that the Crossroads was the name of the loose confederation of towns and villages that included Hero. Still, it had never meant much to her. Almost all the village life of Hero was in Hero.

"Briac," she said. "I've been thinking. I'd like to stay here for a little while."

"Stay here?" said Briac, "are you serious?" He stared at her. "What's here to stay here for? And what about going home to Hero?"

"You probably don't remember," said Anise, "But I promised that I would help the people who needed help." She looked into his eyes. "The people these guards are catching and selling need my help."

She held one hand out, palm turned upward toward the sky. Iggy launched himself into the air. "I may not have the power to bring down lightning from the skies," she said, "but I can do this." Anise launched a burst of flame out of her palm, blasting upward toward the heavens. Iggy flew into the flaming updraft, twisting and turning like a salmon bounding up a mountain stream. The air grew chill around them.

"Burn," Iggy called out gleefully.

"At the least," said Anise, "I can make these Grisput guards regret what they are doing."

# 6

Anise started small. Her goal wasn't to kill all the guardsmen, who, even though they were part of the system, weren't solely responsible for maintaining or creating it. In so far as she had a goal, it was to give the leaders and slavers of Grisput the message that there was a cost to their actions.

She started ambushing small groups of Grisput guards when they were vulnerable. Briac watched and let her know when a suitable target was leaving the city. He was less recognizable than her and could blend in among the people entering and exiting.

They developed a system. Briac would wait by the main gate into Grisput, with Iggy as a wisp of smoke on his shoulder. When Briac saw a likely target for Anise, he would send Iggy off to alert her that the target was coming.

Iggy had at first been reluctant to do this. He hadn't wanted to give up his place near Anise. It seemed like he felt a need to stay close to her. But, Anise and Briac had convinced him that Briac's shoulder was also a welcome and comfortable place to stay.

They had convinced Iggy of this one evening by the campfire. Iggy was settled on Anise's shoulder when Briac started to play his lute. Iggy's body relaxed, his eyes closed, and he started his cat's purr. Anise carefully picked up his loose form and put him on Briac's shoulder, trying not to interfere with the lute playing. Iggy sighed and settled in a little deeper. He started kneading Briac's shoulder with his obsidian talons; Briac had winced and made an effort to keep playing.

Anise had some success with her small attacks. At least the Guard seemed to be recognizing her presence. They stopped coming out in small groups. They started using the other entrances to come and go in a slightly worrisome development. Briac reported that the people he talked to on the roads and near the gate spoke about Death's Daughter quite a bit. Mostly favorably. Not surprisingly, the Grisput Guardsmen weren't too popular among the common folk.

One night around the campfire, Briac expressed some concerns.

"You know," he said, "They're not going to put up with this forever. Eventually, they're going to set a trap for you." He frowned. "I wouldn't be surprised if they try first with more troops, and then if that doesn't work, they'll probably hire some Academy mages to try to bring you down."

"Well," said Anise, "Maybe I should do something bigger before they get that chance."

# 7

S ebastian changed his mind about going straight to Ashton. Death's Daughter had to have something to do with Anise. The description he had overheard in Der Bunte Hund of the creature she had battled sounded just like one of the nightmares he had fought as the Knight of Moon & Shadow.

He searched the local area for word and news of Todes Tochter. He found himself traveling from town to town following news, hints, and rumors.

Hay-bale was very patient with the search. She carefully discussed what they should do with Sebastian in the evenings around their campfires. She would make her recommendations with grunts, whinnies, and neighs, but in the end, she let Sebastian decide what their course of action should be. Anise was his niece, after all.

Sebastian had plenty of time to think about the story he had heard back in Der Bunte Hund. The description of the creature that had attacked Death's Daughter had to be one of the nightmares that Lorenzo had used to attack the Knight of Moon & Shadow back in the day. Recognition of the creature and the method of attack brought him to a realization.

A building fury grew in Sebastian. It was Lorenzo. It had to be Lorenzo. It had always been Lorenzo. How had he ever thought that the jade heart he and Luna had used to transform the man had had a permanent effect? Something was wrong with him.

Sebastian wasn't sure how he knew that he had to talk to Death's Daughter about Anise; he just knew. He wondered if Death's Daughter might be something like the Knight of Moon & Shadow, a channeled creation.

Regardless, the connection with the nightmare had shown him what needed to be done next. The building rage he was feeling toward Lorenzo made him feel torn, but finding Anise took precedence over any revenge.

# 8

B riac was scouting for possible targets. He was under the shade of some trees away from the main gate out of the Grisput. The sun was starting to set, and the area right near the entrance was even darker as the cliffs below upper Grisput were casting their shadows on the city walls.

Briac was thinking about calling it a night. He was about to leave his watch-post to find where Anise had set up camp for the night when he saw a carriage and a group of armed men march out of the gate.

He waved his hand at the wisp of smoke on his shoulder.

"Iggy," he said urgently, "Go tell Anise that there's a group of men ...," he squinted at the troop, "Twenty or so, heading out of the main gate escorting a carriage. They're heading west. The carriage may have someone important in it."

The wisp of smoke firmed up into the shape of the fire imp. Iggy nodded eagerly at Briac, his face taking on a look of pride at the importance of his commission. He launched himself into the air, his wings flapping vigorously.

Anise was putting the finishing touches on her stack of firewood for the campfire when Iggy emerged from the sky. He alighted on her shoulder. The fire imp looked her in the face, pointed west with one obsidian claw, and said, "Burn." His wrinkled, leathery face acquired an expression of self-satisfaction for having fulfilled his assignment so well.

Because they had left the city late in the evening, the carriage and its escort of armed men hadn't gone far before setting up camp. Anise was just outside the circle of their campfires, watching them and wondering why they hadn't left the following day. They could have stayed in whatever cushy quarters they had in the city rather than camping in the woods.

While Anise was watching them, she heard a scurrying in the underbrush behind her. It was Briac. He was out of breath.

"Anise," he whispered urgently, "I'm glad I got here in time," He shook his head, "It's hard to see in the bad lighting, but they're not the Grisput Guard. I only noticed after I sent Iggy." He pointed to the tabards the guardsmen were wearing. Anise squinted to see one. They were not the purple with the black silhouette of the serpent that the Grisput guard wore, but rather the dark blue with the symbol of the wolf that represented the King's men.

# 9

A nise started to step forward into the circle of firelight. Briac put his hand on her arm to stop her, but she shook him off. She flipped her visor down over her face and moved out from the underbrush into the light.

The guardsmen stopped what they were doing and turned toward her. Most put their hands on their weapons. "Death's Daughter!" said one.

The carriage was off to one side of the guard's campground. There was a large tent, whose canvas walls were illuminated from the inside, in the center of the cleared area. Several fires were blazing around the clearing. A couple of the guardsmen stepped toward the tent entrance as Anise started to speak. Iggy faded into visibility on Anise's shoulder.

"I have no quarrel with the king's men," said Anise. With the visor down, her voice was again distorted and deepened. "But, I would like to know what you are doing coming out of Grisput, whose men I do have a quarrel with."

The guardsmen remained alert but didn't make any additional moves toward their weapons. One of the two who were near the tent slipped inside. Another man stepped forward.

"My lady," he said in a tone meant to be disarming, "as you can see, we owe our allegiance to the king and not to the rulers of Grisput." He gestured to the blue tabards with the wolf silhouette that they all wore. "We are escorting the king's Grisput envoy back to Capitol for a meeting with the king."

Briac stepped out of the shadows to stand behind Anise. One of the men started, but the somewhat delicate standoff held.

The man who had slipped into the tent reemerged.

He bowed to Anise. "Your ladyship," he started. Anise wasn't sure where the title had come from, but perhaps they were just being careful. "Your ladyship. The king's envoy to Grisput requests an audience." He gestured to the open tent flap behind him.

Anise nodded and walked into the tent. Briac looked carefully from side to side at the armed men around them, then slowly followed her inside.

It was even dimmer inside than it had been outside. The light of a single oil lamp lit the interior of the tent. A camp bed with linen bedding was against one wall, and a portable desk was unfolded against the other. In between, a man was standing in the flickering light. He looked old to Anise, though she knew she would have to reassess her idea of what old was once she came to terms with having been asleep for fifteen years. He had red hair streaked with gray and startling green eyes that flashed with intelligence in the dim light.

"Death's Daughter," he said. "I've been hoping we'd get a chance to meet."

"Reynard?" said a flabbergasted Anise. Her voice echoed strangely through her helmet's visor.

# 10

The king's envoy to Grisput looked a little taken aback. "Yes, my name is Reynard," he said. "Do I know you?" He peered at Anise through the flickering lamplight. The death's head skull image on her helmet glimmered in the gloom.

Anise flipped up her visor. "Reynard, it is you." She smiled and stepped forward. "It's me, Anise. You remember, from Hero." Anise hadn't seen Reynard since before she had left Hero, which felt like an eternity ago. He'd been one of the first people she had met when she moved to town, as he and his friend William had been on guard duty when Aunt Rose brought her there.

"Hero?" said Reynard, "Oh, you mean Westhavenfieldbrook. That feels like such a long time ago." He shook his head. "Anise. Of course, I remember you. Didn't you have some kind of accident? I heard something about The Girl Who Dreamed."

"I got better," said Anise quietly.

Briac relaxed a little. The tension that had been in the air since Anise stepped into the clearing had eased. He glanced at the guardsmen standing at the sides of the tent flap just outside, and it seemed like they felt the lessening pressure as well.

"So tell me," said Reynard, smiling, "How is it that Anise from Westhavenfieldbrook is Death's Daughter?"

"Only if you tell me how Reynard from Hero came to be the King's Envoy to Grisput," said Anise with a matching grin.

Reynard got several folding chairs and a flask of wine from somewhere, and the three of them sat in his tent. Anise told her story. The relief of finding someone she could trust, someone from home, brought her comfort. She told her whole story in detail. Briac listened with interest as he hadn't heard some parts of what she had to tell. Iggy was less interested and expressed his disinterest with the occasional hiss or quiet seething growl.

When she had finished bringing Reynard up to date on what she was doing and what she was trying to do, he looked thoughtful.

"You know, Anise," he said, "Part of why I wanted to meet with you when I simply thought of you as Death's Daughter is still very relevant." He took a sip of wine from his cup. "I wanted to meet you and talk to you because we have business to discuss regarding your motives and methods in attacking Grisput." He pursed his lips and looked thoughtful. "I was going to try to dissuade you from your attacks on the Guard." He looked up and met her eyes. "Not because I think you're wrong. In fact, the king and I entirely share your motives. The indentured servitude system in Grisput is repugnant and needs to be stopped as soon as possible."

Reynard pressed his fingers together to form a steeple. "No, the problem is that your methods aren't working. The guard and the leaders of Grisput are just digging in their heels. They don't even really see it as connected to indentured servitude. They just see it as an attack on themselves. I thought I understood, so I wanted to talk to Death's Daughter before I knew she was you."

Reynard stood, stretched, and said, "So, if I may give you some fatherly advice." He smiled. "I think I know what you need to do. I think maybe you do as well." He sat back down again and leaned forward. "Twilight and I have the Grisput situation in hand, I hope. We're combining a campaign of education and information about how bad the system is with diplomatic pressure. I think we've been making some headway. I think you need to give up on attacking the Grisput Guard and go back to the Academy and confront Lorenzo. From your description of your adventures, I think it's clear that he is the one behind your troubles. I think he is the villain of your story. You know, I didn't trust him when Sebastian first told me about him years ago. I think it's been him all along."

# 11

A nise met Reynard's eyes. "So," she said, "Thank you for your advice. You've certainly given me something to think about." She smiled. "Now, I think it's your turn. What happened to you after the Knight of Moon & Shadow saved Westhavenfieldbrook? William kept talking about you for years."

"I feel bad about William," said Reynard. "I've been meaning to check on him." He frowned. "It's just I've been so busy."

"So, tell me," said Anise, "Last time I saw you, you were laid up in bed recovering from injuries the nightmare that attacked Hero had given you."

"Yes," said Reynard, "that took a lot of time. I had a lot of time to think." He laughed. "Too much time, I fear. I decided to see the world while I was still young. (And, I was still young. That was twenty years ago)."

He shook his head, "With the foolish imagined wisdom of youth, I decided to just leave. I didn't really talk to anyone. I thought people might try to talk me out of going." He looked up and met Anise's eyes. "There were quite a few times, later in life, when I labored under the bondage of Grisput when I wished they had."

"You were a bondsman?" said Anise. She noticed his left ear for the first time. A chunk of the earlobe was missing; it had healed long ago. She recognized the injury as the way a bonds-person from Grisput was marked.

Reynard put his hand to the clipped ear. "Yes," he said, "for years. There was a time when that's all I thought I would ever be." He wiggled the part of his ear where the earlobe should be with his fingers. "You know, this makes it harder to deal with the Grisput aristocracy. But, I kind of like that." He laughed again. "Rub their noses in it, so to speak. Or, their ears."

Reynard continued, "Anyway, that's jumping ahead

in the story. I left Hero with nothing but a backpack of supplies, a small amount of money, and high hopes."

Reynard stared into his wine cup. "I had some adventures. There were some good times and some bad. They ended, however, when I got to Grisput." He brightened. "At first, in a good way. I met a girl. That's why I didn't talk to William about leaving Hero, by the way. He'd already met Agnes. I didn't want to make him feel torn between her and me."

Reynard lifted his cup, took a sip, then continued, "The girl I met was everything I ever wanted. A copper-haired beauty. We were happy for what now seems like a very brief time. She lived in a little village not far from Grisput. We got married and started talking about a family. That's when the guard arrested me. They claimed for poaching. I heard she died a few years later."

He waved his hand in the air. "Enough about that. I was trapped in bondage for years. My king, my friend, Twilight, saved me from that fate. He saved me, and now we're doing everything we can to save everyone else who is held in this evil city."

# 12

Anise and Briac were sitting by their campfire. Iggy was lounging *in* the fire, relaxing and enjoying the heat. His presence made it harder to add a new piece of wood, but he moved every now and then, which stirred the flames, so they didn't have to use a stick as a poker to keep the fire blazing.

"I put something together while we were talking to Reynard," said Briac.

"What was that?" asked Anise. She was staring somewhat moodily into the fire, her thoughts lost in a morass. She had enjoyed the feeling of purpose that fighting with the Grisput guard had given her. So, while she thought Reynard was probably right, she didn't entirely like it.

"When you told him what Flambé, the dragon, said to you in your channeling dream. The part about the Keep and the Scrying Pool. You didn't tell me that part before."

Anise looked up from the flickering flames. "What about it?"

"The damaged journal of Drun Coeloc that I told you about? It mentioned both of those things. Both the Keep and the Scrying Pool."

"What did it say?" asked Anise.

"Not too much," said Briac, "But it seems significant now. It talked about a place called the Keep of Truth and Deceit. Apparently, it's on the Isle of the Wise."

"There's nothing on the Isle of the Wise but mist, gravel paths, and mystery," said Anise.

Briac shook his head. "Not according to master Coeloc," he said. "And the Scrying Pool? He mentions that too. In fact, though he doesn't say what it is, he makes it sound pretty important. Apparently, the opening of the Scrying Pool is what made him go to the academy. It wasn't clear why, but that was a tipping point."

Anise was silent. They both gazed into the fire. Then, it was Briac's turn to look up and catch her attention. "Another thing," he continued. Anise groaned audibly. "You know it's time. You've been putting it off for too long. I know it's hard, sometimes, to talk to family, but they've got to be worried sick. You need to reach out."

# 13

Something woke Sebastian, and he sat up. He glanced at the smoldering embers of his campfire. He had banked it so it wouldn't spread, but he hadn't doused it completely, as the warmth was still welcome while he slept.

He looked for Hay-bale but didn't see her. Then he noticed some other strange things. The stars weren't the same constellations he was familiar with. And the glow of glimmering light from the coals seemed to form a perfect circle around his campsite.

He recognized this. This was how his dreams had looked when he'd been the Knight of Moon & Shadow. When he'd met with Luna on his quest.

Sebastian rose to his feet and looked around. A figure moved at the edge of the campsite and stepped into the light. A woman's shape, dressed in black, with a skull for a face.

"Death's Daughter," breathed Sebastian. He put his hand on his sword-hilt.

The woman moved closer. She grasped the bottom of the skull visage and lifted it, revealing Anise's face underneath. "Uncle Sebastian," she said. She ran towards him, collapsing into his arms in a deathly tight embrace and bursting into tears.

"Anise?" said Sebastian, holding the sobbing woman in his arms.

"I'm so sorry," said Anise. "I've been meaning to tell you, Rose, and Isabel that I'm all right. There's just been so much going on, and it's been so long."

Sebastian wiped a tear off Anise's face. "It's all right," he said, "I'm just glad you're safe." He looked around. "Are you safe?" he asked. "And, where are we?"

"We're in your dream," said Anise. "I'm a dream walker," she continued proudly.

"Anise," said Sebastian, "Where are you in the waking world? I've been looking for you."

"Don't worry about me," said Anise. "I've figured out what I need to do to end this. I'm going to the Academy, to a place called The Keep of Truth and Deceit. I'm going to confront Master Lorenzo." She shook her head. "He's the one who trapped me in the dream realm."

"When I heard about that nightmare beast that attacked you, I thought it must be him," said Sebastian. "I can't believe I trusted him. I was so sure he had reformed."

Anise looked worried. "Don't try to follow me to the keep," she said. "I need to finish this myself." She touched her uncle's hand. "I'll come home to you, Rose, and Isabel, in Hero when this is all over."

# ASHTON

# 1

T he third dream storm struck during the first hours of darkness. Anise and Briac were asleep at their campsite. Iggy stirred restlessly even before the first crack presaged the crackling sound. Sebastian shifted in his sleep at his own campsite to the north but managed to sleep through the noises.

Anise sat bolt upright when the crack happened. The sound felt like it was cutting into her brain. She put both hands to the sides of her head and pressed. Briac woke a bit less quickly. He looked around the campsite groggily.

There was a loud rustling in the underbrush near them. Anise stood and lit the area with a cool conjured sphere of master Videmon's light.

A creature burst through the trees into the clear, knocking one of the smaller trees to the ground as it did so. Briac leapt to his feet, looking to the ground near the bedroll for his dagger.

It was a nightmare. Like the one Anise had fought back on the road near the Dragon River. Somehow Anise felt like the creature didn't understand why it was here. As if it was lost and confused. It didn't matter, however. It raised its forelimbs and charged toward the embers of their campfire and them.

Iggy launched himself into the air. He maintained a respectful distance as he remembered what had happened the last time he had tangled with one of these creatures. He blasted his fiery breath at the beast. The flames washed over it like water without effect.

Anise faced the creature. The crackling sound filled the clearing. She knew that it was a creature out of a dream. She had a sudden inspiration. Starting with the image of the circle of light that channelers manipulated in their dreams, she formed the glowing sphere she had conjured into a band of illumination. Gesturing with both hands, she moved the hoop of light between her and Briac and the creature. She tried to imbue the gleaming ring with the same connection to the dreaming world that permeated the circle of light in a channeling dream.

Iggy started flapping his wings furiously to backpedal away from the circle. He looked scared. The creature stopped its forward charge and just stared at the glowing band.

Anise thrust her hands forward toward the creature, moving the ring of illumination at and over it. The beast vanished as the light surrounded it, back into the dream it had come from.

Sebastian woke with tears in his eyes and sweat dampening his armpits. He sat up and rubbed his face with his hands. There was some strange crackling sound, faintly sounding in the distance, but it faded as he listened. As the crackling sound faded, Sebastian heard the distant cry of a wolf. He knew why he had been weeping. For the first time in years, he'd had the dream again. He'd dreamt of the day he, Isabel, and their infant son had gone on an outing to the forest. The weather had been so lovely and the day so warm that he and Isabel had fallen asleep on their spread blanket near their food basket.

The dream hadn't ended there, though the next part was less memory and more nightmare. Sebastian dreamt he was somehow following his infant son as he toddled off into the woods away from his parents.

His dream had forced him to watch as his little Twilight bumbled into a clearing filled with wolves. The nightmare had ended with the slavering wolves charging at his little boy.

# 2

S ebastian was riding Hay-bale through the streets of Lakeside. A small town across the lake from Ashton and the Academy, Lakeside had never been very interesting to Sebastian. It was just a town you rode through on your way to the other side of the lake.

This time what struck him about the town was how many clairvoyance students from the Academy had set up shop here. The symbol for a clairvoyant trying to sell their services was a wooden or iron sign of an eye hanging above the doorway. It felt to Sebastian like every second house in town had one.

The shops were shuttered, though it was almost midday. Also, as it had been in Brierstock, the streets were more empty than usual. Though he suspected he might already know the answer, Sebastian asked a passing woman why all the clairvoyants' shops were closed.

"The dreams affected them more than everyone else," the woman answered.

Sebastian nodded. Though it hadn't felt dangerous, not to him at least, the dream that had woken him the night before had been more real and immediate than any dream he had ever had before.

The ride from Lakeside to Ashton was pleasant. The sun shone on the trail and reflected off the lake's waters. Hay-bale was in a good mood and listened attentively to Sebastian's musings.

"Should I confront Lorenzo or try to find the Keep of Truth and Deceit?" said Sebastian.

Hay-bale nickered.

Sebastian looked thoughtful, "You're right," he said. "Anise might be annoyed if I try to confront Lorenzo without her here." He nodded. "I'll try to find out something about the Keep."

# 3

Sebastian and Hay-bale rode into Ashton just as the sun started to set. The Dragon Watchtower stood out against the skyline. There was still some scaffolding on one side of the rebuilt tower, but it looked almost complete. The last time Sebastian had been here, visiting his sleeping niece, the tower's reconstruction had just started. Sebastian thought he saw a ballista standing atop the distant tower.

More people were wandering the streets of Ashton than there had been in Lakeside. The citizens of this town were more used to unusual happenings, being closer to the Academy. Maybe, whatever had happened the day before hadn't had as much effect on them.

Sebastian saw a group of men in the uniforms of the Dragon Watch. The red tabard over a leather jerkin, with the silhouette of a dragon's head on the chest, was familiar. But, these men were acting quite differently than the friendly night watchman he remembered from his first visit here. There were five of them walking close together. At least one of them always kept an eye on the sky, and they all were alert.

Sebastian walked down Dead Man's Alley past the open windows of the Greedy Gull inn. They had just lit the lamps to brighten the darkening twilight. The Inn's common room, glimpsed through the open windows, looked warm and inviting, and Sebastian was tempted to stop in and say hello to Swen, the innkeeper, and his daughter. But that wasn't his destination. He clucked to Hay-bale and pulled gently on the reins to distract her from the warmth and the light.

They turned off a cross street onto Leafdrop Lane a little further on. Sebastian let Hay-bale pick her own pace. He always felt welcomed, but he didn't like asking for favors, so he wasn't in any hurry.

A row of unassuming houses came into view. The one with faded green paint and a battered old oak door with the number thirteen carved into it didn't stand out from the rest. Sebastian pulled Hay-bale to a stop, dismounted, and approached the door.

Holding Hay-bale's reins in one hand, he reached out the other and rapped on the oak wood of the door.

# 4

T he door opened. Sebastian had to adjust his gaze down to the top of a head of bright red hair and a pair of emerald eyes gazing up at him. Hay-bale nickered, hopefully. Unlike Betsy, who had mistrusted new people on sight, Hay-bale assumed they would give her something to eat.

"Sebastian," called out Maeve breathlessly. She hugged him around the thighs.

Sebastian put out the hand that wasn't holding Hay-bale's reins and grabbed the door frame for balance. "Hello, Maeve," he responded a little less emphatically but warmly.

"You're here because of Anise," said Maeve.

"Of course," said Sebastian.

Almost simultaneously, they both continued, "Have you heard anything?"

Sebastian nodded. "I haven't seen her, but she contacted me in a dream." He looked thoughtful. "So I guess I did see her. Though I'm not sure if that counts or not. Anyway, she said she was coming here to go to someplace called the Keep of Truth and Deceit."

"The Keep of Truth and Deceit?" said Maeve. "That's all anyone talks about anymore. Master Lorenzo has been making a big deal about it like he discovered it. He could have asked me about it, and I would have told him where it was."

A young man dressed in a disheveled cook's uniform burst into the otherwise empty common room. He was young to Sebastian's eyes, though he must have been in his mid to late twenties. He was thin but looked strong. He charged over to the doorway where Sebastian and Maeve were and said, "Where is she? Is she with you?" His red hair flopped over his eyes, making him look a little crazed.

Maeve frowned. She turned to Sebastian apologetically and said, "You remember Raphael, our cook?"

# 5

Sebastian looked inquisitively at the young man. "She's not with me," he said. "I haven't seen her yet, but I heard that she's on her way here." He nodded at the young man in his kitchen rumpled uniform. "Didn't you used to be a skinny little kid?"

The young man grunted noncommittally and turned and left the way he came, through the door that led toward the way-house kitchens.

"You'll have to forgive Raphael," said Maeve. "He's been a bit distraught since Anise woke up." She looked thoughtful. "He was quite conscientious about visiting her while she was asleep. I think he made the trip to the infirmary at least once a week."

Maeve met Sebastian's eyes. "Anyway," she said, "Why would Anise be thinking about going to the Keep of Truth and Deceit?"

"I don't know, exactly," said Sebastian. "She said she was going to go there to confront Lorenzo."

"What does she want to confront Lorenzo about?" asked Maeve.

Sebastian looked angry. "It was him, Maeve. He was the one who trapped Anise in the dream world. He's the one who made her lose fifteen years of her life."

Maeve looked shocked. "But, why?" she said.

"There's something wrong about how he's thinking," said Sebastian. "He's obsessed with a prophecy that he heard years ago. He thinks Anise is some kind of dark channeler who will doom the world."

"Well," said Maeve, "that doesn't sound right." She frowned. "Maybe I'll have to talk to some of my connections at the Academy."

"I don't think we should do anything until Anise

gets here," said Sebastian. "I was just going to try to find out something about this 'Keep of Truth and Deceit' for her."

"Well," said Maeve, "the Keep of Truth and Deceit is where Lorenzo spends most of his time nowadays." She made a tut-tutting noise. "Ever since he 'discovered' the Keep, it's all they talk about at the Academy. 'We've found the heart of the dreaming.' 'Clairvoyants now know where their paths begin.'"

"You sound skeptical," said Sebastian.

"Well," said Maeve, "as I said, if he'd asked me, I could have told him that there was a castle on the Isle of the Wise long ago." She shook her head. "But no one thought to ask me."

"If I might ask," said Sebastian, "Where does your knowledge come from?"

"And well, you might," said Maeve. Her voice took on a formal tone that Sebastian hadn't heard before, her gaze grew a little distracted, and she began to recite.

# 6

I t felt a little like Maeve was talking to someone more than Sebastian. Like she was speaking to her people or her family as well, though there was no one else in the room. "This is a tale my people have told since the time before you móra overshadowed these lands. From when our folk filled the land from the sea to the Etenies mountains. It is sometimes called 'the Queen who ruled from Dream.'

"The weak spot between the worlds, the place where dream meets existence, is a fort. It is built of a stone, not from the earth, crafted by someone there before anyone was there. The keep is where dream creatures meet those from our world who wander too far away from wakefulness."

Maeve looked up to meet Sebastian's eyes. "My people have known to shun the keep and the island for ages. We didn't always know this.

"There was a queen in those days, Coblaith. She was the ruler of the clan that lived in this region. Most of the women of my people are wiser than the men, but she was an ambitious prideful woman. She almost resembled a man in some ways." Maeve winked at Sebastian.

"The fort is on the island, and there is no way to get there except by boat. There is no bridge, no causeway, no way to walk. Swimmers don't seem to make it, though it's unknown exactly why.

"At a time when the keep was empty, abandoned, Coblaith took her people, her clan, on boats to the island. They moved into the keep and set up house there.

"For several years, Coblaith's kin prospered and grew strong and populous. They expanded their reach and power, conquering neighboring clans. Corblaith must have achieved some of her ambitions.

"They also grew strange. The people of the

neighboring clans had to work with them and deal with them due to their power and influence, but tales sung to this day tell of how distant and eerily they behaved. As if living on the island and in the keep had changed them somehow.

"The story doesn't end well, as you might imagine," continued Maeve. "One day, the people of Coblaith's clan just disappeared. Scouts from the neighboring clans were sent to check on the island and the keep. They found the fort empty, looking exactly as before it was occupied."

Maeve sighed. "That was enough for my people. We have long memories. None of my folk have been to the Isle of the Wise for hundreds of years."

# 7

**M**aeve looked around the empty common room. "Cian," she called out. "Come greet Anise's uncle!" She turned to Sebastian. "Cian still lives here," she said. "Mostly to keep her old mother company, I think." She winked at Sebastian. "She's done well for herself with her Academy education. She's a house-keeper."

"A house-keeper," said Sebastian, impressed. "We haven't had a house-keeper in Hero in years. I think the Mayor had one a few years back for a little while. But that was mostly for show, and I don't think he had ever been anywhere near the Academy."

Cian stepped into the room from the back hall. She was a larger version of her mother, with the same emerald eyes and flaming red hair.

"Uncle Sebastian," she said. She came over and gave him a hug. "Have you heard anything about Anise?"

"I know that she's alive, and she's on her way here," said Sebastian. Cian looked relieved. "Your mother tells me you're a house-keeper now?"

"She's not just a house-keeper," said Maeve. "She's been hired by some of the wealthiest people in town." Maeve was practically glowing with pride. "She's had to hire helpers. One of the masters from the Academy has been talking about hiring her to keep his house."

"Mother!" said Cian. The exasperation was evident in her voice.

"So, what services do you offer?" asked Sebastian.

It was Cian's turn to look proud. "We're a full-service keeping business," she said. "Security, lighting, maintenance, construction. We can cast a good luck charm to ensure the fortune of all the house's residents or a vigor one to maintain good health. Our motto is 'If you want to keep your house, hire us as house-keepers.'" She frowned. "I know it's not very good yet. It's still a work in progress."

After assuring Cian that he would pass on the information if any news about Anise came up, Sebastian turned back to Maeve.

"So, how do I get into the Keep of Truth and Deceit?"

# 8

**M**aeve looked thoughtful. "Our people do have other stories about the keep," she said. "more myth than history. It is said that the keep used to be the stronghold of the lord of dreams. I believe you móra call him Morpheus. He built it, of course, before the time of Coblaith. Before the time of my people in general, and certainly before yours. He abandoned it, moving on to somewhere else later. His former presence there made the Isle of the Wise a thin spot between our world and Dream."

"That doesn't help me get in," said Sebastian sadly.

"I'm not done yet." Maeve sighed with exasperation. "The main gates are called the Gates of Horn and Ivory. They stand side by side, but the story is that they can only be opened by a mage, a wizard, by magic."

"But, your story about Coblaith and her people?" asked Sebastian.

"Just because my people are different doesn't mean we don't have magic," said Maeve. "It works a bit differently than your Academy trained mages, but it works well."

Sebastian shook his head. "Still doesn't help me." He waved his hands up and down a little mournfully. "Whatever magic I had, if it was ever mine, left me a long time ago when I put the moon back up into the sky."

Maeve shot Sebastian a look. Cian looked away so as not to come anywhere near meeting Maeve's eyes, but Sebastian was oblivious.

"If I may continue," she said and waited a moment. Sebastian didn't say anything. "There is another entrance."

Sebastian looked attentive and quiet, and Maeve continued, "let me tell you a tale of Galan, known, among other names, as Galan dream-stealer."

# 9

**M**aeve started into her tale. Cian's eyes snapped to her mother's face. She focused on her mother's expression and her words. Something *was* captivating about the sound of Maeve's voice, thought Sebastian, as he lost himself in the story as well.

"Now Galan Dream-stealer was a great hero of our people, but this was in the days before that. He was just a young boy on the verge of manhood, living in a village where Lakeside is now. The people of his settlement already knew to avoid the island. Though, this was before the time of Corblaith and her occupation of the keep.

"They avoided the island and the keep because they knew that the lord of dreams lived there."

"I thought you said he abandoned it?" asked Sebastian. Cian's jaw dropped open a bit, and she stared at him.

Maeve looked a little disgruntled. "This was before that," she said. "The lord of dreams still lived there when Galan was young. Perhaps this story has something to do with why he left."

She looked up at Sebastian. He found the expression in her emerald green eyes hard to read. From the way Cian reacted, it seemed she understood it better. "If I may?" she said. Sebastian nodded.

"Now, there was a girl in the village. It's not clear if she was anything special. History and the stories don't tell us much about her. But, to Galan, she was. He thought the sun shone down onto the earth just for her. They were due to get married. Galan was ready to make her his wife and give her the happy village life she wanted.

"But as young people sometimes do, she had doubts. She expressed them to him by describing her dreams. She told Galan that she was dreaming of another young man in the village. This other young man was a successful hunter and quite a charmer, and many of the girls in the village dreamed about him in many different ways. Galan didn't consider whether the dreaming she was talking about might be less than literal. He just took her at her word. He blamed the dream for the problem, not the girl."

# 10

Maeve continued, "Now, being the young man destined to turn into the hero he was to become, Galan didn't react to this the way another man might. He blamed the dream, but he knew where it came from and who had sent it.

"He took one of the small fishing boats that his people used to fish the lake's waters and set out toward the island you now call the Isle of the Wise."

Maeve shook her head. "The people of Galan's village knew better than to approach the island of the lord of dreams. Still, Galan was destined to become a hero, and the difference between a hero and a fool can sometimes be as narrow as a sharp knife's blade.

"The mists were heavy around the island. Perhaps even more than they are now. It's said that the curtain between the realm of Dream and the world was thinner while the dream lord lived in his keep. The mists were heavy, but Galan was resolute. He drew his boat onto the island's shore after a timeless age drifting in the fog on the lake waters.

"He knew what he was looking for. His people told tales of the lord of dream's keep, but the mists were thicker on the shores. There are separate stories told of his time in the mists trying to find the keep," Maeve looked up at Sebastian and met his eyes. "But, I know that you are impatient to get the answer to your question, so I'll leave those stories for another time," she continued.

"Just let it be known that Galan Dream-Stealer, hero of song and story, made it through the mists and stood before the Gates of Horn and Ivory.

"Now, like you, Galan was no channeler, no mage. He was just a boy looking to bring a girl back into his dreams. He had no way to open either gate.

"He tried the gates, both of them. He shook them,

rattled them, and called out until he was hoarse, but the gates wouldn't budge, and there was no one there in the mist but him.

"Once he realized he wasn't getting in that way, Galan started looking for another entrance. To the main gates' right, low on the wall behind some bushes, he found his access, his way in.

"My people call it the Gate of Heros, but it's just a sewer system, a crawlway. Though what or who that lives in the lord of dreams' keep needs a sewer, I don't know."

# 11

Sebastian made a move as if to turn away. "Thank you, Ma ...," he started to say. Cian made a motion with her finger to her lips. She didn't have to make the shushing noise. It was implicit in the gesture.

"You're not thinking about leaving before the story is done," she whispered urgently. Her statement was structured like a question but sounded more like a command. Maeve seemed oblivious. She continued.

"Galan made his way into the keep through the gate of heroes. Once inside the keep, he had to decide where to go. The stories our people told at that time spoke of the Dream-lord keeping watch over the realms of reality and dream from a high room in the keep. So, Galan decided to make his way up toward the top of the fort.

"The keep was like a maze of convoluted corridors and passageways, and Galan's path was complicated by needing to avoid the Dream-lord's servants. Some didn't look too different from the villagers in Galan's village. Others were little winged folk who flapped their tiny bat-like wings as they flitted through the stone corridors about their lord's business.

"Every time Galan came across a stair, he climbed it. Every time he encountered a servant of the dream lord, he hid. Eventually, he reached a large room toward the top of the keep with a wide-open double door. At the entrance to the door was a tall thin man wearing a flowing black robe. He turned his pale face to Galan before he had time to hide and said, 'Ah, Galan, I've been waiting for you. Come with me. I've got something to show you.'

"The need for hiding clearly gone, Galan followed the pale lord of dreams into the room behind him. It was a large room, though the full extent was unclear. The far reaches stretched off to what must be the edges of the keep. The ceiling was open to the sky, though that sky was just a swirling expanse of mist. Both the walls and the floor were covered with doors and portals of every shape and size.

"The dream lord brought Galan over to a stone pool on the floor. He swept one arm over the murky greenish fluid in the basin. 'My scrying pool,' he said proudly. 'I've just built it. Look in. There is something that I think you should see.'

"Galan gazed into the murky fluid. At first, there was nothing but darkness, then his vision cleared, and he felt that he was looking into a clearing in the forest. He recognized the place; it wasn't far from his village. There, lit by the moon's light, was his girl in the arms of his rival, the young hunter. Galan realized that the girl of his dreams wasn't dreaming of him as he was dreaming of her.

"It's said," continued Maeve, "that that moment is what released Galan from a common fate as a villager. That moment inspired him to leave his village and go out and become the hero he was to become."

## 12

Briac, Anise, and Iggy were leaving Brierstock. Anise had gotten a long hooded cloak and wore it when they passed through towns. Her armor and appearance were distinctive enough that she felt it was better to conceal them to remain unrecognized. Iggy did his part by fading into a wisp of smoke on her shoulder. When they walked through the marketplace in Brierstock, Briac greeted everyone and chatted with all the shopkeepers.

As they left the city behind them and set out on the dusty road, Anise turned to her smiling companion. "You know, it doesn't help me keep undercover to have you talking to everyone," she said.

"Sorry," said Briac, though his smile said otherwise. "we haven't discussed what will happen when we get to Ashton," he continued.

Anise frowned. "I'm not exactly sure," she said. "I need to confront Lorenzo." Her brow furrowed. "He's evidently willing to resort to violence to get his way. I hope it doesn't have to come to that."

"Should we just walk into the Academy and ask to meet with him?" said Briac.

Anise shook her head. "I have no idea who's working with him or who to trust. I think we should get in the way I got out. We'll sneak in by the cover of darkness, borrow a boat from the docks, and row over to the Isle of the Wise. If we can find this Keep, and especially the Scrying Pool, we might be able to stop Lorenzo from whatever he's doing."

"Sounds like a plan," said Briac. "My orders are to get you to your final destination, and help you when you get there, so I'm just following you."

Anise's expression lightened. "Thank you, Briac. I don't really know what I'm doing or why. But, you being with me has made doing it a lot easier."

Briac lifted her hand to his lips and kissed it. "That's what I'm here for," he said. Iggy looked skeptical.

# 13

A nise, Iggy, and Briac crossed the Scute bridge over the Dragon River. Behind them was the road that led north toward Meara and the ocean and south toward Brierstock. The way forward led toward Ashton, the Academy, and the Isle of the Wise.

Someone was walking toward them from the other side of the bridge. Anise pulled her cloak's hood forward over her head to hide her hair and the death's head helmet. She and Briac had become a little more casual on the road, especially when passing people traveling alone. But, she still felt the need to not draw attention to herself. Iggy hissed a little and faded from view on Anise's shoulder.

The person approaching them looked a little unusual. He was a tall young man, muscular and fit. He wore a cook's uniform and had a hefty cleaver stuck through his belt. There was an obviously improvised leather sheath around the cleaver blade. The razor-sharp edge was already cutting through the leather. He had some kind of hat perched on his head made out of metal.

As he walked closer, Anise inspected his face. He was handsome. Strands of red hair poked out from under the metal hat. He was tall, and her eyes were drawn to how his shoulders and biceps filled out the beige cook's uniform.

"Raffy?" said Anise.

The young man frowned. "No one calls me that," he said, "except ...," his eyes widened.

Anise pulled back her hood, stepped forward, and hugged Raphael. She felt the strength in his body under his cook's uniform as she squeezed him.

"Anise," said Raphael. "I was looking for you."

It was Briac's turn to frown. "So," he said, "Who is this?"

Anise stepped back a step. "Briac," she said, "You remember Raphael. From the Way-house? Raffy, I can't believe how big you've gotten."

"Of course," said Briac. "The cook's assistant. Didn't you used to be a skinny little kid?"

"I'm the cook now," said Raphael proudly.

"Is that a pot on your head?" asked Briac.

# 14

Raphael flushed. For a moment, his cheek's redness matched the color of the hair wisps that poked out from under the metal. "I lined it with cloth and banged it into shape with a hammer," he said. "I didn't have a helmet."

"Why did you need a helmet?" said Briac. Then he laughed. "Oh, I see. You're a knight coming to rescue your lady fair. How noble."

Anise glared at the bard. "Briac, be nice," she said. "Raffy, I'm so glad to see you," she said to Raphael. "I think your helmet looks very good."

Iggy faded into view on Anise's shoulder. Raphael jerked back and made a motion to reach for his cleaver. Anise reached out her hand and put it on Raphael's. "It's all right, Raffy," she said, "This is Iggy." She smiled at the worry on Raphael's face. "Iggy, say hi to Raphael." The fire imp hissed and focused his cat-like eyes on Raphael. "Burn," he said emphatically.

\* \* \*

"So, out for a stroll, are you?" said Briac. Anise shot him a look.

"I was coming out to look for Anise," said Raphael, "to help. When she left Ashton, I knew she had to be scared of something. Maybe the same thing that made her sleep for so long."

"Well, you were right, Raffy," said Anise firmly. "It was master Lorenzo. I'm going back to Ashton to confront him."

"Master Lorenzo?" asked Raphael. He looked thoughtful. "There *was* something strange about how he stared at you when he came to the infirmary." Raphael gazed at Anise. "I'm coming with you," he said. He spoke quietly and calmly, but the way he said it felt like it left little room for argument. Briac frowned.

Anise looked worried. "Raffy," she said, "it could be dangerous. Lorenzo isn't who he's been pretending to be at the Academy. He's a dangerous man who is quite willing to use violence to get his way." She looked sad. "He killed my parents and left me lost in a dream. Uncle Sebastian thought he had put him right, but it didn't take."

Raphael met Anise's eyes and repeated, "I'm coming with you."

# THE ISLE OF THE WISE

# 1

Sebastian didn't tell the fisherman renting him the boat everything. He felt bad about this, as he didn't like lying. Still, he wasn't strictly lying but simply omitting small parts of the truth. Not everyone needed to know everything.

The fisherman scowled at him. "Don't go into the mists," he said, gesturing out over the waters toward the fog-shrouded island in the distance. "Every now and then, some idiot rows too close to that island. It takes them a long time to come back, and sometimes they don't." He coughed and spat off the rustic wooden dock into the water.

Sebastian had left Hay-bale stabled in the Way-house's stable facilities. Sometimes some of the residents had horses. Maeve hired space for them in a livery barn just down the street from the Way-house. Cian promised to check in on Hay-bale and ensure she was all right. Sebastian rubbed her nose and told her he would be back soon. He wasn't sure she believed him, but she nickered her acknowledgment of his promise.

The boat Sebastian was hiring was a rough-looking rowboat. The fisherman looked even a little rougher than the boat, but the price was right, or, at least, what Sebastian could afford. He hadn't brought much money. Truth be told, he didn't have much. Being the Hero of Hero wasn't a paying gig, and small-town farmers didn't usually deal much in currency.

"You've been in a boat before?" said the man. Sebastian caught himself staring at the man's beard. The hair color had a hint of blue in it. It was a very unusual color. The fisherman noticed his gaze. "I moved here from Meara," he said without further word of explanation.

"Of course," said Sebastian. "My father used to take me fishing." His first lie of omission. His father had taken him fishing a few times, but they'd cast from the banks of the Westhaven river and hadn't caught much. The second lie of omission was inherent in the first. The only time he'd ever been on a boat was one time when he, Gerard, Leonard, and Isabel had stolen a rowboat when they were children. It had been Gerard's idea. It hadn't worked out too well, as they had spent the whole time trying to recapture one of the oars that fell off the side, got caught in the current, and drifted off downstream.

Sebastian got into the boat, trying to look smooth handling the oars as he put them into the oarlocks. The fisherman watched him skeptically. "Don't do anything too stupid," he said as he put his foot against the side of the rowboat and pushed it off from the dock.

Sebastian could practically hear the gears turning in the fisherman's head as he weighed the value of the money he had been paid against the possibility of losing his boat.

# 2

Sebastian rowed the small boat into the lake. He wasn't sure why people made such a big deal out of seamanship; this rowing stuff was easy. It had taken him a bit to get the pattern of pulling harder on one side when you wanted to turn. He had felt the eyes of the fisherman burning into him while he was still close to the dock, but now he had it.

The misty shores of the island felt like they were a long way off, but there was nothing for it except to put his back into it. Sebastian was used to hard work on his farm. Still, the rowing was unfamiliar, and after a short while, he felt like he was using other muscles than he was used to. Also, even though he had a farmer's calloused hands, the oars were hitting different parts of his palms.

At first, it was a relief when the rowboat entered the mists around the island. He had worked up a bit of a sweat in the morning sunshine, and the cool fog felt refreshing on his warm back. He glimpsed trees above the low-lying fog as the boat entered it, so he thought the island's shore couldn't be far. He continued rowing straight through the dense mist, trying to veer as little as possible.

Sebastian kept waiting for the boat to run aground or for there to be something to see other than pearly fog. He turned his head to see what was in front of the rowboat. He had known enough about rowing to sit with his back toward the boat's bow, so he had to crane his neck around to glimpse the front. There was nothing but the milky-white mist.

The sun went from a yellow spot in the fog overhead to a distant glow. The cool mist started feeling less friendly and more ominous. The only sound was the splashing of Sebastian's oars.

It got murky and chill. The dried sweat dampening the back of Sebastian's tunic felt clammy and cold.

He shivered. There was no sign of anything but the impenetrable fog. A strong smell came with the mist, like the smell of freshly unearthed moss from near the roots of an oak tree.

Sebastian firmed his grip on the oars, ignoring his new blisters, and put his back into rowing the boat forward.

# 3

Anise was crouched by the outside of the Academy wall. She was reaching out with her mind to try to contact the elemental strength of the volcano that was the Key to the elements. It wasn't hard. As soon as she reached for it, she felt the flowing lava, the turbulent moat around the mountain, and the surging winds above the caldera.

"I still don't understand why we didn't just walk in through the gates," said Raphael.

"I want to make sure there's no chance that Lorenzo knows we're coming," said Anise distractedly, "He has his ways, and I'd like to not give him time to prepare." She started to route the power of the magma in the volcano into the rock in front of her. A round hole began to form in the flowing stone. Iggy faded into view, launched himself off her shoulder, and did a joyful barrel roll in the air over her head.

Raphael gasped as the smooth stone of the wall flowed and shifted. Briac looked on in fascination. "I've been learning to do some magic with my music," he said. "But, nothing like that."

Anise grunted. Manipulation of elements, especially earth, was a bit draining. "I meant to ask you about that," she said as she rose to her feet. "What sort of things can you do?"

"Another time," said Briac. He glanced at Raphael a little skeptically.

After peering through to make sure that the coast was clear on the other side, Anise squeezed her way through the hole she had made. Briac and Raphael followed. They were screened from the rest of the Academy campus by a small grove of trees. Anise had seen the treetops above the wall.

"I've been meaning to tell you how nice it is to see

you, Raffy," said Anise. "I haven't been able to see anyone from the old days since I woke up."

Briac muttered, "Uh …," and slightly lifted his hand.

"I'm surprised you didn't see Jord," said Raphael. "She was there almost every time I came to visit."

"Jord?" said Anise. "Why was Jord there?"

"Oh, you didn't hear?" said Raphael. "Jord's a master at the Academy now. In fact, she's the headmaster of the new Healing discipline."

# 4

T he boats on the mist-shrouded dock were all locked up. The locks and chains were solid iron, thick and strong. Anise studied them. There was a reason why iron had a reputation as being resistant to magic. It was a tricky material to work with elemental skills. And, it tended to dispel illusions when they touched it. That was probably the reason why it was used on these locks. It would be challenging for the students to "borrow" these boats.

"I can work my way through these chains," said Anise, lowering her voice, "But it will take a while." She shook her head. "Shaping iron is really hard."

The three of them had made their way to the docks on the lake carefully and stealthily. Anise considered trying to hide their appearance with illusions. But, the Academy was the place in Liamec where there was most likely to be someone capable of "disbelieving" illusions. So, it was perhaps the place where they would be least effective.

"Wait a minute," said Briac, "let me." He pulled his backpack off his back and pulled out his lute.

"I'm not sure if this is the right time for a song," whispered Anise urgently.

Briac smiled. "It's always the right time for a song."

Raphael kept glancing over his shoulder in the direction of the fog obscured building at the end of the wharf. He seemed to feel guilty about sneaking around the campus. He looked especially worried about Anise trying to "liberate" one of the boats.

Briac strummed his lute quietly and began singing in a low voice. The song's words were in some language Anise had never heard before, but she felt something, some stirring of power. It reminded her of when Briac had come to the Academy and conjured illusions with a song. Iggy sagged against Anise's shoulder and started making a noise like a cat's purr.

There was a gentle click as the padlock on the iron chain opened. Anise had the feeling the lock had been moved by Briac's voice.

"How did you do that?" she whispered. "I felt something, but it wasn't like any of the magic disciplines they teach at the academy."

"Music unlocks both hearts and locks," said Briac.

# 5

The oarlocks creaked as if they were complaining about the work Sebastian was putting them through. The blisters on his hands got so sore that he took out his pocket-handkerchief, ripped it in half, and bound half around each palm to be able to keep rowing.

Sebastian was confident that he was going straight, but it felt like he'd been rowing for hours, and there was no change in the pearly white fog that shrouded the lake's surface and the boat's gunwales. At this point, he would have welcomed the sound of the rowboat crashing into a rock. Anything to indicate that there was an end to the misty open waters.

Sebastian had plenty of time to think while he pulled on the oars. One thought that kept coming back was, "Why am I here?" Of course, the obvious answer was to help Anise, but he wasn't entirely sure he would be much use.

When he'd confronted Lorenzo before, as the Knight of Moon & Shadow, he'd had lots of help. He'd had Luna and Moonbeam guiding him. He'd had the gifts of his fellow villagers from Westhavenfieldbrook. He'd had his youth. Sebastian sighed. He wasn't that old now, but he certainly didn't have the confidence that inexperience gave the very young.

He pulled again firmly on the oars, ignoring the flare of pain he felt in his palms. It didn't matter. He would do what he could to help, even if it wasn't very much. Perhaps he could distract the enemy. Maybe he could throw himself in front of a fiery blast from Lorenzo's fingers, launched at Anise. Whatever he could do to help, he would.

There was a crunching sound as the boat's prow ran up onto a beach of water-smoothed pebbles. The rowboat came to an abrupt halt, and Sebastian was thrown backward. His palms ached again as he caught himself against the side.

He worried about the fisherman's boat. Sebastian climbed out and pulled it up onto the shore, inspecting the prow as he did. It didn't look like the hull had been damaged by the impact.

He looked around. The milky fog was still thick, and he couldn't see anything much except the boat, the stones under his feet, and the faint glow of the distant sun lighting the mist.

After securing the boat, Sebastian turned and quietly walked away from the rocky shore into the fog.

# 6

Raphael used his oar to hold off the dock to stop the boat from crunching into it. When they got close enough, he jumped off and grabbed the painter line that Briac tossed to him. The dock felt very ordinary. It didn't feel like something in the realm of Dream. It felt like solid plain wood under his feet. He tied the line to a cleat, and Anise and Briac climbed onto the wooden planks.

Raphael looked around, and his sense of ordinariness went away. The thick milky mist felt clammy and heavy, and the sun's light was just a faint yellow glow above them. You couldn't see more than a few feet in any direction. They were standing on a dock above the lake, but they could barely make out the water's surface.

"Anise," said Briac, "You've been here before. Where do we go?"

Anise shook her head. "We always just landed and started walking down the path." She pointed to a gravel paved way that could just be made out through the fog. It started from the edge of the last board of the dock. "After that, things got hazy. There were lots of conversations with master Callum in the mist. It seemed he could talk to everyone, alone, at the same time."

"The Keep?" said Briac.

"I never saw it," said Anise, "No one even mentioned it in class. Though, there were rumors that people used to know more about the Isle of the Wise than the current masters did."

"Well, I guess there's nothing for it, then," said Briac. He pulled the neck of his cloak a little tighter against the chill and started walking down the gravel path. Anise and Raphael followed. Anise felt a shiver run down her spine. The cold, dank mist felt unwelcoming.

# 7

T hey became quickly and wholly lost in the fog. There was nothing to be seen but the gravel path, the faint glow from the sun, and the omnipresent mist. The way twisted and turned, and it kept branching.

Raphael and Briac turned to Anise for guidance at the intersections. She had no better idea than they did, so she picked at random, trying to exude confidence to keep their spirits up. The cold, damp fog and the gloom were disheartening.

At first, they tried to track which way they turned at branches in the path, but there were too many splits. There was no way to record the turnings without a paper and quill. There were too many to remember.

There was no break in the mist. No sights to see other than an occasional scraggly bush or tree. It felt like they had walked for miles, though there was no way to tell if it was in circles or not. It occurred to Raphael at one point that if they had bits of colored cloth, they could mark trees, but they didn't have a supply of bits of colored cloth.

The lighting didn't change. Though it felt like it had been hours or even days, there was no way to tell how much time had passed. The fog smelled of moldy wood and faintly of the waters of the distant lake.

At one point, Iggy flew up into the mist. He scouted around a little, then landed again. "Burn," he said sadly as he shook his wrinkled gray head.

Eventually, Anise got annoyed. With no better idea which way was correct at the next intersection, she muttered irritably, "I'm a channeler. We're in Dream. By Luna's lips, this place should be mine." She lifted an arm to halt her companions and sat on the gravel in a cross-legged position. Anise silently thanked the thick seat of her armor, which protected her from the cold and roughness of the path.

She sat quietly, eyes closed for a few minutes. Raphael and Briac waited, wondering what would happen next.

Anise opened her eyes and held out her arm. A black raven flapped its way through the fog, spread its wings wide to slow itself, and landed on her forearm, its talons digging into the thick material of her armor.

The raven cocked its head to one side, met Anise's gaze, and spoke in a voice between a raven's cawing and a person's speech.

"I wondered when you would get around to calling me."

# 8

Sebastian was even more lost than Anise, Briac, Raphael, and Iggy were. He had left the shore with not even the path they had to guide him. The opaque mist was more featureless without the gravel walkway. Now that he no longer had the splashing of the oars to distract him, the silence was deafening.

The fog was so dense that Sebastian had to move slowly. Each tree or bush sprang out of the mist suddenly, as he could only see a little way in front of him, and he had to ease his way forward so as not to hit something. The trees were little scraggly things. Hardly worth calling trees at all. Sebastian was no expert, but he didn't recognize what kind of trees they were.

He tried calling out once. He called, "Anise!" into the mist, though he had no idea if she was anywhere near the island. He only tried it once. His voice died in the fog, seemingly sucked out of the air by the vapor. He felt that it had been sucked out of his mouth, throat, and lungs as well.

Sebastian had no idea which way he was going. He tried to orient himself by the sun, but its faint glow overhead wasn't much use. It seemed as directionless as he was himself.

After a while, he fell into a slow, plodding pace. He started focusing on just the next step. The mist crept into his brain and made it hard to think of anything else. Then the next step forced his attention on itself. He stepped on something that crunched under his feet.

Sebastian looked down. He had stepped on a human bone. The bleached bones of a human skeleton littered the muddy ground beneath his feet. Sebastian backed off a step. He shook his head in disbelief. The bones had been there for a long time. He shivered. It wasn't just the cold. He thought this could be him if he didn't find his way.

He resumed walking. There was nothing he could do for whoever that had been. It made him sad that no one had been there to bury the body.

As earlier on the boat, he tried to maintain a straight course, but he had no idea if he was succeeding or not.

While he walked, he fell into reminiscing. There was nothing to do but think.

He remembered being the Knight of Moon & Shadow when he was younger. He thought about that time often and wasn't surprised that current events were bringing the memories back to him. Since then, he'd had lots of happy times, along with some sad ones, but nothing else even close to as magical had ever happened to him.

Sebastian thought of his visions of Luna. He sometimes contemplated the picture of the moon that the mayor had commissioned for his mantelpiece and wished that the likeness of Luna was better. He remembered how she had helped him on his quest. "Ah, Luna," he said quietly, "I wish you were here now."

The glow of sunlight in the mist above him started to move.

Sebastian started and looked up. He realized that it wasn't actually the sun's glow but, instead, another light coming toward him through the fog. At first, it seemed to be moving steadily toward him, then he saw that it was bobbing up and down as it came forward.

A light beam burst through the fog to hover in front of Sebastian. It bopped up and down as if on a string. A gleeful high-pitched voice broke through the murky silence.

"Hi," it peeped, "remember me? I'm Moonbeam."

## 9

Sebastian gaped at Moonbeam. As he had years ago when he first met the lunar sprite, he wondered how a little bouncing ball of light could talk. There was a shower of motes of brightness when it spoke, and it felt like its voice reverberated in the mist.

Sebastian shook his head. "Moonbeam," he said, "I thought you couldn't come out during the day?"

"Well, that's a fine how-do-you-do," said Moonbeam, "No greeting. No 'hello.' No Moonbeam, how are you? It's been forever? Just, 'I thought you couldn't come out during the day?'" The little spirit kept on, a cascade of flecks of light accompanying the flash of each sentence. "That's all right," it said, "You've got a lot to think about. Anyway, it's not really day. We're in Dream. Also, the fog keeps the sun away."

"I'm so sorry," said Sebastian. He meant it. "I'm thrilled to see you."

"That's all right," the little light wave repeated. "How did you get here, anyway?" It said. "This is Dream, and you're awake."

"I rowed a rowboat," said Sebastian. He glanced at the ripped handkerchief tied around his hands.

"That's an unusual way to get into a dream," said Moonbeam cheerily. The presence of the diminutive glow of light cut the gloom, and Sebastian felt hopeful. "Follow me," said the dab of moonlight, "Luna sent me to show you the way again." The light blob looked thoughtful, if such a thing is possible, and continued, "Did you ever think that you might have a bit of channeling power? You seem to have summoned me into your dream."

Without waiting for an answer, Moonbeam flashed off into the fog. Sebastian followed as quickly as he was able.

# 10

T he raven perched on Anise's outstretched forearm, looking at them each in turn with its bright, intelligent eyes. Iggy launched himself into the air from Anise's other shoulder. He flew a circle around the group before landing on the ground. Anise got the idea that he was trying to show the raven that he was the winged member of the band.

Anise met the gaze of the raven's beady black eye. "Lord Morpheus?" she asked.

"Of course," said the bird. The raven spread his wings high and wide, still perched on her forearm, and cawed loudly. "Morpheus, Lord of Dream!"

Raphael's gaze got caught momentarily by the dark space under the raven's wings. He suddenly saw a flock of tiny winged people in the inky blackness. Then his gaze brushed past them, and he saw a green grassy field, a warm shining sun, and a place of peace and rest. For a moment, Raphael wanted nothing more than to dive into the welcoming space inside the blackness within the raven's feathers.

Lord Morpheus folded his wings. Raphael shook his head as if waking from a dream.

"Lord Morpheus," said Anise, "If you wouldn't mind. We could use some help getting through this mist."

"Anise," said the bird, "it is more than just the keeper of the underworld who stands to gain from your success. Mortals who rise above their stations can hurt us all." The bird launched himself into the air. His shadow fell over them as he rose above.

"Follow me," cawed the black bird. He started flapping onward above the path.

The companions followed the bird through twists, turns, and intersections of the way. If he flew too fast and they lost him, he circled back until they could follow him again.

The gravel path ended in a clearing. The mist was thinner here, so the companions could see further. The outer wall of a keep rose before them on the other side of the open space. The stones of the keep had a greenish cast. They didn't look like anything seen in the waking world.

There were two massive doors in the wall. Side by side. They looked too thick and solid to be opened by any normal means. The raven landed in the center of the clearing.

"The Keep of Truth and Deceit," he cawed.

# 11

T he stone walls of the keep towered overhead until they were lost in the mist high above. The doors weren't made of the same greenish stone as the rest of the wall. The one on the left was carved from the dark horn of some momentous beast. It glimmered translucently in the mist. The door on the right was polished ivory. It showed its shining surface as white as the milky fog, though it looked as solid as the stones that bordered it. Anise wondered what creatures could have been big enough to have grown the horns and the tusks. There didn't seem to be any seams or joints in the doors.

The raven lifted his head and fixed his beady eye again on the companions. "The Gate of Horn," he explained, "is the one I used to send forth dreams of fulfillment, dreams that brought the truth to the dreamer. He cocked his head to one side. "Though, truth be told, facts are sometimes more painful than fiction.

"The Gate of Ivory," said the raven, gesturing toward the right-hand door with his beak. "Is the door of deceit, lies, and fiction." The bird winked at Raphael. "It's what you saw under my wing," he said.

"There aren't any handles," said Anise, "Not even a knocker." She looked up toward the top of the doors. "And, they're so big."

"You need to decide which door to open," said the raven.

"I don't see how to open either one," said Anise, "And we don't need lies and deceit. I think it's obvious which door we should open."

"Is it?" said the raven. He cawed in a way that almost sounded like laughter, took to wing, and flapped off into the fog.

Anise pondered for a bit in the clammy mist. Briac's ability to click open a lock with a song wouldn't help when there weren't any locks. Raphael and Iggy didn't have any skills that she could think of to help here. And, anyway, she was pretty sure this was a job for a channeler.

Anise spent what felt like an eternity trying various magical tricks to open the Gate of Horn. Briac and Raphael helped by searching for mechanisms, seams, or anything that resembled keyholes, handles, or latches without success. Iggy helped by flying in random circles through the fog, calling out, "Burn," and occasionally splashing the door with a blast of flame.

In the end, it turned out to be simple. Anise, despairing of finding any way of getting the slightly translucent Horn Gate to budge, leaned lightly against the milky-white ivory one next to it. Smoothly and silently, the massive door swung inward. She turned to it and pushed a little more. It swung open wide enough for her and her companions to make their way through.

Anise shrugged and gestured for them to follow her as she walked through the Gate of Ivory into the Keep of Truth and Deceit.

# 12

Sebastian was trying his best to keep up with Moonbeam. It was hard as the lunar sprite flitted through the air freely, and he had to slog through the mire. The ground was marshy, and a thin layer of mud coated the soil.

It was the kind of mud that you don't sink into, but rather that attaches itself to the bottoms of your shoes. The type of mud that forms on the ground in a mist or after the first rainfall in a dry climate. With each step, a new thin layer would attach itself to the bottom of the previous layer. After a few steps, Sebastian felt like he was walking on raised platforms.

Stopping every few feet to knock the mud off his shoes didn't lead to high-speed travel. Moonbeam didn't seem to understand the trials of pedestrians, so Sebastian was very relieved when they crossed a gravel pathway.

"Moonbeam," he called out, "Can you lead us on a path that follows this walkway, please?"

The diminutive beam of moonlight darted back over to Sebastian. It looked at him. Though it is hard to say how it did that without eyes, a head, a neck, or any tangible physical manifestation.

"Of course," it chirped, "I'd be happy to." There was a brief pause. "Well, that is, I would love to," it continued. There was another brief pause. "I mean, I'd like to," it said. The showers of light that accompanied Moonbeam's speech were a bit dimmer with each sentence.

"I can't," Moonbeam pronounced. The little light trace sounded sad. "I don't know anything about the path. I just know which direction it is toward the Keep."

Sebastian sighed. He resigned himself to the mud. "That's all right, Moonbeam," he said. "Though maybe you could fly a little slower?"

It wasn't that much further. The mists opened up

a little, though you still couldn't see the sun. Sebastian followed Moonbeam into the clearing in front of the Gates of Horn and Ivory.

# 13

Sebastian hardly noticed the gates. They were big and impressive, but they weren't what he was here for. He kicked the last mud off his shoes and walked past the doors to the right-hand side along the stone wall.

"A moment," warbled Moonbeam.

Sebastian stopped and turned to the beam of light.

"Uh-huh?" he said.

"I have to go," said Moonbeam sadly. "I didn't get to stay very long this time, did I?" The gleam of moonlight bopped up and down. "Maybe next time we could go on a whole adventure together?"

"Moonbeam," said Sebastian tearing up slightly, "Thank you so much."

The little light wave flitted up into the mist. As it had when it appeared, it looked like it was the circle of the sun showing through the fog before it disappeared, and the light returned to being directionless.

Sebastian started walking along the wall of the keep. The stones radiated a slight cold and reflected the light from the invisible sun, giving the mist an eerie green glow.

He followed the wall, seeing no break or gap in the stones. The moss-colored surface rose above him, preternaturally smooth, broken only by precise seams.

The first break in the uniformity was a line of low bushes growing just in front of the wall. Like the scraggly trees Sebastian had noticed while following Moonbeam, he didn't recognize the variety, but it didn't matter. *I'll call them "Dreamshrubs,"* he thought.

Sebastian pushed his way into the shrubs. Behind them was a low muddy ditch. There, low in the otherwise featureless green wall, was the Gate of Heroes. It was a small round hole in the wall, a culvert. A trickle of brownish water flowed through the gutter into the ditch, where it puddled in a pool of brown sludge.

Lying next to the hole in the ditch was a rusty metal grating. Jagged ends of metal stuck out of the culvert edges where it had been ripped off the wall. Sebastian wondered what kind of creatures would need a sewer in the Dream Realm.

Regretting what it would do to the white linen pants that Isabel had lovingly made for him, he got down on his knees. He carefully made his way over the sharp metal stubs of the broken grating.

Sebastian crawled through the Gate of Heroes into the Keep of Truth and Deceit.

# THE KEEP OF TRUTH AND DECEIT

# 1

Anise stopped after stepping into the entrance hall of the keep. The hall was huge and had once been very elegant. A massive chandelier hung over the room's center, suspended by a thick chain glinting silver in the weak light. The others crowded in behind her. It was quiet and still in the vast space of the open hall.

Anise looked around. What little light there was, was seeping in from somewhere high above. Perhaps filtered by the green stone of the walls, similar to the exterior, the light cast an olive glow over everything in the hall. The lighting was dim enough that the far end of the room was lost in the distance.

The sides of the chamber were lined with chairs that were probably elegant once but were now moldering and falling apart. Tapestries concealed parts of the walls, ripped in places. Cobwebs lined the green surface, with a few web strands stretching from the tapestries to the chandelier. Some of the strands looked as thick as the lines tying up the boat they had used to cross the lake. Anise saw Raphael shiver as he inspected the webs. *He must be imagining the spiders that made them*, she thought.

High above the center of the room, the massive chandelier was formed from crystals that glinted emerald in the light. Above the dimly glittering gems were candles that looked like they had never been used. Anise wondered how anyone ever lit or replaced them. Then she remembered where she was.

Anise focused on the element of fire. It came easily. She only felt the presence of the Key of the Elements distantly, but a more nearby source of fire came surging into her. She remembered being unable to control the elements during her time in Dream. Still, this keep was somewhere between dreaming and waking. The candles burst into flame, flooding the hall with light.

The floor was emerald green, shiny, and polished. It reflected all the points of light from the candle flames above it. It appeared like it should feel slippery, but it didn't.

"Well," said Briac quietly into the silence of the vast hall, "if anyone didn't know that we are here, they know now."

# 2

Anise waited as the light from a hundred candles glittered and reflected off the facets of the emerald crystals and lit every corner of the vast open hall. She was stunned at her own audacity. Briac's quiet words faded into silence, and the stillness resumed.

No one came. There were no other sounds. Aside from Briac's comment, there was no response to the flood of light. Not even a scurrying sound implying that the spiders that made the cobwebs were still around.

After a moment of silence, Anise stepped forward, walked beneath the massive chandelier, and looked up at it. Briac trailed behind her. Raphael and Iggy moved off to the sides of the chamber. Raphael peered with interest at something on one of the tapestries. Iggy flitted up above the cobwebs. They shifted with the wind of his passing, and tiny dust flakes fell like snow.

Anise whispered to Briac, "A little bit flashy for Dream." She pointed upward. "Isn't the lord of dreams supposed to be somewhat subtle?"

"Why are you whispering?" said Briac, speaking in a voice barely louder than a whisper himself.

"It just feels like I should," whispered Anise, "to show some respect for what this place used to be."

"What did this place use to be?" said Briac.

"I have no idea," said Anise, a little bemused.

The light from the chandelier made more of the room visible. Corridors and side passages led out of the hall in various directions. Looking up above the chandelier, there were walkways connecting rooms on higher floors across the space of the chamber. Anise and Briac started walking under the chandelier, down the hall's center towards the far end. They approached a large staircase leading upward. It was a beautiful curving stair made of the same green stone as the floor.

"Didn't the stories talk about going up?" said Anise.

"The things I read in the bard's library talked about the Lord of Dream being at the top of the keep," confirmed Briac.

"I bet that's where we'll find Lorenzo," said Anise determinedly. She put her foot on the first step of the staircase.

# 3

The glow from the fog-shrouded day behind Sebastian faded quickly. The faint light showed green walls with an arched stone ceiling above. The floor, wet with the trickle of brown water, was flat. There wasn't room to stand upright, but Sebastian could move forward slowly, half-crouched. He was grateful that he wasn't taller and thought, for once, that it would be nice to be shorter, as the crouch made him move very slowly. At some point, later on, he was sure there would be sore muscles.

Sebastian moved forward a few feet in his half-crouch and then stopped. The glow behind him was dim. The tunnel before him faded into blackness, especially with his body blocking some of the light. He thought about whether he had anything to help him see in the dark. He didn't have a lantern or a torch. He did have a flint and steel and a little bit of tinder, but that wasn't going to help by itself.

Sebastian wished that he had just a trace of Anise's facility with elements. He remembered her telling him something about a new element that produced light without heat. Sebastian wasn't sure how there could be a new element, but there was no arguing with Anise. She knew much more about this stuff than he did.

He could touch the tunnel's walls on both sides if he reached out, and the floor looked smooth enough, though his feet splashed in the muddy brown water. Sebastian sighed and reached out his arms to both sides. His fingertips barely brushed the tunnel walls. He crept forward into the blackness.

Sebastian moved very slowly, carefully putting first one foot out, then the other, before inching forward. After advancing into the darkness for what felt like a long time, he turned back and looked behind himself. The greenish glow of the culvert opening in the outside wall of the keep was distressingly close. He grunted, turned forward again, and tried to speed up his shuffling pace.

Soon enough, the darkness was complete. Sebastian's hearing became more acute now that he couldn't see. The noises of his own shuffling progress dominated. Still, he also heard the sounds of dripping water somewhere in the distance.

His fingers on the right-hand side lost contact with the wall. He tried to reach a little further and found an opening, a gap, in the wall on that side. Feeling around more, he discovered a branching tunnel, similar to the one he was in, going off to the right.

Sebastian had heard somewhere, he didn't remember where, that if you always followed one wall in a maze, you would eventually find your way through. Even though it meant that he would lose sight of the culvert's mouth behind him, he kept his hand on the right-hand wall and followed the side tunnel.

# 4

Sebastian was getting tired of the darkness. He had experienced it before, of course. Cloudy nights in the fields and his own bedroom's lightlessness after the candle had been blown out, but this was different. It didn't matter if he opened his eyes or closed them; the inky blackness was precisely the same.

He was making progress, he thought, though slowly. He kept his hand on the right-hand wall and turned to the right whenever there was a choice. Sometimes he walked upright through areas where the ceiling was higher. Sometimes there were multiple branches, and it was hard to even tell how many tunnels there were. He clung to the right-hand wall like it was a lover and hoped that Isabel wouldn't be jealous.

It felt like a puzzle why there were so many tunnels beneath the keep of the lord of dreams. Still, Sebastian had never been one to question the ways of the gods, and he wasn't about to start now.

His ears were working harder in the absence of his vision. After a while, he began to regret his newfound hearing sensitivity. At first, the sounds of his own limping progress and the occasional water drips were the only noises. Then he heard a scuttling, shuffling sound at the periphery of his hearing. It came and went. Sebastian was happy when it went. It sounded like something low to the ground clambering over the uneven surface of the tunnel floor. Sebastian felt a shiver run down his spine when he first heard it. It made him think of bugs or snakes.

He tripped over rough spots on the floor or fallen stones a few times. Each time he did, he slowed a little and tried to keep his forward movements deliberate and calm. It was hard when his instinct was to rush forward to get out of the crushing darkness.

Sebastian's relief when he saw a break in the

blackness was enormous. At first, he didn't believe it. He thought it was a trick that his eyes were playing on him. He blinked and peered forward. There it was, a green glow straight ahead of him, a light gleaming in the distance. Trying not to hurry to the point where he tripped, Sebastian moved forward as quickly as possible.

# 5

Anise strode forward confidently without looking back, trying to give her companions the impression that she knew where she was going. The second floor of the keep was a tangle of corridors and rooms. Each doorway she opened felt like it would lead to someplace vital or unusual. Still, each, in its turn, was another disappointment.

She was looking for a staircase up. The assumption that the former lord of the keep had had his sanctuary at the top of the castle was the only thing she had to go on.

The rooms and corridors of the castle were opulent and lush, though they had fallen into disrepair. The walls were all of the same green stone. The floors all showed the same polished surface as the entrance hall, so there was no way to tell if someone had last passed by two minutes or two hundred years ago.

The rooms they walked by contained things that would have fascinated Anise at another time. Some of the rooms had open doors; some of them she opened herself. Either way, the rooms held things that might be mementos of pivotal or memorable dreams.

One room was full of instruments. There were all sorts of musical devices there. Briac's eye's opened wide. Anise shut the door again hurriedly.

She stopped in front of another door. There was a hissing sound from behind it. She glanced at Briac, who shook his head carefully. She opened the door a crack, then slammed it. The room beyond was crawling with snakes.

"I wonder what they eat," said Briac thoughtfully.

There was a room full of treasure. Gold coins, other golden objects, and shining gemstones. Anise tried to shield the view of what was in there from her companions. She closed that door hurriedly as well. *No sense tempting people*, she thought.

THE CHANNELER TRILOGY

Anise opened one door that led into a huge kitchen. The counters and ovens were big enough for many cooks to work and for those cooks to provide food for many people. Or perhaps, other things. Anise thought she would have expected to see a kitchen on the ground floor. Then she reconsidered. The rules of the waking world didn't apply here in Dream.

She turned around and spoke, "Raffy," she said, "can you tell how recently someone has used this kitchen?" She noticed that Iggy's familiar weight was missing from her shoulder. There was no one behind her but Briac. He turned and looked behind himself, a slightly confused look on his face.

"Raffy?" Anise repeated.

# 6

Iggy flitted angrily through the air over Raphael's head. He looked like he was about to breathe a blast of fire. The fire imp had blasted the keep doors with flames when they had tried to get in. Raphael wondered if his improvised helmet would protect his head from the blaze.

"Burn!" said Iggy disdainfully.

Raphael thought for a minute; was it really disdainful? He scanned Iggy's expressionless face and tried to read the emotions behind the features. The big pupils in his catlike eyes were dilated because of the dim lighting. His gray leathery skin covered a face that otherwise looked almost human. Raphael wondered what it would take to get inside that head.

Iggy noticed Raphael looking at him and flapped slightly higher into the air. "Burn," he said again. It still sounded disdainful to Raphael.

"I didn't do anything," said Raphael. "It's as much your fault as mine that we're lost. You're the one who kept flying off down those corridors without looking to see which way they might have gone."

"Burn," conceded Iggy reluctantly.

Raphael looked around. They were at an intersection of several corridors. Off to one side was a staircase leading down. The walls were the same omnipresent green stone, and the floor shone like an emerald. They hadn't seen signs of any human presence since they lost track of Anise and Briac. Raphael had missed his companion's discussion of the lord's sanctuary being at the top of the keep.

"Come on, Iggy," he said with a cheerful facade. "Let's go down. The kitchens have to be on the lower levels, and that's where we'll find traces of life if there is anything to be found."

# 7

Iggy was flying low in front of Raphael. He was selecting which way they went, flitting forward quickly enough that Raphael had difficulty keeping up. Raphael was still trying to reason with him, though he wasn't sure it was worthwhile.

"Iggy," he called out, "It really wasn't my fault. I want to find them as much as you do."

"Burn," replied Iggy derisively. Raphael could tell from the lines of the muscles in the imp's back that he wasn't yet ready to forgive.

The kitchen Rafael had been looking for hadn't materialized. The walls of the corridors on this level were rougher and less finished than on the previous one. The seams between the stones weren't visible here. I wonder if these are tunnels, he thought. Maybe the whole island is made out of this green stone.

The lighting was dimmer. There were occasional openings high in the walls that let in a little faint greenish light. Raphael speculated that they were open to the floor above, expressly to be light tunnels. Still, between the light-tunnel mouths, the corridors were poorly lit.

At one point, Raphael stumbled in the gloom. Iggy turned back, glared at him, and hissed slightly. He turned again and flew forward, but his body started to glow with a muted fiery red glow. Though ruddy and contrasting oddly with the green walls, the illumination was enough to see by.

Iggy kept flitting forward. He flew down corridors, through rooms, and across green-lit murky spaces, hardly looking around. Raphael thought that the fire imp's only focus was seeing Anise's familiar black-clad form again.

"Iggy," called out Raphael again, "We should slow down and look where we're going."

Iggy flew through an ornate wide-open double

doorway into a large room, with Raphael right on his heels. The heavy doors, made of the same green stone as the walls and floor, slammed shut behind them with a thunderous crash.

A spectral voice boomed out, "Die intruders! Thou shalt not pass!" as a tall skeletal figure stepped out into the middle of the room and lifted a gleaming silvery sword into the air.

# 8

As Sebastian headed toward the glimmering green light in the distance, it got brighter. It didn't become any less green, but with the color of the stone walls of the keep, Sebastian wasn't too surprised at that. What did surprise him a little was how the scuttling shuffling sound he had been hearing got louder as he approached the light. What surprised him more was how the glow started moving as he got closer.

It separated out into multiple tiny green points of light. They were moving in some kind of haphazard way. Then, on second thought, Sebastian realized that it wasn't entirely random. He felt like there was some kind of connection between the sounds and the motion of the lights.

Sebastian stopped his inching forward. He looked more carefully, trying to make out what he was seeing. A drop of condensation from the tunnel rocks overhead dropped off and landed in his eye. He wiped his face and peered ahead. The green glow outlined a tunnel mouth into a larger lit chamber, regardless of anything else. He started forward again. The prospect of being able to see outweighed any hesitations.

He was almost at the tunnel mouth before he could make sense of what his vision was telling him. The green lights were dancing around in an oval pattern. The motion of the lights was accompanied by the scuttling sound he had been hearing. The end of the tunnel opened out into a larger chamber, with the skittering lights toward the middle.

What made Sebastian's heart beat a little faster was what he saw above the green lights in the chamber's ceiling. There were three round holes with faint glows of light coming from them. It might be filtered, faint daylight, unlike the glowing dots below it.

He stepped to the threshold of the tunnel mouth. There was a bit of a knocking sound as his foot bumped against an unseen rock on the tunnel floor. The moving green dots stopped.

In the center of the room, with all their bulbous eye stalks turned toward Sebastian, was a circle of green crablike creatures. Each was the size of a large cat or a small dog and had a third sinewy stalk behind their eye-stalks from which hung suspended the green glowing orbs of light that Sebastian had been seeing. The bodies of the crabs were barely visible in the green glows they were producing themselves.

They had been dancing in a circle in the middle of the room. With Sebastian's entrance, they all turned in his direction. The silence was momentarily absolute before the skittering sound resumed as they all started scuttling toward him.

# 9

Sebastian reached for his sword. He still had the ripped half of his handkerchief wrapped around his palm, and he felt the rowing blisters as he pulled the sword from its sheath. He stepped a little further into the room to give himself space to stand upright and swing the sword if he needed to.

Sebastian was pretty sure he would need to. The crablike creatures were all scurrying toward him distressingly fast. The ones nearest to him raised their claws into the air. They started clicking them open and closed. The clicking sound joined the scrabbling sound of their motion to fill the air with noises that made the hairs on the back of Sebastian's neck rise.

He glanced around to get the lay of the land. The three holes in the ceiling were filtering in a little bit of a slightly healthier-looking light. Beneath each hole, in the room's center where the crabs had gathered, was a mound of mossy earth. The room was damp. Water rivulets ran across the floor from multiple tunnel mouths that looked similar to the one behind Sebastian.

There had to be at least twenty of the creatures scuttling toward him. Still, in his inspection of the room, Sebastian saw something that gave him some hope. On one wall of the room, he saw a rusty iron ladder. The bars looked aged, but they might hold his weight, and he imagined that the crabs wouldn't be able to climb the ladder.

The first of the crabs reached him. Sebastian took up a fencing pose like his father had taught him, though he knew this would be a very different fight than a fencing bout. He thrust his sword at first one of the crabs, then the next, trying to get them to stay a little distance away from his legs.

The sword bounced off the tough shell of a crab.

They started to surround him. He felt a pinch as a claw closed on the back of his leg through the thick linen of the white britches Isabel and Anise had made for him years ago.

# 10

A nise gawked at Briac. "Where are they?" she said. "When was the last time you saw them?" They stood in the kitchen doorway, the large room with its ovens, counters, and food storage cabinets on one side and the corridor they had come down on the other.

"I don't know," said Briac. "Was I in charge of Raphael?" He looked around again, "and, who do you mean by them?" He noticed Anise's shoulder. "Oh, Iggy's gone, too," he concluded.

"We have to go find them," said Anise, a note of panic sounding in her voice.

"I have no more idea how to find them than I do to find where we're going," said Briac.

"We could backtrack," said Anise.

"We could try," said Briac.

They made their way through the halls and corridors, trying to retrace their steps. There were countless rooms and hallways, and something about the layout of the passages was confusing. Walking through, trying to find where they had come from, reminded Briac of a distant, almost forgotten dream. When they came to a staircase leading upward rather than the one they had climbed from the floor below, even Anise had to admit that retracing their steps wasn't working.

"They can't be in any danger," said Briac. "There hasn't been a sign of life in the whole place so far."

"I'm still worried," said Anise.

"You know what," said Briac. "We're the ones going to deal with Lorenzo. He's the danger in this place. I bet they're a lot safer where they are than they would be with us."

Anise looked thoughtful. "Maybe you're right. Maybe they're safer not being in the confrontation with Lorenzo."

Briac nodded. "What use was Raphael going to be

anyway, with his kitchen cleaver and his pot on his head."

Anise gave him a scowl before starting up the stair.

# 11

Iggy flapped his wings backward and flopped down on Raphael's shoulder. He made a little deflated hissing noise, whispered, "Burn," and faded into smoke. With the part of his brain that wasn't occupied with the tall sword-wielding figure standing before him, Raphael noticed that Iggy's weight lessened noticeably when he faded. *That's how Anise has been able to carry him for so long*, Raphael thought.

The figure standing in the middle of the room was impressive. It looked like it had once been a tall armored man, but it was now an armored, animated skeleton. Bits of rotting flesh dropped off its grinning skull and off the parts of its bones that could be seen under its armor. It wore a shirt and leggings of chain mail that must have fit tightly when it had flesh on its bones. Now they draped over the skeletal remains. A moldy faded red cloth tabard covered its chest. A black silhouette of a dragon's head was on the tabard on the place where the figure might once have had a heart.

"Which is it?" said Raphael.

The skeleton lifted its sword and took a step toward Raphael. "Huh?" it said. Raphael looked with interest at how its jaw moved as it spoke. *It doesn't have a throat, lips, or a tongue*, he thought, *so how is it speaking?*

"'Die intruders,' or 'Thou shalt not pass,'" said Raphael, "They're kind of incompatible." He pulled his cleaver out of its improvised sheath. "If you're going to kill us," he said, "then the 'Thou shalt not pass' part is redundant. If you're just going to stop us from passing, that doesn't involve killing us, necessarily."

"Shut up," said the skeleton eloquently. It struck out with its sword. The blade glinted in the olive light.

The blow was horizontal. Raphael ducked to try to evade it and, at the same time, knocked the blade upward with his cleaver. It clanged off his helmet as he barely ducked under the stroke.

*I wish Briac was here*, thought Rafael. *He wouldn't be laughing at my helmet now.*

## 12

Iggy faded into solidity on Raphael's shoulder and launched himself into the air. The sudden change in weight and the motion startled Raphael, and he dropped his cleaver. Fortunately, the skeletal guard was also surprised. It fell to one knee, lifted its sword in front of itself, and cried, "Dragon," in a voice that almost sounded excited.

Iggy flared bright red as he blasted a burst of flame at the guard.

A wave of fire bathed the figure. Raphael scrambled to retrieve his cleaver. The faded red tabard started burning, and the chain mail glowed with heat. Iggy flitted back to Raphael and settled onto his shoulder. The skeletal figure rose and advanced on Raphael again, parts of its body flaming. It didn't seem to be hindered by the fire.

"Doesn't that hurt?" said Raphael.

"No," said the skeletal figure. Raphael thought he detected a note of sadness in its voice.

"By the way," said Raphael, "Iggy's not a dragon. He's a fire imp."

The flaming skeleton looked more intimidating than it had before. The tabard was blazing, and even some of the skeleton's flesh seemed to be burning. Waves of heat came from it.

"Maybe, don't try that again," said Raphael in an aside to Iggy. Raphael scrutinized the burning undead figure before him. It occurred to him that this had once been a man. Something had happened to him to make him into this fearful creature. "What's your name?" said Raphael to the flaming skeleton.

"Why would you care?" said the skeletal guard. It thrust forward with its sword.

Raphael noticed the sword again; it seemed polished and well maintained. It didn't match the rest of the guard's aged equipment. He also observed, with relief, that the guard was attacking relatively slowly. He was able to jump out of the way of the thrust.

"Well," said Raphael, "I can't just keep thinking of you as the skeleton or the skeletal guard. That's not very nice."

"My name was Edward," said the skeleton. "Edward of the Ashton Dragon's Watch. My friends called me Ed." It started another swing with its gleaming sword. "You won't have to call me anything for long, but you can call me Ed."

Raphael stepped backward while wielding his cleaver to deflect the blow. "Ed? Does that mean we're friends?" he said.

"No," said Edward.

# THE ROOM OF DOORS

# 1

A nise and Briac reached the top of a staircase. The open space at the top formed a room, which, like the entrance hall, was lined with mildewed, upholstered chairs. At the end of the hall was a broad set of double doors. They stood open, showing another large room behind them. Master Lorenzo was standing in the door frame, leaning casually against one of the side jambs.

Briac reached for the dagger on his belt. Anise dropped into a fighting crouch, pulling her spear off her back and wishing her shield into existence on her left arm. She cleared her mind for quick access to the elements.

It was a younger Lorenzo than Anise had ever met. He reminded her of Sebastian's descriptions of the hearty man he had met on his journey as the Knight of Moon and Shadow years ago. He even had the handlebar mustache that her uncle had told her about. It drew the eye like a magnet. The handles reached out on each side, forming intricate spirals. The spirals of waxed hair bobbed up and down when Lorenzo moved. They shone in the dim light and almost seemed to spin around.

Ignoring Briac and Anise's reaction to his presence, Lorenzo stepped forward and opened his arms as if expecting a hug. "Anise," he called out in a robust youthful voice, "it's so good to see you again. I've been waiting for you." He took in Briac's presence and smiled a warm smile that made it hard not to smile back. "And, who is this handsome young man?"

"Lorenzo," hissed Anise, but she already had the feeling that this wasn't going the way she had expected it to.

"Anise," said Lorenzo, sounding like the purest voice of reason, "Let's keep this civilized." He gestured into the room behind himself, "I've set up a table; why don't we sit down and have a cup of tea."

Briac leaned over and whispered into Anise's ear, "Careful, I think this is a trap."

"Of course it is," Anise whispered back. To Lorenzo, she said, "Civilized? You tried to kill me. You trapped me in the realm of Dream for fifteen years. You tried to kill my uncle. Your actions are endangering the world. They're endangering not just one world, but two."

"That doesn't mean we can't enjoy a spot of tea and maybe some biscuits," said Lorenzo, "You must be starving."

# 2

A nise and Briac followed Lorenzo through the double doors. As they stepped into the room, Anise realized that she'd been there before. It was the Room of Doors from her experimentation with clairvoyance.

The room was just as impressive as it had been in her meditative dream state. The doors, each unique, were strewn over the walls and floor. The large stone pool she had noticed before was not that far away. The back wall of the room was lost in the distance. The ceiling still showed a swirling mist. Anise felt a bit of a chilly wind blowing down from above. There was a startlingly ordinary dining table surrounded by several chairs near the entrance.

Her mouth dropped open. "But this room is in Dream, or clairvoyance, or something," she said.

"Of course it is," said Lorenzo. "As are we."

Anise looked over the contents of the table. There was a pot of tea and a selection of cookies and cakes. She almost drooled. She realized that they hadn't eaten anything since coming to Isle of the Wise.

"So," she said, "What's poisoned?"

Lorenzo looked hurt. "Anise," he said, "You think me that unoriginal? I said that we'd keep this civilized. That didn't work on your uncle, and of course, it won't work on you. You are Academy trained, after all. I remember Master Ernst's lessons on sniffing out poisons as if it were yesterday."

It was true. Anise could tell that there wasn't any poison in the foodstuffs on the table. She took a seat, grabbed a piece of cake like it was a lifeline thrown to a drowning person, and nodded at Briac. He sat as well.

Master Lorenzo took a chair at the head of the table. He watched Anise and Briac eat for a moment, then poured out three cups of tea. He nodded with thought. The spirals on his mustache bobbed up and down intriguingly. "So," he said, "we've got a lot to talk about. Let's talk."

## 3

Sebastian kept thrusting at the crabs, trying to keep them at bay, but there were too many. He felt the nips and pinches of them clawing at his legs. The thick white linen of his britches was being shredded. He had a moment of regret as he thought about how lovingly Isabel and Anise had crafted them for him. Then it occurred to him that there would be more regrets if he didn't manage to change the situation. Or perhaps he wouldn't have anything to regret anymore at all.

He changed his point of attack. Instead of thrusting his sword at the hard-shelled bodies of the crabs, he swung his sword at the third eye-stalk of the nearest, feeling like a boy swiping a stick at a dandelion stem.

His sword struck true. The crab's eye-stalk cut easily, and half of it, topped by the glowing green orb, fell to the ground. There was a high-pitched keening sound, and the crab scuttled off toward the mounds of earth in the center of the room. The rest of the creatures paused. The green orb on the end of the fallen stalk continued to glow for a moment before it started to fade.

Sebastian pressed his momentary advantage. He sprang forward, landing on top of the broad shell of a crab before jumping off, reaching out, and grasping one of the rungs of the rusty iron ladder.

Sebastian climbed quickly, trying to get his legs out of range of the crab's claws. The creatures scuttled forward to crowd around the ladder's base, snapping their claws at his retreating legs in frustration.

The top of the ladder ended at the room's ceiling and a trapdoor, locked with a rusty iron padlock. Sebastian pushed at the door and scrabbled at the padlock, but neither gave way. His legs felt weak. He didn't know how long they would hold him, between the exertion and the cuts and bruises they had taken from the crab's claws.

The crabs beneath the ladder seemed to know this. They snapped their claws, making an ominous din.

*Sorry father,* thought Sebastian. He took his sword and pressed the tip into the padlock's shackle. The rusty iron gave way before the hardened steel. There was a crack as the metal broke.

Sebastian pushed open the trapdoor, climbed the last few rungs, his legs trembling, and dropped to the floor of the room above.

# 4

It took Sebastian several minutes before he could do anything but try to catch his breath. The pain of his cuts and bruises intruded into his attention. He sat up, scanned the room briefly, then inspected his legs to assess the damage.

The lighting was better here, though the green walls made the space feel eerie and tainted. The trapdoor had led into a garderobe. A bench with three seats with round holes in the middle was built into one wall. A door stood open against the other. Sebastian estimated that the holes were right over the three mounds of soil below.

His pants were a total loss. The white linen was shredded and torn. Under it, his legs, though tired and painfully scraped and bruised, were not as seriously injured as he had thought they would be. It reminded him of the line from the old folk song that wandering minstrels sometimes sang when they visited Hero. One of the final lines in the song "Fiona and Irene" was, "The two girls sprawled together, scrapes and bruises, that was all."

Now that the immediate danger was past, Sebastian's mind was left flooded with thoughts by the receding adrenaline. He thought about how sad it was that his pants, though not the original Pants of the Wind, were left in this disheveled state. He thought about how innovative the idea of a garderobe over flowing water was. There had probably been more water flowing in the tunnels below at one time. With the water washing away the waste, you could use the garderobe without encountering unpleasant odors.

Sebastian shook his head. He didn't have time for these thoughts. He had to try to find Lorenzo to confront him.

He opened his backpack, trying to remember what Lilith had told him about the potions and vials she had given him. Sebastian selected a vial with a red ribbon tied around the stopper, opened it, and swallowed the contents. He felt a surge of energy and a bit of relief from the pain in his legs.

He remembered Maeve's story. The Lord of Dream had been in a room on the top floor of the Keep. He had to find his way up.

Sebastian rose to his feet. He felt the air moving around his legs through the rips and tears in the linen. *They're once again the Pants of the Wind*, Sebastian thought. He shook his legs a few times to shake the wobble out of them and left the garderobe to find a staircase leading upward.

# 5

Raphael held up his cleaver to ward off another blow from Edward's gleaming silvery sword. Iggy faded back and forth between smoke and solidity on his shoulder. He seemed to be trying to think about what he could do to help. Raphael was getting used to the weight change.

"I'm not actually an intruder," said Raphael. "I'm just lost. I wandered in here by mistake."

"That doesn't make you any less of an intruder," said Edward. He struck a bit of a pose, his gleaming sword held high. He did look impressive, between the silvery blade and his flaming red tunic. "I've been on guard here for two hundred years. No one has gotten past me in all that time."

"So, Edward from the Ashton Dragon's Watch," said Raphael, "Ed. Two hundred years? That's a long time. What are you guarding? Have many people tried to get past you? How did you become an undead skeleton living beneath the Keep of Truth and Deceit?"

"You talk too much," said Edward. He firmed his grip on his sword. Raphael glanced at the skeleton guard's hand.

"How do you hold your sword without any meat on your fingerbones?" he asked. Raphael wondered if that might be part of why the skeleton was wielding his sword slower than he might have been.

"It was hard at first," said Edward. "I had to adjust my grip."

"Ed," said Raphael reasonably, "didn't your mother tell you that you should be polite to strangers? I think you should answer some of my questions. What are you guarding, and who left you here?"

Edward grinned. Though, with a bare, flaming skull for a face, he didn't really have any other facial expressions available to him. "Don't you talk about my mother," he said, swinging his sword a little more fiercely this time, "She was a saint."

Raphael pressed his advantage while evading Edward's sword. "So, she did," he said. "She told you to be polite to strangers and that you should answer questions, didn't she?"

## 6

Edward's jaw moved in his grinning face. Raphael wondered how much the voice he perceived when Edward spoke sounded like Edward had when he was alive. Though, if he'd heard a living person talk in the same spectral, haunted voice Edward used, he would immediately have run away.

"It was the masters from the Academy," said Edward. Raphael kept quiet; it felt like a dam was about to burst. "The masters from the Academy," continued Edward. "They asked for a volunteer. They wanted someone who wasn't married. They wanted someone who felt that the mission of the Dragon's Watch was more important to them than their life."

"And, that was you," said Raphael.

"That was me," said Edward. Something about his voice sounded sad to Raphael. Though it still had the same mournful unearthly quality of infinite agony that it always had, there seemed to be an element of human grief in there as well.

"That must have been hard," said Raphael sympathetically. "Being stuck down here all alone." He clucked his tongue. "Wasn't there anyone you missed? Anyone you left behind?"

"There was a girl," said Edward. "It was hard to say goodbye." Edward thrust again with his sword, though it seemed that his heart, or whatever was under that part of his smoldering tabard, wasn't in it.

Raphael easily parried Edward's halfhearted thrust. "Did they tell you what you were to guard?" he asked.

"Of course," said Edward. He pointed to the far wall. There was a table against the wall behind the skeleton. On the table was a silver bowl containing a glowing blue crystal. The table, bowl, and crystal looked less aged than the other furnishings, though nothing in that room could be said to look unworn with time.

"What is it?" said Raphael.

"I don't know, exactly," said Edward. "Some kind of magical ward, I guess. I did speak to a clairvoyant before I left Ashton for the last time. She said if it was ever broken, it would 'open the path for the allies of Death's Daughter.' That sounds like a bad thing, don't you think?"

"It does sound bad," said Raphael, thinking the opposite.

# 7

Raphael nodded sympathetically at Edward. They had moved to a stage in their duel where it was almost more a dance than a fight. Edward would make a lackluster attack, and Raphael would make whatever minimal effort was needed to make it look like it had threatened him. The dance steps moved back and forth.

"You must be really bored," Raphael said feelingly. "And tired."

"Chronos' crusty codpiece!" said Edward. "I'm so bored! You're the first person to come here in two hundred years!" He shook his head from side to side. Bits of burning mummified skin flew off. "For the first fifty years, my sword would talk to me, but we ran out of things to say."

Raphael tried to look Edward in the eyes. It was difficult, as there were just two sunken black holes where they should have been. "My name is Raphael," said Raphael, "But you can call me Raffy." He smiled to himself as if at an inside joke. "If you do, you'll be one of only two people who call me that."

"I'm honored," said Edward. Raphael couldn't tell if he was being sarcastic or not.

Iggy sat on Raphael's shoulder, calmly watching the back and forth of sword, cleaver, and words. He seemed to have accepted both his perch and the non-threatening nature of the duel.

"Your job," said Raphael thoughtfully as he dodged Edward's latest thrust, "It's not very good, is it?"

"I have good job security," said Edward loyally.

"No breaks, no time off, no vacation, no pay," said Raphael. "You don't even know if this thing," he nodded toward the crystal, "still means anything anymore."

Edward stopped moving. His arm, holding his gleaming sword, lowered to his side. "I'm really tired," he said.

"You know," said Raphael, "you've earned a rest. Two hundred years is a long time."

"You know," said Edward sadly, "It is."

## 8

L orenzo leaned forward from his seat at the end of the table. He nodded to Briac and then looked Anise in the eye. "Anise," he said, "I know we've put the wrong foot forward first, but I think we can resolve this. I think I have some points to make to help you see things from my perspective."

Anise stared back at Lorenzo. Now that her hunger wasn't driving her anymore, she felt her rage returning. "Lorenzo," she said, "there is nothing you can say that will change the facts. You are wrong. You are wrong about many things. Your methods are wrong, and your goals are wrong. The use of clairvoyance is shattering the border between reality and dream, and you've misunderstood the prophecies that you follow so blindly."

Lorenzo leaned back in his chair. He stroked his mustache. It was hard not to follow his finger's path as it wove its way around the spiral and through the glistening curves.

"Anise," he said, "and you too, son," with a nod to Briac, "Let me try to explain." He gestured to the room behind him, to the doors and the stone basin on the floor. Anise noticed for the first time that the metal cover that had been closing the pool the last time she had seen it was hanging open.

"We need this power," said Lorenzo, "We need to know what's coming. With the power of clairvoyance, and especially now that I've managed to open the Scrying Pool, we will have the ability to predict dangers and disasters that threaten Liamec." His finger kept moving around the spiral of his mustache. Anise found it hard not to follow it with her eyes.

"I'm proud of what I've accomplished here," continued Lorenzo. "I've single-handedly brought clairvoyance back to the Academy. I've found this place and managed to open the Scrying Pool. I've brought clairvoyance, a tool that Liamec vitally needs, back to us. I've been gathering power. Being head of the channeling department is just the first step. Soon I'll be headmaster of the Academy." The spirals on the ends of Lorenzo's mustache seemed to be spinning in Anise's mind. It was hard to keep her eyes open.

Lorenzo frowned. "The only thing I've failed at, so far," he said, "is you." His frown deepened. "I've been softhearted. I need to be tougher. There are no means that my ends don't justify."

Anise felt sorry for Lorenzo. *Why was she making things so difficult for him? He was only trying to do what was right.* With half her attention, she managed to sneak a glimpse at Briac. He was slumped in his chair, his eyes riveted on Lorenzo's mustache. A line of drool descended from one corner of his mouth to somewhere near his belt.

## 9

A nise shook herself. She sat upright and glared at Lorenzo. "That wasn't very nice," she said. She leaned over and slapped Briac across the face. He started, sat up straighter himself, and wiped the line of drool off his mouth. He looked confused.

"I'm sorry, Anise," said Lorenzo. He leaned back in his chair. The swirls on his mustache stopped spinning. "I was pretty sure that wouldn't work, but I had to try." He grinned ruefully. "It worked a little better than I thought it would."

Anise frowned. She pushed her chair back from the table and stood up. She readied herself to connect with the elements to prepare for a fight.

"Lorenzo," she said, "You have to yield. I don't want this to turn physical, but I am prepared to kill you if I have to. I have it on the best authority that you are wrong about the prophecies you have been following. The dark channeler named in the prophecies is you, not me. You're the one who is leading the world toward its doom. You're the one who is cracking reality. The use of clairvoyance and this scrying pool will destroy everything if I don't stop you."

Lorenzo looked confused, like what Anise said was getting through to him. Then, his confident, assured expression reappeared, and he replied, "I know what needs to be done. I'm the only one who knows. We can use the clairvoyants and the scrying pool to fix any problem. We have to use the power we have to fix this, to solve this."

"The solution is to stop using the power," said Anise. "The dream storms are going to get worse until reality fractures. One of the dragons told me …,"

Lorenzo laughed. "The dragons. They don't know anything. You know, clairvoyance was dropped from the Academy curriculum because they were attacking Ashton?

They have some kind of folktale about this and are obsessed with stopping it. The Academy masters two hundred years ago warded this Keep against them. They can't come here. They won't be a problem."

## 10

E dward sat in one of the dusty, faded, upholstered chairs lining the room's walls. He laid his sword on his lap. It gleamed silver. Raphael noticed again how shiny the blade was. The skeleton guard looked like he would have sighed if he'd still had lungs.

Iggy faded into visibility, flew off Raphael's shoulder, landed on the ground, and started peering around the room. Edward hardly spared him a glance.

"Raphael," said the skeletal guard. His voice sounded plaintive. "Do you think I could rest for a bit?" The remaining scraps of his tabard had stopped burning. Only part of the black dragon silhouette on his chest was still detectable.

"Ed," said Raphael, "The masters who recruited you must be dead now. The Keep has been abandoned for hundreds of years. I think you can rest as long and as deeply as you want."

Ed settled back in his chair. His bones seemed to lose some tension. "I'm so tired," he said, "I think I'll just close my eyes for a moment."

Raphael stepped over closer to the skeleton. He rested his hand on Ed's chain mail-clad shoulder. The metal links still felt warm under his hand from the fire. He could feel Ed's shoulder bone through the mail.

"Raffy?" said Ed.

"Yes, Ed?"

"Take my sword when I'm gone," the skeleton's voice grew faint. "She's a good sword. One of the masters at the academy made her for me. Take care of her. We haven't talked in a while, but tell her I forgive her."

"I will," said Raphael.

The skeleton guard settled a little further into his chair, and something seemed to leave him.

"You rest now, Ed," said Raphael. "You have a good,

peaceful rest."

Raphael stood a moment with his hand on the cooling chain mail. Then he picked up the gleaming silvery sword, strapped it to his belt, and walked over to the table with its bowl and the blue crystal.

*Open the path for the allies of Death's Daughter,* he thought. *That's what I'm here to do, isn't it?* Iggy flitted over and landed on Raphael's shoulder again. Raphael raised his cleaver and brought it down on the glowing blue crystal, shattering both the crystal and the sharp steel blade into splinters.

## 11

Anise and Lorenzo faced off near the table. Briac was still sitting in his seat, looking confused, as he tried to shake Lorenzo's control off his mind. The academy-trained mages looked ready to tap into the elements to attack each other. Still, they were trying final attempts to sway things with words.

"Anise," said Lorenzo, "We can't let this opportunity go. We have to use the power this Keep, clairvoyance, and the scrying pool give us."

"Lorenzo," replied Anise, "you have all these clairvoyants telling you the future. You must have seen the coming destruction. You must have seen that the dream storms will get worse."

"They get worse, and the world ends if the dark channeler wins. If you win. The storms get worse if I fail in my endeavors." Lorenzo smiled. He looked almost giddy, almost drunk. "Anise, you have to see it," he gestured toward the stone basin. "The fluid in the Scrying Pool, it's raw dream stuff. It glows with the power of Dream. The clairvoyants gaze into the pool when they pass through here onto their paths, and their visions become even more powerful. It's beautiful. Just looking at it makes you feel that you can control the future."

As Anise glanced at the pool, she could see the contents. It was a seething mass of green fluid. It looked the same color as the stone walls of the Keep. She felt it calling to her; she felt its power. It was beguiling. It was also bubbling fiercely like a pot about to boil over.

There was a noise like the crack of a sail opening, and a wind came down from above. Anise and Lorenzo both turned to look up. A vast dark shape appeared above the open roof of the Room of Doors. Even though there was no apparent direct light source, a shadow flew chillingly across them.

A massive dragon crashed to the floor between Lorenzo and the wide double doors into the rest of the Keep. It reared back, spread its wings, and roared furiously. The greens stones of the Keep shook.

## 12

T he dragon towered over Lorenzo. Anise recognized her; it was Flambé. She had gotten huge. They couldn't see the open double doors behind her with her wings spread. Her roar still reverberated through the hall. The wind from her flapping wings made it hard to stand.

Lorenzo stood unintimidated, not giving any ground. He began readying his elemental magics.

Anise realized that she had no clue about the life cycle of dragons. She had no idea how old Flambé would have been when she was in the menagerie at the Carnival of Wonders, and she had no idea if this was Flambé full-grown or not.

A voice rang out in Anise and Lorenzo's minds. Like on the previous occasions when Flambé had spoken to Anise, she didn't use sound but somehow communicated to them directly. Briac, sheltering behind the table, didn't seem to know that the dragon was speaking.

*Dark channeler*, Flambé said, *Your time has come. Your plans are failing you now.*

Lorenzo looked curious. Anise found it hard not to admire his fortitude faced with the creature in front of him. "How did you get in, beast?" he said. "The wards on this place keep your kind out."

Flambé roared again and stamped one of her mighty feet. The stones shook once more. *Your wards are down dark one. There is nothing for you to hide behind.*

"Those wards have stood strong for two hundred years," said Lorenzo. "I'm not sure how you have brought them down. When I last checked, the guardian still stood, and the crystal was untouched."

*I have done nothing, wizard*, said Flambé. *Your protections have fallen by themselves.*

Lorenzo frowned. "Well," he continued, as he

prepared himself once again to summon the elements, "If it's a fight you want ...,"

The dragon was about to launch herself toward the channeler when they were interrupted from an unexpected direction.

"Anise!" called a familiar voice from behind the vast creature.

## 13

As Flambé whirled around blindingly fast, Anise saw a single human-sized figure standing behind the dragon's black-scaled body in the double doorway. The figure was dwarfed by the dragon.

Anise had a flashback to twenty years ago. It was the knight of Moon & Shadow. Sebastian stood there, his sword in hand, his legs trembling with weariness. He wore his purple thistledown jerkin, though the color had faded with time until it was more pink than purple. His white leggings were tattered and torn. Anise felt her heart go out to her knight, her uncle, whom she hadn't seen except in Dream in years.

Moving faster than Sebastian or Anise thought possible, the dragon launched herself at this new threat, this ambush from behind. She grabbed Sebastian around the midriff in her jaws, lifted him into the air, shook him, and threw his limp body aside into the corner of the room. His sword clattered to the ground. Tufts of thistledown from inside his jacket and little scraps of purple linen drifted through the air.

"Uncle Sebastian!" cried out Anise. She started to run toward the limp figure.

Flambé began to turn back toward Lorenzo, then gagged, coughing and choking like she had eaten something that really didn't agree with her.

Lorenzo took advantage of the confusion and began to summon the winds. "I'm sorry about your uncle, Anise," he said. "You know, I always liked him, even all things considered." He lifted both arms high, swinging them toward the dragon. "But, his distraction has given me time to do this." A mighty wind rose, building as it flew toward Flambé. The dragon was still coughing and spitting.

Anise was on her way toward the limp body in the corner. Briac sprinted from his position behind the table and intercepted her. "Anise," he said, "let me check on your uncle." He pointed behind them. "I really think you need to take care of that."

The hurricane Lorenzo had raised had lifted Flambé's massive body off the green floor. She was being held spreadeagled against the wall by the immense focused wind. While holding the dragon immobile with the gale, Lorenzo used his control of the earth to pry loose a decorative iron bar from a door frame. The bar had a wrought iron spearhead on one end.

With a crack, the iron bar broke loose. The bar, with its spearhead, started shooting through the air directly toward the pinioned dragon's exposed breast.

# 14

A nise cried out, "No!" as she directed her own stream of air across the mighty wind blowing from Lorenzo toward the dragon. She had had less time to prepare, so her gust was a lesser force than the gale flowing from the older mage, and she didn't have time to directly work with the metal spear. Still, the wind was enough to shift the wrought iron bar with its decorative spearhead slightly to the side. Instead of piercing the dragon's breast, the metal cut a hole in her pinioned wing before rebounding off the green stone and clattering to the ground.

Anise's gust also had the effect of lessening the force of the gale holding the dragon to the wall. She dropped to the floor.

Flambé spat one more time to clear her mouth and throat of some bitter taste and launched herself into the air.

Anise took a moment to glance over at Briac in the corner. He was hovering over Sebastian's crumpled body. She couldn't tell anything more about what was happening there.

Lorenzo looked taken aback at the failure of his cast spear. His nonchalance was broken. He splayed his fingers and launched a set of blazing bolts of fire toward the onrushing dragon.

Anise felt the wind grow chill around them as Lorenzo's fire sucked some of the warmth out of the room. She abused the air further by pulling the moisture out of it. She formed a shield of water just in front of the flaming darts.

The fire crashed into the water, making a cloud of hissing steam.

The dragon hovered over Lorenzo, wings spread wide. Anise thought she saw a tiny glimpse of hazy gray sky through the small tear in one wing. Then she folded them together and dove down on the wizard. Anise marveled again at how a creature of such size could move with so much speed. The scene reminded her of a hawk diving down on a rabbit in an open field.

Lorenzo made a last effort and conjured another gust of wind toward the dragon. Still, with no time to prepare and the creature's momentum, it made no difference. There was a mighty crash as the dragon hit the mage and the floor. The hall shook yet again. Anise wasn't sure how anything could have survived that impact. But Lorenzo was still struggling weakly when the dragon launched herself into the air once again, with him clutched in her claws.

Flambé flew to a height just above the top of the walls and shook her prey like a cat shaking a captured mouse. Then she flung the wizard over the edge into the mists outside.

# THE SCRYING POOL

# 1

Ahush fell over the hall. The bubbling, fuming sound from the pool could be heard in the quiet. The dragon flapped her mighty wings and landed in the spot she had risen from. She looked around herself as if to say, "Who's next."

Anise looked over and saw, with great relief, that Briac was helping Sebastian to sit up. There were gleams of silvery-gray metal showing through the rents in his thistledown jerkin.

"My uncle wasn't trying to attack you," she snapped at the dragon, "he was coming to help."

Anise heard the dragon's voice in her head again. *If that's so, I'm sorry,* she thought. *You all look the same to me. Anyway, I regret biting him; he tasted terrible. Dragonsbane and spiders.* Flambé coughed and spat again.

The bubbling, fuming, and spurting noises from the stone pool behind Anise grew louder. It felt like the contents of the basin were about to erupt. Somehow, Anise had thought that the problem would be taken care of with Lorenzo gone. Now she realized that he had merely started something that wasn't just going to end with his absence. Somehow the pool would have to be closed, and the cracks in the barrier between reality and dream would need to be repaired.

"I'm here to help as well," she said. She gestured toward the seething pool. "Can you do something to stop this? Can you do something to stop the dream storms?"

A burst of greenish fluid exploded out of the basin. Anise avoided looking at the liquid as best she could. She felt its power pulling on her mind.

*Can I?* thought the dragon. *Can I? My kind doesn't do such things. We leave such forces alone: we know better. It took your kind to open these cracks; it is on you to close them.*

Briac and Sebastian, with Sebastian leaning heavily

on Briac's shoulder, walked over to them. Anise noticed again the gleam of silvery-gray metal shining through the rents in Sebastian's jerkin. Flambé backed away from the tufts of thistledown falling from it.

Anise pulled her battered uncle into a long silent embrace. Her eyes filled with tears.

# 2

Another spurt of the green dream stuff exploded out of the pool. The bubbling seemed to be increasing with every minute. Flambé looked impatiently at Anise. She tilted her head to one side, and Anise heard her thoughts again.

*There is another dream storm coming*, she thought, *even stronger this time. You'd better hurry.*

"What am I supposed to do?" asked Anise.

*I told you*, thought the dragon, *I don't know. But, you had better do it fast.* She stepped back as if to watch what would happen next.

"Briac," called Anise, "Come help me." She ran over to the pool's edge and started trying to lift the iron lid. It was hinged on one side. The opposite end from the hinge had a solid-looking open padlock.

Briac started trying to lift the other side of the lid. Sebastian came over, walking gingerly, and tried his best to help.

"Don't look into the liquid," said Anise, "It's dangerous."

They managed to get the lid upright between the three of them, but when they tried to swing it over the spurting fluid, the cover bounced back from the dream stuff like it was repelled. In fact, each time the heavy metal lid came close to being in contact with the fluid, it was forced back so fiercely as to make trying to hold it dangerous.

Anise abandoned the attempt before anyone got hurt.

"I don't know what to do," she said sadly, looking at Briac and her uncle.

There was the sound of flapping wings, and a black raven emerged from the mists above the hall's walls. It flew a curving path around the bubbling fountain and landed on the green stone floor at Anise's feet.

　　"Anise," said the bird quietly as it cocked its head to one side.

# 3

The black bird hopped forward on its claws, three little hops until it stood just in front of Anise. It was hard not to think of it as a bird, even though she knew it to be the lord of Dreams. "Lord Morpheus," she said, "can you help me with that?" She pointed to the spurting column of dream stuff.

"Anise," cawed the bird, "you don't need my help. You're a channeler in Dream. You do what you do best." Then the bird tilted its head to one side and continued, "Though I guess that's what channelers do best; they ask for help."

Anise pointed at the top of the wall. "What's going to happen to Lorenzo?" she asked.

The bird made a sound almost like a laugh. "He's fallen into the true dreaming beyond the Keep, not this half-dream we're in here," it cackled. "If he survives Lyssa, I'll make sure he's lost there for at least as long as you were."

Anise turned from the bird and walked over near the spouting basin. She avoided looking into the green geyser of fluid, sat cross-legged on the floor, and closed her eyes. As in the mists outside the keep, she tried to reach out with that part of her mind that she used when she called up a channeling dream.

Trying to channel without sleeping felt odd. Except for calling Morpheus, she hadn't attempted it since before her time at the Academy. Still, she drew on her recollection of her games with Sebastian and Isabel's chickens and her encounter with the wolves when she first traveled to the Academy. Soon enough, she felt herself drifting into a welcome daydream. The sensation of power that flooded into her made her feel strong.

# 4

The familiar feeling of being in her circle of light in a channeling dream flooded Anise. Without opening her eyes or rising, she found herself standing with her eyes open in a room that she immediately recognized as Hades' throne room. On its raised dais at the far end of the room was Hades' ebony throne.

She walked toward the throne. Before she got halfway there, she was charged into by a furry thunderbolt of legs, heads, and licking tongues. When Cerberus put her paws up on Anise's black armored chest, the weight was enough to knock her backward. All three of the dog's heads were licking her face simultaneously.

"Cerberus," called out Hades. "Down, girl!" One of the heads pulled away from licking Anise and turned toward her master. "Down," the lord of the underworld called out again. The second pulled its tongue back from Anise's face. Lord Hades scowled at the last head and said, "And you!"        Cerberus stopped licking Anise and crept back to her master's side sheepishly. All three of her faces were looking at the ground, and her serpent-like tail was between her legs. Hades turned to Anise and said, "Anise, it's good you're here. We don't have much time."

Cerberus pushed up against her master's side. She lifted all three heads and gazed at Anise. Her center head's tongue was lolling out and drooling slightly. The leftmost one panted.

"The doors are ready to open," said the lord of the dead. "Let's go back to the Keep."

"We can't go to the Keep," said Anise, "This is a channeling dream."

"Well, the Keep is in Dream," said Lord Hades. "Or, half in Dream, anyway. All you have to do is open your eyes. We'll meet the others there."

"The others?" asked Anise.

"Open your eyes, Anise," the lord of the underworld insisted.

# 5

A nise opened her eyes to the bubbling seething Scrying Pool. The fluid was fuming even more fiercely than before. The sensation of opening her eyes when she felt like they were already open was odd. She looked away from the pool so as not to be drawn in by the dream stuff. Briac and Sebastian were standing over her, looking worried.

Anise felt comforted by their concern for a moment, then the situation's urgency hit her, and she stood up.

The Hall of Doors looked the same as when she closed her eyes. The raven that was the Lord of Dream stood on the green floor, his beady black eyes fixed on her.

As she turned her gaze toward the bird, something started to change. The raven started getting bigger, growing upward, almost as fast as the spurting dream stuff in the Scrying Pool. The black feathers of its wings spread and widened until they turned into a black cloak on a tall, pale man. Lord Morpheus stood there, thin and smiling, looking just as he had when Anise first fell into Dream.

The Lord of Dream nodded to Anise and might have said something if he hadn't been cut short by one of the nearby doors opening.

It was a silver door, an inlay of a full moon in mother of pearl on its face. The woman who stepped out was dressed in a flowing gown. Both she and her gown glowed with the cool warmth of the full moon on a clear night.

"Mistress Luna," said Anise. She curtsied, only realizing when she reached down for a skirt that wasn't there that the black armor she had on didn't lend itself to the gesture.

"Anise," said the goddess of the moon, "It's good to see you again." Anise felt a flood of reassurance and calm filling her as she looked at the moon's beautiful face.

Luna turned to Sebastian. She smiled at him, then

frowned slightly as she saw his state. The rents in his jerkin and his shredded white leggings made him look like he'd been ground under a millstone. Still, he stood straight and proud and returned her smile. She reached out and smoothed a disheveled lock of hair on his brow.

"And, who is this?" said the lunar goddess, looking at Briac. Briac didn't respond. He seemed mesmerized by the moon's cool glow.

They were interrupted by a blast of hot white light as another door opened.

# 6

I t was a golden door this time. On the surface, etched into the gold, was an image of a chariot pulled by two blazing horses. The god of the sun stepped out through the door frame. "Helios," called out Anise joyfully. Then she blushed, the bright light coming from the sun god's face and crown clearly showing her face's crimson flush, bowed, and said, "It's good to see you, Lord Helios."

The sun good looked as youthful and handsome as ever. His face shone with a bright smile as if he was about to burst out laughing. He looked around the room like it was the first time he saw it, walked over to where Anise and Luna were standing, and said, "Anise." He turned to Luna and continued, "Sister." Finally, the sun god turned his eye on Morpheus. His smile dimmed a little as he said, "Cousin." It seemed that was enough greeting for the sun god. He ignored Sebastian and Briac standing off to the side, and even Flambé. His gaze went beyond the black-robed Lord of Dream to take in the spurting fountain of dream stuff. "I guess we've got our work cut out for us," he said.

Another door opened. This one was black, with the image of a skull on it. Anise was hardly surprised to see Lord Hades, the lord of the underworld, step out to join the assembled group.

Sebastian and Briac were standing to one side, their mouths hanging open. Even if you didn't recognize them, the gods radiated a sense of power and presence. It made it hard to do anything other than standing still, gazing at them in awe.

There was a loud rapping noise. Anise looked around to see where it was coming from. It repeated. It came from a plain unmarked trapdoor in the green stone floor.

When no one else responded, Anise walked over to the door. She opened it. A voice called out from below. "A little help, if you please."

Looking down, Anise saw a hand reaching upward, above a head of short curly brown hair. It was Koalemos. Anise reached down her hand and helped him clamber awkwardly up through the trapdoor. He puffed and panted a little as he collapsed on the green stone floor.

"Just let me catch my breath," he said. "That was a long climb."

# 7

After Koalemos caught his breath and rose to his feet, Hades spoke. "Well," he said, leaning his weight slightly on his bident scepter, "Now that we're all here, we'd better get started." Another surge of green fluid bubbled forth from the Scrying Pool behind him as if to frame his words.

Anise noticed, with some regret, that Cerberus hadn't accompanied her master on this outing. She took stock of the assembled collection of gods and wondered if this could really be her doing. She was somewhat accustomed to speaking to a single god or goddess in a channeling dream. Still, even just one was always an awe-inspiring experience. Five gods were standing around her. She felt like an ant looking up at a mountain.

Koalemos seemed to notice her disquiet. "We needed a powerful channeler to clean up someone's mess," he said. He glanced at Morpheus. Anise thought she saw Koalemos wink at the dream lord before turning his gaze to the ground.

Morpheus turned beet red for an instant. The flush was gone so quickly that it would have been hard to notice if it hadn't stood out so clearly on his pale face. The dream lord stood up a little straighter. "Well," he said, somewhat peevishly, "We can't all be as perfect as you, Koalemos."

Koalemos muttered under his breath, "Cole."

"We needed?" Anise asked.

"Huh?" said Koalemos.

"You said, 'We needed a powerful channeler,'" said Anise. "What did you mean by that?"

Koalemos smacked the palm of his hand against his forehead. "I've said too much," he said.

Hades interjected. "Enough of this. We have an

important job to do and not that much time to do it in." He swept an arm across the pool behind himself. The seething and fuming hadn't calmed or slowed.

Flambé watched the proceedings with a difficult-to-read expression from the other side of the hall. Her expression might have shown skepticism, it might have shown hope, or it might have just been the inscrutability of her dragon face.

Hades met Anise's eyes and said, "Anise, if you're ready, I think you can begin."

## 8

A surge of panic filled Anise. "I can begin?" she practically shouted. "I have no idea what to do to stop this. You're the gods; you need to fix it." Hades looked taken aback. It wasn't clear anyone had ever spoken to him like that.

Luna stepped forward. She glowed with the quiet beauty of a full moon shining down on a flowing river at night. The peaceful smile on her face was immediately a balm to Anise's nerves. "Anise, dear," she said. "We're here to help you. There are rules. Sometimes the gods can't do things that mortals can." She reached out and put her hand gently on Anise's shoulder.

Anise felt a rush of cool calm flooding her body. Through Luna's touch on her shoulder, serenity, patience, and peace of mind flowed into her. *It's all right*, she thought, *it'll all be all right.* She looked around at the group. *Why does everyone look so nervous? We probably don't even have to do anything; the cracks will most likely close by themselves.*

Helios stepped closer to Anise. He reached out to put his hand on her shoulder next to his sister's. "Anise," he said, "Like Luna says, we're here to help you, but we need to act, and we need to act now."

Anise felt her confidence increase. He was right. She needed to take matters into her own hands. It was clear that the gods were not able to act. She had to be the one to make the changes that needed to be made. Action had to be taken and taken now. She started preparing her elemental abilities. *Perhaps I should start by blasting the dream stuff with ice?*

Hades looked nervous, seeing Anise beginning her preparations. It was the first time Anise had ever seen his demeanor crack. She wondered if it was the first time anyone had. He moved quickly over to her and put his hand on the other shoulder from the one the siblings were touching. "Anise," he said, "Let's not rush into anything before we're ready."

Anise felt a sense of control filling her. *Action,* she thought, *but calm, measured action. I will carefully decide what to do, then do it expediently, calmly, and with careful consideration.*

## 9

Anise felt in control. She felt calm, collected, and ready to act, but she still didn't know what to do. She looked at the assemblage of gods. Koalemos met her gaze. He reached out his hand and placed it next to Hades' on her shoulder.

A surge of something else filled Anise. She felt jubilant, wild, reckless. She felt powerful. Anise, the person, faded into the background. Anise, the goddess, looked around the room with new eyes.

"Now, Anise," said Koalemos.

Anise reached out toward the metal cover of the Scrying Pool. Briac and Sebastian lifted it again to a vertical position. She could feel the surging dream stuff on the other side of the metal as she touched the lid.

Everything became very clear to Anise, the goddess. The dream stuff was just an element like Air, Fire, Water, or Earth; she could manipulate it in the same way. The bubbling, seething pool on the other side of the lid still made it impossible for Briac and Sebastian to close the cover. Anise reached out with her mind to pull some reality and truth from the air and use it to calm the turbulent dream fluid.

The fuming geyser of green dream stuff started subsiding. Briac and Sebastian lowered the lid as the bubbling lessened. When the cover dropped onto the stone of the pool edge, Briac ran over and snapped the padlock closed.

Anise stood, her hand still on the lid of the Scrying Pool, the four gods' hands still on her shoulders. She wasn't done. Not even close. She could feel the dream stuff under the lid, still seething and searching for a way to pop free. She could also feel the cracks extending out from here, from the pool, the center of the web. She could see the invisible tendrils of weakness extending from the basin, the hub, out to each of the doors in the room where they began their paths.

# 10

S
he closed her eyes. She would have to use other senses for this next part. The floods of calm, energy, control, and exhilaration from the gods' hands on her shoulders continued. Anise, the goddess, started to wonder if there was any reason she should have to go back to just being Anise, the person.

The spiders' web of broken cracks radiating outward from the central hub of the Scrying Pool surrounded her. Some were thicker and more established; some were narrow paths that only a few clairvoyants had walked. Anise could feel the cracks, and she could feel how they were weakening the structure of the veil between Dream and the waking world.

She felt along the paths. Clairvoyants walked them even now. She sensed each consciousness as a bubble on the crack it traveled. She could also sense how each clairvoyant was deepening and widening the path they walked.

She laughed. The feeling of power increased. With a surge of her manipulation of the element of dream stuff, she popped the traveling clairvoyants off their journeys and back to the waking world.

Anise, the person, had a moment of clarity. *They've trained for years to be clairvoyants. When I'm done, their livelihood will be gone.*

Anise, the goddess, didn't share her concern. *Let them read tea leaves or tarot cards; who cares.*

Anise's spirit hovered over the realm of Dream. The spiderweb of cracks, now empty of travelers, surrounded her. With her distant body back in the keep imitating her mind's gesture, Anise reached out her hand and pinched the first crack shut. She squeezed her fingers together, compressing the split between the realm of Dream and the waking world, and slid her paired fingers along the crack.

There was an enormous feeling of satisfaction as the two sides of the slit merged, and the damage disappeared.

Back in the keep, Briac and Sebastian watched as the doors of the Hall of Doors disappeared one at a time.

## 11

The fluid under the cover in the scrying pool was calm and settled like still water on a lake. Anise opened her eyes to a hall that would have to be renamed. Except for the open double doors at the end of the hall, all the other doors were gone. She still felt the power surging into her from the gods' hands on her shoulders.

She looked around herself eagerly. *What should she fix next?* She could take care of the Grisput problem. She could make sure Lorenzo never returned from the realm of Dream to hurt anyone ever again. She could push the Keep further into the dreaming realm so that no one from the waking world ever stumbled across it.

Anise lifted her hands to make a gesture of power. It occurred to her that she didn't need to do such mundane things as make a hand gesture anymore. With the power surging into her, she could do almost anything with a thought, but old habits die hard.

She started. There was a drop in her power, a reduction in her godliness. Luna had lifted her hand from Anise's shoulder. The calm and peace that she had been providing Anise were gone.

Anise was filled with rage. *How dare they!* With a flip of her wrist, she changed her perspective, and suddenly, she was looking down on the three little godlets that still had their hands on her shoulders. They were nothing. They were ants looking up at the glory of Anise, the goddess!

Anise prepared to blast the tiny things. They had no worth. Hades with his little underworld, Helios with his connection to the sun, Koalemos with whatever he was. They were little provincial powerless beings. She was the goddess of everything.

Helios removed his hand from her shoulder. Anise reconsidered. She would still take her revenge on these little things for trying to take away her power. She would do it methodically, with careful consideration.

Hades removed his hand. Anise started laughing. She had less power, it was true, but she had freedom. She could do with it what she willed.

Koalemos lifted his hand from Anise's shoulder. She blinked, then turned her head toward Briac and Sebastian standing nearby.

Anise took a step toward Sebastian, lifted her hand in his direction, said, "Uncle," and started to collapse as if her legs no longer had any strength. Sebastian caught her before her body hit the smooth stone floor, his eyes filled with concern.

Raphael charged into the hall through the open double doors at the end of the room. He held his gleaming sword. Iggy hissed confrontationally on his shoulder.

"Where's Lorenzo," he shouted.

# EPILOGUE

When Anise had recovered enough to make the trip, she and Sebastian traveled to Capitol. They met with king Twilight and convinced him that he was, in fact, Sebastian's son. Their subsequent journey to Hero and Isabel's tears and jubilation are tales for another time.

Twilight discovered he had a family he had never known, including a younger sister, Sunshine, who he'd never met. He offered to introduce her to the court, but Sebastian and Isabel were convinced that she wasn't ready for that yet.

The masters at the Academy recognized that clairvoyance should no longer be taught at the school. They accepted this partly due to reported events but mostly because clairvoyance simply didn't work anymore. The clairvoyants who'd hung up a shingle with an eye symbol had to close up shop. They found that they could no longer travel the paths of truth, and they also couldn't even find their way to the Room of Doors.

Rafael became a famous hero, with Iggy by his side. He left Ashton to explore the roads and by-ways of Liamec. They became known for their ability to resolve supernatural conflicts civilly.

The realization that the girl of his dreams didn't dream of him as he dreamed of her released Rafael from a common fate as a villager. That moment inspired him to leave Ashton and go out and become the hero he was to become.

Raphael's sword eventually spoke to him. The first thing she said was, "You're not Ed. Where's Ed?"

One of Rafael and Iggy's adventures was a trip to the elemental plane of Fire. Iggy's family was happy to welcome the prodigal flame home.

Briac wrote a ballad called "God Touched." It became one of the most popular songs of the next few hundred years, enhancing Anise and Briac's reputations. It's entirely possible that having written such a popular ballad helped confirm Briac's ascension to the rank of master bard, but who knows for sure.

But these are tales for another time.

J. STEVEN LAMPERTI

**Dear Reader,**

I hope you've enjoyed *The Channeler Trilogy*. I hope that the fates of Anise, Sebastian, Briac, Iggy, and Rafael have mattered to you as much as they matter to me.

If you are curious to explore further—or revisit familiar threads—in the Land of Liamec, you may wish to continue with the *Tales of Liamec*. The first story, *The Wolf's Tooth*, may be of interest to careful readers of this trilogy, as it tells what happened to Sebastian and Isabel's son, Twilight, after they lost him.

The story *Sunshine Over Hero* is a sequel to this trilogy. It features Raphael, Sunshine, Iggy, and other familiar characters, and is also the next book in the *Tales of Liamec* for readers following the series in order.

If you enjoyed this story, I hope you'll consider leaving a quick review on Amazon. Your words help other readers find these stories—and help me keep writing them.

With thanks and wonder,

**J. Steven Lamperti**

# ACKNOWLEDGEMENT

Thanks to my beta readers: Claudia, John, Page, Mary, Harris, and Joerg.

Also, as always, to my alpha, Andrea.

# BOOKS BY THIS AUTHOR

## The Wolf's Tooth

A boy raised by wolves. A world that refuses to claim him.

Torn from the only family he has ever known, Twee is thrust into a world of danger and secrets. Outlaws test his loyalties, a gruff blacksmith forces him to the forge, and a countess offers him an unexpected home at court.

Yet, no matter where he goes, he remains an outsider. And when whispers of a long-buried past surface, Twee must uncover the truth of who he is—and where his heart truly belongs—before the world decides for him.

For readers who love magical YA fantasy filled with humor, heart, and mystery, The Wolf's Tooth is a captivating journey of self-discovery that will enchant you from the first page to the last.

## By The Sea

The sea claimed her brother. Now, it's calling her name.

Years after losing her brother to the ocean's depths, Annabelle Fisher is forced to confront her darkest fears. When a mysterious stranger offers a dangerous proposition, she's plunged into a world of ancient magic and deadly secrets.

A thrilling blend of Greek mythology and coming-of-age fantasy, By the Sea follows Annabelle as she defies the gods, navigates the treacherous underworld, and fights to save her family.

Can she conquer the sea's wrath and reclaim what was lost? Dive into the depths of danger and discover her fate.

## Twilight's Fall

Blood on his crown, betrayal in his court—King Twilight of Liamec faces the collapse of his kingdom.

After a devastating ambush, Twilight and a ragtag band of survivors must navigate a fractured realm where loyalty is scarce and shadows loom large. Among them, young guardsman Corentin harbors a secret that could either be their salvation or their doom.

As Twilight struggles to reclaim his besieged capital and unite a splintered court, he confronts a perilous war against his own people. Guided by his queen Vix through the encroaching darkness, can Twilight overcome the treachery threatening to tear Liamec apart?

In this epic YA fantasy, dive into a high-stakes battle for survival and redemption. Fans of The Stormlight Archive by Brandon Sanderson and The Queen of the Tearling by Erika Johansen will be captivated by this thrilling saga.

## Sunshine Over Hero

In the medieval village of Hero, strange disappearances spark fear of a vampire in the shadows.

Enter Raphael, a renowned monster slayer with

unconventional methods. When Sunny, a farmer's daughter yearning for adventure, teams up with Raphael, their quiet lives are thrown into turmoil.

As shadows deepen and secrets unravel, Sunny and Raphael must confront the darkness threatening Sunny's village. With each passing moment, the stakes rise, and the fate of Hero teeters on the edge. In a world where heroes aren't always what they seem, can they uncover the truth and save their home?

For fans of Howl's Moving Castle and Terry Pratchett's Discworld, Sunshine Over Hero delivers a whimsical, heartfelt adventure where every shadow hides a secret.

## The Pirates Of Meara

Beneath the pirate city of Meara, a secret world awaits.

In the bustling, dangerous city, danger lurks just under the surface. When a daring wharf rat named Mouse rescues a mysterious noblewoman with silver eyes, he's thrust into a high-stakes adventure. Hunted by the ruthless pirate Bluebeard, they flee into the depths of Meara Below, a sunken city shrouded in ancient secrets.

To survive, they must navigate treacherous waters, face deadly foes, and unlock the secrets of forgotten magic.

Ready to set sail on a thrilling adventure? If you crave high-seas adventure, forbidden magic, and unforgettable characters, dive into the city of Meara. The Pirates of Meara is an exciting YA fantasy that will transport you to a world of wonder and danger.

## Endymion And The Fae

A shepherd boy, a girl of the fae, and a love that could heal—or divide—their worlds.

High in the mountain meadows, Endymion tends his sheep where mist clings to the slopes and old songs ride the wind. His life is simple—until he meets Lily, a girl of the Wee Folk with eyes like wildfire and a laugh like spring water.

To her people, she is Wee Folk. To his, she is Fae—a name spoken with fear, as if it carried danger of its own. What begins as a tender bond soon sets two worlds on edge.

When old wounds flare, Endymion must choose between peace and passion, tradition and hope. If he and Lily cannot bridge the divide, their love may cost more than their hearts.

A standalone tale within the Tales of Liamec, Endymion and the Fae is a gentle, slow-burn fantasy romance of first love, meadow magic, and quiet rebellion—for those who cherish cozy folklore, tender magic, and the stillness of high pastures.

unconventional methods. When Sunny, a farmer's daughter yearning for adventure, teams up with Raphael, their quiet lives are thrown into turmoil.

As shadows deepen and secrets unravel, Sunny and Raphael must confront the darkness threatening Sunny's village. With each passing moment, the stakes rise, and the fate of Hero teeters on the edge. In a world where heroes aren't always what they seem, can they uncover the truth and save their home?

For fans of Howl's Moving Castle and Terry Pratchett's Discworld, Sunshine Over Hero delivers a whimsical, heartfelt adventure where every shadow hides a secret.

## The Pirates Of Meara

Beneath the pirate city of Meara, a secret world awaits.

In the bustling, dangerous city, danger lurks just under the surface. When a daring wharf rat named Mouse rescues a mysterious noblewoman with silver eyes, he's thrust into a high-stakes adventure. Hunted by the ruthless pirate Bluebeard, they flee into the depths of Meara Below, a sunken city shrouded in ancient secrets.

To survive, they must navigate treacherous waters, face deadly foes, and unlock the secrets of forgotten magic.

Ready to set sail on a thrilling adventure? If you crave high-seas adventure, forbidden magic, and unforgettable characters, dive into the city of Meara. The Pirates of Meara is an exciting YA fantasy that will transport you to a world of wonder and danger.

## Endymion And The Fae

A shepherd boy, a girl of the fae, and a love that could heal—
or divide—their worlds.

High in the mountain meadows, Endymion tends his sheep
where mist clings to the slopes and old songs ride the wind.
His life is simple—until he meets Lily, a girl of the Wee Folk
with eyes like wildfire and a laugh like spring water.

To her people, she is Wee Folk. To his, she is Fae—a name
spoken with fear, as if it carried danger of its own. What
begins as a tender bond soon sets two worlds on edge.

When old wounds flare, Endymion must choose between
peace and passion, tradition and hope. If he and Lily cannot
bridge the divide, their love may cost more than their
hearts.

A standalone tale within the Tales of Liamec, Endymion
and the Fae is a gentle, slow-burn fantasy romance of first
love, meadow magic, and quiet rebellion—for those who
cherish cozy folklore, tender magic, and the stillness of
high pastures.